"STUNNING!"
—*Starburst*

"HAUNTING...
SENSUAL!"
—*Publishers Weekly*

"RESTORES ONE'S
FAITH IN FICTION."
—*The Guardian*

"SEDUCTIVE!"
—*Library Journal*

"RICH."
—*Booklist*

"STYLISH...EROTIC."
—*Kirkus Reviews*

"ELEGANT."
—*Locus*

WELCOME TO

ABYSS

The Abyss line of cutting-edge psychological horror is committed to publishing the best, most innovative works of dark fiction available. ABYSS is horror unlike anything you've ever read before. It's not about haunted houses or evil children or ancient Indian burial grounds. We've all read those books and we all know their plots by heart.

ABYSS is for the seeker of truth, no matter how disturbing or twisted it may be. It's about people, and the darkness we all carry within us. ABYSS is the new horror from the dark frontier. And in that place, where we come face-to-face with terror, what we find is ourselves.

"Thank you for introducing me to the remarkable line of novels currently being issued under Dell's Abyss imprint. I have given a great many blurbs over the last twelve years or so, but this one marks two firsts: first *unsolicited* blurb (*I* called *you*) and the first time I have blurbed a whole *line* of books. In terms of quality, production, and plain old storytelling reliability (that's the bottom line, isn't it?), Dell's new line is amazingly satisfying . . . a rare and wonderful bargain for readers. I hope to be looking into the Abyss for a long time to come."
—Stephen King

PLEASE TURN THE PAGE FOR MORE EXTRAORDINARY PRAISE. . . .

High praise for

the two-time winner of the World Fantasy Award
and winner of the August Derleth Award
TANITH LEE
who now brings us her first novel of horror
DARK DANCE

"ENTHRALLING . . . top-notch demonology and atmosphere . . . it is Lee's talent for realizing an exquisite and appalling mingling of lust and horror, sexual pleasure and loathing, yearning and revulsion."
—*Kirkus Reviews*

"Lee writes with lyricism . . . ominous wit . . . she is able to effortlessly build to a climax of breathtaking menace with overtones of dislocation and loss."
—*Publishers Weekly*

"Lee's seductive prose and sensitivity to nuance restore the 'atmosphere' to a genre too easily overwhelmed by gore."
—*Library Journal*

"Lee's creations are so rich that one can savor the details."
—*Booklist*

"Restores one's faith in fiction as the expression of imagination and original thought."
—*The Guardian*

DARK DANCE
TANITH LEE

DARK DANCE
TANITH LEE

A Dell Book

Published by
Dell Publishing
a division of
Bantam Doubleday Dell Publishing Group, Inc.
666 Fifth Avenue
New York, New York 10103

The trademark Dell® is registered in the U.S. Patent and Trademark
Office.

ISBN: 0-440-21274-X

Reprinted by arrangement with Macdonald & Co (Publishers) Ltd

Printed in the United States of America

Published simultaneously in Canada

December 1992

10 9 8 7 6 5 4 3 2 1

RAD

'But I don't want to go among mad people,' Alice remarked.

'Oh, you can't help that,' said the Cat: 'we're all mad here. I'm mad. You're mad.'

'How do you know I'm mad?' said Alice.

'You must be,' said the Cat, 'or you wouldn't have come here.'

Alice's Adventures in Wonderland,
Lewis Carroll

DARK DANCE
TANITH LEE

Chapter One

THE WOMAN IN THE FOG:
    It pressed round her, walls of yellow breath.
    She walked in a moving jail. At intervals the
stem of a street light would loom like a great thin
tree, or an angled wall would jut out. High above,
electric windows dim as old lamplight, peering. She
found her way by memory.

The fog had a sad melancholic smell that smothered
everything. There was a feeling in the fog of a pursuer,
but irrational, from every side.

The woman walked on. She was slim in a dark coat.
Her hair was substantial, down her back, very black,
like thick leaves on a bush. A slim white face and
two pale eyes. One hand held her collar. She had
unpainted nails, rather long.

She turned into Lizard Street, past the great
building with lions, and walked into the bookshop.

'Oh, Rachaela. You're late.'

'Yes,' she said.

'Twenty minutes.'

She walked by Mr Gerard and into the back, the tiny
room with its kettle and piled newspapers, the stacks

1

of books either shiny and plastic with newness, or old as dying brittle moths. She hung up her coat.

She wore a black skirt and dark jumper and boots. The shop was never warm except in the sweltering summer when it baked, and only the thinnest of shirts was bearable, but Mr Gerard still pottered in his sweaty jacket and tie. Today he wore the Fair Isle pullover, cheerful under his sour fat fruit of a face.

He left her his position at the counter. 'Price these from my list.'

Rachaela nodded.

This job paid very little, and she was required also to make tea, fetch sandwiches, sweep the floor, and dust the stacks, which she seldom did. She never argued or complained, neither did she apologize for her laxness, her constant lateness. Mr Gerard did not threaten her. She had not stolen from him, she did not answer back. When he flew into a temper at something she stared into far distances, and afterwards seemed to forget. She was as polite as a statue to the customers, of whom there were few. Mr Gerard knew next to nothing about her. A mystery woman.

As Mr Gerard edged away into the back of his dingy, frowsty cave, a man came in to collect a book. The fog swirled vaguely through with him to fill the space, wreathing a thousand volumes.

'Rotten day,' said the man. 'I thought we were finished with these things years ago. Bloody weather.'

Rachaela put his book into a bag and rang up its price on the till. The till was one of the reasons she had applied for the job a year ago. She hated computers, they frightened her. She liked old things. She was not so uncomfortable in this shop.

The customer took his book and handed her the money. Rachaela counted his change slowly, before giving it to him. Figures also bothered her. She was happy only with printed words.

'Excuse me,' said the customer. Rachaela looked at him, seeming shocked. Had she made a mistake with the money? 'You're Miss Day, aren't you?'

She hesitated.

As if admitting a dangerous secret she said, 'Yes.'

Her voice was low, soft and occlusive.

'I thought so. Said I'd bring you this.'

He handed her a buff envelope. Like a spy she took it. She asked him nothing, but her slender, long-nailed hand was reluctant to carry the envelope back to her body, her hand lingered in the air between them.

'Better explain,' he said. He was friendly. 'I'm from next door. Lane and Soames. The boss man asked me to bring it down to you. They've been looking for you, you see.'

She spoke. 'Who?'

'My firm, Lane and Soames. Looking, and here you were all the time.'

She had been hunted, then.

Rachaela brought the envelope into her breast. Her hands were tight upon it.

She had felt a pursuer, silent in the fog.

Day was not her name, but she had used it for years. She supposed it was legal by now; certainly it was the name on her insurance card, and by which she paid her bills.

Perhaps, however, there was a mistake.

'Are you sure I'm the right person?'

'Don't ask me. I'm just the errand boy. Said I'd drop it in to you.'

His jolly eyes were vacuous, he did not like her, her distance, or her beauty, which had a noiseless closed quality, almost to be missed, not exaggerated by bright make-up or dress.

'OK then,' he said. 'Out into the soup.'

He went at once and the door shut and the fog swirled. It was thick in the shop now, and Rachaela remembered *Alice Through the Looking-glass*, the shop with the sheep and the water swirling up. . .

In the back, Mr Gerard was talking on the telephone. 'But I said to him, Mac, old dear, you just can't—' He would be engaged for an hour.

Beyond the windows was that soft, grey-yellow pastelled wall. Behind it might stand anything, the soldiers of an execution, starving beasts escaped from the zoo. Had it been a leopard which had followed her through the fog?

Rachaela saw that her wrists were shaking.

She tore open the letter.

'Dear Miss Day.'

They don't know.

'Would you be so good as to call in at my office, at your convenience.'

Someone, someone knows.

'My clients, the Simon family, have asked me to locate you on a matter that may prove mutually beneficial.'

That name isn't real either.

Unless – something else—

What else could it be?

The easy answer was to ignore the solicitor's letter. But then again, they had come so near.

Lane and Soames, a few yards away through the wall.

Rachaela saw in memory her mother's tired and embittered face. 'Have nothing to do with them.'

She could hear her heart. A drum in the fog.

'Oh come on, come *on*!' roared Mr Gerard to the phone far off over the hills.

At six o'clock Rachaela went out into the street. Mr Gerard locked the shop in a flurry of ancient duffel coat and scarf.

'Filthy night.'

It was growing dark, the fog shadowing, and many bright lights shining through it, smeared and dangerous.

'You mind how you go, Rachaela.'

'Yes,' she said, 'good night.'

'Probably you just dissolve,' Mr Gerard said audibly and angrily to the stiff lock.

Rachaela crossed over from Lane and Soames. The great lions crouched wetly black, but did not spring. No one could make her enter between their paws.

She walked east and came among the vast animal of the evening crowd, bumping and pushing along. At a bus-stop she waited, silent, as people swore and raved at the bus's delay. 'You don't live in the real world with the rest of us.' It had been a blinding accusation. Her mother had furiously believed Rachaela was not hurt by the world.

The bus came.

Men and women thrust in front of her. She let them. The world to Rachaela was mostly horrible and she expected nothing good of it. For this reason she had refused friendships and lovers, although once she had been raped by an acquaintance after a dull party. She only expected onslaughts, upon her privacy, her person. The rape had not shocked Rachaela. She sloughed it.

After half an hour she got off the bus, and stepped back into the belly of the fog. She had now to walk across the wide green in front of the flats. She knew its perils, she did not fear those, they were facts. It was something else she feared.

The fog brought it. It had brought the letter, too. Sitting in the snack bar at lunch time she had thought of absenting herself this afternoon from the shop. But so far she had never done that, not even when she had caught flu, and foolishly she did not want to spoil her record. She was saving her truancy for some perfect day when she would abscond to picturesque gardens or to see a film.

Besides, the letter would have been left for her. She could not have escaped.

Trees passed her, swathed and dripping.

A lit streetlight shone ahead like a living livid moon.

A man stood before her. He was suddenly there. He was very tall, dark, held in a void, faceless.

Rachaela started and her entire body went to water. Then the man was gone. There was only another tree.

'Pardon me,' said a voice. He was by her side, short, in a black overcoat and a woollen hat. She thought he would beg money, but instead he said to her: 'Mr Simon is very anxious that you call at Lane and Soames.'

'Who are you?' said Rachaela.

'A friend of Mr Simon's.'

'Leave me alone.'

6

'But you must go, you know.'

It was usual to be obedient to authority, to obey a legal letter. But Rachaela left her bills unpaid until the threats began. She ignored the money-envelopes stuck through the door for starving children and the sick.

'Go away.'

She did not run. The green ended at a pavement and the lamp filled the fog with an impenetrable vortex of light.

The dark man stared at her. He had a foreign face and gelid eyes. Would he attempt violence?

'You go,' he said, 'to Mr Soames.'

And then he turned and slid into the fog.

Rachaela crossed the road and a boy cycled suddenly by like an apparition.

She climbed the steps and unlocked the door.

The fog smurred into the bleak hall, over its stone floor and the dusty table with letters. She feared to see a second letter lying there, but there was only a telephone bill, not in itself to be dreaded, for she never phoned anyone, the phone had come with the flat or she would not have bothered with it.

Rachaela took her bill and let herself into a tiny space crowded by stairs.

A year ago she had had a cat, a black round cat which was too lazy to come to greet her. But the cat was old and had died in her sleep. So Rachaela had found her one morning on her bed. Rachaela had wept for loneliness, but so far the ghost of this first cat, which she sometimes glimpsed about the rooms, had precluded obtaining another.

Tanith Lee

Nothing therefore awaited Rachaela but the usual walls, cream-washed by the landlord, and a floor carpeted by him in a faint beige.

Rachaela's great bookcase, crammed and crowded by books, many of which now stood and leaned along the wall, did not remind her of the shop. Yet it was her connection to books which had suggested that form of employment. Before the bookshop she had done many flimsy things, served tables in a café and counters in a fabric shop, other things like these.

It was cold. Rachaela turned on the electric fire, a fixture also supplied by the landlord, ugly but warming. She drew the beige curtains against the curtain of the fog. Even this room was touched by it, it had seeped in like pollen or gas through a hundred camouflaged cracks of the house.

In her kitchen area Rachaela opened the fridge. She drew out bread and left it ready to be toasted. She made herself a mug of coffee that she did not really want, but which pleased her as it represented the home-coming ritual.

It was good seldom to worry about a meal. While her mother had lived there had always been a dinner, cheap sausages and black cabbage, watery omelettes, often burnt, and jacket potatoes with prickly eyes glaring out of them.

Rachaela's mother had died abruptly of a heart attack. Rachaela bore the sympathy of neighbours and her mother's friends. She was twenty-five then, and had always lived with her mother and was expected to grieve and fall in little pieces.

But Rachaela went about the bewildering process of clearing up her mother's death without tears. At the cemetery when the joyous young clergyman had promised remembrance of the 'dear old lady' – who had liked to think of herself, when alive, no more than middle-aged – Rachaela had known a terrible ache in all her muscles, not the least the muscle of her heart. It was her body relaxing for the first time in fifteen years. She was free.

She never ceased to be thankful for her freedom. Her aloneness was her pleasure. She missed her cat, who had given her an uncloying and nearly careless love, her cat who never raged or shouted, never told her things, never demanded. But her mother had been a weight of iron. Rachaela had stayed light as air.

Until now.

Because now it was as if her mother reached out for her again. The doom-laden asides of family history, the portion of the unknown father who had revealed just enough before deserting to leave a lifelong stigma of the cheat or the fraud.

His family, not *Simon*, but having a name Rachaela could hardly forget, its oddness lost in repetition, 'Scarabae' – *Scarraby* it was pronounced. A weird name to go with a weird fly-by-night man. 'I loved him, the swine, the sod,' had said Rachaela's mother. She had not taken his name. Her own name was Smith, so foolish that Rachaela, left alone, discarded it.

Rachaela put on the radio, the third station, and heard Shostakovich in an unmistakable clash of silver chords.

She sat by the fire and edged off her boots.

In half an hour she would make her supper, toast and cheese. Tomorrow was Friday and she would fetch a salad and some cold meat from the deli. Perhaps a glass of wine.

Outside the silence of the fog waited.

She had screwed up the letter from Lane and Soames and thrown it in the waste bin at the shop.

Perhaps she had come into some money.

Would she want it if it depended on her father's infamous side?

'He's dead by now. Have to be, the way he carried on,' her mother said loudly in Rachaela's mind.

Four years since the funeral.

'You never came through, did you?' the young man said, accusatory.

She had been trying to avoid him by dusting the stacks, taking out old books that were slightly foxed, and brushing them gently.

'Is it any of your business?'

The young man became flustered. People relied on you not to be rude to them while they tried closer and closer forms of insolence. Rachaela did not play this game.

'No – well, yes. I delivered the letter. Now old Soames thinks I pissed about and never gave it you.'

'But you did.'

'Yes, I bloody well did. Why didn't you go?'

'Excuse me,' said Rachaela, and slipped away around the shelves.

'What's all this now?' inquired Mr Gerard, who had come from the back eating biscuits. 'Something wrong?'

'Er no, this young lady – I brought her over a letter from Lane and Soames and she hasn't taken it up, and old Soames thinks I'm to blame.'

'What letter's this?'

Rachaela did not answer. She dusted a copy of *The Egyptian* and put it carefully back into its slot.

'Something to do with property,' said the young man. 'That's my guess anyway. They're all of a doo-dah over it, damn nuisance.'

The fog was in the shop again. Unrelentingly it mouthed the capital.

'She doesn't have to make an appointment. Just pop up and Soames'll see her. Wouldn't take a minute—'

'You could go in your lunch hour, Rachaela. My God, don't you think you should? It might be worthwhile.'

Rachaela did not speak.

She did not tell Mr Gerard to mind his own business since she had never been rude to him. He paid her small wages.

The young man sighed. 'I'll just take the biography, then. Waste of time, reading fiction.'

'Luckily not everyone thinks so,' said Mr Gerard with dislike. Suddenly unpopular, the young man hastened from the shop.

'What the hell are you doing, Rachaela?'

'I'm dusting.'

'You never dust. Stop it. There's clouds of muck going up. Go to lunch. Take an extra ten minutes. Go and see this Soames.'

It was Saturday morning and the animal of the crowd was out shopping. Its mood was the familiar one, surly and desperate.

Rachaela walked towards the snack bar. A man charging by slammed into her shoulder and almost spun her round. She found the man from out of the fog by her shoulder.

'Miss Day, you will allow me to accompany you.'

He took her elbow and turned her all the way about. They moved against the crowd, which seethed and spat in their faces.

'You're forcing me to go there?'

'No, no, Miss Day. You will be pleased. Come along.'

It was Saturday. Would Soames be in his office? Apparently he was.

Three youths in football colours of some team from Mars collided with them. They were no longer a unit, the foreign man and Rachaela. They were hammered apart.

Rachaela whirled into the fog, into the thick of the crowd, giving herself to its hasty rhythm.

The man did not call out after her. His hand did not clutch and grasp her arm.

She made towards the museum, where she spent her lunch hour among the blue and pink stone of god birds and smiling pharoahs, eventually eating two bananas bought from a stall as she walked to the shop, fog-bananas.

The man did not come into the shop, and the young one did not come back.

Mr Gerard said, 'Did you?'

'No.'

'Silly. Silly, silly girl. Make us some tea.'

She stood on the bus home. The vehicle was full of excited escapees.

The shop shut half an hour earlier on Saturday in order to allow Mr Gerard, also, and his employee the chance to rush away to a bacchanal. But she doubted he had one any more than she did. Mr Gerard

12

remained as thankful a mystery to her as she remained a provoking mystery to him. He lived with a wife near Kennington. She could only visualize a Mrs Gerard who was a female version of Mr, in a Fair Isle woolly or sweaty dress and cardigan, eating custard creams or reading pieces out of papers over the telephone.

The fog hung on the green as intensely as ever, but Rachaela did not anticipate the man. She did not know what she looked for. Something unpleasant.

In the flat as she drank a glass of wine, the other half of Friday's bottle, the door sounded.

No one called on Rachaela.

She thought of some sort of emergency. Perhaps an accident had happened in the street. She might not have heard a squealing of brakes over the storm of Beethoven, not to mention the rock music from the flat below.

'Hallo?'

'Miss Day?'

She did not recognize the voice, isolated and tinny in the receiver.

'What do you want?'

'Miss Day, this is Mr Soames of Lane and Soames. I wonder if you would be good enough to let me in.'

'I'm afraid not.'

'But Miss Day, I've come out of my way to see you on this very urgent matter. It is an urgent matter, Miss Day—'

'No, Mr Soames, I'm not interested.'

'My client, Mr Simon, has authorized—'

'Good-bye, Mr Soames.'

The door sounded three more times after she had replaced the entry-phone.

Rachaela paced her tiny room. Upstairs a tinier bedchamber, and a cupboard converted to a bathroom – this minuscule, expensive flat that mostly her mother's savings had enabled her to choose, and when they were gone, what?

Perhaps it was money Mr Soames offered.

Money was remote to Rachaela. She partly feared it, it carried responsibilities, it caused such trouble and damage. But then.

The phone no longer made noises.

Mr Soames had gone away.

On Sunday she had a long bath, in the afternoon, with a radio play on.

She shaved her legs, as she did every third day, and the slender under-pits of her arms. She washed her hair, as every third day she washed it, and left it to dry in the artificial Africa of two electric bars. These habits were her own. As a child, her mother had washed her hair every fortnight.

Outside a fine drizzle penetrated the yellow fog.

She had a lamb chop for dinner and thought as she ate it of the beautiful white curled creature it had been. This did not sicken her, only made her sorrowful. She enjoyed the meat of the lamb even in some way more because she liked what it had been and pitied it.

She had once in her teens tried to become a vegetarian, but she had vomited and bent double with terrible pains in her stomach for weeks. She gave it up.

Her mother had mocked both her attempt and its failure. She had dragged Rachaela to a dish of burnt fish fingers. 'Stop all this bloody nonsense.'

Her mother had had to bring her up alone.

She was thinking of her mother too much.

It did not hurt, but it unsettled her.

She had never said goodbye to her mother, that was the difficulty, perhaps. The freedom had only been spontaneous. Perhaps she should have kissed the embalmed corpse farewell, on the brow, as in one of the more sensitive old-fashioned horror films. The embalming had not looked like her mother. Something had gone wrong and they had pushed her mother's rather large stomach up into the chest so that she appeared stout and matronly in a way that, in life, she never had. The rouge on her cheeks was patchy. Not dead but sleeping – no: decidedly dead.

She missed the cat, which had been used to sitting on the edge of Rachaela's bath, sometimes pawing the water in surprise. Or on the table, decorous, begging for nothing.

Perhaps she should find a more lucrative job. Where? Who would take her on? She had no experience. She was twenty-nine. Should she work in a wine bar now? She thought of the noise and the hustling, the broken glasses and drunks. No, the bookshop was safe. It had paid for the chop.

Rachaela sighed.

Beyond the curtains the fog was giving way. She could see across the green to a gaudy Sunday bus moving sluggishly westward.

On Monday morning Rachaela walked down a clear grey Lizard Street and up to the black lions. She entered the building and went to the reception desk. Three minutes later she was in the efficient lift which tore her up into the building's cranium.

Without the fog, it was possible to see, from a window, the bookshop cowering under its dirty roof five storeys down. It was dwarfed.

Mr Soames's secretary greeted her brightly and took her at once into the office, like a valued client.

It was a sombre glassy room, whose window looked towards the park. On the trees there was one last faint wraith of lingering fog. The screen was gone. The hunter out in the open.

'I'm here,' said Rachaela.

'Yes indeed. Let me say how glad I am that you reconsidered.'

'It got rather frantic, didn't it? Your call. That little man in the overcoat and wool hat.'

'I'm afraid I don't know who that can be,' said Mr Soames smoothly. He had never had eyes, only glasses. All his face had succumbed to them. 'Won't you sit?'

Rachaela sat in the leather chair. It did not please her to think it had once been a black bull rushing over tindered meadows. Maybe it was only a clever plastic.

She sat with her hands together, her legs crossed. Her heart beat uncomfortably, but Mr Soames seemed more nervous than she.

'Miss Day – first of all, I believe that your name was, until a short while ago, something other. Am I correct?'

'Perhaps.'

'I don't like to stress this, but my clients, the Simons, made rather a point of it. Your mother – a Miss Smith. And your father – well, these things happen.'

Rachaela waited.

Mr Soames twitched at his cack-handedness.

'The Simons are a connection of your father's family. Cousins, I believe.'

Rachaela waited. Her mother had never mentioned cousins, only the Scarabae family, obscure and artistic, darkly ominous, somewhere out of the city, inaccessible, wielding a whip of intent. 'He never stayed with me because they would keep on and on at him.' But of course he had never stayed with her because she had conceived Rachaela. Strange she had never flung that in Rachaela's face. It would have been like her.

'– And even after all this time, hope that you will be willing to visit them.'

She had not been attending.

'Visit them? These Simons?'

'Yes, just so. I have to tell you, Miss Day, a moneyed family.'

'*Is* the name Simon?'

'Yes, Miss Day.'

'Then I don't understand what they have to do with me.'

'Perhaps you should agree to see them. Then you'll discover. As I say, they're prepared to pay your travelling expenses.'

She had not listened, and so did not know to where she was intended to travel.

'I find all this very peculiar. I find it suspicious.'

Mr Soames was ringing for a file.

'I shall show you the correspondence, Miss Day.'

She did not want to see it. She felt no curiosity. She felt threatened.

Their name was not Simon, and God knew where they lived or why they wanted to find her but it made no sense, this coincidence of the solicitors being so adjacent. Unless surely *they* had tracked her down previously, and then placed their business with the firm of Lane and Soames to give it a spurious orderliness and a handy quality. Easy to nab her when she was only next door – it had been perfect for them. And that other one was their agent.

The file came with the glowing cerise-clawed secretary. She teetered in and out as if high on something.

'The name,' Rachaela said again. 'Is it actually Scarabae?'

Soames did not twitch or flinch. He was impervious, a little irked.

'The name I have is Simon, Miss Day.'

He opened the file before her and indicated a lengthy correspondence, lots of long sheets with neat dates and slightly faulty typing, and handwritten letters on featureless white paper. Rachaela could not read handwriting of any kind. Probably its intimacy repelled her. She glanced at the indecipherable address on the handwritten sheets and raised her brows, trying to convey to Soames an air of sensible concentration. She was not responding as he wanted. She felt cornered. The leopard was prowling round the room.

Had she always been afraid these people would one day reach out for her? Why was the idea so dreadful – for it was, it was horrific. Her mother had always maligned them but knew nothing of them. They had been a shadow at the back of her lover, she conveniently blamed them for his desertion. To the child she must have told horror stories now too recessed and entrenched to come forward to the light, embedded like black fossils in Rachaela's subconscious. For she was afraid of the tribe of the Scarabae.

'No, Mr Soames. I'm very sorry. I don't think your clients are being honest, either with you or with me. If they're relatives of my father's there's really no reason for them to be interested in me. I never knew him. I can't help them. That's all I have to say.' Rachaela got up. 'I hope now that I'll be left in peace.'

'I regret you take this view, Miss Day.'

He was pedantic and huffy, he had lost.

Rachaela went out and passed by the secretary who flooded into a terrifying fake smile all teeth and lipstick.

The lift descended.

It was raining in the street.

I must shrug it off now. But she could not. The leopard, invisible in light as in murk, still followed at her heels.

'You're late, Rachaela,' said Mr Gerard. 'Three quarters of an hour. It's too much. I had a rush, ten people, and where were you?'

'I went to see Lane and Soames.'

'Any joy?' cried Mr Gerard.

Rachaela loathed the expression but expected nothing else of him.

'There's been a mistake,' she said. 'The people are no one to do with me.'

'What a pity. Hard luck.'

That week Rachaela continued in her usual way, moving between the bookshop and her flat, doing her slight shopping, eating at the little snack bar, going once to the cinema to see a colourful cruel film which bored her. She bought three books, some shampoo, toothpaste, and oranges, and over all the scent of the leopard was borne to her nostrils. It was still there.

She sensed a tightening cord like a string overwound on a guitar.

She could not appreciate the music which she heard. The noises heard from the neighbouring flats irritated her, and one night there was a party which went on until four in the morning, and she lay wakeful and could not read, the words jumping away under her eyes, the centres of sentences missing.

In the shop she had begun to dislike the entry of any customer. She expected the man in the overcoat or even the fool from the solicitors, or even Soames in person. For some reason she did not visualize one of the awful tribe of the Scarabae. No, they carried on their business from afar. That unknown country written so finely and illegibly on the white paper.

I am waiting for something more.

But what? What could happen. She had refused. It was finished.

On Friday morning she found a letter for herself on the dusty table, one of six identical envelopes from the landlord. Opening this letter she learned that the street was to be widened or renovated or turned inside out in some way. That in six months she would have to find alternative accommodation.

She did not think in terms of coincidence, or even now of destiny. She felt a wave of fright. She stood with her pale hands knotted below her pale face. The complications of the situation, rather than her loss, appalled her.

Then she went to work, late, for she had missed the bus, and Mr Gerard drew her back into the musty inner room.

'Rachaela, I'm sorry, but I'm going to have to let you go.'

She almost laughed at the exquisite counterbalance of her woes.

'You mustn't think it's anything to do with your, well, your rather erratic timekeeping. We've rubbed along all right. Trouble is, this place doesn't pay. I've been thinking about it some time. Saw the old accountant yesterday. No other thing I can do.'

He offered her a biscuit by way of consolation and she took it.

She imagined the agent of the leopard coming in to Mr Gerard with a silken knife, threatening him. She thought perhaps agents had set to work on the landlord of the flats.

She bit the biscuit and ate its tastelessness.

'Stay on the month. I'll give you an extra month in lieu, anyway. I realize it's a bit much. You've been here a year, haven't you? I'll miss you.'

She knew he lied, that secretly he was glad to tread on her spine. All those times he had tried to learn things about her and she had not let him. All the jokes she had not giggled at, the untrue rushes of book-buying customers she had missed by being late. Her lack of apology.

He was well rid of her.

But what was she to do?

She knew what she was supposed to do. It was quite obvious. The leopard sat there, awaiting her,

its inky form wrapped in a garment of fog and
night.

She picked up a fragile broken book, a dead black
moth. Opening its pages she read: 'Her heart lifted
at the prospect of this happy reunion.' And shivered.
It was inevitable, and had been so from the first. She
would have to give in.

None of the other tenants communicated with
Rachaela about the proposed dissolution of their
homes. Perhaps they did not care. Two of the flats
changed hands regularly, and even the rock music
enthusiast had only been installed a few months. She
had previously avoided contact with all of them. But
they would probably know themselves as defenceless
in the face of bureaucracy as she judged herself to be.

She went into work on time, and did not linger over
her lunch hours now. She was scrupulous.

Mr Gerard crowded her at the till. He had come
out of hiding to serve the customers, to get used to
it. He no longer made his telephone calls, but he
ate vast quantities of biscuits. As the week ended
and the end of the month drew near, Mr Gerard
became embarrassed, making awful little extra jokes
and asking Rachaela to sweep up, which generally he
had not troubled with before. He did not send her for
sandwiches but chewed slabs of bread and pickle.

She did not like his proximity. She was seldom
alone now in the shop. She began to long for the
month to be over.

She would have to look for another job. It would be
best to try one of the agencies. They were smart and
brisk. She hated them.

It was raining fiercely and she hurried over the green and almost collided with the overcoated man in the woollen hat.

'Miss Day. I was asked to put this directly into your hands.'

She took the envelope. It was typed. They stood in the downpour confronting each other, both creatures of the jungle who might ignore the rain.

'I don't want this.'

'You must take it. Read it.'

'I thought all this had stopped.'

'Please, Miss Day.'

'All right. Very well.'

She moved away with the letter, the rain thick on her wonderful hair as broken glass.

In the hall she shook herself with a little grunt of defiance. The closed outer door was a barricade. The demon locked outside.

One of the other tenants came clattering down the stairs. A girl in a red coat. Rachaela considered stopping her, discussing the downfall of their house. But the girl did not look real. So young and contemporary she was hardly on the plane of existence, an egg-shaped face, smooth, not a line or an expression to show she had lived, was alive. Rachaela let her pass on, and opened the door to her flat.

The light was bizarre, greenish and electric from the rain. The walls danced. She longed for the warm round body of the cat, to wake her and press her face to the smoky fur with its inner smell of herbs and being. But the cat was gone, only the ghost, conjured by tired eyes, remained to haunt her, indifferently.

Rachaela took off her coat and hung it up. She pulled off her boots. She sat down on the edge of a chair and slit the letter open with a bronze paper knife resembling a dagger.

It was thick white paper.

The letter was typed, as if they knew she could not read their calligraphy, or would not. No chance of a blindfold. Too short to be avoided.

Dear Miss Smith,

By now you will know that we have traced you and are eager to meet with you. Please give us this opportunity. Your mother knew very little of the family and your father, we understand only too well, abandoned you. Give us this chance to make possible amends. The familial connection is complex and we will not attempt to describe it here, but hope to do so before you, in person, at some future date.

Our name is not, evidently, the one given to our agents, but as you have correctly guessed, 'Scarabae'. That name to which you yourself are entitled.

As Mr Soames will have told you, any travelling expenses or expenses entailed in tying up your affairs will be borne by us.

We trust that we shall hear from you soon.

The letter was signed boldly 'Scarabae'. Not even any initial. A dynamic collective which told nothing.

There was no address. The letter was headed solely by the words 'The House' and the winter's date.

Rachaela glanced intuitively towards the unlit electric fire. Her impulse was to burn the letter.

Instead she sat with it in her hands for three quarters of an hour, in the chilly flat, while the rain danced on the windows and the walls, erosively.

'Yes, I've changed my mind.'

'I really am delighted, Miss Day,' gushed Soames. 'I'm sure you've made the wise decision.'

When Rachaela had finished this phone call, she called Mr Gerard.

'I'm sorry, I shan't be completing the month.'

'Oh. Well that's not very fair.'

'You've dismissed me. What difference does it make.'

Mr Gerard began to inform her in detail of the difference, shouting. Rachaela put down the phone. Four days later a cheque arrived. He had not paid her for the extra month nor a penny beyond the day she had last worked for him, which had been Friday. He would have to manage the Saturday rushes of two people on his own now.

She wandered about the tiny flat, tidying it for the last time. If she returned, the flat would be no more. She would store her furniture, the Scarabae could pay for that.

Day by day now the flat became like a prison. She could settle to nothing but packing her two new cases, parceling up the few leftovers for Oxfam. Her plants had died, she could not grow things. The cat had died. She had no friends, no one to bid farewell. She sent the new address to the landlord, who would probably ignore it. The new address was surreal in any case, perhaps invented, a place that did not exist.

A lot of matters she left unseen to. For when she came back.

But it was inconceivable, a return, the outward journey with all its twists and pitfalls before her.

Outside on the green she thought that, twice, she caught sight of the agent in the woollen hat, hiding among the wet trees, watching. But he might be an hallucination.

She hoped the ghost of the cat would vanish from her rooms once she had left. The thought made her cry as sometimes she did, violently, but never for very long.

She had indulged in purely emotionally-sexual fantasies from childhood, at rest or in bed before going to sleep. She pictured unformed adventure, and men almost faceless, tall and black-haired. In the world she never met them, although now and then, for a moment at some street corner, across a room, she might see a fleeting illusion which dissolved as she gazed on it.

Following her mother's death – when Rachaela was twenty-five – she had believed herself too old for these dreams, hazy and incoherent, repetitive and unlikely as they were, meetings in storm and mist, on hillsides, under midnight trees. . . . She put them away. Now and then a book or a film might try to trigger them. She was stern.

Currently her imaginary excursions were all to the place where she was going. She conjured it with terror. It was like a swamp which sucked her in.

Chapter Two

AFTER THE LAST OF THE JOURNEY, many hours long, the traveller was hypnotized, her body still moving with the sway and judder of the train, her eyes amazed by stillness. She stood outside the tiny, half-derelict station among the winter weeds. The sky swept to the land. It was a scene by Turner, great clouds, and suggestions of hills; no break of sun in the vanquished afternoon.

Then along the asphalt road that ran above the station, a fawn Cortina drove towards her.

Isolated in the landscape, she and the car seemed destined for one another.

The Cortina swung into the station forecourt among the weeds and grass. The window went down.

'Name of Smith?'

The driver had an indeterminate alien accent.

'Yes.'

The door opened and politely the driver came to lift her two bags into the boot. Heavy with books, not clothes, he must strain. He said, 'Come for a holiday?'

'No,' Rachaela said, coldly, to exclude him.

Not a driver of the city, he did not impertinently press her, presuming on a wish to talk. He fell silent, opening the passenger door.

Rachaela got in. As the car started up she felt relief. Her body had been in motion so long it now seemed only comfortable if moving.

The car was stuffy and dank yet she sank back against the seat, longing to close her eyes. But the alien driver meant she could not abandon herself. She watched the pale olive green of the country stream away along the road. Dark woodland patched it and occasionally the tobacco-coloured basins of fields, a stone farmhouse, an ancient garage with fallen sign and brilliant rust.

The driver did not speak for thirty miles.

Then he said, mildly, 'I don't know the area too well. I'm from the town. Will you know the place?'

'I'm afraid not.'

'Have to chance it then. Mr Simon sent me a little map. May help.'

She thought of the driver leaving her in the wilderness, running his shabby car home to an electric fireside, a warm semi littered by children's toys and washing, beefburgers for tea, a warm wife and two lively kids, perhaps a toddler. She was jealous a moment, passionately, furiously jealous of this easy normality. Only the mortgage to worry him, the long odd hours of his work, but the warm wife to come home to and the procreative results of former love.

And what am I? How then do I see myself?

She had a vision of a black moth battered through the night, a deer hastening between the fraught shadows. Dramatic, fearfully apt. No warm fireside for her. To what then was she going, where was this baffled driver, himself unsure, taking her? The quag gaped. Rachaela

28

tensed and found her hands clutched together on her limp black bag long ago wrung out. Faint sickness oozed in her vitals, as it had off and on for days, at this prospect. An adventure after all. Maybe it was correct that she should be afraid. *Scarabae.*

Across level fields Rachaela saw the sudden sun, watery and veiled, sinking down into the western valleys.

Bold hills rose straight up from the ground, some with white chalk masks, like the heads of phantom animals, leering, smiling, grimacing, holes for eyes. Trees trailed over rock. Ivy grew along the earth, and festooned old broken walls. Once there had been houses. Now, nothing. Gone away.

'Empty old place,' said the driver, venturing once more into Rachaela's silence, making her start. 'See the sea soon.'

This alliterative phrase snagged on her mind.

She had not known they approached the coast. She was ignorant of everything. The whole world had stayed undiscovered for her, strange names and languages on her radio.

The shop in Lizard Street would be closing shortly. The buses would be scuttling down the highways. A planet away. Lost, gone.

Some seagulls passed across the view.

The road pulled itself up and over, and a sudden break revealed the fish-grey glitter of the ocean. A white cannon-shot of foam discharged itself below. Rachaela's heart rose with it, fell back fatigued and fearful. The sea did not reassure.

They drove above the water and sometimes a stretch of sinuous beach appeared, and once a great tanker was on the horizon like a slowly swimming dinosaur.

'Now there'll be a turn-off here, if I read that map all right.'

Again the voice of the driver snapped at her nerves. 'A turn-off,' she repeated. But he was not now inclined to converse.

The turn presently appeared on their left, winding in amongst a vast bank of trees. Black pines rose along the hill, a sort of forest from a fairy book, in miniature. They sped from the sea, and a cave of boughs brought them shadow. Branches struck savagely at the sides of the car. It was a poor road, bumps, and shingle spraying up as if from machine guns.

'Rough on my tyres,' said the driver.

Rachaela did not say she was sorry.

He said, 'Never told me it'd be this bad.'

They swerved through the forest. Sheer blackness coiled under the trees. The sun broke through with a flash and vanished again.

The road curled over and came to a stop against the flank of a crumbling hill. It was dark, the trees massed all about, listening. The Cortina stopped and in the stillness birds twittered and chimed, a curious primeval noise.

'Look there.'

Rachaela looked and saw a stone signpost. There were two words on it: *The House*. Nothing else, not even an indicatory arrow.

'Must be up the top of the slope.' The driver turned and grinned at her, showing after all the anticipated face of the enemy. 'I can't get the car up there. There's no road. You'll have to walk.'

They went to the boot and he drew out the two heavy cases, which she had ported all day, already spent by them.

'Can you manage?' he asked, unhelpful, recalcitrant.

'What do I owe you?' Rachaela asked.

'Taken care of. They have an account, the Simons. Don't know why, they never seem to use a car, until now. First time any of us has been out here. Mind how you go.'

There was a sort of path leading away up the hill from the signpost, veined with roots and scattered by pine needles. In summer the undergrowth would be thicker, the path perhaps invisible.

In the darkness Rachaela began to walk away from the car. She heard its engine start and the sounds as it reversed on the shingly road. She did not look back.

The cases were heavy as lead, but they contained all that had seemed essential to her. She heaved them on.

She was weary, and the nervous fear slid under her exhaustion, nearly extinct. Did the house not exist, as in half of her daydreams?

She rose above the pines, and cedar trees and massive oaks with mossy, glowing peridot trunks climbed from the soil, great pillars upholding a tracery of dull panes, less light than contrast to darkness.

In such a spot, from among the trees, anything might come at her.

The path eddied from the wood.

She was high up. She heard the rush of the sea.

It was twilight, the sun had gone out inland. The sky was closing. She saw two stars, and away over the open land before her, a building.

There was a tower with a cone of roof. Crenellations and walls slanting. Some last hint of light cast a weird burnish on to ranks of slender windows. It was a large house, and in the dusk it became a masonry vegetable.

31

Beyond its shape the land gave way. Below the sea dashed itself against rock and gulls or silence cried.

Here? She was to confront them *here*? To confront what?

Dizzy with her tension, she had put down the two slabs of lead.

She must cross the formless ground between herself and the house. She must ring a bell or knock some primitive knocker, and then one of them would come. She would go in and so begin to know.

It was cold on this headland. Now she could see seven, eight tinfoil stars, burning icy, thin and hard.

She took up the cases and wands of pain struck at her shoulders. She walked towards the house, stumbling a little on stray stones, the tufted wintry grass.

The house came nearer, drifting over the navy dusk.

She reached an outer wall broken by two posts. No gate. The way was open wide but not necessarily inviting.

Above her, afloat over a tall crowd of garden trees, a window lit up in the house.

Rachaela stared. The light was dull but the window became a fruit of coloured glass, liquid crimsons, dense purples, and damson green.

What did the window propose? Anything? Nothing?

It was not a welcome, rather a shutting out.

The path from the wall to the house was straight. There were massive ancient yews on either side, cemetery trees, where darkness lurked and rustled.

The house too, but for its one lit window, was faceless and black.

A porch became visible. Ebony wood, intricately carved, above five shallow steps, each patterned dimly, which she mounted. No light within the door. A solid wood frame. No bell. Rachaela searched for a knocker, for some semblance of willing communication.

But the door was ajar. It stood open on the empty world, the night and trees. She put down her cases once more and disbelievingly pushed at the door – and it gave.

Blackness and, again, the dim pattern on a white tile underfoot. A black oblong in blackness, there was a second door within the first. Gradually she made out an old-fashioned doorknob, a globe that turned as she gripped it. But the inner door was also open. A smothered red ember of light appeared, so vague, so intangible, like the glim of a dying candle.

She must go forward into this cobweb half-light.

Or stay outside in the cold and whispering darkness.

Inside the second door was a huge open oblong of space, a hall or lobby with a chessboard floor of russet and black marble. It was as wide as a great room and from it there fell away massed shadows that might be anything, doorways, passages, crouching bears.

On a mahogany table softened by a grape-bloom of dust burned a ruby oil lamp, its wick turned low, while from the ceiling hung, unlit, a snow-flake chandelier. Filmy webs knit the glass prisms of the chandelier, which slipped softly to and fro in the draught of the opened doors. Beads of the red lamp caught on it like drops of red ink.

Rachaela could smell the dusts of the house, and the damp vaults of it, but there was too the smell of the oil, a scent like fur, herbs and powders, tinctures unguessable.

She dragged her suitcases into the hall, and turned to close the inner door.

'Please leave it open,' said a flat soft voice.

She moved quickly to face the lobby. A thin, small figure, male, leaning slightly forward, stood at the far side of the lamp.

'The doors are always left a little open after dark.'

This strange statement unnerved Rachaela. She left the door alone. She poised by her cases, for what came next.

'I shall fetch someone for your bags. Will you allow me to show you the room which has been made ready.'

'Who are you?' said Rachaela.

Beyond the lamp she saw a mannequin in a shabby ancient suit, a small pale face with two blots of eyes. Grey hair.

'My name is Michael. I serve the family.'

'And you know me?'

But who else would come here with the darkness?

'You are Miss Rachaela.'

'And – the family?' she said, her hands clenched.

'Miss Anna and Mr Stephan will presently come down to welcome you.'

The flat soft voice and its words did not calm Rachaela.

A flutter in the oil lamp as the man took it up caused all the shadows to take wing, the walls to topple. Extraordinary carvings jumped out and vanished again as the light ran off them.

A stairway was born out of the dark on Rachaela's right. She looked at it in wonder. A wooden nymph guarded the newel post, holding up an ornate light fitment, blind, in her hand. The stairs went up and up, carpeted at their centres in Persian red that the oil lamp made rich.

They ascended in the magic halo of this lamp.

Rachaela counted twenty-two steps. Behind her her cases were swallowed in the deserted blackness of the hall. Only the chandelier caught still red drops among its films of dust.

There was a carpeted landing. A corridor appeared, lighted by another oil lamp on a stand. This lamp was of a pinkish white tone, and abruptly, for a second, Rachaela saw the face of her guide, a cameo between shadow and fire. Not a young man. His eyes were fixed sightlessly. There was a peculiar bloom on them resembling the pollen of dust on the table and other elements of furniture.

They entered the passage. It turned at a massive window, leaded, set with stained glass that had no colour left, showing only the darkness of the night. There were confused pictures on the walls.

The servant of the family opened a door.

'This is to be your room, Miss Rachaela.'

The room, like the house, was gothic. It was green and blue. A lamp with a base of emerald glass and clear chimney was burning on the mantelpiece of a green-tiled fireplace. A fire worked there busily over a pile of logs. In other places plain white candles were lit in sconces on the walls. She noticed, there was not so much dust, perhaps they had dusted here for her, or this oblique servant had done so.

Across the room stood a bed with posts, hung with bottle-green velvet. An indigo cover was pulled back to reveal pillows that looked white and very clean. Perhaps they had bought new linen just for her.

She sensed their preparations. That she was unique, exciting, like a new-born baby.

There was the faint smell of damp, but over this the dry peppery smell of the fire, and a scent like face powder in a compact.

'Your bags will be brought up to you.' The servant Michael indicated the passage. 'The green bathroom is there. We have hot water.'

'Thank you.' Of course the house was old enough to have done without. She wanted the servant to go. The room overwhelmed her yet for a few precious minutes she might hide in it. 'When do Mr Stephan and Miss . . .'

'Miss Anna and Mr Stephan will go down shortly.'

'How shall I find them?' she asked.

'The rooms will then be lit on the ground floor, Miss Rachaela.'

The servant went out and the door shut. A curtain like those of the bed fell back over it.

There was another large slim window beyond the bed, its drapes undrawn; this window too was of blackened stained glass. Rachaela stared and made out the plumed image of a tree, two figures. She would need daylight to see what kept her company here.

She went to the fire. It was appealing, a luxury, and none of the trouble of cleaning or laying it would fall to her. A servant – the Scarabae had domestic help.

Rachaela tried to enjoy the fire.

There were blue iris flowers enamelled on the fireplace tiles. The carpet in the room was very old, Persian probably, blue and rose plants and green birds.

In two places a mirror winked behind the candles, ornately camouflaged by designs of coloured glass jewels. A huge old dressing-table supported a winged mirror whose face was similarly obscured. Rachaela looked at herself through a hedge of lilies, a wild sunset in rays and swallows, cutting her into segments. How bizarre. But it would not matter, she had brought her own ordinary mirror with her.

She sat on the bed a moment, conscious of the dim sound of the sea and of the ticking of a pair of clocks, a black clock on the mantel with two angels, a tiny tower beside the bed. The greater clock told her it was seven-thirty, while on the tower the face showed nine.

Rachaela glanced at her watch, but she had, as so often, forgotten to wind it. It had stopped.

Well, she must prepare for Stephan and Anna.

She could not imagine them.

She got up and made herself go out into the lamp-lighted corridor. She found the bathroom at once, the only other door at this end of the passage.

It was a perfect period piece, for which the rich and famous would pay thousands in the city. Another oil lamp lit up the bath of green marble, the marble wash-basin and wooden-seated lavatory wreathed in green daisies. The vaunted hot water came via an Ascot. White pristine towels lay on a chest sporting eau-de-Nil basin and jug, and a dish of dried petals. The soap was also green with a smell of honeysuckle. New soap, new towels. On the walls mermaids dived over the tiles.

Rachaela looked up. There was a light fitment without a bulb. Electricity had come and gone.

She washed her face, hands and arms, seeing that she was trembling. The mirror behind the basin showed a glass ocean scene with a three-masted ship. She saw her lips, eyes, the blackness of her hair, in fragments.

37

Back in the bedroom her bags had noiselessly arrived. She changed her jumper, took off her boots and put on high-heeled shoes. In the great wardrobe with its mahogany wreaths and flanges, each sealed by a fine pollen of dust, she would later hang her few clothes. She disliked colour on her person, it wounded her. Oddly, the black, grey and cream, the sere faint-green and blue would match her always to this room.

She had again the sense of the validity of her arrival, *their* excitement, and of permanence, that too. She was frightened by these feelings but it was too late to be afraid. She had come to them. They had let her in.

She powdered her face in her mirror and reaffirmed the dark pencil around her eyes.

When she had combed her hair she walked straight to the door. And paused.

She had not heard the coming of the cases, but now someone was proceeding along the passage. It was a peculiar, rhythmic and uneven gait. Then she heard the voice, high and petulant. 'Giddy-up, giddy-up!'

Rachaela thought of a child pretending to ride a horse. An old child playing up and down the corridor.

There was a tiny scuffle. And the horse rearing: 'Whoa there!' And then galloping by and away.

Rachaela opened the door suddenly.

A black shadow cavorted in the passage's end, and rolled from view.

Something lay by the door.

Rachaela bent down, and touched with one finger the body of a perfect long-tailed mouse. It was dead, without a mark. About its body was tied a faded bow of pink silk.

38

Rachaela picked up the gift-wrapped mouse.

She held it in her hand. It did not distress her. It was soft and pitiful, beautiful as a toy in death. She laid the mouse on the dressing-table, took her bag, and went into the house.

Downstairs the lamps and candles had bloomed out everywhere. She saw doors in the walls of the hallway, one with black iron fitments like something from a castle. Burning reflections swam in the marble floor.

An archway gave on to a drawing room, a chamber of immense size and filled by lovely sullen furniture, and by the fine lace draperies of dust. The Scarabae lived in a desert of dust, clearing areas as they must, for here and there a table shone like a black pool.

A fire filled the centre of a white marble fireplace whose icy ends were pillars and heraldic shields.

No one was in the room, it was full of waiting.

Rachaela felt the room receive her, closing over her head. The sea sounded louder.

One of them at least was insane – the mysterious galloper, bearer of dead mice. It had been a man's voice, high-pitched, eldritch, but male. Could it be *Mr Stephan* who had ridden by?

A sound. Michael the servant of the Scarabae entered with a silver tray. Bottles and decanters glinted on the tray. He set it down on one of the dustless pools of tables. Rachaela was reminded of an expensive advert. Through the arch of the doorway now should come two elegant and well-dressed people.

'May I serve you with something, Miss Rachaela?'

Rachaela asked for wine and a glass was filled. The crystal was exquisite, the wine transparent.

Rachaela drank gratefully and the liquor leapt into her brain. An electric awareness made her turn.

Through some other door, or out of thin air, two figures had evolved.

They stood side by side.

They were very old, thin as twine, one female and one masculine, and at the borderline of age where the sexes blend, these two had sustained their genders. The woman's hair was the grey of gunmetal and piled up on her head, held with yellowish pearl pins. Her old dark dress, like something found on hangers in the wealthy clothes markets of the city, hung to her ankles. Her shoes had been in the mode a hundred years before, and were again. A sequin winked, another. She was sprinkled in a sugar of tiny blinks.

The man wore an antique dinner jacket and drained black trousers. His shirt was starched. His hair was thick and white, his eyebrows like iron shavings.

Both their narrow sets of hands were ringed.

Two elderly dolls they stood across the room in the fire and candlelight and their eyes glittered sharply. The eyes of clever rats, not mice.

'It's Rachaela,' said the old man, in a clear desiccated voice and an impeccable actor's accent, vacant of any hint of anywhere, even the country that surrounded them. He did not sound like the galloper.

'It is,' said the old woman. 'It is.'

And they did not move, forward or away. They were so old the absurd flutterings of youth no longer motivated or disturbed them.

Rachaela said, 'You must be Miss Anna and Mr Stephan.'

'Anna and Stephan,' said the woman. She smiled and her face moved like the sea, a wave, layers of pleated skin. Her smile was only a mask.

The old man said, 'How polite she is. No formality, please, with us.'

He did not smile, yet the sculptured motionless creases of his face were also masklike.

Age itself was held up before them, and they peered through, the bright eyes of rats in a wall.

'Later,' said the old woman, 'you will meet all the others. One by one. Here and there. No hurry.'

'*We* dine, you see,' said the old man. He added, 'I like to dine. It's civilized. But the rest . . . We keep to different hours.'

'You'll grow accustomed,' said Anna. 'You must do exactly as you like here. Now it is your home.'

'No,' said Rachaela. She spoke too quickly, violently.

They did not notice, or did not care.

Stephan said, 'We invited you.'

'Which of you wrote to me – the typed letter?'

'Oh, not us,' said Anna. The tide of her face flowed. 'Not *we*.'

'Nasty machines,' said Stephan. He grimaced and brushed the crumbs of the typewriter off his hands.

'The letter—' Rachaela said again.

'Don't concern yourself with the letter now. Now you're here, among us. We are your family, Rachaela.'

The servant entered and went to the tray, and they attended on him in silence.

In the sparkling firelight he brought to the old man a small slender glass of blackness and to the woman a thimble of garnet.

'We shall dine soon,' said Stephan.

Michael bowed, there could be no question of his gesture, bowed, and left them.

'I hope you will like the dinner,' said Anna. 'We eat very simply. We live off the land.'

She crossed to a chair and sat down. The old man continued to stand but when Rachaela seated herself to allow him to sit also, he did not do so. He went to a dusty table where a chessboard was laid out with onyx figures. He moved one carefully and stepped away.

'I must ask you,' said Rachaela, 'why I was invited. You pursued me. Why do you want me here?'

'But naturally we want you. Not only Stephan and I. The others. It's good that you take your place among us.' Anna was unruffled.

'There are many of us,' said Stephan. 'We agreed.'

'Each of you agreed that I must — that I must come here?'

'Of course.'

'We've waited several years. Until the right time.'

'Why,' said Rachaela, 'is it the right time now?'

Anna said, light as gossamer, 'There is a proper time for everything. Knowing it is the art.'

'Miriam and Eric, George and Peter, Sylvian perhaps, they would have had you here far sooner,' said Stephan.

Rachaela recoiled at the pure numerical addition. Were there so many of them, the tribe of the Scarabae?

'But the time was always wrong,' said Anna. 'Now the moment has arrived.'

She swallowed what was in her thimble, the garnet, in one stiletto gulp. She rose, and began to walk across the room towards a door curtain. Stephan said, 'We are going to dine.' And hastened ahead of her to whirl the curtain away and pull wide the door.

Rachaela got up. She followed like an obedient child. When she had been yet unborn, these two had moved on the earth, adult, leading God knew what lives.

Rachaela had never eaten rabbit before. They told her it was rabbit pie, asking her if she minded, if that would be all right. First there was a clear tomato soup. Michael and Cheta grew the vegetables, she was told. They relied as little as possible on the town.

She did not mind the rabbit, it was not unpleasant, rather bland, she thought. She wondered who hunted the rabbits – Michael, with his oddly focusless, blind-looking eyes?

Cheta served them. She was a female Michael, clad in an ordinary dark dress with a brooch at the collar. Its white stones looked real. Her grey hair was dressed in a bun low on her neck as if to show subservience, and her shoes were flat. Her eyes were just like Michael's.

Michael and Cheta were not so old as Anna and Stephan, yet they were old, had a dusty attic quality. They were Anna and Stephan come down in the world.

Candles lit the long table, laid with only three places. Above, lightless, a broken chandelier, snagging firelight from the grate. On the mantel was a golden clock, not ticking, stopped conceivably for decades.

The meal was indeed simple enough. After the pie, served with presumably home-grown carrots and fried cabbage, was dished up a dessert of sliced fruit in an alcoholic juice.

A cheeseboard came and biscuits baked by Cheta, and by another unseen one, Maria.

What relation were Anna and Stephan to each other? Did they bear some relation to the servants, for there was a similarity in all the faces. Rachaela found them disconcertingly familiar. Did this mean that she perceived, too, a resemblance to herself?

She did not want to ask these intimate questions. It had been difficult enough to ask what she had. And they had not answered – or there truly was no answer. Maybe their elderly hearts had only creaked out for her youth.

They were fascinated by her. She saw that.

The little questions they plied her with in turn, to do with the food, what food she liked, if she wished for the salt, were popped into her like polished coins into a magical box, to elicit her responses. They watched her with their bright cruel eyes. They would eat her alive. She only had to be, to feed them. They ate the rabbit with fastidious sharp snaps.

The conversation had been slight.

They were no conversationalists. They had come down here to feed.

As Stephan picked about amid the presumably town-bought cheeses, a curtain rustled, a door opened, and another thin old man came wafting in, weightless and virtually silent, with a book beneath his arm.

He crossed the carpet and slid to the table, but not to dine. He stared at Rachaela greedily, craning a little.

'Eric, here is Rachaela,' said Anna.

The eyes of Eric were the eyes of Anna and Stephan. His crinkled mummy's face showed nothing, the thin dry lips were not parted. Eric made a tiny sound, like a hiccup almost, and glided away and out of another curtained door, which seemed for a moment to open on a garden.

'You mustn't mind them,' said Anna. 'Not all of us are chatty. Eric is a thinker, a reader.'

The door curtain moved again and two old women in fusty beaded dresses blew into the room.

They too swam to the table. They had the eyes.

'Rachaela is here,' said Anna unnecessarily, for the eyes beamed and crackled on the newcomer. 'Rachaela, this is Alice, and this, Sasha.'

'Good evening,' said Rachaela, to test them.

Alice in the plum-sombre red replied with a quick darting movement of her hands. Sasha in a lace collar spoke: 'Good evening, Rachaela.' Like Anna and like Stephan, her voice, which somehow should have had a foreign accent, had none, no accent at all. It was a fact, each of them should have talked like dummies with the dialect of some mountainous European upland.

'Did you have a pleasant journey?' said Alice, abruptly, in the voice of Anna and Sasha.

'Not really,' said Rachaela.

'Oh I'm so sorry,' said Alice, the waves of her face making up concern. 'Travelling is so tedious now. So taxing. Everyone is so unhelpful.'

'Now Alice, when did you last travel anywhere?' chid Anna, playfully.

'I remember,' said Alice, flustered, 'the great black trains and all that steam and smoke. One was filthy. I remember my hat almost blew away, and Peter had to catch it.'

Rachaela found herself picturing a Soviet snowscape, the antique monster of the train flying in sparks and fume.

'It's years since any of us ventured out,' said Stephan from the cheese. 'We have small need now.'

'We were driven,' said Alice to Rachaela. Her face was still a mask, but a mask of confiding. Her eyes gleamed to see how Rachaela would react. 'Driven out.'

'The pogroms,' said Sasha suddenly.

Rachaela caught at the foreign word eagerly. They had given themselves away.

'Ours has not always been a tranquil history,' said Anna. There was no warning or repression in her voice. 'But this is too soon to burden Rachaela with the past. She's never known such things, and perhaps she never will.'

'Old scars,' said Stephan. He pushed his plate from him. 'Old history. The family has borne very much.'

Somewhere, perhaps in the room, a clock struck distantly.

'It isn't the time,' said Anna, still without warning.

Rachaela shivered at the power of unison in this rectangular space.

There were many of them, how many she did not now dare to guess. A swarm, the Scarabae, and heavy with their past which was not hers, and yet which, by relationship, must come to belong to her.

She felt a terrible affinity. She *believed* she was related to them, had somehow come to acknowledge it in the few weird hours she had spent here.

Alice said, faultlessly, 'She will see the library.'

Anna gave a little laugh like broken scales.

'The library!'

'Sylvian was busy today,' said Stephan.

They sighed, each of them, almost as one.

The large house teemed with these creatures, but they were one thing, facets of a whole, an entity.

And she, Rachaela, where did she fit?

Was she to be absorbed, devoured?

'Anna,' she said, forcing herself to utter the name, as if to name them was sorcerous. 'I'm awfully tired. Would you excuse me if I went up to bed?'

'You must do exactly as you want, Rachaela. There's a bell in your room by the fireplace. If you should wish for anything, Michael or Maria or Cheta will see to it. Did Carlo take up your bags?'

'Someone did.'

'Yes, that will have been Carlo. He is our strong one.'

Rachaela rose. She was taller than all of them: Anna and Stephan seated at the table, Cheta and Michael, Alice and Sasha facing her across its glowing length set only with three places. The candles shone and gave heat. Above, sprinkled with reflected light, the second chandelier dropped its mutilated beauty.

'How many are you?' said Rachaela, stemming the alarm of her voice. The sea sounded very loud in her ears.

Stephan laughed. His laugh was the male formula of Anna's. 'Many, many.'

Anna said quietly, 'Now we are twenty-one persons.'

Stephan said, 'You forget—'

'No,' said Anna. 'No.'

The dead mouse had been removed from the dressing-table, but the ribbon left there, neatly folded.

Rachaela sat brushing her hair. Her mother had been used to brush it. She was heavy-handed, seeming to think the thick prolifereration of the hair precluded any feeling at its roots. Rachaela had been a tangled child. Once the mane was lopped for convenience.

Rachaela had wept. She walked in hatred until the mass of hair was regrown.

The house did not make her dwell on her mother. This brusque memory was used, briefly, as a shield between herself and the house. The Scarabae.

On the stairs as she returned to her room she had met another old man in a greenish jacket. He peered into her face with burning eyes.

'I'm Rachaela,' she said. 'And you?'

But this old man scurried away, not frightened of her but unwilling to communicate. Was he Peter, or George, or Sylvian from the library? What did it matter? They were all one, and twenty-one in number.

There was a key in the lock of her door, and after visiting the bathroom, she used it. She had a vision, of course, of other keys which would open the way, and a troupe of them entering in a noiseless procession to observe her while she slept. Cobweb-ringed fingers over her things, her comb and brush, her powder and mirror, musty dresses shuffling by, the flick of an old man's sleeve . . .

It was impractical to leave. There was no means. Besides, she had been doomed to stay. She had nowhere else. All the wide world could not afford her sufficient crannies to hide from them.

For she knew she belonged to them. It was in her bones. She shrank only from certainty.

Finally she undressed and put on one of the pair of nightdresses she saved for emergencies; normally she slept naked. But here she must be protected by an extra flimsy film of man-made silk.

The nightdress was black. She surveyed herself among the marsh of lilies, the sunburst, in the mirror. She had noticed two or three mirrors in the rooms below, each set with coloured glass, ornamented, obliterated. As if seeing oneself must be kept to a minimum.

An empty bookcase stood against the wall. She had already, to ease her nerves, unpacked and peopled it with books. She looked at them. They were hers, her own. How slight her possessions in the house of the Scarabae. How slight she herself against the rooms and corridors, the doors and annexes and inner chambers of this dense-built thing.

Twenty-one, the ancient beetles crept and slipped about their shadowy pursuits.

But she stood alone, compressed by architecture and unusual shapes.

Rachaela got into the white, white sheets and sat up on the clean white pillows, seeing the room framed now in bottle-green velvet.

The fire burned low.

Far away through the house she heard soft groanings of the wood, the breathing of its worn and living heart. The winter night was motionless beyond the window with the tree. The sea was faint.

Rachaela detected old footsteps brushing down her corridor. Then, presently, a woman's round heels, slow and measured, not stopping.

The galloper had not come back.

How should she sleep?

She lay on her pillows, her body throbbing with tiredness. To sleep you must trust, let go. In this cradle she might lie awake a score of nights.

Rachaela heard a clock chiming walls and rooms away.

She had seen several clocks, none of which told the same time as another.

I can't even read. She was afraid to take her eyes off the bedroom, its fireplace, its locked door.

Watch then. Watch all night.

Eventually sleep would be irresistible.

She thought of her flat. It was not hers. Had never existed.

The cat would have liked this house. She would have prowled, scratching lightly at the doors to be let in or out. *She* would have slept, curled there on the indigo coverlet.

Rachaela saw the cat stalking the death of the firelight.

No, she had dreamed for an instant. Going to sleep then after all.

She was safe. They were insane, but so was she to have come here.

'Have nothing to do with them,' said Rachaela's mother, stark in a misremembered room of the past.

'No, Mummy,' said Rachaela.

She closed her eyes and beheld a tall male figure, faceless, black of hair, suspended between floor and ceiling. Rachaela slept.

Chapter Three

AN INCREDIBLE BLITZ OF COLOUR.
The woman in the bed opened her eyes and found herself drowned alive.

It was the window of stained glass, the light of day behind it now, casting down its panes.

Rachaela moved and a pool of blood and emerald slid along her body, turning the coverlet black and scarlet, dying her skin.

The room was splashed, dashed with dyes. A madness of green and red, magenta, gold and sapphire. Where the glass shone white it was opaque, and impenetrable. Nothing beyond the window showed through.

Rachaela saw the picture, hovering over her like a visitation. The tree clove the window, rising into a canopy of foliage from which blood-red apples scalded. Beneath the tree a man in golden armour with great wings tempted a naked woman to accept a fruit. From the extended apple a serpent coiled like a jewellery chain. Beyond the figures was a deep sky and the walks of a formal garden where animals, a gazelle, a lion, a unicorn, calmly

51

reclined. In heaven a rayed sun looked on in rage.

Eve tempted in person by Lucifer?

It was stultifying to wake to it, this bomb-blast. The whole room was in its web. It gave no peace.

Why had they thought the tempting of Eve applicable to their guest? Or did the subject mean nothing? These pictured windows filled the house, she had noticed them in the drawing and dining rooms; outside another marked the turn of the passage.

She would have to live with Eve and Lucifer.

The clock at her bedside said ten o'clock. The black clock on the mantle told her it was eight-thirty. Which was correct she did not know, and even as she thought this, a clock chimed in the house far away. She counted: Five strokes.

Rachaela got out of her coloured bed, leaving the sheets awash. The face of Lucifer reflected on her pillow, eerie and exact. He had the pale and undefiled mask of a saint, this fallen angel.

In the dressing-table mirror among the lilies and the sun, she saw the tree behind her. She was sandwiched in by glass.

She walked to the bathroom. Its window was a sea with shells. She ran a bath.

As she bathed, brushed her teeth, she heard no sounds from the house beyond its continual soft croaks, its joists shifting, plaster cracking, tiles loosening. The house was filthy and in bad repair. Only its lunatic beauty and its twenty-one persons held it together.

As she came from the bathroom an old woman in a brown day dress of six previous decades hurried by, her head tucked in. She paid Rachaela no heed. They were not all interested then. To some she was a threat, maybe, a new varnished toy which might harm.

She dressed and rang the bell, a tail of frayed blue velvet, for Michael, Cheta, Maria or Carlo to come. It was Cheta who presented herself in her dark frock and without her brooch.

'How can I help you, Miss Rachaela?'

'I want breakfast,' said Rachaela. 'What must I do?'

'I'll bring you something, Miss Rachaela. Or you can breakfast with Mr Peter and Mr Dorian. They always take breakfast in the morning room.'

'Bring me something here, please.'

It was a wonder they had not come en masse in the night to her room with knives and forks.

Toast it would seem was possible but not coffee. The family did not drink coffee. Tea, then.

'How do you come by tea?' Rachaela asked. 'You don't grow it?'

'A van comes to the cottages, from the town. Carlo and I buy the groceries from the van.'

'Are there cottages?'

Rachaela stumbled on an incoherent twist of hope. the world was not so far away. But the woman said, 'Six miles off, Miss Rachaela. It's a long rough walk, but we're accustomed to it.'

Cheta's eyes, if it were not inconceivable, would have assured Rachaela that the woman was blind. They were dark, like the eyes of all the people so far encountered in the house, but not sharp and bright; instead fixed, veiled-over, eyes that scarcely moved. Yet Cheta went from place to place with perfect precision. Coordinated, she manoeuvred through the panes of cracked syrupy window-light and went out.

The sound of the sea came and went in the house, vanishing at turns of the walls, behind pieces of furniture or long curtains. In places, conversely, the sea was suddenly loud, the crash of it on the rocks below. It was not to be seen from the house. Nothing was. Every window was of thick hectic glass. The panes were patterned, or they held still lifes: fruit, urns and trailing flowers and skies of crimson, saffron and salmon-pink, viridian and mauve like poisoned ivies, heaven-blue and smouldering red. The rooms were jigsawed with their interrupted reflections. Several of the larger windows contained pictures. Rachaela recognized uncanny and seemingly blasphemous parodies of the Bible: Cain killed by Abel perhaps, over his offering of grapes and wheat, and the slain deer hung around Abel's hunter shoulders, the neck wound like cornelian. And other cornelians in a round window above the stairs where a prince at a wedding changed the yellow wine into blood.

Rachaela was coldly amused by the bad taste of these eccentric scenes, presumably designed to please the family at its inception in the house. Yet she longed for a chink, some square inch of clear ordinary glass, looking out. The house was a box, a church, shutting in. The awful colours submerged the rooms, making them liverish. Gems of fire hung in mid-air, rainbows caught on the dust.

There were carvings on all the wood.

The old woman Anna had assured Rachaela she must do as she wanted. Lacking anything better, Rachaela moved about the building, losing herself in its corridors, finding locked doors, and opening others which gave.

She saw into lavish bedchambers, but presently she discovered in this way two old men playing chess, beneath a window with an angel in white and blue. The tines of their blue hands petrified on the board. The two old mummy faces moved about like rusty clockwork.

'It's her,' said one old face.

'Look at her hair,' said the other.

She was not an intruder but an exhibit. She left them and shut their door.

In other places she came on the Scarabae, or their traces.

Some acknowledged her politely, their sharp eyes eating her up, one or two ignored her, pottering on some crazy mission through the house.

She had become used to these meetings, passings. Their names did not matter – though one stole up to her and said, 'I am Miranda, and you are Rachaela.' Being elements of a whole, the collective name, Scarabae, would do.

They reminded her now of insects, their skinny uprightness and bony quick hands.

It was no worse than being in a fantastic old people's home. Better, for they were all independent and capable of individual governance.

One of them, an interested one, was following her, she became sure of that. Creeping behind her, scraping aside into some empty room should she retrace her steps.

She did not like to be followed, but what else could one expect?

The plan of the house eluded her. It was a shifting kaleidoscope of stained-glass and shadows. The rooms were far darker by day than by night.

Every clock she came on or heard told her of a different time.

Every mirror was choked and occluded. In one corridor a mirror of plain glass was being painted with a skilful if pedantic scene of groves and fountains, meadows and hills. Stacked neatly by the lost mirror were the artist's impedimenta: the tray of paints, palette, brushes and turpentine, rags.

Elsewhere she had seen paintings; but she did not study them. In one a goat seemed to peer forth from a woman's aproned belly.

So there is to be nothing sure here, no day, no time, no view of the self.

It was truly a madhouse.

Lacking time, only a vague hunger guided her. She found her way to the dining room and the long table was laid with ten places, and ten of the tribe were in position.

All looked up at her entry.

There were six old women in ancient dresses and four old men in mossy coats. They were all the same as Anna and Stephan, thick hair brushed back or piled up with pins. Ringed talons at work upon cold rabbit-pie and salad.

Rachaela recognized clothes and jewellery she had seen on her journey through the house – impossible to tell the faces and hairstyles apart. Could it be true that all these old women were herself in a hundred years time?

Should she sit down and eat the leftovers with them?

There was no place laid for Rachaela but a woman in a dark frock – her eyes were blind and bloomed-over and her hair was in a bun low on her neck, yet she was not Cheta, she must be Maria – was rectifying this, laying a place at the head of the table.

Rachaela sat down.

The tribe watched her take a slice of the pie and some tomatoes, lettuce.

No one spoke.

Then one of the old women, it was Miranda, said quaveringly, 'We mustn't stare.'

And reluctantly they ceased staring, returning to their plates, eating with the quick snapping agility of Anna and Stephan.

Rachaela did not try to make conversation. All this was a grim farce. She did not think that she could say anything that would remotely engage them, and yet they would stare at her again, twenty black eyes.

Anna and Stephan must be their leaders. Anna and Stephan were coherent, or almost, had not abandoned all pretence at normal social interaction. These were wild things dwelling in a stained-glass forest. They came to the pool to drink, ate berries and rabbit sitting upright, stared, considered, ran away or pursued. Was it one of these who had followed her?

She could think of no questions to put to any of them. In any case, would they be equipped to answer a question? *Why am I so important to you? A feared treasure, food for your thought?* They would tell her, if they told her anything, that she was supposed to be here. She was a part of them. Here was her destiny.

But actually she imagined them grubbing about her inquiry, pawing it, letting it lie.

They were so old no forms had consequence.

And Rachaela had never much bothered with the form of things, either.

She was not very hungry after all. The nursery of old ones pecked and gobbled, leaving their plates quite clean. They passed fruit between them. Their teeth, she had noticed, though discoloured, were still serviceable.

She listened to the noises of gnawing and sipping, the split of rinds and slicing of peels, spatter of pips.

They did not talk to each other even.

Even the old men at the chessboard had been quite silent.

The window, freed of its drapes, depicted a dragon fighting with a unicorn, but from the loudness of the sea, Rachaela guessed the window should have looked down towards the ocean.

Michael and Cheta came in with two teapots, and a plethora of fine china cups were set out.

Rachaela did not stay for the tea, and as she left the room, the forest creatures looked up and stared her away.

During what she supposed must be the afternoon, Rachaela found a chamber on the upper storey which contained a piano and an unstrung harp.

The harp was large and beautiful and sheathed in dust, the piano also. No one had played it for several years. Rachaela scooped the dust away and touched the keys. Their notes were surprisingly unsullied. She herself could not play. She was an audience not a creator. She longed for music in that moment, and thought of her radio brought from her case that morning. She had only one spare battery for the radio. When it was done, what then? She had seen no evidence here of radios let alone a record player.

How far away was the town? Was any transport credible? Would they let her hire a car and go to the town, or was she, fellow inmate, also now a prisoner?

She found the library too, during the afternoon, a massive room with high bookshelves, everything powdered by dust, but for a round table, polished from use. Here a pile of books was stacked ready, and an ebony ruler, inkwell and pen.

Rachaela went to the shelf and took a book at random, smoothing off the dust.

Opening it, she found that every line in the book was neatly crossed through.

She tried another book, with the same result. Another and another from different parts of the shelves. All the same.

Sylvian . . . busy in the library.

Nothing astonished her. She made one rotation of a defaced globe on the table, and left the library. She negotiated a way towards her room. At the intersection of two corridors, mistaking her direction, she came on a high window with a scene of a baby apparently being drowned among the bullrushes. Below stood a great taxidermist's triumph of a stuffed horse with a man on its back in pieces of armour. The man shook a sword at her and giggled in a thin soprano.

Rachaela stopped.

'Giddy-up,' insisted the rider, kicking the sides of the stuffed animal so clouds of dust were released.

When she had passed him and gone on, she sensed his stealthy presence at her heels. It was this one, presumably, who had followed her, and this one who brought gifts of mice. Maybe he caught them himself. He was not exactly like the others, his hair worn very long under the helmet of the armour. He must have discarded that or she would have heard him clanking through the corridors.

Reaching her room at last she had a weakening sense of relief. She locked her door and lay down on her bed, conscious of the pure face of the Devil reflected on to her own. She slept almost at once, as if a spell had been put on her.

The window was dark and the black clock said seven-thirty. Firelight made the room clandestine.

There were matches by the bed, tapers on the mantelpiece, and she lit the candles, the lamps.

She prepared herself as before, for an intimate dinner with Anna and Stephan. After all there were questions she must ask. The needs of hygiene and vanity – toothpaste, powder. The matter of batteries for the radio. More books without lines ruled through them . . . If she was to stay she must – *must*—

In the corridor, over the undertow of the ocean, Rachaela heard a new step passing. It was not like the others, lighter and more swift. Something brushed against the door.

Rachaela held her breath. Something different was in the passage.

Then it was gone.

She could not make herself go to open the door for almost a minute, and when she did so, nothing, naturally, remained to demonstrate who, or what, had passed.

Add that to the questions, then.

There was a curious odour in the corridor. It reminded her of some pleasant thing. She could not recall.

'You must give a list of what you require to Cheta. The van which comes to the cottages carries most things, most known brands.' This, Anna, in response to the first question.

'But I'd prefer to choose for myself,' Rachaela said.

'Oh no,' said Anna, 'could it be worth it, such a long and difficult walk. It's heathland, you know, beyond the wood. Uphill. Cheta is very strong, aren't you, Cheta?'

'Yes, Miss Anna.'

'But you are not used to such a trek. Seven miles.'

Rachaela noted that the distance seemed to have grown.

'Couldn't I hire a car to take me to the town?'

'Oh, my dear – so expensive. The town is thirty-five miles away.' Should Rachaela believe this? 'Besides, so awkward to hire a car. We have no telephone at the house.'

'But there was a car to meet me at the station.'

'There is a public telephone in the village. Carlo called the company from there. It was still necessary to send them directions.'

Awkward then, but not completely beyond the bounds. But Anna was evidently discouraging her. Let it rest for now. The precious van would supply batteries perhaps, and other basic essentials.

Tonight five places had been laid at the long table. Only two other Scarabae had presented themselves, the two old men from the blue chessboard, Dorian and Peter. They ate voraciously as wasps and now and then stared at Rachaela, not wanting to miss more than a little of her presence. They did not speak beyond a word or two. She was glad she had not breakfasted with them.

Three old women had come into the room during the meal, which comprised a soufflé and fish in a hot sauce. The names of the old women were Miriam, Livia and Unice, which as usual did not mean very much. They did not stay, only filled their eyes with great draughts of Rachaela and pattered out.

'There was something outside my room,' said Rachaela.

'That would be Uncle Camillo,' said Stephan. 'He likes to play tricks, cut capers.'

'Yes, I think I saw him on a stuffed horse. And he's been following me.'

Anna shook her head gravely. 'Camillo is very old,' she said quite seriously. 'Very naughty. But harmless as a silly child.'

'It wasn't Camillo.'

Anna hesitated. She said, 'There is a large cat in the house. A nocturnal beast. We see it rarely, it leads its own life.'

Rachaela shook her head.

'I don't think a cat—'

The door opened.

'Here is Sylvian,' said Anna. 'Sylvian, here is Rachaela.'

The eraser of books came forward slowly, his hands clasped at his chest, eating eyes on Rachaela.

'I've been wanting to meet you,' said Rachaela. 'Why do you rule through all the words?'

'The words,' repeated Sylvian. He looked too fragile to be interrogated but this did not stop her. They were all fragile as the chitinous wings of grasshoppers, and predatory as locusts.

'In the library. And there was a globe with scratches across the continents.'

'Words mean nothing,' said Sylvian, 'they gather like the dust.'

'Words convey concepts and dreams,' said Rachaela.

'Also nothing.'

'So you deface the books.'

'I correct them,' said Sylvian in his cracked firm voice. He unclasped his hands and spread them out, 'When I have finished, the library will be sound.'

'I hope I can find some portion you haven't damaged,' said Rachaela icily.

'The north wall,' he told her, helpful. 'I have yet to work there. A long task.'

'Sylvian does what he feels he must,' said Anna, the translator. 'I'm sorry if you wished to read the books. But I send for books from the town. Allow me to order some for you, if you will give me some idea—'

'Are the books delivered here?' Rachaela asked swiftly.

'Oh, no. The van brings them to the village, and Carlo carries them back for me.'

'I see.'

'And the globe,' said Stephan, smiling benignly. 'That isn't the work of Sylvian. Alice scratched at it with a hat pin.'

'The places from which the family has been driven out,' said Anna.

'The pogroms,' said Rachaela.

'Oh, Sasha uses that word,' said Anna. 'It's a word she finds applicable. It will do.'

'So many countries drove out the Scarabae,' said Rachaela, the globe suddenly vivid in her mind. 'Why?'

'The family is ancient,' said Anna.

'And unpopular,' chuckled Stephan.

'Superstitious fears of the ignorant,' said Anna.

'Of what?'

'We are different,' said Anna. 'You've seen. We keep close, and have our own ways.'

'The windows here,' Rachaela said at random.

'Some have come from our other houses. We are safe here.'

'But the windows,' persisted Rachaela, 'scenes from a Bible of hell.'

'Just so,' said Anna simply. 'Several were broken by the mob and have been pieced together by artisans. Not all are old. Some new ones were fashioned.'

'And you don't like the views from the house.'

Anna said, 'It's the daylight we dislike.'

Rachaela remembered the double doors of the hallway. She visualized Cheta and Carlo on their journey to the village, muffled as if against a storm.

Night creatures then, nocturnal like their cat.

'And you expect me to live like this?' Rachaela said.

'You will come to find it comfortable,' said Anna.

In their places, Dorian and Peter abruptly laughed, as one.

Rachaela said, 'Aren't I allowed to go out?'

'Of course. Of course, Rachaela. By night or day. Oh, let me show you the garden. Come.'

Stephan hurried before Anna to widen the door, already ajar, which Rachaela had seen revealed the previous night. It led into a conservatory of gigantic plants. Ferns towered to the glass roof. Ribbed and ornately paned, the glass was clear.

A stone lion's head stood among the cups of flowers.

'Here is the way,' said Anna, and thrust wide a second door on to the open night.

Rachaela gasped with instinctive relief.

There was the smell of leaves and frost, the night breath of great trees.

A moon hung over the land, an unbroken chandelier. It showed with its blue-white shine the garden of a fantasy, rampant and overgrown. A yew tree, a poplar, a cedar spreading tremendous boughs, and oaks like columns to uphold the sky. A roof of bare stitchwork which in summer would be a parasol of foliage. Ivy mounted the trees, and the rose briars had climbed upon the cedar.

The sea raced and boomed, tireless, on the wall of night.

'At the end there is a little gate. A path leads along the cliff. Quite safe if you are careful,' said Anna. She raised her face of wrinkles and fissures into the balm of the moon. 'Smell the pines,' she said. 'Such terrible trees, they overgrow everything if they can. Carlo weeds them out from the garden, and cuts the lawn in summer.' She flitted forward like an aged fairy. The others ventured after Raphaela, murmuring and susurrating, into the garden. Stephan pushed in among the shrubs to inspect the briars, Dorian and Peter posed grotesquely on the rough grass, Sylvian in the doorway.

There was a moon-dial, the moon's crescent face also a skull. The dial could not tell time, there were no numerals.

Rachaela pushed through the briars towards the gate. She tried it. It was not locked. Outside she saw the free night, the cliff with its clumps of wild flowers, the terrace of pines. The sea beyond the cliff was smooth as silver cigarette paper. Ozone, salt, carbon dioxide.

Behind her the elders stood, pleased at her pleasure, looking on, their sewn faces placid round their hungry eyes.

She woke, and the shock of the window burned her, made her start. The tower clock told her it was ten o'clock.

It occurred to Rachaela that she was waking at the routine time of seven-thirty, as she had done in the days of Mr Gerard and the shop. Ten, then, meant seven-thirty, or the eight-thirty of the black clock of the angels, that meant seven-thirty also.

The reasonableness of this exulted her. It was a triumph over the house.

She threw off the covers, and the body of the golden Devil which had lain on hers as she slept.

Today she need not explore the corridors and rooms. The liberty of the garden and the cliff path were before her.

She would not trouble with breakfast, as in her former life often she had not. She missed coffee with anger. Perhaps Cheta would buy her a jar of instant from the fabulous seven-mile-distant van. It would be playful to send Cheta and Carlo with her rogue list, such things the old ones never needed – batteries and tampons.

The lower house might be empty. Dorian and Peter breakfasted in the morning room – she did not even know where it was.

She went downstairs. The two high windows reflected their violet urns and saffron sunsets into the chequered floor. The wooden nymph was at her post.

An impulse made her approach the iron-bound door. She tried it, it was locked. Recollecting the structure of the house as she had seen it during her approach, it seemed to her this door might lead into the tower. That she found it locked was only in keeping with the capricious mystery of this church of eyeless mirrors.

Rachaela walked through the drawing room and so into the dining room. The table was bare, and Maria was mildly polishing it. Overhead the years-dusty chandelier looked down into its reflection.

'Good morning, Maria.'

'Good morning, Miss Rachaela.'

Maria went on drowsily polishing.

Rachaela crossed to the curtain and pulled it back to reveal the door, closed. Did the conservatory still endure beyond, or had it phantasmally vanished?

As she opened the door a violent smack of whitest light burst over her. It made her mind reel, almost she shielded her eyes. Daylight – already foreign. So quickly the house had blinded and steeped her in its ichors.

She heard an indrawn breath, and looked back to see Maria groping her way from the room.

Rachaela drew herself out into the crystal glare of the conservatory, forcing her eyes to adjust to its brilliance. After two or three minutes her focus returned. She stood and breathed in the light.

The plants were revelling in it, for there was sun today and the glass room was already quite warm.

Rachaela picked her way between the tubular leaves, the green feathers of the giant ferns, the trumpeting lilies out of season.

Although she had found the conservatory door also closed, at night – surely to the detriment of the plants – it stood ajar. The house doors too were kept open after dark. Night was welcome in the house, day not.

There were lily petals on the stone floor by the doorway. No. Not petals. Strong white feathers scattered like an offering. And there was blood.

She thought of the cat Anna had mentioned. But the feathers were large, great quills, surely the cat would not tackle something of this size, perhaps a big gull.

Rachaela moved the disturbance of the feathers from her mind. She refused to be distracted, and opened wide the door, closed it, and stepped out into air.

The winter's day was cool but not harsh. The sun rode in a thin blue sky meshed with vaporous clouds.

The pines were a black wall. They had crept up on the house to this side and, further off beyond the angled steeps of its architecture, they had built on their terrace, staring out across the cliff edge at the sea. The path was well-defined and broad. Quite safe, as Anna had said. Wild flowers starred the border, flowers that had no business there, it being too early for the spring. The cliff bulged before it fell, it curved. In gaps ahead it became possible to watch the splintering of the breakers eighty feet below.

Rachaela walked along the path, exhilarated by the freshness of light and open air. The vistas of the sea made her giddy. She knew the death-wish pull of space, the ease of falling, and kept well to the inside of the path.

Presently it coiled its way aside, in among the pine trees.

She looked back at the house.

Pale grey, stained with drainage of rain, other weather, and the velvet fingering of lichens. The roofs raised their crenellations, the smoke of their chimneys, their parapets, a brace of weather-vanes, which had somehow contrived each to point a different way. The cap of the tower was just visible. The windows did not pierce or breach, though many passed down the face of the building nearly to the ground. They were a solid witches' brew of darkness. Here and there some inner shaft of light sent up a flare in them of yawning rose or stagnant green or the blue of an old medicine bottle. But this was a jewel not an opening. *Keep out* the windows said. A costive house, containing and intemperate. It fulminated in the grey skull of its walls.

Rachaela admired it. It attracted her. All she liked least about it, its imprisoning smother, appealed to her artistically and intellectually, even while the gusts of real air revived her body. She would succumb to the house in time, Anna had been right. Why fight it.

She walked on along the path and in among the black pines. Needles crunched under her boots. The earth was fox-coloured. More feathers were littered about a tree trunk; that was proper, that the cat should do its Goliath-slaying outside in the savage wood.

The trees broke and the landscape altered. The pines had ended with a virile finality on the brink of a rolling grass lawn quilted with heathers and gorse. The sea spread below and the heath above, away and away. She could see distant coves, the cliffs green-ankled and ashed by spume. And too the swell and tumble of the land, pale green and woven brown, the odd tree standing like a mast and closer to hand, a great tilted stone like a descended lightning bolt.

Rachaela walked towards the stone. It was old as the trees, far older very likely. Perhaps it had been here when the Romans assayed these coasts. Perhaps they had marched by and marvelled at it or muttered to their own gods.

Rabbits feeding on the turf shot away as she approached.

The stone was smirched white and carious. Its curious lightning shape hinted at legends of violence. These, like the marching Romans, did not count at all. *Words mean nothing*, Sylvian had said. Of course, nothing did.

Even this. Even Rachaela standing here in her black hood of hair and her London coat, and her white face that was still that of a young woman, even she did not count, or what became of her.

She would catch the virus of age off them. She would grow ancient, gaunt and friable and tough, like them. Perhaps her hair would turn grey, her breasts drop like withered sacks. She would not lose her teeth, for they had not. There was no evidence among the Scarabae of any crippling disease, no arthritis, no limping and twisting. Their metallic snows of hair were as thick as her own. Their eyes more concentrated and feral.

It was stupid to ask herself what she did here. It had been inevitable. Her mother's nagging voice, which never quite went away, continued to warn Rachaela against the Scarabae, but even the warnings had driven her, so it seemed, into their lair. Her horror of them had now melted. She was trapped.

And when she was old like them, what after that?

She was not like them. She was the *unlike* one. That was her purpose.

Rachaela went round the stone. She had noticed strange ripped places on the trunks of some of the pines, and in the soil under the stone were long claw marks, as if from a rake.

Could she walk from here to the village? Six or seven miles. How long would it take her – the going looked very uneven. And she did not know the way.

A bruised cloud, which had been creeping from the horizon, covered the sun. Dark light obscured the heath. She would walk to that hill there and look out. Then she would be tired, for she was not practised in walking. She would go back to the house for food, climb up to her room and switch on her radio for music. Tomorrow she would walk further.

How isolated was the heath. No one in the world but she and the Scarabae.

*

That evening Rachaela wore her green dress and a necklace of green glass beads she had found at a jumble sale.

Anna and Stephan were in the drawing room seated on a sofa, already drinking their pre-dinner tipples. Rachaela helped herself to a glass of the white wine.

71

'Did you enjoy your walk?' asked Anna, comfortably.

'Very much.' Tired out, she had fallen asleep again in the shards of the window, listening to Verdi. 'Which is the way to the village?'

'Across the heath. But it's eight miles. Surely too far for you?'

'I might work up to it,' said Rachaela. 'The exercise will do me good.'

They went into the dining room and three places were laid. Cheta and Maria served them. Maria had recovered from her hurt, the blast of daylight from the conservatory.

There was asparagus soup, and then a meat dish already sliced in a sauce. It had a fishy taste, and was rather stringy.

'What meat is this?'

Anna looked obliging. 'Seagull,' she said. And then, 'I do hope you don't mind it.'

Rachaela had checked and put down her fork. To eat a gull was no worse than to eat a rabbit or a lamb, yet somehow it offended her. She did not want any more.

'I'm afraid I don't like the idea,' she said.

'Our habits spring from necessity.'

Who had hunted the gull, scattering its feathers underfoot? Surely not after all the cat, as she had supposed.

'No, I quite see that,' said Rachaela. 'But nevertheless, I'll leave it.'

There was an apple tart to follow, and Anna urged her to take two helpings, which Rachaela declined. She was used to eating sparely.

After the dinner, they did not speak.

Stephan stared into the fire. Anna embroidered, long flowers and streamers of foliage.

Rachaela sat in the silence and eventually excused herself.

Out in the hallway she sensed a sizzling undercurrent in the drugged air. Something had passed, or lingered still in the shadows. She went to what she took to be the tower door, and tried it again. It did not give.

An old woman in purple came down the stairs and went by Rachaela with a single look. Rachaela did not guess whether or not they had met before. Was it Livia or Unice? Would she know any of them again? Anna and Stephan, perhaps. And Sylvian the destroyer.

In the passage upstairs there was a scent of warmth, of something living, but nothing stirred. No mice lay on the threshold.

Beyond the closed sarcophagus of the house the wind was rising, moaning round the corners. Rain struck the window of the temptation. The cool quiet day had ushered in a storm.

Rachaela imagined the rain splashing in at the conservatory, at the double door at the front of the house, through any other apertures left ajar on the night.

The thunder smote the house like an engine of demolition. The house shook.

Rachaela opened her eyes, lifted herself. The darkened window pulsed and quivered with rain, the wind and the sea between them made a noise in which ancient screaming and the collapse of walls might distantly be made out.

The air was galvanic, a sheen on it like sightless fire.

Rachaela wished she could see through the window to the storm. She sat upright in the bed and waited for the lightning. It came. The picture in the window flashed a ghostly blue and ochre and imprinted itself upon the room, on Rachaela's white arms and features. And in a chair across the room something sat, facing her.

The light was gone.

Had she mistaken it – some trick of shadow?

She reached out slowly and found the matches, the candle on the bedside table. She must strike this primal glow into being, and see.

Rachaela struck the match.

A man sat in the chair, black on blackness, pallor on the black.

Uncle Camillo . . . Camillo the trickster had broken into her room.

Her hands numbed, she put the match to the candle and took it up. Its light soaked out and the man was really there.

It was not Camillo.

He said, 'You like storms.'

'Yes, but I don't like finding strangers in my room.'

'Not a stranger, Rachaela.'

Even seated, he was tall. She could not make out what he wore, dark things. His hair was black, outlining his face, doing no more than that. The face itself was an image of light and shade, clear bones cloaked in skin. He was not old, her age, perhaps. But his eyes were not like the eyes of any of them, black and still as pools of paint.

'I don't care,' Rachaela said, steadily, 'I want you to get out. Now.'

'But I'm looking at you. I've had to wait nearly thirty years. I'm interested.'

His face was devastatingly familiar. It was like her own.

'Who are you?' she said. 'One of the Scarabae?'

'The last, but for you,' he said.

'You're telling me,' she said, 'that you are my father.'

'There's nothing to you of your mother. Did she never reproach you that you looked like me?'

Unbidden, her mother's face rose up in her brain, the unliking look, the hostility always there. A mother who did not confide, never consoled, told stories of dark things, the wolf that blew down the piggy's house . . .

'You're much too young to be my father.'

'I look younger than I am. As you do, Rachaela.'

He said her name as if he tasted it.

She would not pull up the sheets to cover the nightdress, would not look away.

'You must be mad,' she said. 'Mad if you are my father, mad if you aren't.'

'Where else would I be but here?' he said.

The lightning came again then, and the thunder on its wings. Some draught or vibration snuffed the candle as in the most clichéd drama of fiction.

And in the pitch dark, she heard the chair whisper, the door murmur to itself, opened. Closing.

Chapter Four

❀ THEY WERE DRESSED JUST AS she had foreseen, in long coats and boots, scarves about their necks, gloves on their hands. He wore a battered old hat and she a head-square unsuitably brightly coloured. Both wore sunglasses with thick rims. Clad for the Swiss Alps. They poised in attitudes of wonderment.

Rachaela had cornered them in their kitchen, alerted by Anna the previous evening: 'Tomorrow Cheta and Carlo will be going to the cottages. Do you have your list? They will leave early.'

Rather than hand the list to Cheta, Rachaela presented herself in person at eight o'clock in the kitchen, whose whereabouts she had located by watching them head along a narrow passage which led from the hall.

Carlo she had glimpsed in the garden meanwhile, tugging at the winter weeds. The garden was prolific and unruly, regardless of the time of year. He was a big, muscular old man, like a gypsy – but, too, like all the rest of them. The same face, the fixed and dusty eyes of Michael, Cheta and Maria.

'You're going to the village. I'll come with you,' said Rachaela.

'It's a long walk, Miss Rachaela.'

'Yes I know. Nine miles, or ten.'

Cheta glanced at Carlo. How could they refuse her if she insisted.

For a week she had been training her body, walking long distances each day beside the cliffs, across the heath. She had walked as far as the farther hills, and back, a trek which her watch, now rewound, and set according to her presumed waking time of seven-thirty, informed her had taken three hours. She could cope with Cheta and Carlo's long walk.

The kitchen was large, full of sinks, shelves and pans, a black range which was perhaps not used, for to one side there lurked an elderly gas cooker. Gas had come to the house and stayed, but only here and in the Ascots of the bathrooms.

The kitchen floor was stone and the wooden table scrubbed. There were mouse-holes clearly visible. She imagined the forays of the mice by night and the night cat leaping on them. A pantry opened out of the kitchen. The eldritch Scarabae who had not dined would come to raid it in the dark, like the mice. She pictured Uncle Camillo stuffing himself with cold seagull. There were jars of pickled fish and preserves, dark brown and mauve. On the table lay two purple-green cabbages and a great knife. The opaque white windows contained leaves of cabbage-coloured glass, and oil lamps waited ready to light the preparation of food. A weird subaqueous kitchen.

And here the two venturers stood hesitating in their Alpine garments and black goggles.

'A fine morning,' said Rachaela, opening the door. Outside was a tiled passage, and a second door, of course. 'Let's go, shall we?'

They followed her like reluctant dogs, slinking out through the second door into the animosity of the pale sunlight.

After the storm, the weather had been fair all week.

The storm, anyway, maybe had not happened with the violence she had supposed. The dream had been folded away with the storm. In the morning, waking and remembering it, she had lain a long while, trying it over.

There could be no doubt it was a dream, the thunderclap and bleach of lightning, the man who sat in her room.

Later she got up and examined the chair, as if some psychic impression might have been made on it. But really, she knew it for a dream at once. They had come in waking dreams before, the tall dark man and the meeting in the tempest. Naturally she would have such dreams, here. Naturally too she would create her father from the limbs and body of the house. He was the fantasy monster of her youth, the bad black wolf who blew into her mother's life the unwanted seed.

Reason with it as she would, however, the realness of the dream had tinged the days which succeeded it. Lying down at night she had wondered if he would appear again.

But her dreams were only the usual nonsense things. She dreamed of the bookshop and Mr Gerard inserting biscuits into the shelves, or of the flats bulldozed to the ground and swarms of bats flying up with the debris.

Outside the house the path ran along the cliff and back into the woods, towards the heath.

Cheta took the lead along the path.
Carlo went after her, and Rachaela after Carlo.
Three daring explorers in the cold bright morning.

They walked for an hour and a quarter along the half-familiar terrain, then turned inland, down into scrubby stands of pine and barbed-wire entrenchments of gorse.

Cheta and Carlo did not speak to each other or to Rachaela. She did not want them to.

Birds sang in thickets. Gulls wheeled overhead. The landscape was bare and desolate away from the grandeur of the sea. Rocks with gaps in them might conceal strange creatures. It was a place for a knight to come to fight with dragons.

Half an hour later a road, barely more than a lane, appeared, searing aimlessly across the country. Cheta and Carlo got on to it and walked in the middle of the highway. They feared no sudden traffic, and none came.

Leafless hedges shielded the road, and strips of wild meadow, once fields, ran occasionally behind them. Trees rose in isolation, bent by winds. Rooks exploded from a barren-looking copse and the gaunt walls of a gutted farmhouse went by.

An hour more and the road spilled down into a valley, and there was the village.

Rachaela was not tired, which was as well, she had the walk back to contend with, almost three hours in itself. Anna had not perhaps lied about the distance.

The village was disheartening.

Grey stone houses cluttered both sides of the novice road. Dark winter fields stretched up the hills, one with a rusting broken tractor in it. There were groups of abandoned cars, their roofs caved in, and ink-black crows cawing on their bonnets.

They walked down into the street and passed an umber little pub with a creaky board: The Armitage.

There was open ground inside the village and there, already drawn up and ready for business, was the large blue van. No one else was out to buy. The denizens of the drear village must have made their purchases already and gone back inside their bleak stone houses. A phone box poked up beyond the van. From some way off, Rachaela saw the receiver depending useless on its cord. Wires sprouted. She felt a start of unsurprised but actual fear. The phone box, out in this remote nowhere, had been vandalized.

Presumably the houses concealed phones, some of them at least.

She visualized walking the miles to this stone village and knocking on house after house door, and not one opening, and the crows coughing in the ruined cars.

They went to the back of the van and a fat man in an anorak rose up, and a skinny woman with a red nose and chilblained knuckles on her bluish hands.

'Here you are,' said the man, with fake cheeriness to Carlo and Cheta, obviously accustomed to them. 'What can we do you for today?'

He had an accent of London, the city Rachaela had left.

Cheta handed him up a list.

'Just the usual,' said the man.

'The lady will want some things,' said Cheta.

The van man looked at Rachaela, cunning, and she felt the familiar old shame of childhood at having to ask him for intimate items, but there the jolly boxes of Tampax were, blatantly displayed among the soap and bread.

The woman began to pack flour and butter, sugar and toilet paper into the canvas bags Cheta had produced out of her coat and handed up. The man hauled out two huge cans of oil and set them by for Carlo.

Rachaela had believed she would have to carry her own items and had been discreet. But Carlo took up the plastic carrier. He was the servant of the Scarabae.

Cheta said, 'Can you bring some of the brandy next time? Two bottles.'

'If they can get it, I will.' The man totted up the load of goods and read off a price.

Cheta paid from a roll of brown notes.

From where, oh from where, did the Scarabae take their money?

Rachaela was not invited to pay. She was relieved, but not astonished.

At once Cheta and Carlo, now burdened like RSPCA posters of cruelty to donkeys, turned from the van.

There was to be no respite, no pause. Let alone any social chat.

The fat man and the chilblained woman drew away as they walked back over the road.

Rachaela could guess their conversation. 'Well that was a turn-up.' 'Who was she?' 'A young one.' 'No sunglasses.'

The adventure of the village of the vandalized phone was over. Now there was only the three-hour walk to the house.

A wave of exhaustion overcame Rachaela.

What would they do if she lagged behind, sat down on a rock.

Why, wait patiently for her under their loads.

She was not sorry to leave the village.
It was depressing and a disappointment.
The crows laughed among the dead cars.

Defeated by abstract random things, Rachaela found
herself disgorged by the heath, back at the house of
the Scarabae, dog-tired, her stamina used up.

In her absence her bed had been scrupulously made,
as she herself never troubled to make it, only tossing it
together, straightening the pillows for the Devil's face
to reflect on.

She ran a bath and lay there, listening to Mozart on
her radio for which batteries were now assured. The
piece was a piano concerto. It seemed to her she had
dreamed of piano music in this house . . .

Her watch, assiduously wound, showed her it was
three-thirty.

At four-thirty she left the bath and went into her
room. She changed her clothes and lay on the bed,
now only in a bath of music. She thought seriously
about the house.

She had left it alone during her week of external
walking, only trying the iron-bound door of the tower
from time to time, indolently, knowing it would be
locked.

In the passage from her room she had noticed the
paintings more, how in places a top layer of paint had
flaked off from them to reveal other scenes beneath. She
recalled the goat's head thrust from the woman's belly.

And she had found the kitchen with the gas cooker
and mouse-holes.

She thought of the storm, and the dream of the man.

She had begun to imagine, very often, that something followed her through the house. On the heath

she had been free of this feeling. It was a sort of hysteria, she now believed; for the very mad, very old, old man had not pursued her, not popped out or been abruptly encountered. Perhaps he had lost interest in her.

Rachaela began to go to sleep. Well, she could rest until the dinner with Anna and Stephan. She did not mean to miss that. She wanted now to speak to them, to Anna.

It would be simple just to doze and walk and idle the time away here, as if this were all that was asked of her. But she knew it was not. Something was expected. It must be. She was like the sacrificial lamb, kept and fattened against the day of its ritual death. Was it so far-fetched to think the purpose of the Scarabae any different? It was easy to credit them with it, the keeping of her, her ritual slaughter at some pre-ordained phase of the moon. Dragging her screaming at midnight across the heath, strong Carlo and Cheta, their grip merciless; Sylvian with the huge knife from the cabbages held daintily as the ebony ruler. One more word to erase: *Rachaela*.

The room faded. She was standing at a crossroads on the heath, naked but for her blowing hair. She waited, and no one came but the blue van and the fat man, who pulled up and called cheerily, 'Want a lift? Hop in.'

Stephan did not come to 'dine', only Anna came, in her long charcoal frock, her embroidery in one hand.

Michael served her her thimble of garnet and Rachaela her glass of white wine.

It was another rabbit-pie. Rachaela recalled the rabbits she had seen feeding on the heath. There were countless numbers of them, a larder to the

Scarabae. Probably it was Carlo who took them. Yet she had never heard the crack of a gun.

They sat before the drawing-room fire.

On the walls were mirrors obscura, paintings upon other paintings, drawn curtains behind which jostled stained glass images. The figures on the chessboard were in disarray, someone had lost their temper at them; the queen lay on her face. The candles burned and the yellow lamps. Was it cosy by the fire or macabre?

'Anna, I really must talk to you. I mean, I should like answers.'

'Whatever I can do, Rachaela.' Anna was, as always, gracious.

'I went to the village with Cheta and Carlo.'

'You're very brave. But I can see the walk tired you.'

'The village looked quite dead. And the public telephone was vandalized.'

'Oh, dear,' said Anna, embroidering placidly.

'Suppose,' said Rachaela, 'that you needed the phone. Is it sensible not to have one?'

'All that bother of having a telephone installed,' said Anna. 'I'm afraid we're set in our ways. We hate intrusion.'

'But *I* have intruded.'

'You? Rachaela, you're one of our own.'

'Suppose,' Rachaela tried again, 'one of you fell ill.'

'We are never ill,' said Anna. 'Only old.'

'Then that alone—'

'No, Rachaela. The case would never arise. We care for ourselves.'

'And me,' said Rachaela, 'if I wanted to phone anyone.'

'I'm sorry,' said Anna. But she looked up. Her sharp eyes said, *You are alone. You have no one.*

Rachaela said, 'It disconcerts me. The way you live here. And if I stay, the way I must live with you.'

'Forgive me,' said Anna, 'but we know something about you, Rachaela. Your lack of social contacts, your own way of living. Rather like a hermitess.'

'I had a choice.'

'Did you? Haven't you besides made a choice now to be with us?'

'No,' said Rachaela. 'I'll be honest. The choice of coming here was forced on me. And you hunted me, didn't you.'

'Oh yes,' said Anna, 'we will admit to that.'

'I asked you before, and I must ask you again. Why?'

'You belong here, with us.'

'I don't agree,' Rachaela lied. Anna smiled a little. To lie was useless. 'I have no responsibilities. No autonomy here. I'm some kind of puppet. I sense this. That I'm being kept for something.'

'For yourself,' said Anna. 'Don't you understand your worth? We prize tradition. We value the ideal of the family. And you are the last of us. The very last flower on our tree.'

Rachaela thought of his words, in the dream: *The last, but for you.*

She felt a constriction in her throat and spoke through it, crisply.

'And the last before me was my father.'

'Yes.'

'Why,' said Racahela, 'isn't *he* with you?'

Anna said, 'But Rachaela, he is. Of course he is.'

Rachaela thought of the old men of the house. Something sank inside her. Her mother had spoken of him as young.

'Here,' she said. 'Then I've met him.'

'Your father is a hermit, Rachaela. As you are a hermitess. He lives here, but not readily among us.' Anna let her embroidery lie. 'When he was younger, your age, he ran away. He ran out into the world, and we let him go. It was the time for it. He made you, out in the world. Then he came back to us.'

'Willingly?'

'No, not willingly, but with resignation. There was nowhere else for him to go. You chafe at the confines of the house, the two of you. Yet you hate the open places of the outer world, the cities, the people. They offend you. *Life* offends you. You are Scarabae. Here, you're safe.'

'Where,' said Rachaela, and her hands had clasped one another, 'where is he?'

'You've tried the locked door of the tower several times. There. I'm afraid you will have to leave it to your father, the hour of your meeting. You must be eager, perhaps angry.'

'Angry, yes.'

'That is something you must resolve with him. You and he are not like the rest of us. You and he are alike. He will come to you.'

'Tell me his name,' said Rachaela. Her mother had never named her father. He was only faceless darkness, rage.

'Adamus,' said Anna. 'Adamus is his name. It's very old. Traditional to the family.'

Rachaela did not accept the name. It rang on in her head like music in another room.

'And he lives in the tower. Does he prowl the house in the darkness?'

'What a perceptive question. Once he did. He is more rested now.'

Rachaela stared into the fire.

Had it been a dream, then? Had it been real? Or could it be – some vision, precognition, of the facts. The man in the dream was too young. Her father had 'made her in the world' when he was her age now. He would be almost sixty. Touched by age, by the markers of Stephan and Sylvian, Peter and Camillo.

Rachaela felt unable to ask anything more. The flurry of defiance had gone dead. The new flame burned in her. *Adamus*. The name of some saint or demon in a mystery play.

Walled up in the locked dark tower.

'I'll go to bed, Anna,' Rachaela said.

Anna smiled again, and picking up her embroidery stitched in a flower like drops of blood.

In the night, Rachaela sat in the chair, where he had sat, sat in reality not dream. Her thoughts would not keep still. She saw him over and over. He was her *father*.

There was so much she wanted to say to him, cry out at him. She would in his presence be dumb, surely, gagged by all these sentences and accusations.

Her fire burned low and she put more wood on to it from the brass scuttle. All day long Scarabae's servants came in and out of this room, dusting it so the dust flew up off one surface and resettled on another, seeing to the bed, the lamps and candles, the fire, the supply of little logs.

But at night he had come and used a key, for the door was locked.

If she had not woken would he only have sat here a while, watching her? She would never have realized he had been in the room. Had he come back and she not known?

The far-away clock struck. Rachaela looked at the black clock on the mantel. Two – it was one in the morning.

Rachaela stood up. She took the oil lamp with the green base, and opened her door.

As she had foreseen it would be, the lamp in the passage was extinguished. The corridor was black and her own light swung across it, startling things, the pictures, the carved wood of grapes and apples, into glimpsing life.

The Scarabae patrolled the house after midnight, she had heard them often enough.

And he too, despite Anna's denial, for Anna's denials sometimes meant the truth had been hit upon.

The lamp shook a little in her hand. She steadied it. After all, he was what she had feared all along. Not the house, the family, but *him*.

Where to start . . . why not at the tower door, where he himself would emerge.

She went down the passage, and came to the head of the stair. For a moment she was daunted, the entire area of the hall was in blackness. Then she made out a faint soft nothing-light from the drawing room – a lamp or candles there, alight.

She began to descend the stairs carefully, letting her light fall on the treads. How red the carpet looked under the pool of the lamp.

The nymph sprang out, holding up her empty lantern.

As Rachaela reached the level floor of the lobby, the light in the adjacent room went out suddenly. A last candle left burning, now guttered. No one there, for she heard no shuffling or clicking step, no rustle of a dress or scrape of a sleeve.

In the black the hall about her seemed enormous, pouring away from her light to infinity.

But any watchers, crouching unseen in the shadows, could see Rachaela clearly in her spotlight.

It was not unlikely there were watchers.

Rachaela's imagination tried to vault the bounds of her mind. The hall was peopled by things, formless yet sentient, the spirits of the house, hungry as the Scarabae.

And then something came from the corridor and out into the blackness of the hall. It came unseen and noiseless, yet she felt it there. The little hairs of her body lifted erect. This was not imagination.

Rachaela raised her lamp and a wing of the hall appeared, tilted. Two flat green eyes gleamed on nothingness.

A cat. Too high up to be a cat's eyes.

Rachaela heard a soft and slipping step, like a feather brushing the floor.

She went cold and thrust the lamp the length of her arm.

A creature stood with her in the hall. It had the form of a cat, but it was the height of a labrador. Its hair was long, bushy and black, glittering at the light on darkness. Its great cat-shaped head was turned to her, and the eyes shone topaz now, thoughtless and intent and terrible.

Rachaela did not move. She did not dare. Such a thing was not possible, but there it stood, seeing her, so still that its springing would be too swift for her brain to take in. She would merely find herself beneath it, the wide paws planted on her, talons tearing, its teeth at her throat.

'Don't be afraid of him, he won't hurt you.'

The madness of the voice came disembodied, from nowhere.

She did not dare to speak or move.

'He knows you,' said the voice. And then a man walked from the black, bringing blackness with him. He placed his pale hand on the head of the enormous cat, scratching it gently between the ears. The cat made no sound but its eyes half closed. It suffered the attention.

The man was Adamus, her father. He must have come from the tower door, or else from the corridor which led to the kitchen, the direction from which the cat had come.

He wore black trousers, a black pullover, ordinary contemporary garments. No rings on the long hands. The blackness came in about his head, the hair a rim on the wide forehead, outlining the bones of the face.

'He catches your supper, didn't you know?' he asked idly. 'The Scarabae let him hunt for them, only then he hunts for himself. He disdains the mice. He kills them for a hobby.'

Rachaela's body involuntarily relaxed, gave way. She almost dropped the lamp.

'Careful,' he said.

He left the cat and came across to her, and the flickering light cast giant shadows from his tall spare body. He took the lamp from her hand.

'And I thought,' he said, 'you would accept all the surprises here with equanimity.'

The cat watched them, then it turned and padded noiselessly through into the drawing room.

Rachaela remembered all the opened doors. She saw the cat going in and out. She saw it leap upon the gull, the rabbits feeding in the twilight of dawn.

'And you can't speak,' he said.

She said, 'What am I supposed to say?'

'Whatever you like.'

The lamp blazed on his face. The two black eyes were alive and burning, not like the eyes of the Scarabae, nor as she had seen them last, those leaden tarns in the white structure of face. Now she could see the roughness of the male jaw: the mark of normal masculine shaving; the hair-fine lines about the eyes and lips; the individual black strokes of the heavy brows; the lashes beaded by light. The face was thirty years old, no more.

'Who are you?' she said.

'But I told you, Rachaela.'

'And I told *you*. Too young.'

'The family tends to look younger than it is. How old do you think Anna is? Stephan? Add another hundred years, you might be right.'

'This is ridiculous,' she said. She believed him. Anna, one hundred and eighty years. And Sylvian, older. 'But,' she said, 'there's still a discrepancy. If you are sixty years old and the rest of them two hundred, why the gap between you?'

'There were others,' he said, 'they failed. They died.'

'Leaving only you.'

'And now you,' he said. He put a hand on her arm. Her nerves jumped violently at his touch. 'Shall we go into the room there,' he said.

She let him guide her.

In the drawing room a dull red lay dormant in the fireplace. He set her lamp on a table. They sat down facing each other in this oasis, the black all around no longer counting for anything. He was here. And the cat, like his symbol, had passed on into the night.

He threw a log into the grate with the careless vehemence of a young man. And as he turned his head she saw that his hair was not very short but only scraped back from his face, caught at the base of his skull, and falling from there in a coarse black silk rope down his back. A young man's hair.

'Perhaps you'll tell me,' she said, 'why I'm wanted here. Was it you who typed the letter?'

A drift of amusement changed his face, was gone. 'They fear the typewriter. A useful machine.'

Rachaela said, 'Then you wanted to bring me here.'

'It was the time for it.'

'Anna talks like that. The *time*.'

'Yes,' he said. 'Anna's very crafty. You've no idea how beautiful she used to be. I must show you the photographs. Almost as good as you.'

A freezing heat went through her when he said this.

'Strange,' she said, ' a compliment from you.'

'I don't bother with compliments, Rachaela. A fact. The family is noted for its looks. At times it has been notorious for them.'

'So you subscribe to it too, this tribal mystique.'

'Perhaps.'

'Mad people and eccentrics, reckoning yourselves special.'

He said, 'What did your mother tell you about me?'

Rachaela looked at the fire. Was she to betray her mother now, that bitter and frowning, heavy-handed woman.

'Very little. You gave her little enough.'

'Yes, little enough. I don't know if she told you, Rachaela, I was only with her for three nights. Just three. Two in the beginning. One night three months later, when she was carrying you.'

'Why did you go back?'

'To see if she was pregnant, why else.'

'And she was, and you left her.'

'It was done. That was all there was to do.'

'I think you're saying,' Rachaela stated, 'that they let you go, your precious family, to sow your seed. And when you had, they summoned you back again.'

'I came back. I could see by then the futility of anything else. This house is my prison, but I need it. The rest is rubbish. Haven't you found it so?'

'No,' she lied again. 'Actually I valued my freedom.'

He smiled. It was a cold and repellent smile, so that she wished she had not spoken. He intimidated her, but that was absurd. He was one with the Scarabae, a creature of the farce. Was there nothing she wanted to say, did she not want to tell him to be damned? But it was not feasible to think of him as her father. No, she did not credit it. This was some joke they played on her.

She was magnetized by his presence. She could not leave the fireside while he was there. She had never before confronted such an externalization of herself, terrifying and apt.

'I agree,' she said, 'that the house is a sort of prison.'

'Where,' he said, 'do you want to go instead? Who has prevented you? You've only to pack your bags and leave.'

'Easier said than done. There's no transport. The only telephone for miles is broken.'

'I see,' he said. 'They do mean you to stay.'

His face had drawn inward. The eyes were as she had seen them first, still and shadowed.

'Didn't you know?' she said.

'Oh, I expect I guessed. You've no choice then. You'll have to remain.'

'For what?' she said quickly.

'For whatever happens next.'

'Don't spy on me again,' she said. 'You have no right.'

'Oh,' he said, 'rights.' He said, 'Put a chair under the doorknob if it worries you.'

'Would that keep you out?'

'I've seen you now,' he said. 'I'm satisfied.'

'That the family line goes on.'

'You're mine,' he said. 'A natural curiosity.'

'I'm not *yours*. How dare you say something so inappropriate. I'm nothing to you. My mother was nothing to you.'

'There you are correct.'

'Then you can't make any claims.'

'I don't,' he said. 'No claims at all. You're still mine. I created you.'

'Fucking nonsense,' she said stonily. 'You dropped me like a lost coin. Less than that.'

'I meant to make you,' he said. 'I tried with many women. The Scarabae seed is reluctant. It inbreeds better. But your stupid and soulless mother had, surprisingly, the correct ingredients to accommodate me. I knew she would. When I went back to her that night I knew what I'd find.'

'All her life,' said Rachaela, hearing the false desperation in her voice, 'she hated you and what you'd done. It was a constant struggle. She made me pay for you.'

'I'm sorry,' he said, without expression. 'But it's over now, isn't it?'

'Why didn't you leave me in peace?'

'You'd had your peace long enough.'

'You bastard,' she said. But he was not her father. He was a man out of the night who held her there, not touching her, and the fire climbing the log, gilded both their faces. She could not leave. She rose. 'I might as well go to bed.'

'Yes,' he said. 'Sleep well, Rachaela.'

To her consternation tears scorched into her eyes. He spoke without tenderness, and he was nothing to her, and yet it was as if, across the twenty-nine years of her life, this simple and insincere wish had lain in waiting, gathering true sentiment.

She had no reply.

She took the lamp, and left him in the firelight, while the great cat hunted somewhere through the pitch-black night.

Through the lilies and the sunburst, she regarded herself in the winged mirror.

She was naked, framed in black hair.

Her white body, creamed of all its down, only the sable fleece at her groin. Long and slender, like something carved from a bone, but full-breasted, the little sweets of the nipples dilute-rose. A blue-green shadow reflected on the whiteness, something undersea.

She stared at her body, what she could make out of it portioned by the mirror, trying to know it as her own.

Rachaela had never seen her mother's nakedness. Her sagging defeated frame had stayed swathed in zippered day clothes, and nighties and tent-like dressing-gowns. And once the knock on the bathroom door and her mother's harsh frightened voice, 'You can't come in.' Her mother had been scandalized that Rachaela slept naked. In the same way she had been scandalized at the frequent hair washing, and Rachaela's habitual lateness at her places of work. All the same, all condemned.

Her daughter was a being from Venus.

She had bought Rachaela sensible nightdresses and marked the shampoo bottle and set the alarm clock in her own bedroom to wake her so that she might come in and shake Rachaela awake. 'They won't stand for it. Do you know you used almost the whole bottle when you washed your hair? Why don't you get it cut and set?'

A lily stood up against Rachaela's navel, its green glass stem bisecting her pubic fleece.

She turned from the mirror and got naked into the bed.

She had placed a chair under the doorknob.

This was foolish. He had seen her.

She did not sleep for a long time, and twice muted steps went through the passageway, and she thought of the great cat slipping past, brushing the door with its flank, something dead in its mouth.

Rachaela was standing at the base of the tower.

There was no light, but glass lilies grew between the treads of the stair, which was scarlet, moist, littered with feathers.

He stretched down his hand to her.

She would not take his hand.

She climbed up and up the tower. The ascent was endless. All the while some terror was tight in her throat. She meant to reach him and was afraid to do so.

At last she came into a wide round room under the cone of the roof. To her amazement there were windows of clear glass. They showed the woods, the cliff and the sea.

Adamus, if so she must call him, was not there. The room was vacant. And Rachaela began to cry.

*

The picture in the corridor window was a dreadful one, a lion slaughtering a sheep, and its vivid colours were strewn everywhere by the excluded sunlight.

Rachaela was searching the house aimlessly.

The corridor was very long and it seemed to her it led to the library, but she could not recall for certain. Sylvian would be busy in the library, crossing out the words, or Alice would be there, scratching with a hat pin at the globe.

She saw the Scarabae hounded over the face of the globe. Burning houses glowed behind them as they fled in the snow, and the snow was red from firelight.

Someone was following her.

Was it the cat? How would she deal with the cat, alone? She would not dare to touch it.

The corridor was so very long. She had passed so many doors, some of which she tried, and they were locked.

What was behind the locked doors of the Scarabae?

She heard a rusty panting behind her, a giggling like that of a naughty child.

Camillo.

Was this a cause for relief? Lost in the byways of the house with a madman snuffling behind her. Did he have the sword?

The corridor turned, and rounding the turn, Rachaela saw it ended in a door.

The door was bound in black iron. Could it be another way into the tower? Locked also then.

At that moment Camillo's steps became pronounced, flapping down on the carpet behind her. He was running. Running, this mad old man, to catch her up.

Rachaela shrank against the wall and naughty insane Uncle Camillo sprinted by. He giggled as he passed her, and ran up against the door.

He had a key, and with it he unlocked the door, and an oblong of blackness appeared, night in day.

Camillo bowed, holding open the door for Rachaela on the oblong of night.

She lifted her eyelids and saw her room in the frenzy of the window of the temptation. She had only been dreaming again. Uncle Camillo had not opened the way into the tower. But she had not dreamed her encounter with Adamus. He stood out as solidly as a lighthouse in the sea of nightmares. *Sleep well*, he had said.

Chapter Five

IN THE LIBRARY, SYLVIAN WAS BUSY.
He did not glance up from his work. Rachaela
stood and watched him, placing the ebony ruler
precisely, dipping the pen into the ink. Drawing a
neat thin line. Another phrase gone. Another thought
obliterated.

Rachaela went up to the table and, pulling out the
chair, sat down opposite to him.

'I wish I could make you stop.'

'No, Rachaela. I can't stop. This is necessary.'

She sat watching him. A desire to scream rose in
her. She damped it down. Only another mad old man.
Elsewhere these books thrived and were read. But
perhaps not. Some of them were decayed and ancient.
The only copies left in the house of the Scarabae and
Sylvian ruling them through.

'Why am I here, Sylvian?'

'You belong here,' he said, not stopping even now,
but just a flash of the spiked eyes.

'Where should I look to find Camillo?' she asked.

'Uncle Camillo goes here, there and everywhere. A
will-o'-the-wisp.'

'*Uncle*,' she said. 'Is he your uncle, Sylvian?'

'The previous generation.' Like Anna, Sylvian said. 'He's very old.'

'Two hundred, three hundred,' she hazarded lightly, her heart beating in her side.

'More, more,' said Sylvian absently. 'Uncle Camillo remembers the flight from the last city. Another country. Long ago. I don't recall the date. I was a baby then.'

As in the dream, Rachaela saw in her mind's eye a burning house. A mob shouted and smashed the coloured windows with stones.

'Tell me your age, Sylvian.'

'Oh I forget.'

'How old is Adamus?'

Sylvian ruled through a sentence, lovingly. Seen across the table the face of the page had assumed a beautiful matrix quality from the carefully spaced lines.

'Adamus is your father,' Sylvian said.

'So he tells me. How old?'

'You must ask him. I forget these things. Time drags on, yet it goes so quickly. A year passes like a month. A day becomes a year.'

'And you won't tell me about Camillo.'

'He moves about the house. He followed you.'

'Not any more. He's lost interest.'

'Anna may know,' said Sylvian.

'I never see Anna in the daytime. Hardly any of you, apart from your servants. What are they? Some lesser branch of the family?'

Sylvian had ruled over the final page. He put the book aside and drew another towards him.

Rachaela could no longer watch.

She asked them, those Scarabae she came on, where Camillo was. She believed in the augury of the dream. Camillo would show her the way into the tower. She could then break in on him as he had done on her. Beyond that point she did not venture. It was only that she did not like her powerlessness, the sense of which was growing on her.

Then again, the dream might be and probably was a wild illusion. She misled herself. But she did not know what else to do.

She went down to the kitchen. She meant to make her inquiries of Cheta, Carlo, Michael, Maria. None of them was there. They too had vanished.

She guessed at their whereabouts, the caverns of unlocated bedrooms, or narrow cells where they stood upright in the dark, propped on the walls.

The house was the tomb. These day-fearing things did not need to creep into a box. The double doors and sugar windows contained them.

She re-found the corridor with the drowning baby in the reeds and the stuffed horse. Camillo had left no traces, not even the armour.

She passed the painted mirror again. More hills had appeared. And the goat in the woman's belly was indeed the result of one picture beneath another.

In the room of the dusty piano and unstrung harp someone had rested on a peg a yellow guitar. The window in the music room, which she had not looked at before, revealed an orchestra of beasts: tigers which played flutes; an elephant in charge of an organ; a crocodile with a viola. Perhaps meant to induce laughter, the window seemed decidedly frightful, like an hallucination in infancy. Somewhere else there had been a Noah's Ark awash on the flood and two golden unicorns left behind. But the lion and the sheep were a product of the dream. Unless it was some clue her sleeping brain had provided.

Maybe Uncle Camillo did not know the way into the tower, had forgotten, or would not say.

A lion devouring a sheep . . . *the wolf also shall dwell with the lamb . . . the young lion and the fatling together. . . .* It would be like them to have such a window. *And a little child shall lead them.*

A child. Where would a child go?

Rachaela raised her head. The naughty child Camillo – playing overhead in the playroom of an attic.

There was sure to be one. Dust and cobwebs and antique toys of the Scarabae when they had been young, centuries before.

She had seen no evidence of a way into an attic. She did not want to go there. If Uncle Camillo was there with his games and keys to the house, to the tower, he must stay undisturbed.

Rachaela waited in her room until she judged by the clocks the hour of luncheon had arrived. Then she went down to the dining room.

Somehow she had known and was not amazed on opening the door. The table was full. Not ten places but surely sixteen. She stood in the doorway and counted them aloud. They raised their old heads of silver and white wire, glanced once with their gunshot eyes.

Rachaela went to the head of the table, which was empty, stood there, and said off all their names that she had heard of, could call to mind, randomly, yet like a schoolteacher checking attendance:

'Anna, Stephan, Peter, Dorian, Sylvian, Alice, Unice, Miriam, Sasha, Eric, George, Miranda, Livia—'

And when she ceased, like good children, the three she had missed spoke up shrilly:

'Teresa.'

'Jack.'

'Anita.'

About the room were the other four, Michael and Cheta, Carlo and Maria. The two women were serving cheese omelettes, Carlo saw to the fire, Michael laid down salad.

Their behaviour was insectoid. They had gravitated to this spot like running water. Only Camillo had not come, the one she wanted. Camillo and Adamus, age and youth – for to them Adamus was a boy, and she – she was a baby.

Maria was beside her and began to set extra eating utensils for Rachaela, where she stood at the table's head.

Rachaela sat down in silence, and ate what was offered her.

And the Scarabae began to chatter. They twittered and chirruped amongst themselves like a nest of small, harsh dangerous birds with razor beaks.

She heard odd words only, the hubbub was so great – *lace, omelette, chesspiece.*

And Anna, the usual spokeswoman, was talkative, and once or twice she directed at Rachaela a pitiless smile. *You see how we can be*, it said. *Do you like this better?*

On the edge of insanity the room crackled and vibrated.

Rachaela sat mesmerized, in a shrinking fascination. It was like being in a demented music-box. A twist of a key would silence them. But which key was it?

When the plates were polished clean, the fruit had

Tanith Lee

gone round and been demolished in its turn, the
teapots came, three this time.

Rachaela sat on in the aviary of noise. She drank
tea.

Alice and Sasha were the first to rise.

Rachaela rose also and went up to them.

She had recognized Alice, who wore a plum-red
knitted cardigan, a long string of crimson beads.

'Alice, tell me about the attic.'

'Oh, the attic,' Alice said at once, like clockwork.
'Full of trifles. A dress of my mother's—' weird notion,
this one had had a mother'—on a dummy. And the
old rocking-horse, do you remember, Sasha?'

'How does one get into the attic?' said Rachaela.

'A stair,' said Alice. 'We'll show you.'

The others watched as they went from the room. The
noise did not subside.

They walked up to the landing and turned to the
left. The corridor curved like a worm, branched. Alice
chose left again. They passed through an annexe with a
window of Salome dancing with the head of John—or so
Rachaela interpreted the saffron and cerise glass. There
were bare floorboards beyond, closed doors, a narrow
stair going downwards and another up, uncarpeted.
Rachaela had never come this way. It was gloomy,
sulkily lit by glimmers of Salome, old reds of dying
sunfall on a peeling wall.

'Up there,' said Alice. 'Now you know.'

Sasha said, 'Watch out for Uncle Camillo. He stores
wine in the attic.'

'Oh, yes,' said Alice, 'he made ever such a lot. Quite
horrible it was, very sour and acid. Undrinkable. But he
said he liked to do it, make the wine. In the kitchen the
corks kept popping. So now he stores it up there.'

As Rachaela stepped on to the stair, Alice waved to her, 'Goodbye, goodbye,' as if seeing her off on an epic train journey.

The attic door was free of webs, in use. There was a lock, but it stood ajar. She pushed it. The two women had gone.

The attic ran long and high. It was crammed with things. She saw chests, old wardrobes, stuffed birds, indeed a dummy with a scarlet musty dress, the rocking-horse in blood and snow suspended in a shaft of light. A window pierced the end wall, round and spoked like a wheel. The glass, dusty, greenish, was clear. A dream window in the wrong place. By its shining illumination she gradually saw the ranks of brown bottles standing up everywhere, and at last Uncle Camillo seated in a rocking-chair he had perhaps mistaken for the horse.

He was out of the shaft of light, yet the attic was sprinkled by it. It touched white sparks on his clasped and wiry hands, three rings, and lit the long hood of albescent hair. His eyes were shut, but as she stared at him, he opened them.

'Giddy-up,' he said to the rocking chair, and made it go. The creaks were like emanations of his etiolate body.

'The light,' said Rachaela.

'You'll have to put up with it,' he answered. 'Avoid the direct beam.'

'It doesn't worry me.'

'It will.'

'And you,' she said, 'aren't afraid of the light.'

'Too old,' said Uncle Camillo, rocking. 'Do you want to go down to the sea?'

'No,' she said. 'Is there a way into the tower?'

'Adamus locks the door,' said Camillo. 'Adamus ran away. Into the outside world, alone. Then he came back.'

'You know the way into the tower,' said Rachaela.

'Easy,' he said. 'Over the roof.'

He pointed at the window. Rachaela walked into the full glare of the murky glass. There was a catch, the window might be opened. Outside lay a flat roof with a parapet of stone. One of the weather-vanes balanced at a crazy angle, it was a dragon. Beyond the flat roof was another, and then the cone of the tower. Under the lid of the cone a tall dark window, dyed glass and leading. It looked inaccessible.

'Have some wine,' said Uncle Camillo.

He did not sound as mad as she had thought him. He did mad things perhaps to camouflage an awful misfit sanity.

'No, thank you.' She opened the window. It was quite possible to climb through. She surveyed the roofs, the window beneath the cone. He might close and secure the window when she was outside, stranding her. He rocked, placidly. She did not think he would. He would, as he had advised her, avoid the direct beam of the light. 'I'll need to come back,' she said. She did not believe she could get into the tower this way. She did not think that, even if the tower window might be opened, the man Adamus would open it.

She got through the window and stood out on the open roof.

Other roofs of the house spread below, hints of walls, and then the tawny ground, the trees of the garden and the wood. The sea gaped to one side, green today and restless. A thin drizzle fell.

She crossed the roof, stepped over on to the second.

As she approached the tower, she heard a piano playing, coarse brilliant strokes, a line of angry melody that matched the writhing of the sea, the boom of the foam.

She thought of a radio or record player in the tower. He was like her, he wanted music, and allowed modern machines to bring it to him. In there too the typewriter had clicked.

She reached the window. Following the heavy leading, she saw the shape of a lion standing over not a sheep but a warrior in armour. The dense colours were not to be made out. There was no apparent means of entry.

Rachaela rapped harshly on the window. Then drew back her fist, alarmed at what she had done.

But the piano music continued. Nothing moved in the tower to indicate she had been heard.

Rachaela went back through the rain. The attic window leaned open, Camillo was still rocking.

She climbed in more awkwardly.

'Yes, I'll have some wine.'

'You're welcome. Help yourself.'

'I can't open the bottles.'

'Then you will have to go without.'

Rachaela said, 'You have a key to the tower door.'

Camillo said, 'Was he playing the piano? There's a way in. Did you knock? Perhaps he didn't hear you.'

She sat down on a low chest in the dust. Camillo rocked. He said, 'I'm the oldest of them.'

'They told me.'

'Like to hear my age?'

'Yes.'

'Can't. Can't remember. Giddy-up,' he said to the

chair, and closed his eyes again. Then he said, 'I know a way down to the beach. Walk by the sea.'

To humour him, she said, 'All right. I'll go with you.'

She expected another rebuff. Instead he got instantly out of the chair. He ducked with a skittish agility beneath the ray of light. A pile of armour glinted in the corner, a sword. He had taken the mouse out of the big cat's mouth.

'Come along then,' he said, 'Rachaela.'

Beyond the place where the path turned back into the wood, bushes overhung and obscured a flight of steps cut into the cliff. They were slippery and dangerous, and Rachaela descended with caution. But Camillo went down them like a ferret, fearless and coordinated. Beneath there was a high stranded beach, a cove, while either side the sea came in and cast itself against the obdurate skirts of the rocks.

'At low tide,' said Camillo, with the kind of air of one giving desired information, 'Carlo catches fish.'

'I thought the cat caught all the food.'

'Gulls, rabbits,' said Camillo. 'Once it caught a robin and let it go. I saw.'

'Mice,' said Rachaela.

'Did you like the mouse? It was perfect.'

'Yes it was. Someone cleared it away, Cheta or Michael.'

'Probably put it in the stew,' said Camillo. He gave his high pitched madman's giggle, as if he had left it too long.

They were in the daylight. Camillo did not bother with it any more than he bothered with the fine rain. His skin was like thin paper, the bones like a framework of hard sticks. He did not look frail.

'Why does the family avoid daylight?' said Rachaela.

'It doesn't agree with them.'

'And you?'

'Nothing agrees with me. I like the colours by day. Once I couldn't bear them. I remember a night ride that ended in the dawn and I hid my head and wept.'

'Somewhere else,' she said.

'Far away.' He spoke very fast in another language. It might have been Russian or some Serbian tongue. He cackled. He said, 'Shan't tell you the family history. It's all muddled up in my head. I remember a cathedral on Christmas Eve and a dunghill and two hundred women and all the dogs, but I forget where or when. Why should I care? I'm not interested. Not even in you. Just a brief glimmer at first. But you're so predictable, girl. Exactly what I would have guessed. Wandering about in your black clothes and your white skin. You'll run away too, but you'll come back. You're the one. Like him.'

'Adamus.'

'The boy.'

'Is he my father?'

'If he says so,' said Camillo. He crouched on a rock like a gargoyle and his long white hair fluttered in the wet wind. The sea burst and sank, like hopeless anger.

'Why am I important?'

'A gene,' said Camillo. 'We all carry it. It comes out in some. Adamus. You.'

'What do you mean?' She felt a stab of fear.

'There were others,' he said, 'but they died. Only the two of you left. The rest of us would have liked to have had it. Glamorous and wicked. At first the family drove out the black sheep. Then it harboured them. The family revels in its differences.'

Suddenly Camillo sprang up. He executed a little gallop round and round on the strand. He used a whip. He neighed and the cove echoed with the equine human sound. The madness was his garment but he had put it on so often it claimed him. The mask had become the skin.

Rachaela frowned impatiently, waiting for the horse dance to end. But part of her wanted to gallop with him, make believe. She had never had a childhood. At eleven years the one doll she had had, a hard ungiving model child, was taken from her and deposited at a local charity shop. There Rachaela saw her in the window for a week; then someone bought her.

Camillo the sea horse rested.

'He has to come to you,' he panted, 'or you go to him. It's a pattern, unavoidable. And so you want to go to him, break in on his mystery.'

'He watched me asleep,' said Rachaela.

'Unforgivable,' said Camillo. Then, 'I'll show you the way into the tower. Any of them could have done it, but they love a game. Cheta or Maria or Michael would have taken you.'

'I dreamed you have a key,' she said.

'A young woman dreams of me. I'm flattered.'

They went back up the treacherous steps. Rachaela slipped and saw the cliff and the sea whirl. She completed the climb nearly on all fours, in terror.

But Camillo did not fear death, darted straight up and did not slip once.

They went back into the house by the side door Camillo had used on leaving. It led via a passage into the morning room where Peter and Dorian breakfasted, and now sat post-luncheon, both slumbering in chairs before a fire. In sleep they looked dead. Camillo paid them no attention. The morning-room window showed a queen picking green grapes in a vineyard – Jezebel?

Camillo did not take her back to the attic. He took her as far as the annexe with the Salome, and there pointed down the descending narrow stair.

'Leads to a corridor, which ends in a door. Open the door and go into Adamus's tower. Knock first.'

'He didn't knock when he spied on me.'

'Don't knock then.' Camillo hopped upstairs.

Rachaela hesitated and then went down.

The corridor was unlit save by the stairwell, a pink sauterne Salome light.

She passed shut doors, webby, which she did not want to open. The corridor bent round, and the light faded into a depressing eerie darkness. The ultimate door appeared, as in the dream straight ahead.

Rachaela reached it. She listened. The piano still played, something of Brahms, it seemed to her, a piano concerto without the orchestra.

She was not ready.

She turned away and hurried back into the light.

Rachaela put on her pale blue dress and a brooch of twisted silver she had once found lying in the rain outside the flats.

She went down to the drawing room and stood by the white fireplace, waiting for Anna and Stephan. She was used to eating with them by now in the evenings. They did not come.

Michael entered belatedly with the tray of bottles and decanters.

'Where's Anna?'

'I don't know, Miss Rachaela.'

111

Just as they had been unexpectedly at the cheeping lunch, now they would not appear.

Rachaela dined alone on a fish casserole and gooseberry tart.

The fire cracked and flared in little spurts as heavy rain came down the chimney.

After dinner Rachaela found her way back to the unlit morning room. No one was there, the hearth black.

Rachaela sat for an hour before the dining-room fire. No one entered. She spent ten minutes in the drawing room, where the golden clock kept silence. It had no hands.

No one entered any of the rooms. It seemed to Rachaela that through the dregs of the afternoon no one had passed along the passage outside her door.

Michael, who alone had served her at dinner, had now vanished.

The house mewed and tossed like a tree in the rain and rising wind. It might now have been empty, but for herself.

Rachaela returned upstairs. She went to the bathroom and prepared herself for bed. In the bedroom, she sat in one of the nightdresses before the fire. Outside the unruly weather sounded like a storm at sea. She heard the ocean itself rolling in on the land.

Rachaela took a book and tried to read.

She read the same paragraph over and over.

The clock with the angels told her it was one o'clock: it was midnight.

Rachaela got into bed.

For an hour she tried to sleep.

Beyond the wall and the window the storm of wind increased. The corners of the house shrieked and the glass was lashed by metal splinters of rain.

If the lightning began it would be impossible to sleep. A pallid flash, the picture of Eve and Lucifer and the viridian tree imprinted themselves on the room.

On such a night . . .

Rachaela left the bed. She lit the lamp, dressed, powdered her face and crayoned in her eyes. Her black lashes cast shadows on her face, her mouth had a red ripe colour in the lamplight. It was *the time* for it.

As before, she carried the lamp out with her, and as before the passage was in darkness and all the carvings of fruit dipped and swerved. She was afraid of meeting the abnormal cat, but this nervousness did not dissuade her.

She went to the left and followed the corridor to its branch, went left again and found Salome leaden in the dark.

Spiders clung on the narrow stair down, catching the light in their filigree webs.

In the lower corridor the lamp glowed steadily, the ranked doors passed, and the other door manifested like a black oblong. Was this, too, locked?

She came to it and without pausing tried the doorknob, which turned obligingly.

As in the dream, inside was only blackness.

Was he asleep, the one who lived here, lying in the sea of black while the storm roared about him? That would be justice, coming on him like Psyche on the monster in the legend, letting fall the scalding drop of oil from the lamp. But Rachaela would not be so careless. If she found him sleeping perhaps that would put the balance right.

The light found a stair inside the tower, and Rachaela mounted it slowly.

There was a faint reddish film above, the shade of a low-burning fire.

She came up into a room. The lamp described the dark interior of the lion window she had seen from outside, and across it the black levels of a piano with dim paleness on the keys. He then, not any machine, had made the music which she heard.

She turned away and let the lamp slide over the beams of the ceiling, the furniture of the room, to the hearth.

The great cat lay there, watching her from half-moon eyes.

Then a second light struck against her own.

Three candles on the mantelpiece had come to life. She saw Adamus standing there in his black clothes, and the match quivered down into the fire.

'I couldn't sleep,' she said, as if taking up again their previous conversation.

'Nor I.'

He looked the same, as if always he must look the same. He leaned to ruffle the big cat's ebony head, and lights streamered over his nonconformist face before shadow dippered it. He sat in a chair before the fire. His face was a stranger's that she knew.

'Come here then,' he said, 'sit down and say whatever you have to.'

She walked forward and set her lamp upon the mantel. There was a mirror there covered by iron-black scrolls; a white clock which, she saw, was quickly running backwards.

'I don't have anything to say,' she told him.

'Then why are you here?'

'I'm interested,' she mimicked, 'I've had to wait nearly thirty years, to see my father.'

He observed her as she sat in the chair opposite to his own. The form of the cat lay between them, a living rug, head lowered now to paws. It was simple after all to accept the domesticity of the cat. Not his.

On the edge of the hearth, on the tiles there, was set a bottle of red wine. There were two glasses, one full one empty. He leaned down and filled the second glass from the bottle. He handed it to her. She took it. He had been expecting someone, presumably her.

'You knew I'd come here. You spoke to Camillo.'

'I rarely speak to any of them. Camillo especially avoids me. He finds my – youth offensive.'

'Anna and Stephan didn't eat dinner with me. They always have. Yet at lunch they were all there. Even the servants. They chattered, *tweeted*. The noise was peculiar.'

'Another game,' he said. 'They're playing with both of us. You'd better understand.'

'But you,' she said, 'typed the letter to me.'

'Anna asked me,' he said. 'Anna can be very winsome, persuasive. She dictated the words.'

'Who signed it?' Rachaela asked.

'I did.'

'*Scarabae*.'

'My name.'

She said, 'You have a very melodramatic name. What did my mother think of it?'

'She believed I was called Adam. In a way I am.'

'*Man*,' said Rachaela.

He shrugged. Each of them, perhaps not meaning to, sipped from their glass at the same moment. The wine was rich, a deep metallic taste.

'So here you are,' he said after a while.

'Yes. I thought I'd return your call. And Camillo told

me the other way into the tower.'

'It's usually locked.'

'An oversight.'

'I knew you would come.'

'How?'

'I don't know,' he said.

'I don't believe you.'

'Then that's your problem, Rachaela.'

'Why,' she said, 'do you say my name that way?'

'I enjoy your name. It's a family name that I offered your mother as a title for you. She naturally originally rejected it with scorn and repulsion. She thought I'd come back to make an honest woman of her.'

'Yes, she'd have preferred to be married. But I think she'd have settled for your support. For your being there.'

'I couldn't be there,' he said. 'I had no interest in any of it. It was something the family had brainwashed me into thinking I must do. I spent two years out of my prison and I hated them. I got you, and that was that. I needed to go back to earth, here.'

'And you had no interest in me.'

'No. As a child you were nothing to me. Something I'd accomplished.'

Rachaela swallowed with the copper wine the bitterness of her mother, the twenty-five years of being with that warped and irate woman. There had been only those magics stumbled on by accident – classical music, books, the things her mother despised. So often the radio switched to the pop channel to cancel her dreams, or the book was snatched away: 'You can wash those dishcloths through if you want something to do.'

'You left me,' Rachaela said, 'in a desert.' She thought

of a childhood where a tall dark man led her by the hand through a park, swans on water, bread for the ducks. She thought of a man's voice reading to her. A shadow playing a piano. And the daggers of tears were in her eyes. She blazed with sudden pain. 'But it would have bored you. A child.'

'I must try to find you now,' he said.

'You're too late. I don't want you now. I don't need you now. You've wasted it. I won't let you in.'

'But you're here.'

'Like you, I'm curious. To see who it was that abandoned me twenty-nine years ago when I was blind and dumb.'

'Don't, Rachaela,' he said.

And in his face she saw too an answering pain, his young man's eyes and lips drawn with it.

'It's a lie, anyway,' she said. 'I still don't believe you're my father.'

'There it is.'

They sat in silence, and the cat rose up between them, stretching, its glorious coat rosy from the dying fire.

'He wants the night,' said Adamus. 'I must let him out. Come on,' he said quietly to the cat, which followed him from the room and down the stair, presumably to the lower door.

Rachaela stared round her at the unequally lighted chamber, the blackness beyond the radius of the lamp and candles, where things sorcerously caught the red glint of the fire, the green umbra of the glass of the lamp, like eyes or thoughts.

A taste of salt now in the wine.

It was foolish for emotion to crowd in on her. She had not expected that, for surely it was all a sham, this interview with a pretend father.

She supposed it was possible, if the Scarabae lived as long as they declared. But even that was probably a lie, some senile device between the wishes to amuse and to alarm.

The darkness howled beyond the window. The lightning had died.

She did not hear him come back. He appeared out of the air, the light not properly reaching him. A tall shadow.

Instead of coming towards her, he went instead across the room. He seated himself at the piano.

Unable to prevent herself, Rachaela held her breath.

And in the dark he began to play.

The music drifted up in long chords above the gunfire rattle of the rain. The sombre lower register lit with the white rivets of the higher notes. She did not know the composer of this melody racing across octaves. The storm of music covered the tempest furling round the tower.

Rachaela shut her eyes.

She sat in the chair, floating on the tide of sound, the glass of fire held loosely in one hand. Against her will she felt herself surrender to what he made.

At last the tide drew out, separated in retreating rills. Ended.

Not opening her eyes, she said, 'Play again.'

He said nothing. But after a moment the fast stanzas of a Chopin Prelude flighted into the room.

What would she have been if she had had this in her childhood?

The tears ran slowly down her face. She let them, drowning in the music.

'You were asleep.'

He stood before the hearth. The fire was dead. The lamp shone crimson in the glass of wine as he drank. The length of his bound-back hair astonished.

'I heard it all.'

'I know. You only slept when I stopped playing.'

So soothed. The pain had left her in a flood. The petty anger and the greater anger, these too.

'You have to let me come back,' she said. 'I want to hear you play again.'

'Why not.'

Like a child she pushed the hair from her face.

The clock whirled from half past four to three o'clock and on towards two. It must be late into the early hours of morning.

She did not want to leave but she was cold, and all at once afraid. How close to him she had come. And close to what? She did not know him, what he was, or who. He could see in the dark like the cat.

He leaned forward and took her hand, and helped her lift herself to her feet. His hand was new. Male and warm. She marvelled at it – it was gone. She stood alone, exhausted.

'Which door?' she said.

'Whichever the lady prefers.'

The idea of walking to her room weighed on her tiredness. She must be quick and run away. She did not know what she was thinking.

'This will do.'

He walked with her back across the room, carrying her lamp.

He handed it to her politely at the stair head. She took it and stepped through and down the stairs to the upper doorway, and into the overpowering close darkness of the corridor beyond.

The door shut behind her, she listened for the scrape of a key, but did not hear it.

Rachaela dreamed of her mother cooking a Sunday dinner which every six months or so she had done. There was always great business. Rachaela stood at the sink peeling endless sprouts, marking each one as instructed with a cross against Satan. Her hands ached.

From the kitchen door, blurred in the dream, he called her.

'No,' said her mother. 'You finish those sprouts.'

But Rachaela left the sprouts in the bowl.

At the door the man waited with outstretched hand.

'You're not to,' said her mother. 'You keep away from him.'

But Adamus picked her up, although she was adult height, he picked her up and bore her away.

Rachaela woke with this dream behind her eyes, very real, disconcerted.

The tower clock said twelve-thirty-five. Ten, she supposed. She had slept late.

She went to run a bath and found outside the door an exquisite thing lying on the carpet, a necklace of small shells, pale fawn and rose and ivory.

Another gift from Camillo perhaps, out of the treasure trove of the attic.

She stood with the shells in her hand, then set them on the dressing-table.

When she came back from the bath, drugged rather than revived, she dressed and brushed her hair lethargically and the shells lay there.

On impulse she took them up and held them, one by one, though they were too small, to her ear.

Her mother had told her of this trick when she was a child, but at first it had not seemed to work. It was at a stall somewhere at the seaside, where they had gone for the day. It had drizzled and the wind from the sea was sharp. Rachaela fell over on the sands and cut her knee on a piece of glass. In the mother's fish tea was a large bone, about which she had been incensed.

There was of course no voice of the sea from the shells. The sea voice was already faintly in the room.

Yet when Rachaela took the shells from her ear, a wave, a *sound* came.

Rachaela.

She heard her name on a whispered roar, as if the room, the stones of the walls, had spoken it out.

A stupid illusion. It startled her.

She put the shells down again. She thought of the stick of rock she had wanted because other children had them, and which the mother grudgingly bought her. 'You'll break your teeth.' She thought of her mother, squashed into the wrong shape, lying in the coffin, dead as a door nail and patched with rouge.

The tears came out of her eyes again, as on the night before. She wept wildly for a few minutes, and ceased. That was goodbye then. To something.

Chapter Six

❀ NOW THAT SHE KNEW A WAY to the beach, she
sometimes nerved herself to the slippy steps,
and got down. She explored the limited cove,
which at high tide the sea covered, leaving behind
seaweeds, driftwood, a dead jelly fish, flotsam she
could not identify.

Otherwise she kept up her arduous walks along the
heath, tracking through the gorse and dry bracken,
the rabbits fleeing before her and the gulls screeching
overhead. She made herself walk, for sanity's sake.
She had nothing to do. It was all one long hypnotized
holiday.

She walked the house too, trying to fix its angles
and parabolas into some coherent plan, but it stayed a
labyrinth, even where she could find her way through
knowledge. She had begun to try the doors again, and
once or twice found Scarabae under these stones:
old Anita knitting at a red and violet window, the
funeral of a king, Miriam and Unice sorting through
huge albums of photographs, beneath a jade window
– perhaps Jonah riding on the whale.

Miriam and Unice had drawn her in and shown her

hundreds of the photographs until she was numbed. They revealed beautiful waxworks of men and women in bygone clothes, posed before scenery and palms in urns. There were no recent shots, nothing in colour. Rachaela found herself surprised the photographs had been able to catch the figures at all, for surely they must be as invisible as ghosts to the eye of a camera, just as, presumably, they did not reflect in their multi-ornamented mirrors.

One morning she breakfasted with Peter and Dorian in the morning room. They did not speak.

Once she met Alice flying through the house in a shawl like the mad White Queen, her quest unexplained.

She avoided Sylvian in the library, re-reading her own books.

She listened to her radio. There was a phase of opera she did not like. The human voice intruded on the music.

At night Anna and Stephan had reappeared in the drawing room. They behaved as if nothing were different, yet Anna especially bore the look of a cream-fed cat. They were pleased with her. Their whole manner was congratulatory. She asked them nothing.

Camillo she did not see. The others only briefly, as they flitted about.

After seven days and nights she went one afternoon to the tower door by way of the backstairs and ominous corridor. The door was locked. She rapped and no one answered. An almost violent rage overtook her; she had been diffident, nearly ashamed.

On the eighth evening, after dinner, she found the enormous cat in the hall, scratching at the lower tower door. A bright spurt shot through her. She went to the cat, and smoothed its head. The fur was savage and full of electricity, but the cat did not show displeasure.

'Shut out,' she said, but she tried the door. Always previously fastened against the house, now it gave. The cat snaked through, and Rachaela followed. Two closed doors flanked the stairwell, which she had not the extra temerity to touch. She ascended to the landing where the second door was placed, and so up into the wide upper room of the piano. The lion window rose dark and barren, but a lamp burned now on the piano's top, another on the mantelpiece. The fire was high, and there on the table lay the remains of an eaten dinner. Adamus had left all this evidence but was himself absent.

The cat stalked to the fireside and lay down familiarly.

Rachaela sat at the piano and walked her fingers gingerly over its keys.

Adamus did not come into the room and after perhaps an hour, Rachaela vacated it. The cat slept by the fire.

She did not see Adamus for fifteen days and nights. She tried both doors on three further occasions, to find them locked.

It occurred to her that he was as afraid of her as she of him.

She wanted never to go near him again, but was drawn as if by a golden rope.

One morning brought a typewritten envelope under her door. She had been addressed as *Ms R. Smith*. This tone of lightness made her bristle, as if he mocked her. At first she did not open the letter, the only mail she was likely to receive in the house of the Scarabae. Finally she did so.

'Rachaela – I smelled your scent in the room. One long black curling hair was on the piano. Something from your mother after all, the slight curl in your hair. A visit, and I wasn't there. Come today in the afternoon. What would you like? Chopin? Prokofiev? Ravel? I'll expect you.'

This time he had signed himself 'Adam'. The letter was false, but inviting.

She was like a schoolgirl who had played truant from school – sickly excited, her heart beating.

Well then, she would not go. To punish her greed.

She put on the green frock and the glass necklace. She never wore perfume. Her scent . . . it could only have been the scent of her skin and hair, alien in his tower.

She went when the black clock said four-fifteen, about a quarter past three in the afternoon, as if for an appointment. Which it was.

She used the secretive backstairs door, and found it unlocked.

The coloured window, the fulvous lion and rusty warrior, stabbed through the air of the room, transfiguring it. The ceiling beams were edged in yellow. He stood before the fire, reading from a book, old and mildewed black like the derelicts of Mr Gerard's shop. As she entered he put the book down, not marking his place.

'Here you are.'

'Yes.'

She was shy and awkward at his long hair and his youth. Her dreams had come between their last meeting and this. She wished he had been old like the book, or that she had not agreed to see him.

'Come to the fire,' he said, so she advanced.

As she reached him, he moved away.

He's afraid. He was afraid of her, awkward as she was. Their one area of ground, the music.

'Will you play Prokofiev?' she said, grudgingly to assist him.

'Whatever you like.'

'You know so many pieces?'

'Some days, some nights, all I've done is play the piano.'

She thought of him in the dark tower, the sea-brushed air furious with notes, harmonies.

The cat was absent. She had come to associate the cat with him.

She sat in the chair she had taken on the last occasion. Did the lines of his body relax a little? He went to the piano and the music began at once.

It was as if he spoke to her. Soft cadences, a stormy undertow, a resolution in swift chords. The development wandering across the black and white plain.

She turned in the chair to watch him.

His hands moved in possession, quicker and slower. The muscles fanned across his back beneath the dark shirt, and the long jet of hair shifted and spread.

She seemed to see his aura. It was cold and pale as steel, the essence of his darkness.

What would it be like to stand behind him, to touch his shoulders lightly, and the back of his neck, beneath the tempest of hair? To feel that power of the hands and the body vibrating through his skin to hers?

'Adamus,' she said under her breath.

The piece concluded or became another. The harmonies were acidulous, the tempo raged. Her heart beat so quickly it seemed to hurt her.

Who was he?

Glimpses of his profile, the features turning with the waves of the melody. His face intent and fixed, the eye of the profile burning and the lips now and then moving. Anger in the face, and desperation. Only once had such a face been before her, not pure, not handsome like this one, but in a lighted room at two in the morning: a maddened face blind to everything, every plea or threat, until it had been pointless to do anything but lie still and think of when it would be over. Torn and bruised beneath the ugly forcing of that face. And this face so unlike and yet reminding her, the face of a rider in the night.

She stood up in sudden terror.

'Stop!'

He lifted his hands instantly from the keyboard. He did not look about. The air thrummed.

'What is it?'

'I don't know.'

'You know,' he said. With his back to her and face half averted, he said, 'Tell me.'

'It – frightens me,' she said, before she could prevent herself.

'Yes,' he said.

'The music leads to a brink,' she said. 'I don't want to go over.'

'It's the only choice we have. To fall.'

She clenched her hands, and he got up from the piano. He came towards her. He seemed to blot out all

the light from the window. She was in a lake of gold
and honey and brown and this blackness swinging
down on her. She could not see his face, only the two
eyes, both burning now, black fire.

'No,' she said. And stepped backward.

The hearth was behind her, raw heat. Between the
Devil and the deep red flame.

He reached forward and the blackness swept in on
her. His hands were two blazing circlets on her arms
as he held her back from the flame.

'You'll fall.'

'You said it was the only chance,' she said.

'Rachaela, stop struggling. You'll hurt yourself.'

'You'll hurt me,' she said. 'You will.'

'Probably.'

'Let me go.'

He drew her forward. Her breasts came into contact
with him, the hard flat masculine front of him like a
plate of fleshly armour. Where their bodies met the
flame was, now. The room spun slowly. She drowned
in the lake and only he could save her, only he could
hold her up—

She struck at him with her fist.

They had separated.

There were six feet between them.

'And what now?' he said.

'Nothing now,' she said, 'what did you expect,
Daddy?'

'But you don't believe that.'

'I don't know what I believe. Anything may be
likely, here.'

'That's true,' he said.

His face was blank. As in all the dreams, he was
nearly faceless. The eyes dull pools of paint. The lips

compressed and puritanical.

'I'll go,' she said. 'I'll go and I won't see you again. I'll put the chair against my door. If you get in I'll fight you. I'll kill you.'

'I won't come into your room. Poor Rachaela,' he said, 'where else do you have to hide?'

She turned and walked over the room with carefully placed steps, and down the stair. Outside the door the horrible passageway seemed filled by some miasma. She walked on steadily, back into the light of the Salome window. That was her flight.

An old figurehead had been washed up on the beach.

It was a merman, with green and orange paint still stuck to it. Its tuna-coloured torso ended in a post of tail. It carried a trident, bent and buckled out of shape.

Camillo would like the figurehead, she thought. It leaned against the cliff, waiting for him.

She sat in the cove, watching the sea. The sea had no answers, even its flotsam was a sort of jeer.

What she should do now was to pack her cases and walk to the village, find a house with a phone. Then a hired car would come to take her somewhere. But where? And more practically, how could she carry the heavy bags so far? She would have to jettison everything in order to escape.

Doubtless, he would now leave her alone. If she did not go to him, invited nothing. It was her fault. Not like the rape, which had been inflicted on her. She had encouraged this man, not knowing what she did. That must be it.

Another inch, another minute, and she would have dropped over the brink.

She wanted to get away.

Ironically Cheta, bringing her breakfast, had told Rachaela that in a day or so Carlo and she would be making the trek to meet the van.

She could not persuade Carlo and Cheta to carry her cases. They too were in on the peculiar plot to keep her here. They could not make a fuss, but they would evade helping her. She was the family's.

Last night how cream-fed Anna had been. Stephan had executed several moves against himself on the chessboard. Anna especially represented the Scarabae. Her smile of approval was the beneficence of the tribe.

They're playing with both of us. You'd better understand. So he had said to her. Was she to think him also caught up, helpless in their net?

The sea charged the cliffs and shattered.

Rachaela rose, and made her way back up the precarious stairway. What would happen if she slipped? An end to their schemes of familial continuance.

She reached the top.

A curlew cried over the heath. She could not see it.

She returned into the house by way of the conservatory. Carlo was there, bending to a tub of mauve flowers, muffled.

No Scarabae in the dining or drawing rooms. A clock striking somewhere, thirteen times.

She came up into the hall and found eight Scarabae standing in a group, quite motionless: Eric, she thought, Peter and Dorian, Unice, Livia, Miranda, George and Jack.

Something was happening. What?

There was an omission of light where the coloured

windows shone into the chequered floor. At first she could not make it out. Then she saw it was an old man in a mossy jacket lying face down, his thin old limbs in a bundle, his hands like screwed-up paper.

Miranda turned to Rachaela. She said slowly, 'He just fell down.'

'I saw it,' said Unice. 'He came down the stairs and fell over. Just like that.'

'He's ill,' said Rachaela, nonplussed. Their fragility of cast iron was after all flawed.

'No, not ill,' said Jack across the hall. 'He's quite dead. I felt him.'

'We're sure,' said Miranda, 'quite sure.'

'This is the way,' said Livia.

'All at once,' said Miranda.

'But—' said Rachaela.

'It happens like that, with us,' said George. He put his hand on the shoulder of Jack. 'Better fetch Carlo.'

'He's in the conservatory,' said Rachaela. 'Shall I—'

'Yes, yes,' said Miranda, 'you go, my dear.'

Rachaela turned in a daze and left them all there, standing like models of shocked old people, with calm withered faces and dense black eyes.

In the conservatory Carlo moved among the ferns like an ape with a mister-spray.

'Carlo. Sylvian's fallen in the hall.'

Carlo put down the mister and came without a word. His face was expressionless. She followed him back into the hall.

Three more had arrived and poised on the stairs, Anita, Sasha and Alice. The same faces. Even as

Rachaela looked, another one, Miriam, appeared on the landing above. Up the passage from the kitchen came Cheta with an apron over her dark dress, and Michael and Maria like an echo.

Without a sound or cry, they knew and gathered.

Carlo went to Sylvian and picked him up at once.

It would be useless to warn them of care. They spurned medicine, doctors, any reasonable treatment. Sylvian was dead, according to them. And probably they were correct. Rachaela remembered his neat wire hands in the library, ruling through the books. Had the books of the north wall then been spared?

Carlo mounted the stairs. The Scarabae went unhurriedly after him in a procession.

Rachaela followed, daunted.

Down a right-hand corridor, Carlo negotiated a door, presumably that of Sylvian's bedroom. Sylvian was borne in, the rest trooped after. They made no noise apart from a faint shuffling of their garments, slippers and shoes.

Sylvian was placed on a bed. The window reared above it, some sort of battle, horses and plumes on a cochineal sky. The room was winey from the light, and there Sylvian lay on the big, grey four-poster bed, his shoes on the coverlet and carven head on the pillows. Carlo arranged his hands in relaxation at his sides.

'No, no, Carlo,' said Miriam, 'put the hands over his body. It will be easier later.'

Carlo obeyed this odd, sinister injunction.

Only Anna and Stephan, and Camillo, had not come.

The crowd gathered round the bed.

They looked hard at Sylvian, as if to be sure after all.

It was certainly a dead face, the whites of the eyes just showing, and the mouth agape. Almost like an old man asleep, but not breathing. Perhaps they had tested for the beat of the heart, or not needed to. Was this how they all anticipated their ancient ends? After so many hundred years, between one step and another, a clotting of the breath, great silence and utter darkness, this undignified dignity left behind.

'I'll close Sylvian's eyes,' said Alice.

She went forward and did so briskly. She tried to shut his mouth too, but obstinately it dropped open again.

'Better leave it,' said Jack.

Alice left it, stepped away.

One by one, two by two, the Scarabae began to retreat, to go out of the room.

Rachaela watched this egress, puzzled and at a loss.

They were all gone before she could think of what to say to them.

She was alone with dead Sylvian, and outside the corridor was empty.

She caught up with Cheta on the landing.

'Cheta, what will happen now?'

'Happen, Miss Rachaela?'

'About Sylvian, obviously.'

'Miss Anna and Mr Stephan will see to it.'

Cheta moved off and went down the stairs.

There was so much to be done. A death certificate, a burial to be arranged – Rachaela recalled the several duties of the living at a death.

The remote house would be breached, disturbed. She visualized them all in some rustic graveyard, twenty-one black crows about the grave. It did not seem conceivable.

Rachaela went to her room, and switched on her radio. The music pushed out of it to fill the space, but the music did not help and the window intruded.

Their lack of fear was uncanny. This symbol of cessation: They did not seem to care. She was offended at seeing her own reaction to her mother's death – her *dis*interest, perhaps even her relief – acted out by the Scarabae, who should have wailed and trembled.

'Are you there, Camillo?'

The attic window was blue with dusk, a blind of stained air. The rocking-horse rose like a double hill against the dying light. The bottles winked.

The rocking-chair was empty.

She saw the form of Camillo seated on a cushion on the floor, working upon something.

'Come to tell me, have you?' he said. 'I know.'

One of the others had climbed up and given him the news.

'Sylvian,' she said.

'Despoiler of books.'

There was no sign of compassion or fright, either, in Camillo. She had not expected them. She had expected something.

'None of you feel anything,' she said. 'It's nothing special. I thought you were all part of a whole.'

'Yes,' said Camillo. 'A flower head. One petal drops.'

She defined in the half-light that he had Sylvian's ruler in front of him. White on black, he scratched something on the ebony.

'And the burial,' Rachaela said.

'You'll look forward to that.' Camillo tapped the rocking-horse. It tipped into a rolling static gallop. 'Hope you enjoy it.'

'Am I likely to?'

'Horsey, go like the wind.'

She found she wanted to speak to him of Adamus, but what could she say?

'Why are the Scarabae the way they are, Camillo?'

'Are they? What way is that?'

'Not even a doctor when a man dies.'

'Old as crumbs,' Camillo said, 'tucked down the side of the armchair of life. Mouldy. But not so old as me. Like to know my age?'

'You can't remember.'

'Sometimes I can.'

'But not today,' she said.

He cackled. 'Not today.'

'What will they do about Sylvian?'

'Something.'

She faltered. She said, 'Will Adamus come out of hiding to see to it?'

'I don't think so,' said Camillo. 'When Adamus was a child, Sylvian started crossing out the books. Adamus tried to stop him. There was a scene in the library. A child shouting and an old man. Anna intervened. She was sometimes about in the daytime then.'

'Adamus cared about the books.'

'Then.'

'What does he care for now?' She shuddered.

But Camillo only said, 'Ask him.'

'I intend to avoid him.'

'Avoid him then.'

He was scratching a skeleton on the ruler.

'You won't tell me anything useful.'

'Go, horse, go.'

'Is that Sylvian you're drawing?'

'Anyone,' said Camillo. 'Touch your face and feel the skull beneath the skin.'

'I know,' she said.

'You're all right then.'

'No, Camillo. Camillo . . .'

'Horsey, gee up.'

Rachaela left him, and went back to her green and blue chamber.

She looked at the temptation of Eve. What was so alluring in an apple?

When Anna and Stephan came into the room Rachaela tensed, to see if all the others would come after them, as they had gathered for the weird lunch. But no one else appeared. It was a night like any other.

Michael served the drinks and went away.

'Anna,' said Rachaela, 'what are you going to do? Will Cheta go to the village, find a phone?'

'You mustn't worry about this,' Anna said.

'It will be taken care of,' Stephan added.

'But you'll need a doctor for the certificate of death. When will Cheta go? Tomorrow?'

'Cheta will go tomorrow to the cottages. The van will be there.'

'And she'll phone for a doctor?'

'Rachaela,' said Anna, 'don't concern yourself. Everything will be seen to. You must understand. This has happened before and will happen again. We are old. We die.'

Anna's face was serene, her voice coaxing. Winsome and persuasive, Adamus had said. She smiled, consoling a peevish infant.

'No,' Rachaela said, 'I don't follow you. This utter indifference—'

'He's gone,' said Anna.

'He's gone,' said Stephan.

'He's upstairs,' said Rachaela, 'in the grey bedroom with the violent window. Something has to be done about him.'

'Of course, of course. Why such vehemence? We're used to seeing to such things.' Anna sighed. 'Can you even imagine how many we've lost? And young ones too.'

'The young are the worst. A waste,' said Stephan, drinking his black drink. He looked into the fire.

'But Sylvian had lived a long, full life,' said Anna.

'And so you don't grieve,' said Rachaela, stung by their equanimity, wanting to see them show her something which made sense, and was not like herself.

'Grief is superfluous,' said Anna. 'It is over.'

She got up and she and Stephan walked into the dining room.

Rachaela saw. No extra places were laid, only the habitual three.

Anna and Stephan took their seats.

Rachaela too sat down.

And Cheta and Maria came with a tureen of cabbage soup.

They ate in silence. Some emotion inside Rachaela scratched and gurned, the anguish and alarm she had felt since yesterday, when she had fled him, given a focus now.

'And the funeral,' she said, 'where will the Scarabae bury Sylvian?'

Anna looked at her. The eyes of these people were no longer predominantly hungry. The famishment had settled to something else. It was credible to see the likeness between his eyes and the eyes of Anna. Pools of deep black liquid. Tarns of eyes.

'Don't let what's happened distress you, Rachaela. Nothing need trouble you. We have our own ways, older than the house. You must let us deal with our dead.'

'How?'

Anna said, 'As we see fit.'

Winsome, persuasive, hard as cold flint. There was no method of getting past her. She spoke for them all.

The soup was cleared.

Michael brought a fish-pie.

Anna and Stephan began to talk of the excellence of the winter vegetables, the cleverness of Carlo and Michael in growing things out of season.

Rachaela listened. She felt the sense of depression and fearfulness which they, *they* should have felt. Above, the dead one lay on his bed. The house reeked as if with smoke.

She was excluded. She had no place in these rites. They would not invite her to the funeral. For death had nothing to do with her; she, like Adamus, was the new life. The sinful incestuous bloom they had nurtured with their smiles and creepings by.

Rachaela began to be angry. But that too was pointless. Not only was she their pawn, she was their adored afterthought. If grief were superfluous here, then so was she.

Stephan and Anna ate portions of the pie. Rachaela picked at the food.

Stewed fruit was served.

Rachaela said nothing else, and when she had finished toying with her plate, she left the two of them, and went upstairs.

What could she do but sit in her room and play her radio for comfort, pretend this was some cosy house at which she lodged, the fire and lamps some lovely old-fashioned niceness, and nothing dark anywhere, no shadows, the window clear and ready to let in the coming day.

A sombre symphony of Mahler's added to her gloom. She turned, as she rarely did, to a station of speech, to hear a normal human voice.

Men and women talked knowledgeably about politics. Rachaela sat mesmerized. Out there, the world, dangerous and real. She could not believe in it, and clung to the talkers in an effort to credit them. In how many ordinary places did those leading normal lives attend to these words which now to her were like snow swirling past a precipice. She had never learned the strategic points of maps. Tonight other countries were like dreams, the capital city an illusion.

There was only now, and this.

At midnight she heard them moving in the house like water in a pipe.

She patrolled the room back and forth before the hearth. She knew they were seeing to Sylvian, some ceremony of their own, having nothing to do with doctors, ministers, the church.

She opened the wardrobe on instinct and took out her coat.

She went out of her door and stood in the passage, listening. She could barely hear them now, and then a little burst like bats squeaking. They were on the stairs, on the red Persian carpet, going down. And Carlo must be there, strong Carlo the porter, with his load.

Rachaela walked firmly to the landing. She saw them below her in the hall. They were all there except for Camillo. Camillo and Adamus – too old, too young, to be a part of this.

Would they send her back? Entreat or threaten?

As she descended, the iron head of Livia turned; Miriam and Jack lit her with their bright rat eyes. But not a word was said.

She was family. Not included, but not to be shut out. A witness.

They went across the lobby, into the drawing room. The fires were dead. Already the rooms were cold. Into the airlock of the conservatory. Carlo was ahead of them. He carried something Rachaela did not need to see to identify. They brushed by the towering plants. This time petals did fall. Rachaela recalled what Camillo had said to her, the flower head . . .

Outside the night was frigidly cold, achingly still, but for the rush of the sea.

The tide was out, the moon up. Perhaps they had been waiting for both these phenomena, as much as for the coming of the night.

She watched them file ahead of her along the path where the unseasonal wild flowers grew.

She kept a little distance between herself and the last of them, who now was Miriam.

They sidled round the cliff, went beyond the path, beside the wood, slanting back to the sea. They were going to the slippery steps. *Easy is the descent to Avernus—*

Those ancient brittle bodies on those stairs of slime. She caught her breath for them, but they did not hesitate, they crowded to the edge.

And now Carlo bowed to some task. She saw a length of rope slide out, and something bumped drily on the face of the cliff.

They had tied up the body of Sylvian, and were lowering it ahead of them, it grazed against the rock again and again, and Rachaela heard it with a chill of the blood.

She pictured dragging her mother's corpse behind her, out to the dustbins, and gall filled her throat.

But they were lowering Sylvian to the beach, to the sea. What would they do with him there? Give him to the ocean like a Viking?

The old men and women began to descend the cliff.

They moved with care, but not with extreme caution. They did not stumble or slip but felt their steady way like worms.

None of them had dressed for a funeral. In the blue-white light of the moon their coats were patchwork, they were draped and tailed with scarves. Alice with velvet violets in her hat and Miriam with a toque of white fur.

Coming behind them, it was Rachaela who knew fear. She took her own unsure paces down the rock, clutching at hand-holds, skinning her palms, tearing a nail, frightened.

They were already spooling out upon the beach when she was half-way down.

She stopped, and stared at them.

She forced herself on, downwards.

Their witch-like voices came up to her abruptly, and she paused again, gripping the cliff, her feet at angles.

What were they doing?

For a moment the scene swayed and bloomed out like a sail in the wind.

Rachaela held the cliff and drew in three long breaths.

She could go down no further. She opened her eyes and saw the small figures moving busily like ants in sugar.

On the rocks of the cove the drunken figurehead of the merman leaned, waiting for Camillo. Carlo and Michael climbed towards it.

The body of Sylvian lay directly below, flat on the strip of sand as it had lain on the chequered floor. The Scarabae came in to it and went away, bringing it things from the shore.

She must get nearer.

Rachaela tried four more steps and froze once more. The moon had made the stair more slippery, like a dousing of water. She would after all, have to get up again, ahead of them.

She eased her body over and managed to find some respite from the cliff. Her whole frame shook and her mouth was dry.

She could see and hear them, but they were small and foreshortened and no words came clear.

Round Sylvian now the offerings were piled. Cheta, Jack and George were placing things from a sack, and by the side of it a black rectangle stood upright with a smear of the moon on its top.

Meanwhile Carlo and Michael had reached the merman. They crawled about it, took a grasp on it.

Like workmen or loggers they began to manhandle it down towards the beach. They could not quite manage. Rachaela heard Carlo give a warning shout.

The merman tumbled and rolled over the rocks, bouncing down as Sylvian's corpse had done, on to the beach.

Carlo leapt after it, and Michael hurried at his back.

The figurehead came to rest on the beach. The two men came up with it and began to drag it on towards the corpse. They hauled it level with the body, laying it out beside Sylvian.

Would they tie Sylvian to the trunk of the merman, set them afloat together at the lip of the sea, to attend on the returning tide?

The Scarabae pleated in again.

She anticipated some quavering chant, some hymn of wildness to rise from them, but there was no sound.

Far out the sea made white flounces.

A tangerine flower budded in Carlo's hands. It was a match. The soft moist wind guttered it out.

Rachaela saw Michael lift up the black rectangle, unscrew its cap and pour the libation over Sylvian and all the driftwood they had packed about him, and the little logs.

'They're going to burn him,' she said aloud.

Without a prayer or a song, like old clothes or refuse, so they would cremate their dead at the rim of the sea.

A second flare woke in Carlo's hands. It flew down upon the pyre. For a few moments, nothing, and then a great wash of blue and fulvous flame going up from the petrol.

Some of the Scarabae stepped back a little way. Some stretched out cold hands to the fire. Warmed by death.

Rachaela smelled the true smoke, and with it the awful smell of burning human flesh. She turned her face into the cliff and gagged. But the wind blew the smell away. It was too cold for it to linger in the nostrils.

One of them, Eric, had gone off a few steps, and came back now with another gift. Heavy and white, a dead gull hung from his hand, picked up from the shore.

He cast it down into Sylvian's bonfire. A rage of sparks sprighted up. And then some of the feathers, caught in a whirlwind of the heat, fluttered up on fire into the air. Quill pens for the crossing out of the books of flame and night.

When the fire had consumed him, they would come away, and leave the slender bones of Sylvian for the tide to take. The ocean would have them, polishing them for ever, changing them to corals . . .

The merman cracked and the fire gouted from his tail and belly.

She must go back up the rock.

Rachaela stood against the cliff, the bonfire of the dead reflecting neon yellow in her eyes.

Chapter Seven

MORNING DESCRIBED CHETA CABBAGE-GREEN.
She was stowing the heavy canvas bags, much
folded, in her coat pockets. Carlo stood by, and
behind him the gas cooker shone in the cabbage-sea
windowlight.

'You'll be coming with us again, Miss Rachaela.'

Rachaela nodded. 'Yes.'

Maybe she slowed them down. Too bad.

They set out along the path, and went away from
the place where the evil steps led to the cove and the
remains of Sylvian in the water.

It was a hard, sunny, icy morning, the mufflers and
sunglasses did not look so incongruous on them.

Crystallized bars of sunlight hit the landscape.
Birds sang in the bushes as before. The heath was
the same, lit and bleak. The prospect of the long
walk enervated Rachaela and at the same time eels
of tension slithered in her stomach. She carried the
black shoulder bag casually. It weighed on her.

They passed through the dragon areas and came
to the empty road. As before Carlo and Cheta
walked at its centre. There would be plenty of

time to hear anything coming, but nothing ever came. Some type of thistle was bursting out of the asphalt.

They went between the hedges. Rachaela longed for the landmark of the gutted farm, but it did not come for an age. Her whole body ached as if she had not walked for weeks.

Finally, at last, the road ran over and the valley opened like a dirty green basin. There were the rusted cars, sunken fields and stony houses.

Cheta and Carlo, as previously, had not spoken.

Rachaela could not help herself. She said, 'The van will be here today?'

'Oh yes. This is the day he always comes.'

And Rachaela realized that in her cunning struggle to keep hold of time, its minutes and hours, afternoons and mornings, she had lost the days. What day was it? If she asked Cheta, would Cheta say? Rachaela could not bring herself to try.

They walked down the street and passed the dismal pub with the creaky sign.

On the slope of open ground the blue van sat just as before. And in the background, unmended, the vandalized phone box.

No one else was there, as usual.

In the back of the van the fat man was reading a paper. He seemed definitely to be waiting for Cheta and Carlo.

The skinny woman was knitting something pink and fluffy.

Rachaela took particular notice of them on this occasion. She saw the wedding ring among the chilblains and that the woman's eyes were a faded-jeans blue. Hairs poked from the man's nose and under his anorak he wore a jumper, perhaps knitted by his wife.

'Here you are,' said the man, as he had before. 'Almost given you up today. What can we do you for?'

Cheta handed over the list. 'And the lady will want some things.'

'No,' said Rachaela, 'I don't need anything today.' She smiled stiffly at the man, who looked suprised. 'Many more stops for you after this one?'

'This is the last,' said the man. 'Then back to town and put me feet up.'

The skinny woman sniffed. 'And that's when *my* work starts.'

'A woman's work is never done,' said the van driver, clearly pleased at this adage which shored up years of male indolence and buck-passing.

The cans of oil were coming out for Carlo, and some petrol. Of course, they had used up a lot of petrol on Sylvian.

Seeing Carlo tote the cans, Rachaela recollected him hoisting the merman off the rocks, lugging it over the beach.

Cheta, her bags loaded with soap and soda, dettol, oatmeal, said, 'Did you bring the brandy?'

'Could only get one bottle. Just a tick.'

The man squeezed into the back of the van, slightly displacing his knitting wife like a stack of cornflakes, and returned with the black bottle.

Stephan's drink. Doubtless the abstemious consolation of some of the others. The Scarabae were not great drinkers, but they liked their little comforts.

'Couple of books too, for the missus,' added the driver, giving to the preposterously laden Cheta a parcel tied, old-fashionedly, by string.

Cheta produced the roll of brown notes.

Rachaela thought of the envelope of brown and turquoise notes in her own bag.

'Any chance you could give me a lift into town?' said Rachaela, bright, innocent, an offhand request.

At her side Cheta altered, it was impossible to be certain how – astonishment, alarm or menace.

'Well . . . It's a small van, this one.'

'I'd be happy to pay.'

As she had expected, easy money tempted him.

'What do you say, Rene? Shall we help the girl out?'

Rene folded up her knitting. 'It's all one to me.'

'I'll see you later,' Rachaela said, lying, brightly, innocently, to Cheta.

Cheta and Carlo stood on the slope, saying nothing, doing nothing, their blank faces and bloomed-over eyes quite fixed. She had gambled they would not make a scene before the van driver and his spouse, and she had been right.

The facility of her escape went to Rachaela's head. She got in at the front next to Rene, who was instructed to 'squash up' on the long seat. The van man shut the van and came around to fill up the cab.

It would not be a comfortable journey, but she had never thought it would be.

'Longish drive,' said the van man. 'Have to ask you for a fiver. It's the extra weight and the petrol,' he explained rather sheepishly, bulging Rene and Rachaela almost off the seat.

Rachaela looked back from the open window as the van started. She saw Carlo, the great cans in both hands, bowed and leaning forward, staring after her as she was borne away. Growing smaller.

The van man and his wife talked incessantly during the drive. Rene asked Rachaela to close the window, and the van became hot and stuffy, dense with the smell of groceries and washing powder. Behind them things bumped and shifted like ogres balancing in the back.

'There go those Knight's Castile. I told you they wasn't properly secure,' said Rene.

Their accents were not local, but London, like a signpost, perhaps.

Rachaela tried to keep her mind set on what she was doing, but the flight had made her queasy and excited, and the constant chat and questions distracted and wore her out.

'And I could just fancy a nice bit of silverside for dinner,' said the van man, at intervals.

'It's fishfingers or go without,' snapped Rene each time. 'You don't mind me saying,' she said to Rachaela, 'but they must be a funny old lot at that house. You working there?'

'That's right,' said Rachaela.

'Must be a real pain, stuck off up there. What do you do, then?'

'How do you mean?'

'I mean what work they got you doing?'

'I'm typing a book,' said Rachaela, at random.

'Oh God, you don't mean to say they do books.'

'Memoires.'

'Oh, memoires.'

How much did they know of the house? Not much.

'Odd to see servants, i'nt it? This day and age. Who'd do a job like that? Demeaning. Just two or three old ducks and them servants running round.'

A cow passed in a field, only one, and not a house in sight.

'See that cow? I could just fancy a bit of silverside.'

'It's fishfingers or go without.'

Eventually the desolation of the countryside was filled by villages, not derelict and malign like the place of dead cars, but quite pretty, with gardens and ivy in baskets, washing, here and there a swing or a child on a lawn playing with a dog.

The fields were sown, neat and kempt, with windbreaks of tall trees. Hedgerows lined the road which had changed to something broader. After an hour, now and then a car passed them, and once a country bus.

At length a broad highway received them. Houses followed the road, stone, but also plaster and pebbledash, bright red front doors, driveways with motorbikes.

'What road do you want?' asked the van driver.

'Just the town centre.'

'We don't go there,' said Rene quickly.

'I'll let you off at Market Street,' said the van man, 'it's simple enough from there.'

She paid them their fiver and the van pulled up in a wide, ordinary street, dominated at one end by a high, brown cathedral tower.

'Just go towards the church,' said the van man, whom Rene had never liked enough to name aloud. 'Glad to get a bit of time to yourself. See some new faces.'

'Yes.'

Rachaela got out, her heavy bag, holding all necessities, on her shoulder. She stood bewildered in the street as the blue van closed like a clam and made off up the road. 'Well she was a funny one.' 'Not much to say for herself.' 'Close-mouthed bit.' 'I could just eat a bit of silverside.' 'Fishfingers.'

The plan was straightforward. To reach this town, and from here to retreat to London. There was nothing to stay for, everything to avoid. It was true that London posed problems, for nothing was secure there, no flat, no job, money in a state of levitation. But it was what she knew. It was away from the Scarabae.

She had been crazy to come anywhere near them.

And the first part of the plan had worked better than hoped for. For the van driver might have refused her, or Cheta and Carlo seized her like warders.

So, she was free.

Free, and here.

Rachaela felt agoraphobic, almost afraid. The street, the town, were now alien. She had been shut up so long in the coloured dark of the house, only the sea and the heath for exercise.

The street was long, and over its sides crowded other roofs going uphill.

People hurried by with baskets and carriers and prams. Cars drove to and fro.

There was a sensation of movement in all directions, as if the ground shifted underfoot.

It would be incredibly stupid to be influenced by any of that.

Rachaela began to walk towards the tower of the cathedral or church.

There were shops, and crowds on the pavement. A child screamed and a chocolate bar went skidding by her foot. 'Sammy I told you!'

The street turned and gave on another. The tower canted aside. It was on the left now, and no route through.

Rachaela nerved herself. She must ask the way. At the centre of the town information would be available.

'Excuse me. How do I reach the church from here?'

The woman looked at her as if she were an imbecile. 'Just go down there and then across and up.'

'Thank you.'

Rachaela crossed the road and took to a tiny alley. The crowd pushed up the alley against her, overtaking her. A minuscule post office offered picture postcards of the town. Two or three off-season visitors pondered the cards, congesting the alley further.

Rachael emerged. There was a zebra-crossing and a street running uphill. The tower and pieces of the church roof appeared over houses.

The crowd wandered, and shoved.

'And I said to him you'll have to hang it.'

'What does he expect.'

Unlike the van people, the town had its accent. Perhaps Rene and the beef-fancier had lived here years, still ostracized as foreigners.

The street ended in a public library, grey stone and firmly shut. The street ran both ways below the church tower which was partly hidden again by intervening roofs.

Rachaela turned to the left and walked along the street. The shops were quaint here with bow windows and jolly holiday wares, painted milk jugs and carved animals, and the first crop of Easter eggs.

A policeman idled along the road. Rachaela mistrusted uniforms but that too would be stupid. She was lucky to find him.

'Excuse me.'

'Yes, madam.'

'Is it possible to get a train from here to London?'

'Why no, madam. You'd need to change at Fleasham,' she was sure he said *fleas*, 'and then at Poorly, on to the London line. Not a very regular service, I'm afraid.'

Who after all would wish to leave here for a spot like London?

The other station by which she had arrived would have been easier, only one change involved, but it was out in the wilds and she suspected, being unable to give them directions, no car firm would locate it successfully. Unless she found the original car firm which had picked her up, and she could not recall seeing their name. Besides, the Scarabae might assume she would attempt that station. They might send someone to intercept her, as once before. Here, there were the crowds, the out-of-season holiday-makers.

Her eye went back to the Easter eggs. Would it soon be spring? Would spring provide a camouflage?

'Can you tell me the way to the station?'

'I can, madam. But I can tell you, too, there's no train connection at Fleasham to Poorly today. Not until Friday.'

Dare she ask him what day it was? No.

'Where is the station, anyway?'

'Top of Wagon Street. Over the river from St Bees.' She was sure too he said *Bees*, as if all the names here were toytown names, designed to confuse and ridicule.

'And that's the church, there.'

'Yes, madam.'

'I've been trying to get to the church.' Did it matter now? Yes, she must find her bearings.

'You go down there, take a left at The Baker's Arms and you'll come to it directly.'

'Thank you.'

She did not believe him.

But he might watch her, and so she set off the prescribed way.

The manner in which he spoke of 'Friday' indicated a long wait. Surely the van would not visit the desolate village on a Sunday, day of rest? Nameless murmurs of a beef dinner were cravings, not symptoms of a Sunday lunch. Was it Monday then? The crowd was thick, female and male, and often sluggish, and it was by now one o'clock, early afternoon. Saturday?

She reached The Baker's Arms, a pub of crocodile green from the interior of which fruit machines flickered. A narrower road, tree-lined, led out into a cobbled square. It seemed likely. She went down it. At the street's end the square spread out, rimmed by even quainter, cuter shops bursting with curiosities and furry toys.

The church-cathedral faced modernity across the cobbles, a brown-and-molasses structure pocked by carving and warted by gargoyles who leaned precariously towards the earth from their heights.

Across the square stood a hotel. It was too smart and would cost too much, but it made her think along the proper lines. She must find shelter, until the day of the train.

That was settled then, her plan augmented but not broken.

At four o'clock Rachaela had located a small hotel which offered bed and breakfast. It lay in a warren of streets behind the church, a whitewashed Georgian building, joined to others, another symbol of her goal: London. She was, by the time she found it, at the end of her tether. Empty of food, tired beyond belief, she sank on the lean little bed and lay with her eyes shut.

She would have to go out again for anything to eat. They had refused her a sandwich; only breakfasts were presented in the rooms between seven-thirty and nine.

Already the dark was coming, the glittery day closing itself in leaden cloud.

From her window, Rachaela could see a yard, drainage pipes, a window opposite veiled in white curtain, which obviously gave the same view as her own – yard, pipes, window.

That was immaterial. She had found out the day from the hotel register. It was Tuesday. Only two days then of this. Then the train to Fleasham and so to Sickly or Poorly or whatever, and the capital. Where she must lose herself for ever to the Scarabae, with their eccentric intimate burnings of corpses on the shore. Lose herself to the man who claimed to be her father, whose own black fire had seared her, set her running.

She tried to breathe more easily, her chest was so tight it was sore.

No longer excited.

But there was nothing to fear.

How could they find her? She had muddled even herself, twisting and turning about the ghastly town, asking in shops, sitting down once in a café but unable to drink the tea or eat the bun.

She must calm herself. She had succeeded.
Nothing to fear.

She went out at eight o'clock, entered the little café down the street, ordered an omelette and chips and was able, with the glass of wine, to eat some of it.

Rachaela did not want to return to the featureless cramped room but she had no choice. Neither did she want to wander again the peopled town.

There were floodlights on the church – St Bees – by night. The cars had white eyes flashing and ducking. The inhabitants and the visitors walked about, laughing and gesticulating.

She was in another country.

She had forgotten what the world was like.

What had he said? *The house is my prison. Two years out of my prison and I hated them . . . I needed to go back to earth.*

But she did not want the prison of the house.

No.

She had left all her books behind, but two. Her choice had been profligate, frantic. Books that meant something, difficult to get hold of, perhaps the wrong choices. She might in the future be able to prize her abandoned possessions from the Scarabae. Or would they incarcerate those, lacking her? Surely she would never have any contact with the family again.

What had truly caused her to run?

Sylvian, or Adamus? Or some other, more insidious thing?

The lamps would be alight now, and the candles.

Anna and Stephan would be dining. Fricassee of seagull. A gift despite everything, the bird Eric had dropped in Sylvian's pyre – they might have eaten it.

What would Anna and Stephan say?

Rachaela is gone.

Had she smitten them a terrible blow?

She would not think of them.

Rachaela went back to her room at the small hotel.

The bathroom was down the hall but she had been told, at this time of year, there were no other guests, she would have it to herself.

She ran a bath. She shaved her body and washed her hair, worried all the while that someone would come knocking, despite the reassurance.

Finally she washed out her underclothes and took them back to her room to dry.

The central heating in the room was tepid.

She got into bed. She was cold.

It began to rain on the town, and she was glad. All those pub crawls and pizza suppers spoiled by a dousing. The sound of wet cars slashing through puddles came ceaselessly.

At midnight she heard the church clock chime.

The clock agreed with her watch, and this was Tuesday. In the mirror over the chest she might see herself.

She lay coiled into the foetal position, shivering in the icy bed.

Sleep well.

In the morning the dustmen woke her, crashing and bellowing at the front of the hotel.

It was seven-thirty.

She got up and dressed, and at eight a grudging breakfast, rolls and warm coffee, was brought to her by a pasty, lipsticked girl.

Even warm, the coffee was a pleasure. Yes, it was.

Now, what to do with her day.

She could hide, of course, like a spy in a novel, but the thought now of a further ten or so hours cloistered in this bedroom brought her to the point of mild hysteria. Besides, they would want to do the room, and anticipated that guests would absent themselves.

She must absent herself.

Rachaela put the heavier articles from her bag into the chest drawer. Her toothbrush and paste, her cosmetics and other items stood along its top like toy soldiers. She fought off the urge to take everything with her.

Outside the day was grey and yellow. Umbrellas marched on the pavements. There was no lessening of the crowd, men with shoppers and women with pushchairs, babies zipped in polythene environments, staring with contempt at the buffeted and unprotected adults they were due to become.

Rachaela walked carefully, trying to hold a half-formed map in her head.

She went into the shops, and inspected fifty-year-old antiques, woolly coats, blue ducks with flowers on their backs.

At lunch-time she went into a snack bar and ate a dry salad with drier ham. But she had not tasted ham in some while. It was salty, fatty. She had forgotten ham was like that.

At sea. It was all right. Only today, and one more day, and then she could take the train.

She should try to find the station. Behind the church, over the river, Wagon Street. She had memorized the address of the hotel and could find her way back.

158

There were Roman remains in the town. She had looked for them vaguely, and not found them.

The station was more important.

She got to the river, wide and yellow-grey as the sky. Boats went up and down, slick and trim or rusted and moribund. A bridge humped over the river, and beyond, the streets sprawled and flared into and out of each other. She asked the way twenty times. It was certain, there were those in the town who sent you on a wild-goose chase. Baiting an alien.

Finally, at a quarter to four, she came into Wagon Street and saw the brick and iron façade of the station like El Dorado.

She hurried up and went inside. It was very clean and plastic, with litter bins, and lavatories labelled in the London way, the woman with only one leg.

No one in the ticket office. No one on the wide windy platform where the darkness now began to fold its wings.

At last she knocked on a 'Staff Only' door. But nobody answered.

It was as if the station was a sop, merely. A ploy to prove it was feasible to get away, but inoperative in fact. Who would wish to leave?

No trains went through along the shiny tracks. No lights changed. The lavatories did not flush and the litter bins were devoid of mess.

Never mind. The station existed. It was there, and could be used. On Friday she would come very early, before eight, foregoing her lukewarm breakfast if need be. She would wait and if she had to, she would question the driver of every train that stopped. Fleasham, Poorly. The great sightless, careless city that sucked one in and buried one. To be buried. That was it.

Rachaela made her way back cautiously from the phantom station. The sun was setting in a slum of cloud.

On the streets the umbrellas still glided.

She was lost three times before she reached the street with the hotel. Nevertheless she reached it.

Her possessions were in place, her bed had been made with mindless starched precision, and tucked in like a straightjacket.

She had jettisoned Wednesday.

Now there was only the evening, the night, Thursday.

She could cope with those.

At the house, they would be lighting the lamps.

They were carrying him down to the beach. There were no steps, but a long slope. Carlo and Michael had him between them. Camillo walked behind, his long white hair dancing on his shoulders. Alice had a mouse in her hat.

'You mustn't cry,' Anna said to her.

But she was not crying, shedding no tears, sloughed of everything.

They would burn him. His slim man's body, the clever hands, the face of bones, the rope of black hair. Fire in his eyes for sure.

She would need to look at his skull, after the fire, before the sea claimed it. She wanted to know. Only his skull could tell her.

They were on the beach. Adamus lay among the driftwood and the logs. Michael and Carlo hauled the piano over the rocks towards his body.

Rachaela woke.

It was the middle of the night. The cars were quiet. She almost heard the mechanism of the church clock turning silently over towards morning. It rang only for noon and midnight.

She fumbled after her watch and by a dim non-light through the window read off four o'clock.

Why had she dreamed Adamus was dead?

Because she feared him. His death would be an apt solution.

She had felt something terrible in the dream, not grief or loss. Worse than those.

She composed herself to sleep again and lay until it was seven-thirty and the green rat light came creeping to the window.

Rachaela shopped pedantically. She bought a beige sweater, a packet of new cotton panties, tights, a paperback book. She bought a large black bag to put everything into. She would have to buy clothes, books, a radio, in London. When she was settled. There were some funds left. She would find another job. Anything would do.

As the days in the town had passed, even so few, the urgent city had grown remote. When and if.

She had to get there first.

The day listed by, toppling slowly from hour to hour. She ate another salad at the snack bar, which was cheap, and later walked out and sat by the river. The afternoon was clear. There were ducks on the water, she had not noticed them before. Bread for the ducks and the warm hand holding hers. It was almost a memory, invented and out of time.

She came across a cinema and went to see the film. It was meant to be funny, and sometimes the old-age pensioners in the front rows laughed querulously. How unlike the Scarabae they were – how much younger. Cracked and bent, warped and wounded. Pitiful. The Scarabae were not pitiful. Not even Sylvian on his pyre.

Rachaela left before the film ended.

The church clock and her watch gave evidence it was five o'clock. Thursday was almost done with. She braced herself with the idea of Friday now. She felt a little sick when she thought of it. A tearing of the strong cord. A scissors-cut. When the train pulled out the parting would occur. How would she feel then. My prison. Gone to earth.

In the evening Rachaela carefully packed the new black bag with the sparse items of her getaway. Then she went out again and ate a watery spaghetti bolognese at the café. The wine was like vinegar and did not help her to eat, but it made her quite tipsy for half an hour, during which half-hour all the recent events became funny. This passed into depression in time for bed.

She tried to read the paperback but real life was omnipresent and she could not suspend her personal consciousness.

Did Adamus know she was gone? Had they told him? How had he reacted? Probably with relief. It was all a ritual, something the house coerced him into doing. Those singeing moments before the fire – had she imagined that as his intent, or was this the ritual too? How could she think of him as a father – he had never been one. He was a stranger, and the phantasm of her daydreams.

It was her fault. She had provoked it. If it had happened.

She slept and dreamed of Sylvian under the sea, full fathom five, with fish swimming in and out of his eyes. The dream was peaceful.

She woke up and saw the sense of what they had done. He was dead. What they did to his body did not matter. And anyway they had cremated him. Very hygienic and modern. After all she was running away not from the burning on the beach, or from the man and what had been about to happen with the man, but only from the constriction of the house. Running actually from security. Her clothes and radio and books left behind. Like a six-year-old leaving home.

It was Friday.

She had paid her bill yesterday evening. Now she had only to rise and dress and go.

She did not want breakfast, her stomach churning. She drank some water, which tasted of chemicals, visited the uneasy bathroom, and was ready.

At a quarter past seven she went out into the street.

The morning was rainy again, the streets shining like wet sealskin, a streetlamp or two still bewilderedly alight in the dark day. The cars sloshed and splashed up and down as usual. The shops were blank. People began to emerge like agitated rabbits, going early to work, and lighted buses streamed into the streets.

She knew the way. She crossed the dappled river with confidence and climbed into the skirl of streets above. She mistook a turning, but only once, then came to Wagon Street. It was ten past eight. Surely the only connection of the week to Fleasham would not leave so prematurely? She had not judged the time properly. She hastened into the station building.

Thank God there were people on the platform, on both platforms indeed, standing as if for execution in bowed resignation among the dripping umbrellas, soggy papers.

In the ticket office was a man.

'What time is the Fleasham train?'

He looked at her, frowned. 'Which?'

'Fleasham. It only runs today. The connection to Poorly. I want to get to London.'

'Oh that's Bleasham you want.' The man produced a Bible and consulted it.

It might run at six o'clock tonight for all she knew. Never mind. She could wait.

'That's at ten forty-five am.'

Rachaela smiled. 'Then I haven't missed it.'

The man laughed confidingly. 'Well, in a manner of speaking you have. It goes on a Tuesday morning, not a Friday. It's the Fletchers Junction that runs today.'

'Is there any other way,' she said, 'I can get to Poorly?'

'Not by train. And there's no London connection at Poorly until Tuesday. Tuesday or Thursday. Eleven-fifteen.'

The day she had asked the policeman. That had been Tuesday. And he had told her Friday.

Her circumstances struck her like a weight of bricks.

She had nowhere to go and four more days to wait.

Well, she would have to wait them. What else could she do.

She did not thank the beaming man, radiant with his bad news. He would say to his mates, 'Some bloody woman here wanted the Bleasham for Poorly, and she's expecting it to run to suit her on the Friday. I told her. Nothing till next week.'

She would find another bed-and-breakfast hotel; not, *not* the same one. A waste of valuable cash, but there. And she would waste away the days, the horrible noisy Friday, Saturday, the deadly church-bell Sunday, and on Monday it would only be one more day. If what this one had told her were actually true.

Outside the station a hot pulse of fear came over her. It was not fear of the house of the Scarabae, or of their pursuit. It was a fear of the town. Its streets and people, the cars, another institutional room overlooking drains and glaucoma window-nets.

Don't be a fool. It's all right.

But it was not. She had had enough. The world seemed in a plot to mar her escape. As once before.

Rachaela had gone into a café and tried to eat some toast, drink some coffee. She had managed the coffee. Then she had to look for another, a different hotel. She was not successful, and gradually her road led her back into the cobbled street before the cathedral-church.

She stood and looked up at the gargoyles.

It was easy to picture the men working on the church, clad in medieval garments, on scaffolding. The making of the devils and demons, the grotesques, the foreman's face used as a model, or the local old woman supposed to be a witch.

Looking up made her giddy, the gargoyles swung
out, ready to leap down on her.

The thought came that she might go into the church
and sit down, out of the street and the way of the
crowd, without the need to eat anything, pretend
anything.

Rachaela carried her two bags in under the carven
porch, through the wooden door.

Inside, at once familiarity swept over her,
oppression, an undeniable sense of relief.

It was the coloured windows. A great dim space
filled by polished wood, a stone floor, and light
trapped in cages of red and viridian and indigo blue,
then scattered in pieces over everything. Even the
smell of incense was not unfitting, like the powdery
smell of the house.

Rachaela made her way to a pew and sat down. The
whole interior softly murmured like a shell, or as a
shell was meant to.

There seemed no one else in the church, not even
visitors to peer at the organ and the choir, squint at
the windows.

No one even praying.

There were embroidered cushions for the knees.

Rachaela had an urge to kneel down and pray. For
what? She remembered school prayers, for which
she was increasingly too late, *Our Father which
art in Heaven*, the propitiation of a bad-tempered
and jealous deity called always compassionate and
with a need for praise worse than an insecure
adolescent's.

Was there any God? Logically not. No one to lean
on then. No one to understand or to be implored. She
was on her own as usual.

Rachaela leaned, instead, achingly on the pew. Her whole body seemed to have been racked, her back and neck were stiff, her head held red-hot wires that wound and bound.

Four days. Oh God, nonexistent father, four days.

She watched the scarlet sunlight break through a cloud beyond the window. The pictures were not insane here. Christ changed water into wine and infants were set afloat not drowned in the reeds. And the lion would lie down with the lamb.

There was a leopard in the church.

It moved so quietly, kept so still between steps she had not known. She had been lulled.

But now it came towards her and she scented it, not knowing what scent betrayed it, heard it, hearing nothing.

She did not turn her head.

Through the blue reflection of the Virgin, the leopard's shadow passed and put out the light.

He was here.

Of course, where but here would he wait for her, away from the sun, under the shadows. Where she must come eventually. Or had he known to the moment, her hand on the door, her body slumped upon the wooden pew.

She turned after all, and saw Adamus standing above her.

Chapter Eight

ONCE WHEN SHE WAS ABOUT five she had been
separated from her mother in a department
store. Someone had eventually taken her
through the bustling, towering giant world of the shop
to where her mother waited. The impression lingered
that her mother had not come to find her, and that her
mother had not been pleased to have her returned, for
Rachaela was instantly slapped.

'How did you know,' she said, 'I'd come here?'

'You like old buildings. Sanctuary.'

'How long have you been searching for me?'

'Not long.'

'And in the daylight too,' she said archly.

He wore a black leather coat, too young for him if
he had looked his age. But he did not. He wore no
sunglasses. They would be in his pocket, ready for
the day. Glad of the overcast? But the sun had come
out now.

'I don't like the light,' he said. 'I can cope with
it.'

'And it was imperative that you found me.'

'You were lost.'

His words fitted so exactly her own approximation of her state.

'No I wasn't lost,' she said. 'I meant to get to London.'

'That's rather complicated from here, I seem to recall.'

'One train a week and they told me the wrong day. Or I'd have been *gone*.'

'Then I should have had to wait until you came back.'

'I would never have come near you.'

'You think not.'

'I know not. You can't make me go back with you. If you touch me I'll start to scream.'

'That would be noisy.'

'I mean it, Adamus.'

'How medieval that sounds in your mouth. Interesting. Anna only makes it sound Victorian.'

'I won't play any more games. I'm going to a hotel. I'll catch the train on – when it comes.'

'All right,' he said. 'If you want.'

'So you've chased after me for nothing.'

'Except the pleasure of seeing you again.'

He sat down beside her in the pew. His blackness shut off the blue window, the blessing hands of the Virgin. It would.

She should edge along to the pew's other end and get out, but she was excruciatingly tired. She had nowhere to go. He would follow her. Walk up and down at her side, perhaps politely take her arm. How much grey sunlight could he really stand? She could only rely on that, his wearying before she did. And she suspected he would not weary.

'You must let me go,' she said.

'Why?'

'You've no right to try to stop me. I'll go to the police if I have to.' She thought of the helpful policeman who had told her the wrong day for the train.

'I'm not going to drag you away,' he said, 'kicking and screaming, by the hair. If I hurt you, it would be in other ways.'

The inside of her body pulsed and moved, leaving the outside a thin cold integument, stranded.

'Shut up,' she said. 'Don't talk to me.'

He sat in silence, calm, every aspect larger, towering, almost as in the uncontrolled moments in the upper room. Not quite.

She said, 'I really am going to leave. Do you hear me.'

'I'm allowed to speak?'

'I can't stop you.'

'No, you can't really. If you leave, you leave. Where are you staying?'

'As if I'd tell you.'

'You've checked out of one hotel and have yet to find another.'

'You – were following me?'

'No, Rachaela. It's obvious, isn't it? You checked out, or even ran away without paying your bill for all I know, in order to take the train. But the train didn't materialize. And here you are sitting in the church with two bags.'

'If you come after me I'll do something to prevent you.'

'That might be entertaining. It's all right. I won't come after you. I'll sit here and let you get away. I'll stay an hour, you look as if you can only move at a crawl.'

'Another game. Hide your eyes, and then try to find me. You won't.'

'I won't try. After all, I need only find out the day of the proper train and waylay you again on the platform.'

'Do it. See what happens.'

'Nothing would happen. I'd kiss your cheek and you'd wave me goodbye through the window. *Brief Encounter.*'

Rachaela tried to slow her breathing. She was desperately excited. She wanted to strike at him.

'You're saying then that when I walk out of the church I'm on my own.'

'Completely.'

'Free of the Scarabae.'

'No, you'll never be free of the Scarabae. You're one of us. That goes with you. And that will bring you back.'

'Live in that hope.'

'I know from my own self. I got away. I came back. You're already tainted. It's too late.'

'So you think I'd prefer to be walled up in that mausoleum – that *grave* of a house.'

'What is so preferable to it?'

Before she could circumnavigate, the whole of her future jolted before her. The trains, the city, her search for some grubbing, nasty ill-paid job, a room somewhere, the noise of neighbours, the teeming streets, the overt viciousness of the capital. She saw too the length of days, the black-bullet chambers of the nights. She saw her aloneness, now loneliness, and she saw the vista of age, which she had never contemplated before. She was shiftless, had made no provision. She had lived as if awaiting rescue, her mother's money, the arrival of the Scarabae.

'It will be my life.'

'It's yours, wherever you are.'

This was fundamentally a fact.

She would have to get up and leave the church. The longer she stayed here the more power he had over her. It wove like a web.

But she was so tired and her heart beat so quickly. She did not want to go. She was glad he was here, his strength beside her on the bench, keeping her safe with his darkness from the blue sanctity of the Virgin.

The red window was a dark rose. The sun had gone in again.

'How did you come to the town?' she asked, to prevaricate.

'I hired a car. How else? Do you think I'd walk all the way, like poor Carlo?'

'How did you call the car?'

'That was Carlo. Or Cheta. Someone in the village I imagine gave them use of a phone.'

'The car didn't come to the house.'

'As you know, the road doesn't go so far.'

'Why did you come and not the others?'

'I'm the young one, remember. And I'm the nearest to you in blood.'

'In blood,' she said. 'The blood of the tribe.'

'Your blood and mine are different.'

'How?' she said again.

There was a long interval. She felt him gather himself like a beast on the powerful springs of its limbs. He said at last, 'Come back and see.'

She said, 'You want to sleep with me. That's what it is. You say I'm your daughter, you *believe* it, but you want to fuck me.'

From the corner of her eye she saw his face turning towards her. As if moved by a key, her own head turned until she confronted him. His face was like a blow. She could hardly breathe.

'Yes, I want to fuck you. Come back and be fucked by me.'

'Now you're speaking the truth, you bastard.'

'Now I'm speaking the truth. What's the problem? The family will be thrilled. They'll revel in it. It's happened over and over, mother with son, father with daughter. Brother and sister. Two thirds of them are inbreedings of one kind or another, several twice over. A charming little intimate orgy has been going on for centuries. Secret pleasures of the house. And what other values hold you back? The criterion of the church, of morality and the world? It's nothing to you. Come to me and let me give you what you want.'

'I don't want that.'

He put out one hand, long-fingered, bone-pale, feathered lightly with dark hair. The hand moved in slow motion. So slow there was all the time on earth to avoid it, and she was not quick enough, and the hand caught her, behind her neck, the fingers in her hair. A liquid electricity ran down her spine. Her stomach turned to ice and her skull to fire. She could do nothing. 'Let,' she said, 'let me—'

The shadow flung forward and fell upon her with a slow, deep violence.

The eyes had become a jet-black bar that flamed. She tasted his skin, his mouth, cool and unknown. Her eyes shut. She was blind, whirled down and under, turning. Only the pressure of his hand behind her head anchored her in the rushing of the storm.

She had rarely been kissed. Never kissed on the mouth. Never invaded and possessed.

His mouth moved in hers. Her head sank backwards. She let him drown her in the deep water, too weak even to raise her hands to cling to him. Falling and falling through measureless ocean.

When he lifted his mouth, he held her still with his hand.

At first she could not open her eyes.

When she did so the church was a blur of colours and streakings of light. The white faces of saints had grown insane and bloated, their purity profaned.

His face was calm still, only the mouth gave evidence of change, the lips parted.

She turned towards him on the pew and put her hands up and caught his collar. 'Kiss me again.'

'Again?' And he laughed at her like a boy.

He was laughing as he possessed her once more, and the laugh died on the point of a knife.

Her whole body now flowed and spun. She gripped his clothing to hold her up, and plunged fathoms deep, mindless, soaring. She pressed herself to him, dissolving into his flesh, the hardness of him, lost, she was lost. 'Don't stop.'

'Not here,' he said.

'Where then?'

'Where do you think Rachaela.'

'I don't care,' she said. 'I'll go with you.'

The car was waiting in a side street.

They went to it and got in.

The driver, oblivious to them, started the engine.

Adamus had not put on sunglasses. He sat with his arm about her. The arm, its pressure, dislodged her reason. She wanted the car to stop. She wanted, as the strands of trees drew out, to be beneath him in the bare and leafless brown of a wood. She had never felt such things, only the vaguest intimations. Daydreams.

She longed to laugh at the stupidity of the driver, not knowing. Excluded.

It did not matter that they were going back to the house of the Scarabae. What could it matter? Nothing was important but to give in again to the onrush of his mouth.

The landscape ribboned past.

The journey was so long.

But they reached the house, or rather the road below, and when Adamus had paid the driver – no account was mentioned – they walked up the crumbling slope in the shadowed midday light, and came out among the wet green oaks, and the house appeared. And Rachaela sobered.

There were the roofs, the ranks of windows, the cone of the tower.

'I'm here again,' she said.

'You agreed to it,' he said. He did not attempt now to touch her.

'Yes, I agreed.'

Her body was forgetting his. The warmth, the freezing and the vertigo of sudden want had drawn away. She observed them, anxious.

They reached the porch and the double door. Adamus used a key, something so ordinary.

They went into the chequered hall. It was silent and deserted. She seemed to see it too from far away.

'Don't go,' she said.

'You must be patient,' he said, 'and so must I. The one rule. Night-time.'

'There are no rules. You told me.'

'Yes.'

Ridiculous as a bride on her clichéd honeymoon, she must wait until the accepted hour. She did not credit this. This was some cruelty or other test of his.

'I may change my mind.'

He stood looking at her, and she was drawn towards him, pulled by chains. She kept still by an effort.

'Don't,' he said.

'I find this silly and insulting.'

'I'm sorry.'

'I hate this house,' she said.

'No. Go up to the bolt hole of your pretty green-and-blue room. Go up and wait for me.'

'You're a tease,' she said acidly.

He grinned at her. A boy's grin, like the laughter. Did an elderly man grin and laugh like that still? Perhaps normally it was only hidden and distorted by the combered flesh, the yellowed eyes and teeth.

'You want me so much now,' he said. 'I'm glad.'

'It will pass,' she said.

'I hope not. Trust me. Tonight.'

She turned and walked away up the stairs, bemused. Here she was, back again.

Her room was just the same. The bed made, the surfaces dusted. In her wardrobe were her clothes, on the dressing-table her radio. She looked at them with pacific surprise. She was dazed. What had happened to her in the church – and in a *church* – and with him.

Camillo had told her she would run away, and come back. But she should have got as far as London. This was absurd.

She sat down in a chair by the hearth. The fire at least had not been lit. They had not been positive.

She lay back in the chair and he went out of her like alcohol. It was like the brief tipsiness from the glass of vinegary wine. It had lasted longer, but then she had still been touching him.

She had truly made a fool of herself. She had been *seduced* back into the house, and now everything was to do again.

Again . . . Kiss me again. She had said *that*.

A burning blush poured up from the pit of her loins into her breast, throat and face.

She was abashed at herself, her triteness.

But also so tired. She had slept so badly in the small hotel.

She got up and switched on her radio. An easement of music rose into the room. How she had missed it. She lay on the bed and pulled the coverlet up over herself and the golden Satan shone behind her closed eyes. She was comfortable, and warm. She fell asleep.

That evening she bathed, put on her skirt and the new jumper, and went down to the dining room.

She did not know what she expected, but only Anna and Stephan were there.

'Welcome,' said Anna. 'We're so glad to see you are here again.'

'You missed me,' said Rachaela.

'Yes, of course. Everyone missed you.'

'Apart from Sylvian.'

'Ah yes. Apart from him.'

'I ran away,' said Rachaela. 'To buy this jumper.'

'You should have told us you were so eager to go to the town.'

'I was eager to go to London.'

'Such a long way. Can't your business be done by post – Cheta will take a letter to the village.'

'It was an escape,' said Rachaela. 'As you realize.'

'Perhaps.'

'I ran off like Adamus, and Adamus brought me back. Persuaded me with a fatherly kiss.'

Anna smiled and lowered her eyes.

Stephan hummed a little tune and stirred his soup.

It was sure: they knew.

'I don't,' said Rachaela, 'understand you all.'

'So long as you're becoming comfortable among us.'

The town had been horrible. Its throng of people, the misdirections and falsehoods. Like a nightmare. The house was safe. It made its own crazy sense.

No. The house was a madness. Only the outside world was real.

After the soup there was a vegetable casserole with toasted cheese. A gooseberry cream to follow.

Rachaela ate hungrily. The food was tasty and good. She was indoctrinated.

She sat by the drawing-room fire with them.

Alice and Unice came in and gave her little nods, and sat down and knitted.

Eric wandered through, he of the seagull, with a book.

Jack and Dorian appeared and disappeared.

There were other slight to-ings and fro-ings, flutters on the edge of the eye that were doubtless Miriam and Sasha, Anita, Teresa, Miranda and Livia, George, Peter.

Carlo came in once with logs.

Maria, Cheta and Michael had served the meal.

'Oh, Michael, a fire must be laid in Miss Rachaela's room.'

'It's already seen to, Miss Anna.'

A fire. The luxury, the cosiness.

She did not want him now. She wanted to be a little girl in the safe balmy house, with the dear old grannies and grandfathers, and the big pussy-cat, and the doll's house beds and all the lovely windows.

Keep away, she thought.

Nothing must smash this cloud-cuckoo world. Nothing so absolute as sex.

It was strange, she thought, as Unice knitted and Anna sewed and Alice consulted her pattern, and the good old granddaddy Stephan watched the fire, strange she had never properly felt sex before. It was as if she had been cordoned off from it. It had not been for her.

She would not think of kissing and being kissed before the white eyes of the Virgin.

'Michael,' she said, 'I'd like another glass of wine.'

All the old grandparents in the room beamed on her. A favourite child.

She was to uphold the family tradition. She was to lie with her own father.

She stripped her body naked and got under the covers. It was almost one by the tower clock, about ten-thirty. Early to bed.

The coy bride on the bridal night.

She had locked the door. It was a token. A needful token. He had, after all, a key to all the doors.

Perhaps he would make her wait until midnight.

She tried not to think what would happen. She guessed at it, alternately disconcerted, aroused, angry. Even amused.

She had seen his face when he made love to the piano.

The radio had a play. She had switched it off. Other dramas could not engage her.

An hour passed. The single lamp burned on the mantel.

She heard the breathing of the sea. No one had gone by in the corridor. The house muttered and shifted its joists, the windows crisped in their leading.

Of course. He would not arrive at the door. The night would come and go without him.

Rachaela made a sound, her throat, her body, a protest that her mind had not ordered or allowed. And the handle of the door turned. The door opened. Outside was darkness, and as usual the dark came in with him on hair and clothes. He shut the door, locked it again. He stood looking at her.

There was nothing in his face that she could interpret as affection or even as desire. It was the face of a high priest at the moment of offering. And she – she must be the altar, for he came towards her spontaneously.

'Rachaela,' he said, 'do you want the light, or not?'

'I want the light.'

He had come in barefoot. Now he lifted the pullover off over his head, unbuttoned the shirt and dropped it, the trousers and underpants sloughed gracefully and quickly, as if he were very practised in this. His body in the lamp and hearth light was tawny as an icon, the white changed to gold, long and thin and leanly muscled, the belly nearly concave, the ribs evident as carving. The legs were long and strong, like those of a runner, the shoulders wider than they had seemed when concealed.

The hair at his groin was blue-black, and there the serpent lay, which she knew of only from literature, a rape, and the daft little things of little boys in childhood. Like amber, the snake, soft still and quiescent; the thought of her, then, the sight of her under the covers, had not yet woken it.

Only when he was naked did he take the edge of the covers and draw them gently off her body.

She believed she lay before him as golden-white as he, the amber budded on her breasts, the fleece of her groin indigo-black, closed and secretive as his was not.

He looked at her, and she saw him come erect, the magical mechanism of the male penis, lifting and filling out to a great rod the colour of a dull sunset.

She slithered to one side of the bed, and he moved through the gilded air, angling his body down to hers. He lay beside her and she knew a primal terror, old as hills – older far than the Scarabae.

'I'm afraid.'

'Yes.'

Supporting himself on one elbow he leaned over her. His face was grave, composed. A dual creature, the rod of appetite and the priest's face. He touched her lips with one finger, then bent his head and put his mouth against hers. With the other hand as he kissed her this chaste cool kiss, he reached back and shook free something from behind his neck. A shower of black rain. His hair, coming unbound, washed over her, over her breasts, like a deluge of rough silk.

'Your hair,' she said, 'your hair,' and reached up and took sliding handfuls of it, and the kiss changed, became the kiss of before.

The terror flared up and engulfed her. It was not terror.

His mouth left hers. She turned after it and a line of his hair, flavoured with night, ran across her lips. She bit at it as his mouth strayed down across her throat and found her breasts.

His tongue tattooed them with circles of heat. He took their centres in his mouth and sweet tremors ran through her body. A harp string plucked in her loins, chains of stars running in highways of feathers and lights from the points of her breasts into her centre, her groin, the soles of her feet, her brain.

He moved down her, the hard smooth flesh of his body, the velvet rasp of the hard penis as it rubbed against her belly, her thigh . . .

His hands were on her breasts where his mouth had been. The music was fiercer, glissandi of fires.

He kneeled in prayer between her thighs, his face cruel as an angel's. His head was lowered.

A rhythm began like breathing. The core of her body was in a moment melted. Long waves of pure ecstasy washed through and through her.

She groaned and threshed on the bed in an anguish of pleasure, redness behind her eyes, her ears singing, sea in a shell.

His tongue described valleys and hillsides, the coil of rivers. Waves poured in like the ocean.

She was carried up and flung outward. She heard herself cry aloud, as if she had left her body, expelled by the spasm which shook it.

He lay beside her again, looking at her, quietly stroking her ribs and stomach.

She watched him, not wanting to speak.

The movement of his hand was soothing now. She calmed under it. It was as if she had let go of a great burden.

She heard the sea under the cliff, low and ceaseless.

He took her hand, drew it across his body to the hardness of his sex.

She touched this totem carefully, gaining confidence as it quivered and tautened. She played with him as he had played with, played her. He lay back and she stretched her body over his, leaning to his mouth and parting his lips with her tongue. Where their flesh touched she became one thing with him. She gave herself to his body and her own, and to her instinct.

His hair was spread behind him like a black raiment. She slipped her hands through the strands of it, and along his sides.

He gripped her and swung her over, reversing himself along her body. The black cloak of hair streamed now over her hips and legs.

She felt again the dagger dart of his tongue, like a flame lapping at her core.

She kissed and mouthed his belly, the firm cavity of the navel. Her own tongue moved on him in sympathetic sorcery. She found the burning rod and tasted its length, the swarthy tower-head, like a smooth-skinned fruit swollen with juice.

She was lost in him, the textures, tastes of his flesh, the exquisite torture of what he did to her with mouth and fingers.

Everything else forgotten.

She was solely feeling when he turned again and leaned above her. His golden shadow fell on her from the lamp. He spread her thighs with a tender ruthlessness.

She was no longer afraid, but opened herself for his invasion.

Nevertheless she was rammed, split. She had only known one man, a moronic battle in neon light. That had torn her, now she was torn afresh. She did not care. She forced her body wide and pressed up the length of him. Red pain lanced through the sweetness, and a deeper pain like thunder.

She moaned and lay beneath him, quite taken, filled to her brim, impaled.

He kissed her mouth and breasts. Shallows of the sweetness flooded her.

When he moved again the pain flared into a glorious friction.

Again she pressed herself to meet it, was wounded, rose again.

She grasped his body, his hair, clinging to him on the brink of chaos.

His face above hers was also shadow, but she saw the savagery of it, to match her own.

Then he lay down on her, his weight sinking her in the bed as if in sand.

She worked and leapt to meet his onslaught.

The pain was gone in an agony of ascent.

His mouth was on hers, at the line of her jaw, blazing on her neck.

In the tumult, rushing, she felt the second invasion, the sharp bite of two merciless teeth, and tried to cry out his name, but she was choked and vanquished.

She experienced the pull of her blood into his mouth like threads of silk drawn up from her vein.

He ravished her like a lion, thrusting into her, his lips drawing out her life.

She felt herself unravel from her flesh.

To the first pleasure this was a cataclysm.

Rachaela screamed. She was flung up into madness, as she rode the whirlwind. Panes of light and darkness shattered before her. She was crucified, obliterated. And as she fell she sensed him plunge to meet her like a meteor on fire, heard the sound he made against her sundered throat.

'The lamp's dying,' she said. 'Cheta didn't put in enough oil.'

'Lie still,' he said.

He was touching her even now, smoothing out her body, caressing her breasts, brushing back her hair.

A tiny flower of blood, like the one Anna had embroidered, lay on the pillow.

'Like virginity,' she said. 'The first time, I bled for a week.'

'You can't compare that to this.'

'He didn't drink my blood.'

Adamus lifted himself. He put his lips softly to her neck and mouthed the little wound. Delicious, the sensation, another melting.

'Do you need it?'

He raised his head. 'No.'

'But it pleases you.'

'Very much.'

'How long . . .?'

'Your mother was the last.'

'Something else she never told me.'

185

He drew again on her vein. The stars lit through her body, following the pressure of his mouth. She tensed and shivered and his hand slipped between her thighs, the fingers daintily probing after the sparks of delight. She climaxed instantly, startlingly.

'Do it for me,' he said. He licked at her throat hungrily, closing his eyes.

She snared the tower of him, once more erect and satin-hard, rubbing, tickling, feeling the tremors of its second almost separate life.

She felt his urgency as he moved against her and his breathing caught against her neck. The flaming juices of him burst into her hand.

He kissed her. She tasted salt, the spice of her own blood.

'What will happen?' she whispered.

'Nothing. A love bite.'

A faint noise, beyond the dark world of the room, in the corridor.

'Is it the cat, looking for you?'

'The cat never looks for me. He comes and goes.'

'Would they be voyeurs?'

'The family? No, they've seen it all. Done most of it.'

Rachaela eased herself up from the bed of sheets and pillows, skin and hair.

'Don't,' he said.

'I want to see.'

She lit a candle from a bedside match, went to the door and unlocked it.

Outside, something lay.

'One of Camillo's gifts,' she said.

She bent down.

It was a peculiar, twisted heart, made of driftwood.

Camillo was the wicked one.

She reached to take the heart and it crumbled, fell to bits.

'Oh.'

She came back into the room and shut and locked the door.

'What had he left you? A cat turd in foil? He's been known to do that.'

'A broken heart.'

'I see. Not just a comment on our morals.'

She set the candle down. Its wavering light lit his long body, ice-white now on the lake of hair. He looked like a prince from an uncensored story, a Beardsley illustration of male perfection. Even to the sleeping phallus, which doubtless Beardsley would have fashioned upright.

'Why a heart which breaks?' she said.

'He's a romantic. Did he tell you about his flight by night from a besieged city?'

'No,' she said. 'He's like an old baby. Mischievous and clever. He cares about nothing.'

'Maybe he cares about you.'

'It's my heart, then. The breakage.'

'Come here,' he said.

She went to him slowly.

He drew her down and again she lay the length of him, over him.

She was accustomed to it now, the torrent of feeling.

'Tomorrow,' she said, 'I will be ashamed.'

'Tomorrow it will be too late.'

'Yes.'

He circled her with his arms.

She rested her head in the curve of his neck. She mouthed him, as he had done to her before the bite of his lust.

'You've made love to me five times,' she said.

'You're counting.'

'We haven't slept.'

'Sleep tomorrow,' he said, 'when you're ashamed.'

He rolled their bodies over and pinned her beneath him.

'I can't any more,' she said.

'Once more, for old time's sake.'

Beyond his shadow, she saw the dim shapes of the window of the temptation.

'It's getting light.'

'That happens.'

She did not want the day, the day of shame and confusion.

He pierced her without prologue. Used to him now, her open body received him easily. He moved in her slowly to the rhythm of the distant sea.

The deep melodious ache began in her. She could not ignore it.

They rose and fell on the beach of silence.

Behind him the window merged through silver into a dusk of green and chrysanthemum. The red blood drops of the apples appeared.

'I want to see you,' he said.

He drew out of her and she groaned at her deprivation of him. He stood back, blew out the candle, watched her as the body of Lucifer was spread out over her own.

'The apple lies on your groin. Appropriate.'

'They will have placed the bed so that it would. Come back to me,' she said, 'quickly, quickly.'

He lay down on her and penetrated her again so that she gave a cry of relief.

She danced beneath him, writhing on a spindle of galvanic motion.

'Go faster.'

'Not yet.'

He held her in waiting between earth and heaven as the window bloomed into its insanity of dyes. The surf pounded in her head. His mouth came gently to her neck and she gave herself again to the lion.

She could not even scream now. The window boiled. She had forgotten everything, past, future. And outside, tiny creatures ran from the driftwood heart.

Chapter Nine

'How many miles to Babylon?
Three score and ten.
Can I get there by candlelight?
Yes, and back again.'

A thrush or some brown bird answered from a thicket. Rachaela watched it, and walked on. The bird sang a few more notes and flew away.

'How many miles, how many miles?'

Where had she heard the rhyme? Not from her mother. It came now because it was applicable. She had been to Babylon, and come back.

How canny of her to have chosen a new sweater with a roll neck. This and a little piece of elastoplast denied the most outrageous element of the visit to Babylon. The blood had stopped, had been dry when she woke up. He was gone. But her whole body, strained and bruised as if he had beaten her, that was the monument to his reality.

She was not ashamed. Not embarrassed. Not angry or bewildered or happy. She was nothing. Vacant. He had scoured her out.

He must have removed the remains of the heart from

the carpet, or Michael or Maria had cleared it up, like the mouse.

What do I feel?

Surely she must feel something.

But he had drunk up her feeling with her blood.

The heath was rinsed by fitful sun. Sometimes it clouded over with rays of darkness.

'Yes, and back again.'

She sat down on a rock. From here she could see to the house, the standing stone between like a lightning.

No rabbits today.

She began to cry, silently. Some feeling after all then.

The sea boomed.

The heath took no notice of her.

Rain fell for days and nights. It washed away the markers, the clawings of the cat in the earth, the tenuous little flowers beside the path, the webs upon the outside of the windows. It dissolved memory. For this was what the immediate past had become.

He had come in at the door, he had lain down with her, he had been her lover. And before that he had brought her back from the world, home again into the enclave of the Scarabae.

The doors to the tower were locked. She had tried them after two days. She had knocked.

She knew intuitively Babylon had been only for one night. He had wanted her only for one night. If he had even profoundly wanted her at all. It was the act the house drove him to, a completion. Even her blood was not enough to entice him. If it was true, he had gone without, a monk, for thirty years.

She did not want to leave the house now.

In misery she clutched at it. The cheerful fireplaces,

the masks of the windows. She could hide here, burrow, and be safe. No worries, no living to earn, no people to deal with. How dangerous the house was, a great stone cradle lagged with cotton-wool to wrap her.

She existed with the firelight and the radio, and most nights she went down to 'dine' with Stephan and Anna, and now and then others appeared. She knew them all now.

She had never gone back to the beach.

But the rain washed the beach, too.

They were all there, at the dinner table, all of them but Camillo, who had never come. Sixteen Scarabae, and the four who served.

Wine was brought with the fish.

From this, if she had not guessed, she saw it was a celebration. Her blood turned to ice.

And they all smiled at her from time to time. Little biting smiles of their old strong teeth.

Then she felt the trap again. It was not a cradle she was in.

Upstairs she had another hot bath, too hot, it almost made her sick.

She performed the set of exercises she had taken to, on the carpet by the bed.

She should have drunk more of the wine.

In the bed she lay and imagined that she had never come here, that her life went on, between the shop of Mr Gerard and the flat. There would be monetary compensation for the loss of the flat. She had heard nothing, but how could she, here?

She waited, for the door to open.

Of course it did not.

Five by the tower clock at the bedside – three-thirty in the morning.

The rain, the restless sea.

The rain had ended, and only Anna had come to dinner.

This seemed if anything as purposeful as the gathering of the clan on the previous night.

She was meant to confide in Anna.

'I was thinking,' said Rachaela, 'I may need to get away to London for a while, after all.'

'How should that be?' Anna did not look astonished or even feral. She was bland.

'Some money matters I should have sorted out.'

'Surely, a letter would do.'

'No mail comes to the house.'

'The van brings it. Cheta—'

'I really think I'll need to attend to it personally.'

'Well, if you must.'

No refusal then. And nothing to assist.

Rachaela looked into the fire. She saw no pictures there, not even of Sylvian's funeral pyre.

'As you know,' Rachaela said, 'I've slept with him.'

'Oh, my dear,' said Anna. Obviously there had been a breach of etiquette.

'It was what you all wanted and anticipated. I thought you'd like to be certain.' Anna did not say anything. 'I've seen nothing of him, since then.' Rachaela had not meant to say this.

'Adamus is very secretive,' said Anna. 'You must allow him time.'

'I was the innocent, not he. What does he need time for? He's had thirty years.'

'He doesn't communicate easily,' said Anna, indulgently. 'I myself haven't seen him, except briefly, for a great while. You must be patient.'

'So you said before. Why must I be patient?'

'What else can you do?' said Anna simply.

'Yes, I see. Plainly nothing. How long do you think he'll hide from me? Two months, three?'

'I don't know, Rachaela.'

'Or perhaps this is now a permanent state. Maybe I should get Michael or Cheta to take me into the tower with them when they deliver meals.'

'That would never do. You can't force yourself upon him.'

'He forced himself on me. You all forced him on me.'

'No, Rachaela. There was some measure of acceptance on your part.'

'This is a game,' said Rachaela, 'as I suspected.'

'Not at all. More . . . more a dance, Rachaela. A changing of partners through time.'

'Left alone on the dance floor,' said Rachaela, 'and the band's gone home. When the last little star has left the sky,' she added, quoting with banality, 'and not still together.'

'He is as he is.'

'I see that. Where am I?'

'You are quite secure, Rachaela. You have all of us.'

Rachaela quailed. 'But you're all mad.'

Anna smiled her smile. 'What can I say to that.'

Rachaela saw a picture in the fire. It was Camillo riding on the back of the great black cat.

'Well, I'll go to London.'

Anna said, 'Wait a while.'

'For what?'

'Perhaps something will happen.'

'But it has. I told you.'

She thought, *Has anything happened? Another dream.*

She thought: *London, have I the strength to try again?*

She knew the days now, she had retained a careful count of them. On a Saturday she went up to the attic. It was two weeks and a day, since he had brought her back, since their episode on the green-and-blue bed. The doors into the tower had stayed locked. She had been busy, walking and walking, sometimes in the fountains of the rain, doing her exercises. Some nights she drank three glasses of wine. She did not talk to Anna, only responded mildly when Anna spoke to her.

Camillo was not in the attic. It seemed he had lost all interest in that too. The rocking-horse stood still as a rock, she tipped its back to make it move. Three bottles had exploded off their tops and there were wine stains on the walls.

Rachaela sampled the wine. It was sour, as the old women had told her. Sour, but potent. She might try this brew, in preference to the civilized wine Michael dished up.

She searched the attic, and found a hammer lying between a sewing machine and a stuffed bird. As if in readiness.

She opened the clear window and climbed out.

The sky was blue, muddied with vast banks of cloud like cumulus from a volcano.

She walked across the two roofs and came to the tower and its window.

No sound. The piano was not being played. How quiet he was. Was he even there? Where did he go to when he disappeared? She had seen, he would brave the daylight. Was it only their affectation, to be afraid of it, as if it was expected of them.

She knocked courteously with the hammer's hilt.

Was he there, and only dissembling. Burrowed in the tower, safe from her.

Nothing. Only the noises of the sea.

Rachaela rested against the tower wall. She longed to be elsewhere, to be another person. Anyone would do. Some spotty check-out girl, some sock-washing wife. Anything, anything rather than this.

She swung the hammer lightly. At her first swipe the glass cracked in the lion's head. She lashed again. Pieces of yellow crystal dropped out on to the roof like strange sweets.

But she had not breached the tower. There was more glass, or some other thicker substance, behind the jagged hole she had made.

She smashed down hard against it with the hammer and the window shook, tiny cracks appeared like earthquake faults. The substance beyond and between the glass did not give.

She might have guessed. The stone-slinging mob had taught them. The glass was provisioned against attack.

She left the broken shards lying and took the hammer back into the attic and set it down neatly by a bird of paradise in lime and cherry feathers.

A useless aggression.

She had been shown. They were impervious to her.

And she was not a vandal, it was not natural to her to destroy things.

She went back to her room.

In biro, she wrote on a piece of paper taken from an ancient stack in a bureau of the morning room.

Adamus, it is unfair of you to shut me out. I want to speak to you. This isn't some idle whim. How long are you going to hide yourself, or can you?

Then she tore up this letter, and the two or three which followed it, and burned them in the fire.

Adamus was the Prince of Darkness. He would not answer at her call. A capricious and malevolent spirit, thing of shadows. He had imposed his will, or the will of the Scarabae on her. Now she must loosen their shackles. She must. She could. It was simple.

In fear she sat and thought of everything before her. She had been an imbecile and deserved nothing more kind.

She had better find the strength. She had better.

At about four in the morning, by the light of one candle, she thrust two more books into the new black bag, tested its weight, and did it up.

This time she had squashed some of her clothes inside, and several of the lighter books, the paperbacks. Into her everyday bag went make-up and toiletries. She could not take the radio, but as before she had acknowledged that. The quantities of books she must leave behind.

It was Tuesday, she had kept careful count.

The day of the van, perhaps, but that was not relevant. The van could not be used again. Surely Carlo and Cheta would prevent it, now.

She put on her coat and hauled the new bag up on to her back like a knapsack. It was heavy but tolerable. She would have to endure. The lesser bag she slung on to her shoulder.

Rachaela opened the door on the usual night-time blackness. She gripped the candle firmly.

The carvings swung, and up there an owl of wood stared at her among the leaves.

There was something wrong.

She knew it before she had reached the landing. A light burned in the hall, the red lamp.

She came out at the head of the stairs and looked down.

They were all there. All the Scarabae. She looked them over one by one, Unice and Alice, Peter and Dorian, Jack and George and Eric, Stephan was there and Anna, standing to one side, Teresa, Miranda, Anita, Sasha, Livia and Miriam. And Uncle Camillo in his armour with the lamp shining on the breastplate and helmet, and the vizor down so you could not see if he were laughing.

Rachaela had halted in her tracks.

She confronted them, waiting for one or all of them to speak.

How had they known?

Even, there, near the passage, the four servants, big Carlo among them. Ready to seize and stay?

'I'm going,' Rachaela said loudly. 'I won't be stopped.'

She held up the candle and began to descend the stairs.

A little ripple went over them, and she braced herself, but otherwise they did not move.

She was strong and they were old. How would old Carlo react to a kick on the ankle, her teeth in his wrist. The candle might be used as a weapon.

She got down into the hall. They were a wall in front of her, between her and all the doors.

She moved towards the drawing room and walked right at them.

She thought of striking them, the matchstick sounds of the breakage of old bones. She would do it if she had to—

Eric and Stephan stepped aside. They let her pass.

She went into the unlighted room, the candle bursting on the ridges of furniture. The door to the conservatory veered at her, half-open as it always was by night.

They were coming after, creeping forward with a susurrus of materials and soft shoes. Creeping after her as if they stalked her. But would they spring?

She pushed wide the door and edged through the lanes between the great plants, black and white and grey. They brushed her like strengthless and accusing hands. Rachaela thrust them off, and the stems broke, the petals showered like confetti.

She gained the door on to the night and pushed it and stepped over the sill.

She walked across the garden, over Carlo's weeded lawn, under the girders of the cedar. Only the little gate now.

She put down the candle and left it burning there. She glanced back as she shut the gate behind her.

All the Scarabae – all but one – were crowded in the garden. They watched her. Their grim old faces gave away nothing. Like elderly kiddies at a play they did not understand yet knew to be important, they regarded her as she stood behind the gate.

Goodbye, she thought. *Goodbye for ever*.

With a feeling of great cold, almost of terror, she turned away from them, brushing a spray of their petals from her coat. Who would believe this flight by night. She thought of all their eyes glittering in the candleshine. Eyes like beetles caught on the bushes. She resisted the temptation to look back a second time.

Rachaela walked along the path, in among the pine trees with the sullen roar of the sea to her right. When

199

the trees broke, she came out on the uncut lawn of the heath. The sea lashed between the bulkheads of the cliff. The standing stone rose white in the darkness. There was a thin moon, a wrack of cloud. The night was noisy with its own nocturnal sounds.

Now she must remember the way that Cheta and Carlo took. She needed to find the village in the dark.

She moved along the heath, and from a tuft of darkness something came out and stood in her way.

Last of them all, it was the cat.

Rachaela slowed her pace but did not stop. The cat eyed her. It was sleek, its ears raised not flattened. Did it know her still or would it turn on her now she was an outcast? Was it some supernatural sentinel of the Scarabae?

She came level with the cat, stretched out her hand, and the cat sniffed her. She smoothed its great barbaric head.

'You're a beautiful monster,' she said, 'are you going to let me by?'

The cat withdrew from her like a sooty ghost and stole away along the slope towards the standing stone.

From a distance of thirty feet she heard it clawing the earth. It was not concerned with her. She was through all the ordeals now, and had only the journey to accomplish.

There was a kind of separate fear on her as she walked.

The vast heath was full of stillness and life. Noises were continuous, chirrups of unimaginable creatures, the sudden flush of something in a bush, the beating of wings. Once three night birds rose into the blue-black of the sky.

She disturbed the pattern of the nocturne.

There were stars, brilliant and manufactured, so many of them, ridiculous to believe that they were suns and planets. The cloud formed the shape of a skull beneath the moon, huge eyeholes of sky glaring down. Anything might come out of the sky.

Or off the ground.

Rachaela walked stolidly, the weight on her back like the sins of the pilgrim in some religious tale.

What were her sins? Incest, for one. But the word meant nothing. *Do what you like so long as you don't get caught.* But there—

Perhaps the long hard walk would help her. Shake loose the sin.

Silly to hope for that. She had acted unthinkingly and was punished.

Was it a sin to leave the Scarabae?

Were they still standing like statues in the garden? Had Anna and Stephan led them in?

She must forget the Scarabae. Forget Adamus.

Her mother had never managed it. She would have to be different.

It was not difficult to recollect the route Carlo and Cheta had taken. Certain landmarks had been unconsciously remembered. She had turned inland at the right spot she was sure. Yet where was the road now?

Out of a stand of pine a slim grey beast emerged. It checked and looked at her. The markings about its eyes made it savage, wolf-like, but it was only a fox, more discomposed than she at the meeting. It trotted briskly away.

Beyond the pine trees the road ran, desolate and haunted black.

Rachaela did not like the look of it by night. She

walked carefully to one side. Some colossal thing might come from the dark, storming down on her.

The gutted farmhouse appeared, silvered by the moon. Uncanny lights could have blazed in the windows, but they did not. A black rook or crow sat in the hedge, as if to challenge her. She saw the glitter of its eye. All things here were Scarabae. But the rook paid her no attention, did not fly at her crying in a human voice *Go back*!

How the night worked on her imagination.

The village might be gone, or dead, or all the inhabitants turned to stone like the houses.

No, the village was only that. It obeyed the laws of normal things. There were telephones, and they would answer if she knocked loudly enough.

She had only to follow the road now.

Nothing walked or ebbed behind her.

The moon was setting, the cloud like streaming hair or bubbling steam.

She did not recall that wood there by the road. Could she somehow have taken a wrong turning on the straight, unbranching surface? Had part of the land been lifted up and spirited away?

But there, she remembered that derelict wall. Beyond that rise, the village would be. Probably.

She achieved the crest of the road and saw it spill over, and the village in the bottom of the valley, silent as if drowned a hundred years beneath a lake.

The door to the pub called The Armitage was of thick wood, lacking a bell or knocker. A side door was streakily painted and had two sorry pots of weeds beside it, and a bell and letterbox.

The sky was higher and the stars had lost their

clockwork effulgence. Dawn was near. Wakey wakey.

She rang the bell brutishly, keeping her hand on it, and flapped the lid of the letterbox.

After a long while muffled sounds came from above. A window lighted.

As she had supposed, it had been best to take them by surprise.

The window went up. A bald but tousled head poked out.

'Is that you, Sandy?'

Rachaela cleared her throat.

'No. I need your help. An emergency. Your telephone.'

'There's a telephone up the way,' said the aggrieved being above.

'Vandalized,' said Rachaela. *As if the bastard doesn't know.* 'Please. It's urgent. I'll pay you for the use.'

'This time of night,' said the man.

'Please,' said Rachaela.

'Are you from the farm?'

'No.'

'Just wait there.'

The sky was bluish-grey, vast films of darkness seeping out of it.

From outposts of the dirty village, wild birds began to sing their lawless aubade.

She pictured the man stamping down through his pub, irate and duty-bound. Who was 'Sandy'? Another who knocked them up before daylight.

The door was unlocked and scraped open.

'Now what is it you want?'

'Your telephone.'

'I don't know. Who are you?'

'It's very urgent. I must call a car.'

'A car? What do you want with a car?'

The man, she had noticed, had a London accent, like the van people. Another outsider.

'It's an emergency,' Rachaela repeated.

'All right. You'd better come in.'

Racahela moved through. The hallway smelled beery and unclean.

'I need the number of a hire car,' said Rachaela.

'Wants the phone and wants a bloody number an' all.'

'I'm sure you have some numbers.'

'Maybe, in the bar. I'll have to go through. Wait there.'

The man went off in his brown dressing-gown.

From above, a woman called plaintively, 'What is it, Harry?'

Rachaela stood in the dark and threadbare hall. She gazed at the telephone. She felt drunk. Perhaps it was the smell.

The man came back and thrust a card at her.

'That'll do. I'll ask you two pounds for the call. Don't be more than five minutes.'

Rachaela took the card, opened her bag, and put down the money on the smeary table. The man scooped them up at once.

'Harry!' called the woman.

'What the hell is it?'

'What's happening, Harry?'

'Some girl here wants the phone,' he shouted. 'Get up and make us some tea. You women,' he said to Rachaela in disgust.

She picked up the telephone receiver, disbelievingly, and dialled the number of the card. *Quickies*.

It rang. It rang and rang.

Twenty-four-hour service said the card. Perhaps they had gone to make tea also, or to the lavatory.

'Quickies Cars.'

Rachaela caught her breath.

'I need a car to get to the town station.'

'And where from?'

Where from. Rachaela said, 'Just a moment.' She said to the man, 'What's the name of this place?'

'What, here?'

'Yes, the village.'

'You don't know?'

'No, I don't.'

'Bidgely,' he said. She thought he said.

'Bidgely,' she enunciated cautiously into the phone.

'I'm sorry,' said the man on the line.

'Bidgely. Can you spell it for me?' she asked the pub owner.

He spelled the word. It was 'P–i–t–c–h–l–e–y'.

'Don't think I know that one,' said the car-hire man.

Rachaela said firmly to the impatient pub man, 'Would you be very kind and give him directions?'

'Well you've got a bleeding cheek I must say. Getting me out of bed at this hour, wanting me to give directions.'

Rachaela handed him the phone.

To her relief he took it and did as he was bid. The advice sounded incomprehensible to her but when he handed her the phone receiver back, the car man said, 'OK, I've got that. Be about an hour. That's the soonest I can make it.'

'All right. Thank you.'

'What number is the pick up?'

'By The Armitage public house.'

'Right-oh.'

Quickies clicked into the void.

'There you are then,' said the man.

His woman was coming down the stairs in a blue candlewick dressing-gown and her hair in curlers.

They watched Rachaela off the premises and slammed and locked the door.

An hour, and an hour perhaps to get back into the town – still plenty of time, as she had judged it, to catch the ten-forty-five for Bleasham.

Suppose it was not Tuesday that the train ran.

It was. It was and she would be in time. Somewhere someone had to tell the truth. She was determined now. She would make it happen.

Rachaela sat on the ground, on the slope of unbuilt land up the street, where the van came when the van came.

She watched for the car.

The village started half-alive about her, lights went on in some windows, then off again as the daylight strengthened. A woman came out of her house and apparently poured a pot of tea around the base of a bush. Another one put washing on to a line, gaudy bedclothes and sombre shirts.

A car or two, the wrong ones, took off down the street in the direction of the town.

A dog barked.

The village was, as she had thought, a dump, where time was whittled away in some vintage manner. Tainted by Scarabae.

But the car would come.

The car was late.

It was half past nine and the car had not arrived.

Rachaela stood up. Was the driver lost?

The driver would not be lost.

An old green Ford Zodiac materialized on the road, driving down into the village. It went past Rachaela, and pulled up outside the pub.

Rachaela ran.

'I have to catch the ten forty-five at the town station.'

'I doubt if you'll do it, miss,' said the driver sadly. 'You're late.'

'It's the traffic, you see. Should have ordered the car sooner, miss.'

'I did.' She got in. 'Will you try?'

'The Poorly connection is it you want?'

'Poorly, yes. For London.'

'Your best bet is if I drive straight over to Poorly. Cost you a bit more, but you'll get the eleven-fifteen London train for sure.'

'All right. Do that then,' she said recklessly.

'You understand, I'm trying to help you out.'

'Drive to Poorly.'

'Don't want you to think I'm just angling for extra fare.'

'It doesn't matter. So long as I get the train.'

The village reversed, took off and poured away.

After all, this was the moment of severance.

The car raced up the road. Rachaela felt a flare of mad joy. As if she could leave all her troubles behind. But they were only just beginning.

The driver was talkative. She let him go on, offering the proper monosyllable here and there. He wanted to tell her his life-story, not hear her own.

Perhaps he had lied about missing the town connection. He had four children, two parents, and a weak-willed sister.

The colour of the car, grey-green, the country rushed by. They passed houses and fields and a number of prettified pubs, all showing that the influence of the Scarabae had been left behind. Churches rose in meadows, picturesque, with leaning gravestones. Faint blossom was on some trees like wispy bridal veils. Spring began here too.

She had lost the months as well. Was it March?

They turned through lanes, and joined a motorway and left it. It was ten thirty-five. Certainly too late for the town train now.

A sign said *Porlea 6 miles.*

Rachaela almost laughed.

Perhaps everything would change like the names once she was out of their net.

Nobody stood on the platform for the despised means to London, but in the ticket office the man had assured her that all was well, or at least, sane.

The station was bright with lots of red plastic, but cartons lay in the litter bins and a discarded magazine loitered on one of the seats.

Birds sewed back and forth over the line.

Then the train came, massive, filthy and real.

An announcement informed the vacant platform and Rachaela that this train was the London via somewhere, calling at something and elsewhere and who cared at all? In an ecstasy of selfishness she got into the magic train.

It was quite crowded but in her pleasure Rachaela did not mind. She found a seat and placed her bags at her feet.

Thank God. Oh thank God.

With a gliding forward-thrust the train achieved its truth. It was bearing her away. Everything would be all right.

The woman with the shopping basket cuddled on her lap made her fifth attempt upon Rachaela.

'Don't you find these long journeys are a nuisance? It's the motion. I can't settle to anything. I brought my knitting. Do you knit? But I drop stitches, I find. Knitting a cardy for my granddaughter. Very fancy pattern. I can show you my grandchild. I always carry a photo. Such a bonny child. Not like my daughter at all. More like my mother's side. Such lovely hair. A proper blonde. Of course it will darken. I never let my daughter do anything to her hair. You leave it the way God intended it.'

Have it cut, said Rachaela's mother, *and a nice set. Easier for you to manage.*

The photo was produced and given to Rachaela. A fat, pale child with yellow hair, smiling, jam on its upper lip, unless it had also a red moustache.

'Yes,' said Rachaela.

'Do you have any children?'

'No,' said Rachaela.

'A pity, I always think, not to have them while you're young. It's the best time. I had my Janet when I was eighteen. And then John and Kieran. I love children, don't you?'

Rachaela did not answer.

Fields and pylons passed. Distant houses with crimson roofs. A far-away river with a castle on its bank. Oh, to be there. To have some destination. There was only London. And until then this woman.

'Hurry up and give me a grandchild, I said to her. Oh Mum, she says, I'm only twenty. I had you when I was eighteen, I said. I expect you're waiting for Mr Right,' said the woman to Rachaela. 'We've been together, my

Martin and me, twenty-four years. A perfect match my sister used to say. I just wish, she used to say, I'd had your Martin, and your lovely children. What do you think you'll like, dear, a boy or a girl, for your first? A girl's best. Keep the boys in order. Like a second mum my Janet was.'

Rachaela stood up. The woman was not affronted. Her universe contained only one, the rest were bit players, successful or not.

Rachaela dodged her way to the lavatory.

The lock was whimsical. She got it shut, and leaning with difficulty to the jolting bowl, she vomited colourless fluids from her empty stomach.

Was this the truth after all, even so early, the proving of the facts? Not the train, not London, but this?

As her head cleared, Rachaela propped herself against the wall. She voided the lavatory, and ran cold water in the basin, laving her face, hands, wrists.

Too soon surely to panic.

It was only fear.

Chapter Ten

❀ A POSTER ON THE WALL showed a bleeding rose. *Tetanus: it doesn't have to be a rusty nail,* the caption read. Beneath, a handwritten notice pleaded: 'If you or your child feel sick, please tell the receptionist.'

The surgery was crowded, a plague ward. Children sneezed and cried and ran about in a fever. Men and women coughed and evacuated their noses, blue germs puffing from their mouths in the chilly room. The chairs were hard and the magazines few. You were not encouraged to come.

The buzzer went angrily. Who would dare to be next.

'Miss Day? Go through please.'

Rachaela walked through into the doctor's room, which was quite large, with netted windows over a garden.

The man wore a suit and tie. He was slim and fit with well-brushed thinning hair. He gave Rachaela a neat and ironed smile.

'What can I do for you?'

Rachaela sat down on the chair he indicated.

Tanith Lee

'I need an abortion.'

The doctor put his smile away and raised his brows.

'Let's not put the cart before the horse, shall we? So you think you may be pregnant. What leads you to believe this?'

'My periods have stopped. I've been sick several times.'

'How many periods have you missed?'

'Two.'

'Have you brought a sample of your urine taken first thing in the morning?'

'I did a Predictor test.'

'I see. Well as you're here, we'd better take a look at you.' He pressed at the intercom. 'Mrs Beatty, come through please.' He said, 'Just slip off your under-things behind that screen. Keep your slip on.'

Rachaela did as she was told, and came out to the examining table, very white with something on it like a large paper towel.

Fat Mrs Beatty entered and sat down in a corner beyond the screen.

'Knees up, please, ankles together. Just relax.'

The last time a man had touched her it had been a pleasure, a miracle of sensation. This one was rough, knowing how tough the female body had to be, how much it could take.

'Yes,' he said, 'um.'

And he poked and prodded at her vagina and her belly. He stared in behind a light, like a miner.

'All right. You can put on your things now.'

He washed his hands, soiled by her, at a sink, and Mrs Beatty slunk back out of the room.

'Well, Miss – ah, Miss Day. I'd say you're definitely pregnant.'

212

'I know.'

'Everything,' he said, 'seems very healthy. Let's have a look at your blood pressure.' He attended to this, checking his gauge. They waited in silence. 'That's excellent. You're a very healthy young woman.'

His congratulations did not thrill her.

'I want an abortion.'

'There's absolutely no reason that you should. You're what—' he consulted her statement before him, 'twenty-nine? That's not too late. There are tests that can be run if you're worried the baby—'

It's not a baby. It's a thing, a parasite, lodged in me.

'I don't want it.'

'But, Miss Day. It's not as simple as that. You have a responsibility. The child has been conceived. A life, Miss Day, which you are carrying.'

'It was an accident.'

Could she say that? She had not taken any precautions, nothing had been further from her mind. The gate left open, and the fertile Scarabae seed, better at inbreeding, sown in one of five vortices of ecstasy. Yes, she was responsible.

'I'm afraid, accident or not, the child is a fact.' He ran his eye over her. He smelled of disinfectant and aftershave. 'Do you have any family?'

'No.'

'And I take it your boyfriend isn't interested.'

Boyfriend.

'I left him.'

'I see. An awkward situation. But people come through worse. You must be brave. In this day and age things are made quite easy for a young mother, a single parent. I see you have an address in quite a nice area.'

She had just gained the small flat via the proceeds of the compensation for the other. It had taken weeks to sort things out. Thus her delay in coming to this man. This man who believed in the sanctity of life, *its* life, not hers. Hers was immaterial.

'My address doesn't matter. I don't have any money—'

'There are means of support for women in your situation.'

'But I tell you, I don't want it. It – it was forced on me.'

'Surely not.' He allowed himself to show a measure of distaste.

'I can't – I can't have it, care for it.'

'You can decide all that when the baby is born. And you'll change your mind. Children are wonderful things. Special.'

'Not to me.'

'Well, Miss Day, I'm sorry but I see no excuse to recommend you should opt for a termination. Of course we need to go into your history. But judging by what I've seen and what you've told me, I see no reason why you shouldn't square up to this and assume your responsibility. Think of all those women who long to bear a child and are unable.'

'I don't care about that. I care about my own body. I want my freedom.'

'Then I'm sorry, Miss Day. I can't help you.'

'Then where do I go?'

'You'll have to find that out for yourself. I'm not here in the position of a butcher. Life's important to me.'

'I'm desperate,' she said.

He flushed. He said, 'You people make me sick.'

He rose. Rachaela got up too.

She struck him violently across the left side of his face dislodging all expression. He gawped at her, his left eye watering, and the imprint of her hand bright-pink across his clean-shaven, aftershaved cheek. So he would have to confront the next patient.

Heavy as lead, she walked from the room.

The main chamber was ten feet by fourteen. The walls and ceiling were white with a hint of peach, and the carpet dove-grey. She had known all this before she moved into it, from the estate agents' sheet.

The bathroom was boxed off, giving a tiny entrance lobby as you entered the flat. The suite in the bathroom was white and the floor black-and-white tiles. There was a frosted window. The kitchen area also opened off the room, without a door. It had a black floor, white cupboards, and a stainless-steel sink and drainer. The one window in the kitchen and the two in the main room were on the same end wall. They looked across the lines of houses and the blocks of flats towards a distant handkerchief of park with tall bare trees. In summer they would be green, as the agent had cunningly pointed out.

Rachaela had expensively rescued her furniture from store. She spread the bed with a blue and crimson Indian blanket, put up lampshades, hung blue curtains.

The flat was not unpleasant. For one. It was only for one.

The radio stood on the kitchen work-top.

She turned it on. Haydn, clipped and safe, with only the passion of melody.

She had been so frightened. It had taken all her strength to go to the man who thought children were special. Why were they special? They were unformed dough, unfinished things, due to be warped into the general useless and dangerous mass of human adults.

Rachaela touched her stomach and took her hand quickly away. It was in there. A growth, busily feeding on her, swelling second by second.

It would take so much courage to find another doctor, and she would surely have to go to a hospital to do so. She feared hospitals. She distrusted the uniform of the white coat. And then she might meet another one like the one today.

Could she do something herself?

She had tried all the sane home remedies she had ever heard of to dislodge it. Gin and hot baths, exercises. She could not bring herself to fall down the house stairs. The commotion, and people running out, a broken leg.

She was afraid, too, of the abortion. To have the thing scraped or vacuumed out of her womb, the very thought of it last night had sent her to the bathroom, heaving over the modern white lavatory.

But she must find someone. Someone kind who would put her first.

As she had told herself she must not, she saw the Scarabae reaching out, their agents in the surgery, the doctor listening, nodding.

This was not a plot. It was simple bad luck.

The tradition of the family. Continuance.

No wonder he had left her. He had seen to her as he had seen to her mother. He had been more certain with Rachaela.

She sat down in her chair and threw its new blue cushion to the carpet.

How pretty the flat was. She could live here, surely, at peace, alone.

And she would need to work. There was the cafeteria in Lyle and Robbins. Old-fashioned, not too demanding, and no drunks. Then again the Pizza Eater on Beaumont Street was a better bet for tips. No bookshops. Computerized tills. These things could be sorted out and surmounted.

But not this.

She lay back in the chair.

She was so tired.

The clear windows showed the roofs of London, the redundant chimneys and the crop of TV aerials, the spring sky. An aeroplane. She recalled no aeroplanes flying over the heath. Out of time and place, that spot.

Perhaps something will happen. Anna had said that.

She had meant the pregnancy.

Was it wrong to kill it?

It was a monster.

In the blustery dark descending the well-lit centre of the house, Rachaela found a woman had stepped out from a doorway, a neighbour from the floor below.

'Oh, Miss Day. I picked this up by mistake. I'm afraid I think it's only junk mail, but it's addressed to you.'

Rachaela took the glossy envelope.

'Thank you.'

'You can never tell these days. It might be something you want.'

The woman was conciliatory in warm fawn. Her

hair was a greying fair, thick and shaggily cut. She had a square face and large brown eyes, smiling. She wanted to be friends.

'How are you finding the flat?' she asked.

'It's fine.'

'I find it's so small,' said the woman. 'But then, I've had all these years to accumulate rubbish.'

Rachaela waited, her heart drumming and her stomach rife, for the challenge of the street and the night.

'Well I mustn't keep you. Take care,' she added kindly, 'it's a nasty old night.'

Rachaela went on down the stairs, stowing the piece of junk mail in her bag.

She forgot the woman outside. The wind struck at her, the sky was choked with dark blue churning cloud.

Rachaela walked down the street and caught a bus at the corner. It twisted and turned and bore her into an ominous and derelict suburb, stark in the orange street lights.

Where she got off, the buildings had been knocked down, great rattling walls of corrugated iron, striped with bills, separated her from yawning cavities. She walked past the rowdy pub which had been described and up a hill of council houses fish-boned with fake shutters, gardens spattered by gnomes, and windmills that whirled with weather. The street ended in waste ground. Some youths in leather and day-glo socks were holding a meeting on the gloomy grass. One shouted at Rachaela, a ritual of menace. She walked on and came to a one-storey building surrounded by a cordon of wire fencing.

Through the gate and over the lumpy ground, and she opened the door and went into a long drill hall with a clacking wooden floor.

The air was hot and sour, the room crowded, the lines of wooden seats around the walls filled by women of all apparent ages between the virgin and the crone. It was a place of women, a mocking slightly sordid club. And from a yellow door issued a man in a white coat, and the eyes of his harem of suppliants went to him, the click of knitting needles hesitated and pages of rustling magazines halted.

He joked briefly with a woman in a lilac cardigan at a desk. Then he was gone, like the god.

Rachaela went to the desk.

'I've got an appointment for seven.'

'Oh yes. Miss Day is it? That's right. If I could just take your address.' The woman entered details and nearby the nearer women listened. A pallid girl with round frog eyes watched Rachaela, popping a boiled sweet into her rosy, fatty mouth. 'I'm afraid we're a bit behind tonight. It may be a bit of a wait.'

'All right.' Rachaela went from the woman and found a chair at the end of the line.

About thirty in front of her. Surely some of them were together. It was ten to seven now.

The frog princess was the nearest to the yellow door. Presumably when one went in, they all moved up a chair, into the heat of the previous sitter, intimately. We are all women. We are bound to protect ourselves. The cap and the pill, the scrape of the spatula taking our smear, to save us from semen and from cancer. We are the responsible ones.

But there were children with the women here and there, subdued children eating chips or drawing on pieces of paper on the floor.

Fourteen-year-olds with kids and thick mascara, slim with strange fat faces that had not lived, but had overseen, screaming and crying, the birth of offspring from the trunk below.

Certainly, none of them looked afraid. They were all quite comfortable in their evening club, the Family Planning Clinic.

I'm afraid I haven't planned. Heavy with child I come to ask for an extraction.

Would this one listen?

Was it to be the man from behind the yellow door? She had hoped it would be a woman on this visit. A woman's touch would be less horrible, perhaps.

But these were all women. Look at them.

The needles of that one clocking like Madame Defarge, her soiled yellow hair piled up on her head and red lipstick like a gaping wound. And there one writing, probably a letter, holding the paper sideways and chewing her nails.

The hall smelled of women, too. Cheap scent and costlier scent like fly spray, sticky underarm deodorant, hair lacquer, babies and washing-up hands.

Rachaela felt sick. If that happened, where was the lavatory? There must be one. She should have asked.

She could feel *it*, pressing against her belly from beneath, like solid indigestion.

Try not to think of it. She took slow breaths of the nauseating air.

A girl in a purple suit began to talk to her friend beside her.

'I don't like this waiting. Gets on me nerves.'

'Yeah.'

Yes, thought Rachaela.

'Don't know what he'll say this time. I reckon he fancies me.'

'Don't be daft.'

'Well why not?'

'It's more'n his job's worth.'

The purple girl toyed with a packet of cigarettes beneath the 'No Smoking' sign, playing with them like a toy. If she could not consume them at least she could hold them.

'He keeps on, give it up. I've tried ain't I? I started with all that worry.'

'Yeah.'

'All them counsellors and psychiatrics. Was I sure? 'Cause I'm bleeding sure. Can't have another kid can I? Can't afford it and he'll leave me.'

'Oh Lyn.'

'Well he would have. We was in a fix as it was. An' I took the bloody pill. I did. Regular. And then I goes up the shute. That would have been number three.'

'Lyn, you always go on.'

'It's this place. It reminds me. All them psychiatrics at the hospital. I had to see four of them. Like a bloody judge and jury, trying to persuade me to have it. I can't have it. I've got two already.'

Rachaela listened, her eyes on the wooden floor. To one who had travelled before her.

'Well, you got rid of it, Lyn,' said the unfriendly friend.

'It was a struggle. And then the way they treat you. And the pain. Christ, I thought it would be all right. I've never been right since. You know I ain't. I couldn't bear him near me after.'

'That was psychological. They told you it was.'

'No it weren't. They done something to me, the clumsy buggers. They treat you like shit when you go in for it.'

The yellow door opened and a slim, fat-faced young girl came out, looking satisfied.

The god emerged again and went to the desk. He gave instructions and vanished once more.

'Miss Garland,' sang out the woman in lilac, and the frog princess, sucking her sweet without fear, went forward and inside the door.

The Defarge woman dropped a stitch and cursed.

'I'm going outside for a fag,' said the purple girl. She got up and left the hall.

A new picture. Probes for the body and others probing at the mind. The team of psychiatrists, trying to delve the reasons of the would-be terminator. Would it be enough to be afraid? No. The dream she had had, lying on the beach and the sea coming in, split open and fire running out of her guts, that would not be enough.

Of course, they would not make it simple. It must not be easy. She bore a life. She could not merely flush her body like a toilet bowl.

The girl next up from Lyn's friend was discussing food. 'A nice cut of steak and fry it up with onions. I could give him that every night. It's no good me saying, Tony, it's bad for you. You'll get a heart attack. And try giving him salad. Chips with everything. Our ceiling's black from frying chips. Running with grease. He makes me sick.'

She had done the favour for Rachaela.

Rachaela rose and walked quickly out of the hall.

Outside the night came thankfully cold, a smell of external houses and open street. The glare of the nauseous streetlights which made the world faceless and colourless.

The purple girl, now in black, stood by the fence smoking greedily. She glanced at Rachaela and away.

It was not possible to ask her questions. In any case, everything was now revealed. A difficult business. A humiliating struggling business. Ending in harsh treatment and pain, and a lingering scar.

She could hear the adjacent streetlight sizzling like a radioactive isotope. The earth was alive with poisons, and surrounded by the threat of outer space. What use was anything.

The abortioned girl stared after Rachaela as she walked out of the gate and back along the street. There was a faint affront on the girl's face, as if she knew Rachaela had denied herself a similar vileness and suffering, the secrets of the female club.

Over the Beethoven concerto, the door was knocked upon.

Rachaela lay in the chair, listening to the echo.

Why should she go?

It was no one. Some mistake. When she had been here three days a man had trailed up the stairs, let in by another tenant, hammering on her door. 'Do the Chambers live here?' She had told him they did not. He was disbelieving and finally she shut the door in his face.

The door was knocked upon again. A muffled woman's voice. 'It's only me. Downstairs, Flat Five.'

Rachaela lifted herself from the chair.

223

Was this too some part of the Scarabae plot? For yes, there was a plot. Of course there was.

She opened the door. It was the fair, greying woman from below.

'Sorry to disturb you. An absolutely ridiculous request. You couldn't let me have a little milk? I've been so chilled all day, made myself cup after cup of coffee and tea, and I've run out. The milkman delivers tomorrow. I can let you have it back quite quickly.'

Rachaela said, 'There's only carton milk.'

'Oh that's perfect, if you can spare it.'

Rachaela went into the kitchen and opened the fridge. She took out her three-quarters-full carton.

The woman stood on the grey carpet. 'How attractive you've made it,' she said, 'and no clutter. I truly admire that. I'm afraid mine's a cross between a library and a curiosity shop.'

Rachaela thought of all her books left behind.

The Beethoven played on, oblivious.

'Can you spare all this?'

'Yes.'

'Well, thank you so much. As I say—'

'Don't bother. I've another carton,' Rachaela lied.

'But I must.'

The woman paused. 'That's Number Three isn't it? I'm a fan of Beethoven. I love his fury. Why shouldn't the poor thing get angry, going deaf as he did?'

'Yes.'

'I'd better introduce myself.' Rachaela only looked at her. Undaunted, apparently, the woman said, 'Emma Watt. Mrs. Not that that counts any more. My poor old love died two years ago. I sold the house and took the flat. Tried to squeeze myself really small.

We all have our own funny ways of trying to deal with pain.'

And the pain. Christ . . .

'Anyway,' said Mrs Emma Watt quickly after all, 'I expect you're busy. Thanks again for the milk. I'll pop up and put a bottle outside your door tomorrow.'

'There's no need.'

'But I must.'

She went into the hall and brightly down the stairs with a brave self-sufficient smile, for Rachaela's benefit.

What would it be like to be Emma Watt, fifty years old, sad and alone and brightly squeezed into her too-small flat?

What would it be like to be the purple girl, frigid from anxiety, and child-bearing behind her?

There was no escape. She was Rachaela, here and now.

In her belly the thing lay, embedded, coiled.

The Pizza Eater took on Rachaela, gave her a red dress and a pale green apron, and asked her to put up her hair. She plaited it, which seemed to satisfy them.

She worked from ten in the morning until six, or from three until eleven-thirty. Some of the late customers were drunk, but normally well-behaved. Often, delayed by the clearing up, she did not leave the premises until midnight. In addition to serving the wood-plastic tables, she cut sandwiches, grilled steaks, scooped out ice-cream, piled pizzas in boxes for a take-away service, and now and then washed up.

She grew accustomed, as she had before, to her feet hurting and burning, to the rudeness and tiplessness of many customers, and the matey chatter of her fellow workers of both sexes. She received lunch or dinner free from the restaurant, but the food did not really appeal to her. Sometimes she managed a rare steak or else ate salad and ice-cream. It saved her efforts at the flat.

She came to terms with the computerized till, which often she had to deal with. One afternoon she gave a pound short on the change which had showed up in emerald numerals before her face. The customer did not notice; and by the time she realized, he had gone. On her own at the till, Rachaela removed the extra pound and kept it.

The Pizza Eater was only twenty minutes walk away from the flat.

For the first seven weeks she was meticulously on time. Then, when she was late, it was never more than ten or fifteen minutes, which the other employees frequently bettered, coming in half an hour over the odds due to tube delays or traffic jams.

Rachaela thought of the job as temporary. Something more soothing would present itself. Meanwhile the money was not bad, and forgetting the occasional pound in change proved a useful means of saving. Only once had the customer checked his money and informed her she had short-changed him. Rachaela looked flustered, apologized, and fished the extra note out of the till. 'That's all right,' he said blithely. 'Anyone can make a misnnetake.'

The other mistake she ignored.

At the time when most women, so a solitary book from the library had informed her, began to experience sickness, Rachaela stopped. She had no symptoms, except that no monthly showing of blood took place. Her waist widened a little, her hips. She took care of that by moving the buttons on her skirts, then buying a larger size. She bought loose T-shirts. So far the red dress, always too large, fitted.

The weather verged through a blustery spring into a rainy May. The trees in the distance of the windows flowered into mop-heads of shining green. The grey and stormy skies made them if anything greener. Chickweed pushed through the pavements. The city was all cracks and crevices wetly fruiting, burgeoning. The weather lied. It was nearly summer.

She did not think about the thing inside her now. She put it out of her mind.

As if to compound her plan, it gave no real evidence that it was there.

Perhaps her greatest defiance, the extravagant music centre she had ordered from the junk mail, arrived when she was out at the restaurant.

Arriving home at half past twelve at night, Rachaela found it in the downstairs hall, another tenant had obviously taken it in.

Rachaela proceeded to lug the boxes upstairs three flights.

On her last journey, as she was passing Number Five, the door opened and Emma Watt looked out.

'Good heavens, I thought it was the broker's men! Oh goodness, you shouldn't be carrying that, let me help you. No I insist.'

And so, aided by Emma Watt, Rachaela carried the last box up to her flat.

'Do you mean you brought all those up too? And some of them look quite heavy. These firms nowadays, they're so bad. Couldn't the man have brought them up? In your condition – oh, I'm sorry,' said Emma Watt, blushing. 'That sounds so nosy. I mean you hardly show, but I couldn't help seeing, you're so slight – and well, I had three myself, and I've seen my daughters through it. I hope you don't mind that I said anything.'

'No.'

'You must be careful,' said Emma Watt. 'I'm sure it's all right this time, but you shouldn't carry anything heavier than a handbag – that's what my old love used to say. He used to add that my handbags would make a strong man blench.'

Rachaela, as if by suggestion, felt suddenly weak. She sat on the bed.

'There you see. You've overdone it. Can I make you a cup of tea?'

'I'm quite all right.'

'I will any way. Don't worry, I won't stop, just a quick cup of tea. Your kitchen's through here, isn't it, like mine? You just relax. Put your feet up.' From the kitchen the sound of water and a surprised, 'You don't have a pot – just use the bag then. They're so convenient, aren't they.'

Rachaela stared at the boxes. Would she ever have the strength to undo them.

'What's in those?' asked Emma, coming back out. 'Is it a music centre? Can you put it together yourself? I'm hopeless at anything like that. If you have any trouble try the little man in Horsley Street, the electricals place. He's splendid. He wired all my lamps for me and fixed my washing machine.'

'I'll remember.'

'Kettle won't be a moment. Oh you must be so tired. You work late, don't you. I often hear you come in – please don't think you disturb me, you're very quiet, and I'm always up till one or two. Terrible sleeper. I've got some pills but they make me feel like a rag in the mornings. And I love the mornings. I get up at seven. Always have. Oh, please don't think I'm prying, but I'd love to know. When is your baby due?'

Rachaela reeled off a book-established fact.

'December.'

'A Capricorn. They're lovely. But good lord, you're in your fourth month. You're very small. My middle daughter was like that, tall and slim and you could hardly tell. It used to annoy her the way everybody took no notice. She said she wanted to "sail upon the land" like Titania's handmaiden. My oldest daughter, poor girl, swelled up like an elephant. What does your chap say at the hospital?'

Rachaela said, 'Apparently everything's the way it should be.'

'Yes, of course. And you're so young too. It's exactly the right age.' Emma Watt blushed again. 'All the same, it's rotten for you, having to manage on your own.'

'That was my decision.'

'Yes, but it's courageous of you. And so wise to go ahead and have the baby, if you want it.'

'I didn't,' Rachaela said, 'I don't.'

And wished she had not spoken.

Emma Watt did not look shocked, but only tremendously sad.

'But that's terrible. Why—'

'I went to the wrong doctor.'

'You poor girl. But couldn't you – no, I suppose not. And you're resigned to it now. I still think it's

229

best. When your baby's born – they're so rewarding. I loved it. When they're little, watching them grow. And I love them, I love my children. It's such a pity they're so far away. I hardly ever see them. They phone me up, of course, but it isn't much good. They're always so scared I can't cope after their father died. I have to keep proving to them that I can.' Emma smiled valorously, proud of her façade. Her eyes were moist. 'I've missed all the grandchildren, too. It's awful. I just love babies, children. They fascinate me. These tiny helpless little things that just come to life day by day, until they're people. Oh, I'm sure you'll be glad.' She raised her head. 'There's the kettle.'

She went to make Rachaela the unwanted tea.

She made none for herself, but left Rachaela at once with the mug in her hand.

The room darkened oddly, perhaps a trick of the electricity.

The summer came at the beginning of August.

The city baked, the trees turned coppery. Ochre dust rose from the blazing pavements.

A blue sky of cobalt made a lid for every stink and fume. Everything smelled and tasted of asphalt, petrol, car exhaust and sweet ice-cream.

Rachaela's back ached continually. She could put this down to her job. The red dress was firm but the apron hid it. One of the girls made a crack that Rachaela had put on weight due to the food.

One day she amassed ten pounds from those careless customers who did not count their change.

The man from Horsley Road had fixed the music centre. The radio was not very good but the tape and record players were excellent.

She bought books and lined the shelves of her bookcase.

Emma found excuses to appear, but not very often. Emma still did not know her first name.

September was a tawny month, tanned, cooked skin on the streets, brown crispness on the leaves.

October yellowed, banana sunsets cut with gilt, lemon first-light as Rachaela, cramped and sleepless, saw the dawn begin, and the trees in the park like topaz flags.

Storms at night. Downpours of hot rain.

Sibelius, Mozart, Shostakovich.

No need to think. So sluggish. She would have to give up the Pizza Eater. Her back shrieked, and when she bent to serve the late-night customers with their breath of beer and Cinzano, her head swam. Nobody had noticed she was pregnant. They thought she had got fat, a good advert, on the succulent nosh.

The summer ended on the first night of October. Hail thrashed the roofs and glass windows.

Rachaela had called in sick and sat at her window and watched it, her back packed with cushions and pillows.

She had an hallucination of a tall dark man on the street, striding through the hail. Adamus in a cloak of thunder, come to claim her again for the Scarabae.

But all that was over. It was a dream. She had conceived immaculately and here she was, the slave of this molten tumour in her womb, and it was real.

Chapter Eleven

From the larger stores along the high street, carols wailed and jingle bells jingled, compulsory joy.

It rained heavily. There was a lot of flu about.

Rachaela had given in her notice at the Pizza Eater and left just as the free balloons began to be given out and Christmas pudding appeared on the menu. Children had knocked over the tree of green and red glitz, and everyone was picking it up; that was her last image of the restaurant.

Emma Watt came out of her door like a cuckoo from a clock.

'I've bought a bottle of really nice sherry, and some wine. Will you come down and have a drink with me? To toast my little tree. I always have one. One must. Christmas is so important, it's important to salute it, even if, well even if you're on your own. Are you going anywhere for Christmas?'

'No.'

'Just quiet by yourself. Yes, you must get all the rest you can. Anyway, do pop down. About six?'

'All right,' said Rachaela, to shut her up.

Rachaela had never bothered with Christmas. It had only meant one more day of privacy. She heard distant bells ringing and the strange silence of the streets. The radio had Christmas music which often she did not like, huge oratorios and quasi-religious peculiar plays. Once she had listened to a Christmas service out of curiosity. She knew the hymns from school days, the tunes at least.

Her mother had believed in celebrating Christmas too. There had been a dinner cooked, turkey or chicken with sausages, roast potatoes and stuffing. It had entailed much the same fuss and anger as the now-and-then Sunday dinners: Rachaela recruited to peel vegetables, make crosses on the thousands of sprouts. One Christmas her mother had scalded herself on the turkey fat.

Neighbours would come in for a drink and boxes of chocolates and handkerchiefs would be exchanged.

After the neighbours and the dinner and the Queen's speech, depression would set in from the rich food and the gins and tonics.

Her mother gave Rachaela sensible presents, a new blouse or shoes that pinched. Once there had been a fairy costume from a neighbour. Rachaela had played in it for hours, she was six, it had been oddly magical. But somehow the wings got torn, like a symbol. Her mother scolded her and made her ashamed.

Rachaela did not mean to go down to toast Emma Watt's tree. So far she had avoided the interior of Emma Watt's flat.

Rachaela sat in comfortable misery before her electric fire, her back wedged with cushions, sipping a glass

233

of her own wine. Her back was excruciating and she
had also taken three paracetamol. Despite the pain she
began to go to sleep.

She was woken by bright little squirrel knocks on
the door: Emma Watt.

'Damn her.'

Best go to the door and tell her she was not
feeling well, could not come down, an early night
and so on. Left unanswered, Emma Watt grew
anxious and knocked and called; it had happened
before.

As Rachaela got up something seemed to tear
inside her all the way down, between her spine and
stomach. In puzzlement she stood there, waiting for
some sequel, but nothing happened.

She reached the door and opened it.

'Are you all right?' asked Emma Watt. 'Oh my dear,
you look dreadful.'

'Yes. I'd better not come down,' said Rachaela.

A pain like the worst toothache clutched her vitals.
She felt herself wither.

'What is it?' said Emma.

'Just a pain.'

'What sort of a pain?'

Dazed, Rachaela told her. She had to hold the frame
of the door. For the first time in months she felt very
sick again.

'Excuse me, I have to go to the bathroom.'

She made it. Her body emptied itself in all its
chambers. She came out shaking, and Emma Watt
was still there of course, standing in the middle of
the room.

'My dear,' she said, 'I think you've started.'

'Started what?'

'Your baby's coming. Oh don't be frightened. This will soon be over, and then the marvellous part begins.'

Rachaela sat down. The pain came again, griping her hollow guts, twisting her body like a cloth.

'Must you be so stupid?' she said.

Emma brushed this aside.

'Say anything you like,' she said, 'call me names. I know this bit isn't particularly nice. I'll phone for you. The hospital – is it St Mary's? What's your doctor's name?'

'Oh, that,' said Rachaela. 'No doctor, no hospital.'

'What?'

'I haven't been seeing anyone. That was just your happy little fantasy, Emma. Nobody knows.'

'But my God, my God,' said Emma. Panic took her all apart, and then she gripped herself together again. 'Never mind. I'll get an ambulance.'

Rachaela watched her, smiling. She took a mouthful of wine, but it came straight back up. This time she did not make the bathroom.

'Don't drink that,' said Emma through a white blur. 'Take my hand. That's it. They won't be long.' The pain came and crushed her away. 'My God,' said Emma, 'they'd better be quick. Just hold on. Hold on, darling. It's going to be all right.'

'Now push,' said someone, some mad woman. 'That's it. *Push*. Good girl.'

Were they speaking to her, these lunatics?

She lay on a scarlet beach and Uncle Camillo bent over her. He hauled the crimson obstacle from her womb. She felt it go as if her body had been disembowelled.

So this was the abortion. The pain was terrible. Much worse than that girl had said.

'One last try. Push.'

She could not push. What did it mean?

A fearful rhythm like galloping horses – stopped.

It was so quiet.

There was so much light, but growing darker.

'You can rest now.'

Who were these people, so many of them, crowding round her in a white hedge. Had she fallen in the street?

The pain had ended. There was another pain, but it was different, slow and closing.

Something cried like a savage animal in the wilderness.

It was alive.

The thing had been got out of her, and it lived. It made noises, horrible and unhuman.

In a sort of aperture she saw a white baby hanging upside down from a nail of light. A single, blood-red ribbon marked its back, shining.

'A girl. You see? She's quite perfect.'

*

Emma Watt sat by the bed. She was bright-eyed and faintly flushed. She had brought pink roses and a bottle of apple-juice, and grapes, and sweets in coloured wrappings.

'You're not to worry about a thing, Rachaela,' she must have found the name out from a nurse. 'I've seen to it all. Everything. We can sort the money side out later, but I don't want you to worry about that either. It really doesn't matter. I have more than enough, my old love saw to it I was comfortable. And I know, well – let's not talk about it now. The baby clothes are pink, of course. That's one good thing about not getting anything until we knew.' Emma hesitated. 'They'll be along soon, won't they.'

'Yes.'

'I can't wait to see her again. Oh, Rachaela, don't you feel clever? A gorgeous little girl.'

'I don't feel anything.'

'Well that can happen. Have you told them how you feel?'

'It isn't any of their business.'

'But Rachaela, it is. They can help you to feel better.'

'I feel all right.'

'But you said—'

'Emma, I told you. I didn't want this – baby.'

'But she's here now. And she's yours.'

'Yes.'

'Are you wishing,' said Emma cautiously, 'that he—'

'No. He wouldn't be any more interested than I am.'

Emma looked away. After a moment she said, 'Have you been luckier in feeding her.'

'Luckier? Do you mean can I breast-feed her yet? No I can't. Apparently I haven't got much milk.' Rachaela fought down her disgust. 'I find it repulsive. It's bad enough with the bottle.'

'I'm so sorry,' said Emma.

'Emma, you've been more than kind, but you don't understand.'

'No. I'm sorry about that too.'

'It's all right. I can't do anything about it. I accept that I can't.'

All those months swelling up, the pain and weight, and pretending it did not exist. But it had arrived and was actual. The pain had taken on a form, which cried, and dribbled from every orifice. A white hospitalized package smelling of faeces, urine and sick. Something she was expected to love. Aliens might have placed it in her, it might have burst out of her body rending her – it had done so. It had enslaved and damaged her. Now it was to rule her life. Why should she love it, this demon?

The nurses were coming with their Father Christmas sacks of snivelling and screaming babies.

'Here you are, Emma. Your moment.'

And Emma's unhappy face had freshened. She was not however indiscriminate. She rose and took Rachaela's child from the nurse with a gliding 'May I?', a sort of sleight of hand. Emma held the baby exactly as it should be held.

'Hallo, precious. Hallo, my sweet.'

Emma loved it. But dutifully she passed the bundle down into Rachaela's cold white arms.

Rachaela peered into the gnomic face.

It had lived in her, used her, but it was not hers. It was theirs. The Scarabae.

She could even see it in this thing, the pallor of it, the fine dust of jet black fur. The eyes were dark already, not yet focused, but questing. No teeth yet. Not yet.

Rachaela glanced about her. The ward was full of fulfilled and cow-like women waiting to give their udders to their young. In the wings waited the proud husbands, boyfriends and parents. The nurses on the ward were strict but applauding.

The room rocked with the howls of babies now being put to the breast, stilled. Rachaela had seen. The small mouths avid, the hands punching and grabbing. Tiny vampires, all of them. But this one, this monster, would have to make do with a bottle.

'You don't like it, do you?' she said to the monster as it sucked. 'Bottle or go without.'

She hated it. When it cried she stared on it remotely. She who had been its suitcase.

The room had altered. There was a cot. She could put the baby into this miniature prison and it crawled there in the trap.

Sometimes she had to lift it out, feed it, and change its nappies, thick with excrement.

The room stank. She kept the window open and the fire on. As the weather eased she left the fire off.

Emma came in and out. She arranged the feeds, trying the temperature of the milk. She took the baby out of the pen, and played with it. She had bought it blue and pink fluffy toys. The baby watched the toys with increasingly beady eyes.

'Isn't she pretty?' said Emma, perhaps to encourage.

The baby was not pretty. It was a baby. Primeval and unfinished, crawling about like a busy white slug.

All night the baby cried.

Rachaela got up and fed the baby. She rocked it roughly, loathing it, and the baby grew hysterical. It was strong. With every day its voice got louder, its punches and kicks more hefty.

Rachaela touched it as little as possible.

In the end she left it to cry.

It screamed for hours, probably waking the entire house. Near morning it burned itself out.

Rachaela got up and looked at it. Its bluish-black eyes seemed to focus on her for the first time. It had learnt something.

They took the baby for rides in the pram, to the shops, and up to the tiny park with its three or four flowerbeds and margin of trees. Cold winds knifed at them but the baby was snug in its portable bed, the blue and pink rabbits bobbling between its face and the real world.

'Lucky she wasn't born on Christmas day,' said Emma. 'She'll still miss out on presents, poor little sweetheart.'

The baby now had a name. It was called 'Ruth'.

'Rachaela and Ruth,' said Emma, and to the baby, 'Whither though goest, I will go.'

Emma had actually named the baby, reeling off name after name, pausing to assess their merits, recommending, persuading, until at last to stop her, Rachaela assented.

It sounded like a Scarabae name. It was unavoidable, Biblical. Ruth, daughter of Adamus.

'You must be getting awful cabin-fever stuck in all day,' said Emma, as they pushed through the lancing wind. 'I know what it's like. My oldest nearly went mad with Richard. She used to ring me up, just to hear an adult voice that could talk.'

Rachaela thrust the pram between the bare trees.

'So if you want to go off on your own for a bit, and you'll trust me,' said Emma, 'I can look after Ruth.'

'Thank you,' said Rachaela. 'But what I really need is to get a job. The money's run out fast.'

'But you can get assistance, Rachaela, and you must.'

'Yes.'

'It's foolish to try and manage on your own.'

Rachaela had not repaid Emma for the plethora of pink clothes, the blankets and toys, the pram and cot.

Emma had told her several times she did not wish to be repaid. Ruth was payment enough. Her 'share' of Ruth. They connived together: Emma taking a little more of Ruth at intervals; Rachaela gladly giving a little more.

'I need space to think,' said Rachaela.

'Let me have her, then. As I say, if you can trust me . . . I'll look after her if you want to go back to work. Only if you're sure . . .'

'Yes. I'm no good with – her. You're marvellous,' she added stonily, a meaningless accolade.

But Emma flowered in the winter park.

'Well, I've had three. And I did see a little of Pauline, when she was small, just enough to remind me. She's lovely, Rachaela. You know I'll take care of her.'

She had already seen the new bookshop. It had opened in the high street. 'Isis Books'. Feminist tracts and slim novels lined the windows. It already had a tatty, dusty look that reminded her of Mr Gerard on Lizard Street.

She went in and bought a novel set in India, whose prose appealed to her, and the heat and dust and cinnamon smells of somewhere else.

A soft fuzzy girl was at the till.

'I'm looking for work. I used to work in a bookshop before I had my baby.'

'Oh a baby,' said the assistant. Women were the mothers, protected of Isis.

'I'm wondering if you need an extra person.'

There had been three girls and a woman at first, now there was only this one.

'What, part-time?'

'No, full-time.'

'Well, with your baby.'

'A friend looks after her.'

'Oh is it a girl? How nice.' The fuzzy one gave Rachaela her change, correctly. The till was not computerized. 'You need to see Jonquil. She's not in today. She'll be here tomorrow morning. Why don't you drop by and have a word with her.'

In the morning Rachaela returned, leaving Ruth in her pen in Emma's crowded flat.

Jonquil came from the back. She was about thirty-seven, tall and spare, with spiky grey-streaked hair. She wore jeans and a large jumper, cowboy boots, one stainless steel earring.

'OK, I can certainly give you a job. Denise is here to all hours. We don't pay top rates, can't afford to.' Her eyes were a pale, thin grey, her face weather-beaten. 'This is about women. If it helps, then that's good. We don't employ men.'

The wages were indeed low. But it was money. And Emma would take care of the child. The child would spend all day with Emma. Emma was already expertly weaning the child. At night the child would sleep in the same room as Rachaela, that was all. Some nights Emma would keep the child.

Jonquil showed Rachaela round the bookshop.

Every book was by a woman.

'And you've got a baby? Swine left you, I suppose. Never mind. She's a girl. She might have a chance, things are changing.'

Sometimes men in mackintoshes stared in at the bookshop windows as if building up to a flash. Usually nobody came in.

Rachaela sat by the counter and read, making herself coffee. At lunch-time she closed the shop for an hour or longer, and shut up at five-thirty.

Jonquil came in every few days.

On Thursday and Saturday, Denise joined Rachaela. Denise was fallen. She had a live-in boyfriend to whom she devoted most of her time and energy. She confessed she could not wear red as Keith did not like it on her.

'You want to tell Keith to take a running jump,' said Jonquil.

Both thought they knew Rachaela's life and so did not ask many questions.

When Rachaela was late in the mornings to open up, no one was there to see. One morning Jonquil had got there first. 'Baby hung you up,' said Jonquil. 'No sweat.'

'She can walk,' said Emma, rosy as if tight. 'She really did it. I know you've only just got in, but come and see. I'll make some tea. It ought to be champagne.'

Emma's flat was chaos.

To the fat chinz chairs and divan, the second divan which changed into a bed, the clocks and ornaments, old dolls, and skeins of photographs, fresh flowers and coloured-glass paperweights, was added now the parked pram and the pen, the fluffy toys scattered, a great teddy-bear, the baby.

The baby would not walk for Rachaela.

She flatly refused.

Her smooth black eyes were vague and innocent. She sat on the floor.

'Oh, you naughty thing.' Emma picked her up and dandled her. 'You bad sausage. Not to show Mummy.' And Ruth laughed, as with Emma she often did. 'I'm sorry. It really happened. I didn't imagine it.'

'Well, I suppose she will eventually. Walk, I mean. And say words.'

'She should be saying things now. Oh, I don't mean anything's wrong. Pauline was slow. It's just how their temperament goes.'

'She doesn't speak because she doesn't need to,' said Rachaela. 'Telepathically you anticipate all her demands.'

'Do I? Do I, sausage?' Emma asked the chortling baby.

When its face screwed up with laughter it looked very old. Scarabae-old.

Rachaela put on the kettle and made tea for Emma and coffee for herself. She was used to Emma's flat by now.

'You ought,' said Emma softly, 'to spend more time with her. Oh, Rachaela. You're missing all the best parts.'

'Is she a nuisance? Do you want me to take her off your hands?'

'Rachaela, you *know* she isn't. I love her.' Emma held Ruth close, protectively, possessively. 'I only meant—'

'It doesn't interest me.'

'Oh Rachaela – you don't know. You haven't tried.'

'I had to carry her. I had to birth her. That was enough.'

'If only I could make you see how wonderful it is.'

Rachaela said, 'If I could see that, Emma, I'd cling on to her the way you do. You wouldn't get a look in. We wouldn't be here now.'

Emma went white. Her face crumpled, straightened itself out with difficulty. She swallowed.

'Yes. You're absolutely right, of course.'

'If I loved babies.'

'If you loved Ruth I wouldn't have been able to – I wouldn't have looked after Ruth as I have.'

'And you do love her.'

'Yes I do.'

'So it's lucky,' Rachaela ended pitilessly. 'Lucky for me, and lucky for you.'

'Yes,' said Emma.

She sat down and put Ruth on to the floor with her toys and the soft blanket.

Emma sat looking at Ruth.

Rachaela drank her coffee, and presently left Emma and Ruth alone together, for Emma to give Ruth her revolting gooey tea.

On Sunday they went up to the common, a performance; lifting the pram, Emma still insisted on for the sake of Ruth's spine, into and off the tube, the escalators.

Rachaela did not know why she had participated.

The trees were umbrellas of leaves and brilliant poppies dotted the grass. Where had the year gone? It was as if she had spent it underground, the hibernatory flat, dusty Isis Books.

'She's enjoying it,' said Emma. 'Look, Ruth. Tree. Doggy. Say "doggy", Ruth.'

Ruth stared from her eldritch eyes, Anna-eyes and Uncle-Camillo-eyes. Not the eyes of Adamus. Too old.

They wheeled the pram up the paths. The sun was hot and the common flooded by people. Dogs charged about grinning, plunging into the green pond, emerging to shake off volleys of water.

At the café on the common they had coffee. There were red horses in a field. 'Look, Ruth. Horsey.'

245

'I don't think she cares,' said Rachaela.

'Of course she does. It's all bewildering and new.'

Rachaela thought they must look a very normal family group: Emma the fond grandmother; Rachaela the mother with her black-haired baby. She wondered how many of the other normal-looking groups were also fakes: that man perhaps with the glasses, a wife-and-child-beater; the two lovers with their shared ice cream, brother and sister. But it was crazy to expect oddness from the day to match her own. Her child should wear a notice round its neck: *Conceived from my father while he drank my blood, suspected of being a demon*.

Obviously Ruth was not a demon.

Emma did not think so.

There was no need to trouble about it anyway. Emma had taken charge.

They wheeled the pram over the golf course.

When Rachaela had control of it, the child's black eyes went to Emma for reassurance. Who was this stranger moving her along?

Emma encouraged Rachaela with little inanities.

'She knows it's you.'

'She doesn't like me,' said Rachaela. 'Why should she? I was just an envelope.'

An intense golden light blared from the sky. It was five o'clock and they began the trek homeward. The tube was full of tanned and excitable travellers going home or *en route* to inner London. A sort of pollinated bloom was on them of dust and sun. The air smelled of deodorant and skin. A man in a bowler hat helped Emma with the pram.

When they returned to the house, they went into Emma's flat.

Emma took the baby out.

'My goodness, aren't you hot, you poor little thing. You shall have a nice cool bath.'

While Emma bathed Ruth, Rachaela sat on the chintz sofa looking at the Chinese statuettes and blue glass animals. In pride of place above the electric fire was a paperweight of a giraffe on which inappropriate snow fell when you shook it. Pauline had sent this last Christmas.

The splashing from the bath ended.

'She really is very hot,' said Emma. 'I think she's a bit feverish. They get these little things. It's nothing to worry about.'

'Better not move her, then,' said Rachaela.

'No, I'll keep her down with me for the night.'

The child kicked off her sheet fractiously. Her usually pale face was red. Perhaps she had caught the sun.

Upstairs Rachaela put on a tape of Brahms and laid out some leaves of lettuce and slices of tomato, a cold chicken leg from the deli. She ate without hunger, absorbing instead the music.

Later she sat and watched the golden sky turn to ruby over the roofs, the distant trees of the park blacken and fade.

This is my life then. It amused her. She did not let herself think of the Scarabae. She had become adept at avoiding them. Avoiding him. She would pick up the thought and put it outside her mind. When it came back, she removed it again.

She turned on the radio and listened to a Greek play which she did not understand but liked.

At about ten-thirty when she was running a long bath, Emma knocked on the door.

247

'Please don't be worried,' she said at once, 'but I think I'd better phone the doctor. He won't be there, of course, but they'll have someone. She's terrifically hot and she keeps crying. You know she never cries. I'm sure it's nothing, but I want to be sure.'

'All right,' said Rachaela. 'Do you want to bring her up here?'

'No, no. And I can phone from downstairs. I'll come back and tell you what they say.'

'Yes.'

When Emma was gone, Rachaela got into the bath. She shaved her legs and underarms, and shampooed her hair. Emma knocked again. Rachaela went to the door in a towel, and with a second towel wrapped round her head.

'Someone's coming out. They said about an hour.'

'I see.'

'You'll come down, won't you,' said Emma.

'If you think I should.'

'Yes you must, Rachaela. She's your child.' Emma looked pale and distraught.

Rachaela said nothing and Emma went away.

Rachaela rinsed her hair and wrapped it up in another towel. She dressed and put on her shoes and went down to Emma's flat.

Emma held Ruth in her arms. She sat down and fanned the baby gently with a Japanese fan. Ruth looked like a radish, as if her blood were slowly boiling. She snivelled weakly, on and on.

They said nothing, but sat facing each other.

The rest of the hour ticked by.

'It's Doctor Chatterjee,' said Emma at last. 'I've never had to call him out, I don't know what he's like. Poor man, he must dread these late calls. Doctors have a very rough time of it.' She fanned Ruth. 'You should have taken her to the clinic, Rachaela,' she said, without accusation. 'You never did.'

'No.'

'She would have had regular checks, and any shots. They give them so much protection nowadays. But Ruth hasn't had any of it.'

'She's strong,' said Rachaela. It was instinct which made her say it.

'Of course, of course she is. Silly old Emma getting in a state about nothing. Poor sausage, poor pretty.'

The baby was feebly sick on herself and Emma's cardigan.

Emma rose without flurry or distress to clean this up. She spoke to Ruth, explaining what they were doing.

Rachaela sat on the chintz chair, and asked herself if she felt anything, any pang. But nothing was there in her. It was as if Ruth were truly Emma's child and for some reason Rachaela had had to come down and witness this scene. The baby's sickness turned her stomach, affronted her. Ruth had frequently sicked up her bottle milk, as if on purpose, like the endless stinking miasmas of the wet nappies.

While Emma and Ruth were still in the bathroom, the door sounded.

Rachaela got up and answered the phone, pressed the button and let in Doctor Chatterjee, who presently arrived in the flat.

He was a small, fat Indian with a fussy manner and clever eyes.

Emma brought him Ruth and he examined the baby carefully.

'Yes, you did right to call me,' he said, to Rachaela. 'This is a very sick child. I am recommending that we take her to the hospital immediately.'

Emma exclaimed in horror.

Doctor Chatterjee looked from one woman to the other.

'You are the mother, yes?' he said to Rachaela.

'Yes.'

'To save time we will go in my car.'

'Thank you,' said Emma humbly.

She wrapped Ruth up too thoroughly in her fear, and the doctor loosened the blanket a little.

Rachaela took her damp hair out of the towel.

Emma brought two of Ruth's favourite fluffy toys.

Outside the night was hot and compressed, waiting for a storm. Chip papers strewed the pavement and a buckled can of Sprite lay by the back wheel of the doctor's Sierra.

They drove fast but wisely to St Mary's, the great brick façade like that of a prison, the chimney of the incinerator.

As Ruth was admitted, Emma's eyes disgorged two tears. She controlled herself sternly, forcing her face into a puffy obstinate shape.

They sat for a long time on brown plastic seats in a white corridor.

Nurses busily went up and down, sometimes pausing to exchange words and careless laughter. A trolley was wheeled past by two brutish-looking orderlies chewing gum. This was a disconcerting contrast to the chambers of sickness all about, the bodies lying in white bleached wards with pieces of themselves cut away for ever, the hidden grey figures struggling in the last embrace of life.

Rachaela cringed at the hospital. She had never liked them, perhaps taught by her mother's obsessive fear. People did not go to a hospital to be cured but to be killed or maimed.

She wished she might go home, leaving Emma to watch and wait. But this would be beyond all bounds. It was not possible. She, Rachaela, was the frantic mother. She must stay and try to play her part.

What did she feel? Nothing, nothing.

It was like Ruth, to bring her to a place she hated and loathed, and make her sit here for hours with wet hair.

The Scarabae were never ill.

Was Ruth then not true Scarabae after all?

The sister came in her evening blue.

'Hallo, Mrs Day? We're doing all we can, but she's a very ill little girl I'm afraid.'

She hesitated for Rachaela to scream, weep or swoon. Emma obliged by bursting into tears.

'There. Please try not to be too upset. We've got a good chance.'

'I'm sorry,' Emma apologized, as if her tears put them all in jeopardy. 'I'm being silly.'

'I expect you'd like a cup of tea. We'll see what we can do.'

'Thank you, that would be lovely,' said Emma. When the sister had gone she said, 'They're all so kind. These people are saints. I'm sure it will be all right.'

Later, they let Rachaela, alone, go to look in on her baby.

The room was full of apparatus, empty of doctors. Then one came in, looking harassed.

'You're Ruth's mother? That's right. Well I'm going to be honest with you. We're rather concerned.

We're going to try some further measures to get the temperature down and they may have to be a little drastic.'

'I see,' said Rachaela.

Probably he took her nothingness for the numbness of shock. She hoped so. She did not want the hostility of these people in their robes of snow.

He told her some more, including complex words she could not follow and which she was sure she was not meant to. In the hall of the magicians she was supposed to remain a novice.

Afterwards she went back to Emma and gave her an expurgated version.

Emma was ashen. She had not been able to drink the tea, although she had tried, so as not to be ungrateful.

They waited through the night in the white corridor.

At five am, the harassed doctor appeared and came towards them slowly.

Emma stood up and reached convulsively for Rachaela's hand.

The doctor frowned. He said that the latest measures had been a success, that Ruth's temperature had dropped and her breathing loosened. In half an hour Rachaela would be able to go and sit with her.

Emma cried again. She thanked the doctor so earnestly his mundane face lit up with the impatient awareness of a saviour.

Rachaela was shepherded into the room to sit with her pale, saved child. She sat down. She had wanted and hoped that Ruth would die. There was no reason to lie to herself. Is this what her own mother had wanted? Had she looked at the living Rachaela as now Rachaela looked at Ruth?

Chapter Twelve

✤ THE CHILD IN THE SNOW:
It lay around her like a Christmas card. The street was transformed by whiteness, fluffy and fresh on the buildings. Already there were trampled paths of icy black. The child walked along one of these, towards the house.

She was thin, a small seven-year-old, with two thick plaits of raven black caught in blue toggles. She wore a red woolly hat and scarf and gloves, which Emma had bought her, and a dark belted mac. Her feet were in little red boots that matched the hat, also Emma's idea. She had a satchel. Just another home-going child from the primary school.

Rachaela watched her from the kitchen window of the flat. It was a coincidence she was here at the moment the child turned on to the street.

At first Emma had taken Ruth to the school twice a day, and fetched her home at midday and at night. But most of the other children came and went alone. There were no main roads to cross, for a child it was a quarter-of-an-hour walk.

Ruth would almost certainly not come up to the

253

flat. She would not expect Rachaela to be home in any case and always had her lunch and tea with Emma.

Today Jonquil had suggested that Isis Books be shut at three o'clock, due to the snow. The pipes had frozen and the tiny electric fire did not do much good. A male plumber would have to see to the pipes. This had annoyed Jonquil and set her steel earring swinging with temper.

Rachaela saw Ruth come to the door of the flats and disappear. She had a key.

Rachaela made her coffee and came out of the kitchen. She looked at her flat as she always did, her flat, and Ruth's area. Generally Ruth slept up here, although now and then she would come politely to ask Rachaela if she could stay the night on Emma's sofa. It was Emma who insisted Ruth always ask. Rachaela and Ruth knew it did not mean anything. The moment of asking was one of their few times of agreement and understanding.

Ruth's area had been Emma's idea also.

The child's bed, draped in midnight blue, stood behind a wicker screen with a crimson shawl cast over it. Bells hung on the inside which occasionally Ruth, when in residence, would strike. Behind the screen too was a chest of drawers, whose top was used as a table for Ruth's treasures, her paintbox, and her teetering tower of books.

Emma had taught her to read before school, and now the chest was piled with golden and rose fairy books, *Winnie the Pooh*, *Alice in Wonderland*, and other things which perhaps Ruth did not yet grasp or should not yet be reading: *Lord of the Flies*, *The Lion, the Witch and the Wardrobe*, *Cleopatra*. Rachaela did not oversee the books and Emma believed in stretching a child's mind.

Any homework Ruth saw to at Emma's flat, or sitting on the dark-blue bed. She had also had a pot plant on the chest called David. The plant, robbed of light, did not do well, and eventually David was moved down to Emma's windows.

Half an hour after Rachaela had seen Ruth into the house, Emma's knock sounded on the door.

Rachaela let her in.

Emma looked uneasy and at the same time glowing. Perhaps Ruth had done something especially stunning, as when she had been made chief maid of honour to the school's May Queen. Emma had insisted Rachaela go with her, and they had stood outside the railings, in the biting May breeze, watching little girls in pink frocks and shivery legs strewing paper petals, while Ruth, in the red party dress Emma had bought her, crowned a pretty smirking child with tinsel.

'Ruth's eating her tea,' said Emma, 'I got those sausages she likes, and tomatoes.'

'Thank you,' said Rachaela automatically.

'There's been rather a development,' said Emma.

'What's she done?'

There had been the time, too, when Ruth made a painting of a dragon devouring a knight which had apparently scared another child. Someone had come from the school and seen Emma, who had laughed them to scorn.

'Done? Oh, it's not Ruth. I'm afraid it's me.'

'What have *you* done?'

'I don't know where to start. It's thrown me completely. Out of the blue.'

Emma sat down in the chair, near to Ruth's area.

'It's Liz,' she said.

Rachaela had to wrack her brains. Liz was one of the daughters, the eldest.

'Liz,' she prompted.

'She's sent me an extraordinary letter. She hardly ever writes, and now this. It's wonderful, but she's got herself into a state. She's found she's pregnant again. Not planned – she's thirty-six. She wants to go ahead but she's afraid she can't manage. And apparently Brian has suggested I move in with them. There's a large room with en-suite bath I can have, and Brian says he'll fix me up a kitchenette. It's a lovely house. I haven't seen it for years, of course, but they built a big extension. The garden's marvellous, like something from a show place . . . It's just bowled me over. Cheltenham! She says she needs me. I remember the last time, she got so big. And of course she'll have to have these wretched tests to be sure the baby's all right.'

Rachaela took in Emma's sprinting words belatedly, hearing each sentence over again in her head.

'But haven't they neglected you?' she said.

'*No*. Never. They've got their own lives to lead. And I can cope beautifully. My independent streak.' Emma shone. 'But she's my daughter. I can't leave her in the lurch.'

Rachaela stood in the window, the white snow behind her, feeling the weighted floor falling out of everything in slow motion.

'So you'll go.'

'I must.'

'And how long will you be gone?'

'Well, I rather think it's a permanent arrangement. After all, once the baby's born, a baby-sitter is going to be useful. They've got to be able to have a break. And as Brian points out, well, at my age a little security might be reassuring. It's a fabulous chance. I can't sit back and let Liz get on with it.'

Liz has let you get on with it.

Pointless to voice the selfishness of others, it was her own selfishness which was about to suffer.

Rachaela said, 'Have you told Ruth?'

Emma looked crestfallen through her shine.

'No. I haven't had the courage. And I wanted to tell you first. She's amazing for her age. I'm sure she'll understand. She's fond of me, she'll be glad for me.'

'She loves you,' said Rachaela.

Emma squared her shoulders.

'It's probably the best thing, Rachaela. You and she need to spend more time together.'

'Well, we'll certainly have to do that.'

'Oh, dear,' said Emma. 'I don't know what to do.'

For once her tone was insincere. She knew quite well.

Compared to her own flesh and blood, what was Ruth? Only a substitute. Now here was the real thing.

Swept aside.

Rachaela felt a bitter pity for her daughter, this blow about to fall like an axe.

Ruth would not be glad for Emma. Ruth also was self-centred and selfish, with all the ego-life of a child.

'Hallo Mummy,' said Ruth's clear pale voice from the doorway. And then, familiarly, 'Emma, I finished, and I put the plate in the sink like you said.'

'Thank you, Ruth.'

'Why are you up here?' asked Ruth.

Here was obviously somewhere one did not go unless one must.

'I had to see your mummy.'

'Are you coming back down now?'

'In a minute, darling.'

Rather than leave, Ruth crossed the threshold into the room and went inside the screen to her own area. The bells jangled and Emma jumped.

She looked at Rachaela appealingly.

'Why not tell her now?' said Rachaela, shrinking and cruel at once.

'Do you think—? Oh lord, I suppose I should.'

Emma stood at a loss.

And Ruth came back from behind the screen with a white paper in her hand, brightly painted green and mauve.

'Here's my seahorse, Emma. I forgot to show you. Have I done the tail right?'

'Oh yes. He's perfect, Ruth. Shall we put him up with the others?'

'I want to put in some shells and seaweed first.'

'All right, you do that, and then we'll pin him up. It's becoming quite an art gallery. Would you like to go to a real gallery, Ruth, to look at some paintings?'

'Will you have time?' said Rachaela.

A hopeless anger, a kind of fear roiled in her. She wanted it to be over. She wished Emma would take the child downstairs, do it there. It would be nicer to behead her with a carving knife. Would Ruth scream? They had said at the school she had had a screaming session. Nobody knew why. Emma suspected some of the other children had harassed her, but even to Emma, Ruth had been close-mouthed.

Emma had picked the school, Rachaela only signed on the relevant line. The first day Emma had escorted Ruth to the gates and come back with a red nose.

But all that was behind them now.

'Ruth, lovey, I've got something to tell you.'

'What is it?' Pleased, the child looked up into Emma's shadowed glow.

Ruth was not pretty, no Queen of the May. Her skin was ice-white and flawless, her eyes large and luminously black, fringed by reed-thick lashes. Her features were well-shaped even so early, and the jaw placed finely on the white neck with its blue flush of springing hair. Ruth's hair was straight as falling black water. Something of her father after all.

It was hard to be sure why she was such an unattractive child.

Taken piece by piece, the face was lovely, almost ethereal, but taken all in all it was far from beauty. And in a rage – when some painting eluded her, when she was frustrated or puzzled – it was an ugly, bestial little face.

Soon it would be ugly.

'You see,' Emma was saying gamely, 'my own daughter Liz, you remember Liz? Liz is going to have a baby.'

'Yes,' said Ruth, seriously, interested.

'And Liz wants me to go and look after her. And Liz lives in Cheltenham, which is a long way away.'

Ruth nodded. She understood.

She said, business-like, 'When are we going?'

'Oh darling,' cried Emma. 'Oh darling.' And could not manage any more.

Rachaela said, 'You won't be going, Ruth. Emma has to go. Her daughter needs her. You'll have to stay here.'

'No,' said Ruth, reasonably, 'I'll go with Emma.'

Emma said, 'Darling, I'm afraid – you can't. You can't come with me. I wish you could.'

Liar, Rachaela thought.

Ruth looked blank. She held the seahorse out and gazed at it, as if searching its curves for an answer.

'You must stay here,' said Emma, 'and look after Mummy.'

'No,' said Ruth, quietly.

'*Yes*, Ruth. That's how it's meant to be. I've just been borrowing you. It's been so lovely. And we'll stay good friends. I'll write to you every week. I promise. I'll tell you all about Cheltenham.'

'No,' said Ruth. She had not screamed.

'And I expect I'll come and see you,' said Emma. 'I'll bring you wonderful presents.'

'No,' said Ruth.

'And maybe one day you can visit me. Rachaela can bring you on the train.'

'No,' said Ruth.

'Oh dear,' said Emma, 'darling you must try to understand. It's very hard I know. I'll miss you dreadfully. But poor Liz, I have to go. She's my daughter.'

Ruth said nothing.

She took her picture back with her behind the screen. The bells did not ring.

Emma looked at Rachaela.

'I'd better leave,' said Emma. She rubbed her forehead. Plainly she had a headache. 'If she wants any of her things . . .'

'When will you go?' asked Rachaela.

Ruth must be listening behind the screen.

'She did say as quickly as possible – Brian will pick me up at the station. Then he said he'd arrange to get my stuff moved out. Liz is pretty desperate.'

Desperate.

'A month?'

'More – more like a fortnight,' Emma faltered. 'Oh, dear,' she said again, and went out.

She had not cried. Naturally. What had she to cry about? Ruth had not cried either. Perhaps the outburst would come.

Rachaela looked out at the dusk on the snow street, and the snow piled up against the walls, the pedestrians slipping and sidling along the ice.

The silence in the room was deafening.

The child no longer came home at lunch-time. She took sandwiches and ate them at the school. This was an extra task for Rachaela, the making of sandwiches for the child. Sometimes Emma had given Ruth breakfast too, but breakfast was fairly easy, cornflakes or toast. The evening tea was more irksome. The child required and was used to cooked food. She would let herself into the flat and be waiting for Rachaela behind her screen. She would never speak first.

'Hallo, Ruth.'

'Hallo, Mummy.'

Rachaela hated cooking Ruth's teas. Usually they were not things she herself wanted and so two meals had to be arranged. Rachaela tried to give Ruth what she had had with Emma, things she liked or which would be good for her: sausages and chips, chicken and broccoli, real carrots, grilled fish with cheese and baked beans.

Ruth was used to a dessert too, and Rachaela bought her fruit pies and ice cream, but Emma had made plum tarts and custards, crumbles and baked apples.

Rachaela stocked a large blue bowl with apples, oranges, pears and bananas for the child to eat, as Emma had done.

There had to be orange juice, Lucozade and Pepsi in the fridge.

The fridge was crowded. It was costly, feeding the child.

Luckily the washing machine coped as adequately with Ruth's clothes as it had been doing for the past six years. Emma had ironed Ruth's blouses. Rachaela bought new ones which did not need ironing.

After the evening meal, Ruth would retire to her area. She would do her slight homework if she had been given any, or paint wild garish pictures, forests of lions and castles on fire, duels in deserts, ships in tempests. Her imagination was obviously being fed by the school and by the books. Twice a week she went to the library, usually on her own.

She caused, apart from the expensive, awkward food and the constant renewal of clothing, very little trouble.

She slept noiselessly. In the night it was difficult to know that she was there, but for the wall of the screen.

Emma's flat stood empty for six months before anyone else moved in.

They were unfortunate arrivals: two young men who played loud pop music during the evening and sometimes had noisy rows – including the landing in their sphere of operations.

Ruth did not react to this alien influx. She had never cried over Emma.

At first, Emma's notes, on brightly coloured paper, had come on every ninth or tenth day. Ruth would retire behind her screen to read them and stored them in one of her drawers. She never made any comment on the notes, seemed neither upset nor glad to receive them. After a couple of months, the notes dwindled. Neither had Ruth ever answered them.

'If you want to write to Emma,' said Rachaela, 'just take some paper and an envelope from the cabinet.' She had got them in specially. 'There are plenty of stamps.' Ruth said yes, she knew about the paper and the stamps. She did not use any.

After four months, Rachaela herself got a letter from Emma. Emma was in heaven, full of news of Liz, but she asked after Ruth. 'Children are so bad at letter-writing. I remember I used to be a horror.' Rachaela answered the letter after a week. Ruth and she were well, nothing had happened, Ruth had a lot of homework just now. Ruth sent her love. Rachaela had not asked Ruth if she wished to send Emma her love. Probably Ruth did not. Emma was over.

This trite communication put an end to Emma's overtures and she began to fade from their lives.

One day Rachaela found all the coloured letters from Emma to Ruth in the waste-bin under the sink.

In the very beginning she had sat down with Ruth at the small table.

'I'm sorry about Emma having to go. It's hard for you. But we'll just have to do the best we can.' Ruth had not replied, nor looked at her. She was making a drawing of a tall woman in flowing sleeves. 'You know I can't give you as much time as Emma. I'm at work. But if there are any problems, you'll have to tell me, because Emma won't be here. Do you understand?'

'Yes,' said Ruth after a gap.

Rachaela did not say she would leave the child alone as much as possible and that she in turn would expect to be left alone. It was tacitly agreed between them from long experience.

Rachaela thought that the mistake her own mother had made was in her brainwashed attempts to care for and become involved with a child she did not want.

Ruth and she had instead a disarmed neutrality. They would never be friends, but by keeping a great distance, they might not become enemies.

Rachaela no longer hated Ruth. Ruth was now a sentient being, that could visit the lavatory alone, wash, feed and clothe itself, amuse itself without recourse to her.

Since Ruth had not cried, there had been no onus on Rachaela to extend a prosthesis of sympathy and warmth she could not feel.

For her part, Rachaela tried not to curb the child, but let her go her own wild, silent way.

Ruth never showed Rachaela anything – her art work, her homework or a book – but Rachaela gave her the use of the bookcase, overloaded now, and once or twice when money had been freer had bought Ruth books of fantastic art, Kay Nielsen, Vali Myers. Ruth took these gifts politely, but she pored over them in her burrow.

Emma had left her two glass paperweights and a blue glass cat. For her eighth birthday Rachaela bought Ruth something from the local Sunday market, with misgiving and a knowledge of unassailable rightness. It was a mirror inset with purple iris flowers, peacocks' feathers, shells of pink opaque glass. 'Oh,' said Ruth when she saw it. She thanked Rachaela coolly and bore the glass into her cubby.

The plant, David, had died although Rachaela had put it in a window. Now Ruth began to collect, with saved-up pocket money, false flowers of enamel, and finally a birdcage with a painted wooden linnet.

Glimpsing into her daughter's area – the strip of wall now hung with strange prints in clip frames and Ruth's own latest exotic work, the mirror, the bells and shawls, flowers and cage and even, just above the chest, the white face of a clock which did not go – Rachaela saw Scarabae. Perhaps she had encouraged it, or not. Ruth was a living plant which put out stained-glass flowers. You could not snap them off, as perhaps Rachaela's own mother had tried to do. For how much of the shadowy Scarabae had she seen in her daughter, and tried to poison with her haircuts and crosses on the sprouts?

Beyond the windows, out in the streets, the coloured glass of the seasons came and went. The distant park was like a calendar. Green, yellow and brown the pages fell from its trees, black spider-web bareness and another ice age of pure snow.

Emma was never mentioned.

The school took Ruth to museums, art galleries and gardens; the seaside.

At night and the weekends, they sat in silence but for the music centre and the thump-thump from the flat below.

It was easy yet impossible to forget the child was there.

Jonquil was in the shop when the young woman came in. She was about twenty-two or three, with glasses and a washed young face. She walked up to Rachaela.

'Mrs Day?'

'Yes,' said Rachaela.

'Ms,' said Jonquil, 'Mzzz Day.'

'Oh, well,' said the young woman. 'I'm Miss Barrett, from Ruth's school.'

'What's happened?' asked Jonquil.

'Oh, nothing – well, something. But I mean Ruth's quite all right. I'm sorry to bother you at work, Mrs Day. But I wanted a word with you when the child wasn't there.'

Jonquil swung her boots off the counter.

'Go through to the back, Rachaela. Take Mzzz Barrett with you. I'll see to those magazines.'

They went into the back room. It was crammed with boxes and piled by books. Letters overspilled a tray and the old typewriter squatted among the coffee things. Over a radiator hung three pairs of Denise's tights, long dry.

'As I say, I'm sorry about seeking you out, Mrs Day, but I felt it would be best to talk to you without Ruth. If you prefer I can come to your flat at a convenient time.'

'When I'm there, Ruth is always there. What's the matter?'

'Well, I don't want to alarm you. It's probably nothing, children get these strange little fancies. One shouldn't make too much of them, but then again, they need watching. I wonder if you've noticed anything like it.'

'Like what exactly?'

'It was play-time, and I saw a huddle of children near the sheds. I left it a while but they didn't break up, so I went over to see what was going on. There was a ring of children, they were giggling, but some of them looked a bit frightened. Sitting on the ground was Terry Porter who'd apparently fallen over and cut his knee quite badly. Instead of coming up for medical attention he was just sitting there, looking white, and Ruth was sitting next to him. As I got there she put her hand on the cut and actually squeezed it, so the blood ran out quite violently, all down his leg. She said, "Make it bleed again, Terry".'

Rachaela felt a strange delayed horror, moving so deep in her she scarcely knew what it was. She said nothing.

Miss Barrett, having waited for her, said, 'Has Ruth ever done anything like that at home?'

'No,' said Rachaela.

'Perhaps it's never come up. Ruth's had the usual odd spills and scrapes herself, but never anything very bloody. Sometimes children do get fascinated by blood.'

'Yes.'

'Maybe you should have a word. Or perhaps you've been telling her about when her periods will be due. Sometimes that sparks it off.'

'No.'

'Well it is a bit early.'

'What happened?' asked Rachaela. 'I mean with the boy?'

'Oh, Terry. Well, I just told Ruth not to be a silly girl and got him off to Nurse. Ruth is sometimes a bit, well, a bit unusual. The things she draws. And if we ask them to tell stories or act out little plays, Ruth's are always rather gruesome. I sometimes wonder where she gets her ideas from.' Miss Barrett looked at Rachaela with keen glasses.

'I don't censor her reading,' said Rachaela.

'No. Well, maybe you should be a little more strict. We're very careful what we let them have.'

Rachaela remembered a drawing pinned up in Emma's flat.

'But you tell them about the crucifixion of Jesus Christ.'

'Well of course. That's Religious Knowledge.'

'It's also a very grim subject and Ruth painted it.'

'Well I have to admit,' said Miss Barrett, trying not to look at Denise's tights, 'I know they're all fairly bloodthirsty little savages. They go on and on about the nails.' She cheered up, having reassured herself. 'That's all it was, really. I thought you should know and keep an eye on her.'

'Thank you.'

'Don't mention it,' said Miss Barrett.

'Typical woman,' said Jonquil disapprovingly, when Miss Barrett had gone.

Ruth was drawing behind her screen when Rachaela came in.

Rachaela took off her coat, and washed her hands, and began to arrange Ruth's tea automatically.

'How did it go today at school?' Rachaela asked.

A pause, perhaps of astonishment.

'It was all right.'

'What about yesterday?'

'That was all right too.'

Rachaela thought of her mother, so many lectures over the table. Meals should not be interrogations.

She turned the steaks slowly.

Tonight they would eat together. Steak for both; mashed potatoes, tomatoes and peas for Ruth; lettuce and avocado for Rachaela.

When the food was ready she called Ruth to the table. They ate in silence, the drawing dividing them, to which, between mouthfuls, Ruth added a stroke or two. Upside-down, the drawing looked ominous, some bleak landscape under a cloudy sky, some beast coming from a lair.

'What would you like now, pie or ice-cream?'

'Both, please.'

Ruth was always polite. She was also a greedy child. Even when Emma had gone her appetite had not slackened. She stayed wand-slim, yet, in past weeks, Rachaela had begun to note the points of little breasts. She was only nine. Everything would need buying again, including a tiny bra. Would Ruth be embarrassed? Rachaela never saw her in the bath.

When the meal was finished, Rachaela washed up and made coffee, and Ruth retired behind her screen.

'Do you have any homework tonight?'

Again the perhaps-astonished pause.

'No.'

'Will you come out, Ruth, for a minute. I want to talk to you about something.'

What would Emma have done? Emma, with all her experience, might not have cared. 'It's a phase they all go through. Don't you remember it in yourself? Don't draw attention to it. She'll work it out.'

Ruth emerged, with her drawing. She sat down again at the table and worked on steadily.

Rachaela said, 'Tell me about Terry Porter.'

Silence.

Eventually Ruth said, 'I don't like him.'

'Why not?'

'He shouts things at me.'

'What sort of things?'

'That I didn't have a dad. That I came out of an egg.'

'Of course you had a father. He doesn't live with us, that's all. Emma told you about that.'

Emma's name was ignored.

How nastily inventive of Terry Porter to say Ruth came from an egg. Perhaps he had heard mention of the reproductive cycle.

'So you were glad,' said Rachaela, 'when Terry Porter cut himself.' Ruth said nothing. 'Why did you make the cut worse? To scare him?' Ruth drew on. The landscape, like all deserts, had a familiar look. 'Please say something, Ruth.'

Ruth said, 'It bled.'

'Is that what interested you?'

'It was very red.'

'You've seen blood before,' said Rachaela. Had she? She must have done, she had been born in it.

'It was very red blood.'

Was there relish in the statement? Was there, more to the point, thirst and incipient sexuality?

Ruth shaded in an area of her beast.

'Why doesn't my dad live with us?'

'He didn't want to.'

'I don't have a nanny or a grandpa, either.'

'No. I'm sorry. There's just us.'

'Didn't they want me too?' The inquiry was not plaintive. It was brutally matter-of-fact.

I didn't want you. Don't want you. You are a little animal, muddling up my life, that expects to be fed and clothed, that has to have schools and presents. That has

270

*to be thought about. Not loveable, like a cat. Skin and hair
and voice.*

But the Scarabae *had* wanted Ruth. *Oh* yes.

Lie about it now? She tried not to lie to the child,
as *she* had been lied to.

'I expect they did want you, but it wasn't their
choice.'

'Do I have a nanny?'

'Maybe.' Had Anna been Adamus's mother, as
Rachaela suspected? 'But they're a long way away.'

'Like Emma,' said Ruth, surprisingly.

'Much further than Emma.'

'They don't write to me.'

'No.'

'I don't expect they want me,' said Ruth.

She had successfully sidetracked Rachaela from the
subject of the blood.

Rachaela said, 'About Terry Porter. You mustn't
do anything like that again.' Ruth did not ask why.
'You understand that, don't you? You must be careful
not to give people bad ideas about you. Don't trust
anyone. Don't give yourself away. Try to behave like
other people.'

Ruth nibbled at her coloured pencil.

Impelled by instinct, Rachaela took the drawing up
and stared at it.

Ruth had drawn the heath, the Scarabae heath, the
dragon parts, and the dragon coming forth to kill its
knight. On a slope was a weirdly shaped rock – the
standing stone?

'What gave you the notion for this?' Rachaela said.

'Don't know.'

Ruth was looking at her at last with sharp, bright
black eyes. Her unlined milk-white face was ancient.

'It's a very good drawing.'

'Thank you.'

Rachaela handed back the heath and the dragon. Through that place she had walked, Ruth a thing coiled inside her. How else had the child seen?

'Mummy,' said Ruth, 'can we have a cat?'

'No, I don't think so. I'm sorry, but there's no garden and we're out all day.'

She did not want Ruth to have a cat. She did not know why. Surely Ruth would not hurt the cat, for she stroked them on walls. Rachaela had seen her. It was something else.

Ruth did not whine or try to get her way.

She took the heath and went back behind her screen.

A storm raged over the house.

Rachaela dreamed of Adamus bending over her, his hair a black cowl. The lightning caught him, faded.

She opened her eyes. Ruth was seated at a window watching the storm.

A blue flash like an incendiary, the child did not start, but leaned closer to the pane.

Ruth had watched storms since she was three or four.

The thunder bombarded the capital.

Rachaela got up, and in the light of the street lamps through the uncurtained windows, padded into the kitchen.

'Do you want a drink? Milk? Coffee?'

'No thank you.'

Rachaela did not turn on the light. She filled the kettle and set it to boil. The saffron-azure of the gas flame starred the orange dark. The lightning came again.

As she drank the coffee something made her walk about the room. The child ignored her. Reaching Ruth's area, she saw the beads and bells, clock and paintings, sear in another flash. So much that glimmered. And there the mirror she had given Ruth. The mirror had changed.

Not entering, Rachaela craned to see.

'What have you done to your mirror?'

'I painted it.'

Another blast of blue. All the glass was covered, fields and meadows, flowers and clouds, and distant mountains in a mist.

Chapter Thirteen

SHE HAD BOUGHT THE BATHROOM mirror soon after moving into the flat. It hung the length of the wall. As the bath ran, a fog of steam began to cling to its surface. Rachaela wiped it away. Through the frosted window blazed the cold light of winter morning; sidelight, the most harsh. Rachaela examined her face and body.

She was forty. She did not look it. She looked the same as when she had been twenty-nine, before the birth of the child. Even that had not touched her. No stretch marks, no cellulite, the belly and thighs firm and white and smooth, the breasts full and yet high, the nipples small and rosy. The neck was unlined, the face unlined, the brow and cheeks. The chin was firm. No pouches about the mouth or under the eyes. The face and body of a young, young woman. And in the black hair, the black hair of the groin, not a single silver coil.

It did not please her. She tried not to let it unnerve her. She was used to it, saw it every day. She accepted such remarks as Jonquil's, 'But you're only a kid.' Even Denise had aged a little, got heavy and puffy in her thirties, from the big cooked dinners she made for hungry Keith. Jonquil had not herself changed very much, her skin had only grown harder and more obdurate, she had swapped the steel earring for an earring of bone, and all her hair was grey.

Probably I'll age suddenly.

That might happen. It happened in books.

People did not notice youngness when they saw you constantly, the same as the alteration into age went largely unobserved, only picked out in sudden revelations.

'What are you, you must be about twenty-eight now,' Jonquil had said last year, not bothering with an answer.

The child had changed, of course.

Ruth grew out of all her clothes with punctilious regularity. She had breasts and two small brassières that must be hand-washed.

Rachaela had explained to Ruth about her periods, sitting at the table with her while Ruth drew, asking if she understood. Rachaela's mother had not told her anything but had given her a rather serious book. The blood had come in the middle of the night and she had still been appalled. She had had to wake her mother up to ask for sanitary pads, and her mother had grumbled. Rachaela put pads into Ruth's drawer, among her underclothes, in front of her.

Ruth showed no resentment, no excitement. 'I heard about it at school.'

'From the teachers?'

'From a girl.'

'Tell me when you start,' Rachaela felt bound to say.

'All right.'

What did Ruth look like, unclothed? Rachaela never saw her. She would go nightly into the bathroom in her skirt and blouse and come out in a cotton nightshirt.

Rachaela slept in a nightshirt, too. Ruth's decorum had somehow imposed it on her.

The bath was full.

Rachaela let the mirror veil itself in steam and stepped into the water.

'Hi, you're late,' said Jonquil airily as Rachaela entered the shop. 'That kid of yours mess you up? Is she at her secondary yet?'

'Next year, when she's eleven.'

'I suppose you've got that all mapped out.'

'It will depend on some test,' said Rachaela vaguely. She was used to answering occasional questions about the child, who perhaps Jonquil did not really think existed after all.

'I see,' said Jonquil. 'Used to be the old eleven-plus, but that's all different now. You wouldn't remember.'

Rachaela made coffee, and tea for Jonquil with one of her herbal tea bags. Jonquil fussed round her. When they sat down, Jonquil stood up again.

'You've been here a long while, haven't you, Raech? What is it – five years?'

'A little longer.'

'Denise too. Poor old Denise. That bloody awful feller she's with. I hoped he'd leave her in peace but he knows when he's on to a good thing.' Jonquil drank some tea and sighed gustily. 'I'm afraid we're going to have to shut up shop.'

Rachaela looked at her. This had been on the cards from the very beginning. She was only surprised Isis had lasted so long.

'I'm sorry,' she said.

'Yeah. It's a shame. But there's never been much interest around here. Dozy hole. I've got a chance to go in with a women's group up Manchester way. So I'm all right. But it means curtains for Denise and you. Will you be OK?'

'Oh, I'll find something else.'

'Some skivvy's job. Or running round after some bloody male in an office.'

'Probably.'

'I wish I could do something.'

'How long?' said Rachaela.

'End of this month. It's rotten timing. It'll be Christmas next. But it will give you a bit more time with the kid.'

'Yes.'

Relieved by unloading her bombshell, Jonquil began to move about the forlorn little shop, examining books.

The hot water pipes gurgled as they had done for ten years.

It was not the end of the world. Thanks to Emma's years of extreme beneficence, Rachaela had managed to save a little, and now there was some interest which would tide her over, perhaps until the new year. The child was an expense, of course, but she seemed up to date with her garments, her school trips.

Lyle and Robbins were advertising for staff again. Perhaps that would do. Or there was the antique shop in Beaumont Street, only one flummoxed woman who was always shutting for 'ten minutes'.

Not a problem.

Rachaela remembered how Mr Gerard had fired her, and how relevant and ominous it had been.

Things were different now. Or she was.

On Thursday, her half-day off from the shop, as Rachaela was sitting in her chair listening to Tchaikovsky ballet music, the door sounded.

'Yes?'

'Oh Mrs Day. It's Miss Barrett. Perhaps you remember me?'

'No, I'm afraid not.'

'From Ruth's school.'

'Yes?'

'I need to see you about something.'

Rachaela recalled Miss Barrett, just over a year ago, the scrubbed clean face and essential glasses. Terry Porter and his knee.

'You'd better come up.'

Miss Barrett entered the flat in a strawberry-red coat with a white fur collar, a yellow wool hat and brown fur gloves without fingers. She carried a pink umbrella.

'Oh, Mrs Day. So glad to catch you in.'

'Please sit down.'

Miss Barrett sat in the chair, and Rachaela sat down on one of the hard chairs by the table.

Miss Barrett shed her gloves and hat.

'What a nasty day. I shouldn't be surprised if we were in for some more snow.'

'What has Ruth done now?' said Rachaela.

'Oh dear. It's always such a worry, this sort of thing,' said Miss Barrett. 'Mr Walker thought, as I'd come to see you before, it would be best if I came again. We don't like to make too much of it. Unless it goes on, of course.'

'What has Ruth done?'

'It's really what she hasn't done. She hasn't been coming to school, Mrs Day. I take it you haven't been keeping her at home and just not sent a note? We must always have a note, you see. There's a lot of colds about, I know.'

'Ruth never gets colds.'

'No. Well then I take it she isn't here.'

'She isn't.'

'Mrs Walker thinks that she saw Ruth in Woolworth's.'

What a mundane place for the escapee to be. Why Woolworth's? Sometimes when Rachaela shopped in the Saturday lunch-hour, Ruth went with her, and into Woolworth's too, never showing a symptom of interest in the toys, sweets or loudly drumming music section.

'Mrs Walker thinks that Ruth was trying on make-up,' said powderless Miss Barrett, her unpainted eyes and lips wide with shock.

'Perhaps she was,' said Rachaela, for a moment almost intrigued. She herself had done something similar when she had played truant, but then she was thirteen or fourteen.

'The thing is, Mrs Day, this is very serious. You must speak to Ruth and impress upon her that she has to come to school. She's been absent several days this month. She has an important test next year, and she needs to pay attention. She's very much a dreamer. A lot of talent in art, though some of her paintings, well. But she needs to pull her socks up. She must attend.'

'I'll speak to her.'

'Ruth must come to school. If she doesn't, Mr Walker will have to take further steps.'

'I see.'

Miss Barrett was rouged after all by indignation.

'Throwing her chances away,' she said. School was very important, a life jacket in chaos. She looked actually frightened.

Rachaela had not offered her anything to drink, and let her go to the door unaided, pulling on her ridiculous gloves, until she looked like a parody of a bear.

'And if she has to stay away,' said Miss Barrett, 'we really must have a note.'

Rachaela ate tomatoes on toast for lunch, and pictured Ruth eating her sandwiches on some wall or in a park.

She must finally have become bored with school. Rachaela knew she could read well but was virtually innumerate. This had been so in Emma's day, and was so still, for once or twice Ruth had asked Rachaela some arithmetical question which Rachaela also found impossible to answer. Ruth had trouble even in adding up. 'How many apples are there left?' Rachaela had recently asked her. Ruth studied the bowl. 'I don't know, Mummy.' There were seven. The child paid for things in shops by giving always a large coin, or a note. She would bring her loose change to Rachaela for translation into fifty-pence pieces and pounds.

Perhaps it was wrong to feel empathy with Ruth simply because she too had played truant.

Yet Rachaela saw the brief daylight ebb with a slight amusement, waiting for Ruth to appear punctually, as if just coming home from school.

The child manifested in the cold street. Rachaela thought of the day she had seen her in the snow, the day Emma had bowed out from their lives with urgent smiles. Poor useful Emma.

How different, now, was Ruth.

Her hair was no longer confined in plaits, but hung down her back to the base of her spine. It was thick and almost crudely black, with a shine on it like molasses. No hat any more, or gloves, the white long-fingered pianist's hands playing with the buttons of her dark-blue coat. The satchel still there, incongruous. Despite this school bag of deceit, the white knee socks and little-girl shoes, Ruth was like a tiny woman on the street: a midget, quick rather than graceful, and with that strange white face of an elf.

When the flat door opened, Rachaela was sitting at the table.

'Hallo, Ruth.'

'Hallo, Mummy.'

'Put your bag down, take off your coat, and come and sit here.'

'What's for tea?'

'I haven't thought about it.'

'Can I have chips?'

'You had chips yesterday.'

Ruth came to the table in her charcoal skirt, blue jumper and scarlet blouse. Rachaela allowed her to choose her own colours. She had, certainly, better dress-sense than Miss Barrett.

'You haven't been to school,' said Rachaela.

Ruth looked at her, assessingly. She did not attempt to lie.

'No.'

'Why not?'

'I don't like it.'

'Did you like it before?'

'It was all right.'

'And now it isn't.'

Ruth said nothing.

281

'Are the other children,' said Rachaela, 'bothering you?'

'No.'

'A woman came here today from the school. A Miss Barrett.'

'Batty Barrett,' said Ruth.

'You were seen in Woolworth's.'

'Oh,' said Ruth.

'Why Woolworth's?'

'It was raining.'

'What do you do when it doesn't rain?'

'I walk about,' said Ruth. She paused, then said, 'I go in the big graveyard and look at the stones.' She added, 'Sometimes I take a bus. I get lost. I always make sure I get back in time for tea.'

'Yes I know.'

'Are you going to say I have to go?' said Ruth. She looked blank. She did not suspect Rachaela of complicity with the authorities, recognizing her as a fellow, though alien, outsider.

'It depends what you want,' said Rachaela.

'I don't want anything,' said Ruth.

'You'll never get a smart job,' said Rachaela. 'I expect they've already told you about those.'

'They said what did we want to be.'

'What did you say?'

'I said a library lady.'

'Is that what you want?'

'No.'

'If you really don't care,' said Rachaela, 'I'm not going to force you.' She recollected her mother's furious wobbling face: *'You've got to pull yourself together. You'll end up in the gutter. You go to school, do you hear me? I won't be disgraced like that again, you bloody little beast.'*

'But we have to work something out,' Rachaela said. 'You'll have to go in some of the time. When you want a day off tell me, I'll write you a note.'

Ruth considered. Her privacy had been penetrated, but she seemed to accept the inevitability of this.

'Will you?'

'Yes.'

'All right,' said Ruth. 'Thank you,' she said.

Rachaela sat looking at her eldritch elfin child. Was Ruth also like her?

'Will spaghetti on toast do for tea?'

'With cheese.'

'With cheese.'

Rachaela got up and went to set out tins on the work-top in the kitchen. Ruth followed her and stood in the doorway.

'What would my dad say about me not going to school?'

Rachaela checked. 'I don't think he'd give a damn.'

Ruth said, 'Will I ever see him?'

Rachaela made herself look back at the white face of her child.

'No.'

'Why not?'

'He wouldn't be interested, Ruth. I'm sorry.'

'How do you know?'

'Because I knew him. He wasn't interested in me, either.'

'But the grandfather and granny,' said Ruth.

Your grandfather is also your father.

'There isn't any grandfather or granny. It's just a big shapeless family of old people. You wouldn't like them.'

But how could she be sure?

Ruth was in their image. Ruth had done what they did.

She must not try to picture Ruth in that house. The house which had faded to a ghost with the years, but still lingered there, a lump of fog, on the edge of her mind. The mirrors, the windows.

Ruth said, 'I might like them. I don't mind old people.'

'They're very far away.'

'Couldn't I go?'

'No, Ruth.'

'But I want to.'

How had the conversation veered into this? Rachaela put down the can opener and emptied the spaghetti into the saucepan.

'*No*, Ruth.'

'I dream about them,' said Ruth.

Rachaela stopped what she was doing.

'What do you mean?'

'I dream of them in a big house. And I walk down a corridor and I go in a door, and they're there.'

Obviously, through the years, Rachaela had let things slip. She must have done. The child had her fantasies, like any child.

'I don't want to talk about it, Ruth. I don't want you anywhere near them, and that's that.'

Keep away from the Scarabae.

Rachaela saw again her mother's congested face.

Ruth said, 'Why can't I? Why not?'

Rachaela said, 'They're mad. They're mad people. And they're a sort of vampire. Or they think they are.'

Don't say any more.

'Vampire,' said Ruth. 'Like Dracula?'

'Not like Dracula. They're bad people.'

She stirred the saucepan, waiting for the next assault, which did not come. When she looked back, Ruth had retreated again, behind the screen.

I shouldn't have said that.

Too late.

She had a vision of Adamus walking up the wall of the house in the black of the moon, his pale face lifted and a trickle of blood running from the corner of his mouth. A sexual pang shot through her core, amazing her. After so long, after so much that was base and stupid, after *Ruth*.

She put the bread under the grill, and her hands shook. From a decade of cobwebs and dyed glass she felt old leaf-like hands reach out and brush her.

The shop was bare, the books packed in boxes or sent away.

Denise was crying softly and fuzzily.

'Come on, come on,' said Jonquil. 'Have some more wine.'

They sat drinking, perched on the wonky stools, as outside the non-customers, now excluded for ever, stalked past on the wet, dark pavement.

'Do you remember that old lady who kept coming in for Roald Dahl, saying he was a woman?' sobbed Denise.

'What about that man who kept buying copies of *Fight the Good Fight* by Angela Truebridge?'

'And the Angela Carter fiend?'

'And that girl who never knew the author?'

They nodded reminiscently.

'It's been a funny old job,' said Denise, and blew her nose. 'I start at the Co-op next Monday, just till Christmas. Keith's furious. He'll have to get his own breakfast.'

'Lazy sod,' said Jonquil, 'do him good.'

'But he'll make such a mess,' wailed Denise. 'And he never washes up.'

'You want to get shot of him.'

'Well, I met this really lovely bloke on the bus last week. I see him every night.'

'Out of the frying pan,' said Jonquil. 'You never learn.'

'What are you going to do, Rachaela?'

'I haven't decided yet.'

'If you want to come up to Manchester,' said Jonquil, 'just drop me a line. You can doss on one of the girls' floors till you find somewhere.'

Outside two young men peered in at the lighted women with their bottles and Jonquil's cans of Carlsberg. They leered and made signs until Jonquil strode towards the door.

'Rubbish,' said Jonquil, as they fled. 'There ought to be some sort of dustbin for them.'

'I'll have to go,' said Rachaela, slipping down from her stool. 'I have to get Ruth's meal. I told her I'd be late but it's already seven.'

'Yes, OK, Raech. You whizz off.'

Denise embraced Rachaela, wetting her with fresh tears. 'Drop in at the Co-op. I'll get you a discount.'

Jonquil shook Rachaela's hand. Her pale grey eyes were resigned. 'If ever you're Manchester way, look us up.'

They saw her off into the splashed black and rainy yellow night.

Spears of light, long aprons of neon reflected in the pavements. Beyond the block of shops the street-lamps spread like broken egg in the puddles.

The rain was dense, trying to turn to snow. The wind flurried.

Lit windows in the flats, the houses made into flats. How often she had passed them, in rain and shine, on the summer evenings in the dust and diesel, on the white snow where every step portended a snapped ankle.

Already one or two trees with garlands of coloured bulbs. There in that blue window the same old 'Merry Xmas' which appeared doggedly year after year.

Soon a birthday present for Ruth, and then a Christmas present. Jonquil had pressed some books on Rachaela, unsuitable for anyone. Oxfam could have those.

Someone behind her.

Nothing in that.

One night a drunken man had staggered after her the length of Rosamunde Street. He had taken her arm and she had thrust him off. 'What's the rush, darling?' he had said, and she had pushed him hard. He lost his balance and fell against some railings. 'Bloody tart! Fucking whore!' he had warbled, but no more than that.

There were generally people about, harmless people, perhaps concealing lives of molten depravity but offering no threat to the single woman on her way home.

A man with a dog now, coming up the road. Cars zoomed by in wings of water.

The one behind her did not fall back, or pass her.

His step was very soft. Somehow she knew the step – not its author, but its meaning.

Her stomach tightened. She was being silly.

The man with the dog drew level and went by.

Ahead, the traffic lights at the end of Beaumont Street were in sight. Green, amber, red.

Black snow drifted over her face.

It was like before. It was like the time when she had been hunted.

No, that was absurd. How could they find her now?

She reached the lights, had to wait. The shops showed a blaze of colours. She could turn, look up the dark road, and see who had come after her.

There he was. A man standing about forty feet away. Hesitating, as if trying to make out the numbers on the house fronts, which were perfectly clear.

Her heart tumbled down a stairway.

A short man in a dark overcoat and woollen hat.

It was frighteningly stupid. For people did not keep on wearing the same garments, not for eleven, twelve years. People did not stay the same.

She had. The mirror had told her.

She had not changed.

She thought of the green before the flats and the sudden figure. *'You must go, you know.'*

'Go away,' she said. But later he had come back and handed her the letter, the letter Adamus had typed, from the Scarabae.

He was too far off to be sure, the foreign face which maybe had not aged by another line, the gelid eyes, invisible.

She needed to see him more closely, to be sure. And even then, could she trust her memory?

It was impossible they could have found her this time. Even if they had been trying all the years between. She refused it.

The lights changed and the cars grudgingly screeched to a halt.

Rachaela crossed over the road.

She looked back and saw the man stop dithering before the houses, and cross further up the street, just before the cars took over again.

He came on, walking in the same direction as Rachaela, the dilute snow sparkling in his hat like sequins.

Rachaela walked along Beaumont Street. The garish front of the Pizza Eater blossomed. Should she go in for a drink? No, they would not serve only a drink, she should recall that. Where then? Somewhere to halt, to see what he would do.

It was a coincidence. He was some stray who had reminded her of the Scarabae agent. That was all.

The launderette was open, lit dead-white and empty.

Rachaela pushed open the door and went in.

She sat down on one of the seats, and waited for the man in the woollen hat to come up, see her, and check.

A woman emerged from the insides of the launderette.

'Do you need any help?'

'I'm just waiting for a friend.'

The woman looked at her suspiciously.

'Not doing any washing then?'

'No.'

'Well I suppose you know what you're doing.'

She began to fiddle with some clothes from an open machine, dropping pairs of briefs and socks on to the floor.

The man appeared. He went by the window, without a glance, and moved on into the night.

The light from the launderette had shone upon him like an arc lamp. He was the man she had seen all those years before. She was sure of it. *Sure.*

Rachaela got up.

'Off now then?' chirped the woman, dropping another sock.

Rachaela went out into the shiny black, the confusion of slanting lit rain, streetlights, headlights.

Where was he? He had vanished.

She had imagined the likeness. He was just some man. The Scarabae had been preying on her mind, as in patches they always did, and so she had conjured up the memory to fit a stranger.

For they could not have gone on haunting her. They could not still want her now.

She trod cautiously along the street.

Knots of people scurried in the snowy rain.

Rachaela turned left and walked more briskly. She was borne away from the lights, and on the stretch of darker pavement, she stopped and looked all round. But no one was there save for a woman with an umbrella, a cyclist going wearily along by the kerb. Overhead a red window concealed some ordinary pleasure or wretchedness. She too began to hurry home.

When she opened the door the flat was in darkness, but sometimes Ruth, alone, would sit in the dark.

Rachaela crossed to one of the windows. It was open, the curtain wet and blowing.

Rachaela shut the window.

She stood in the darkness, gazing out at the street.

Traffic went by now and then. A man passed, but not the man she had seen.

No one, so far as she could tell, hugged the doorways, folded into the shadows. No one was there, watching, ready.

She turned and switched on a lamp.

A sort of sleepy stirring came from behind Ruth's screen.

'Hallo, Ruth.'

Ruth came out.

Rachaela was startled; wholly, disconcertingly unnerved.

Ruth was draped in the blue and green shawl, leaving her legs, her snow-white shoulders bare. Through eyelets of the shawl, white flesh stared. Beneath this thin covering she was naked. Her hair poured round her, strands sticky with electricity.

Her face was made-up, not inexpertly as one would expect, but like a painted doll. Coal-black lids, mascara sooty-thick, the lips exactly shaped and red as holly berries.

She looked drowsy, as if she had been asleep. Yet a kind of current emanated from her, she was like a live wire. She had not been sleeping.

Rachaela found her voice. 'Is that the make-up from Woolworth's?'

'Yes.' Ruth's own voice was mild. She was neither embarrassed nor uneasy.

'You've done it very carefully.'

'Yes.'

'What were you doing?'

'Waiting,' said Ruth.

Of course she had been waiting. Rachaela delayed at the shop, later than she had intended.

But did Ruth mean that? Waiting for her mother?

'Why was the window open?'

Ruth said, 'To let in the night.'

Perhaps it was a line from a book. Ruth did not lie to Rachaela, neither was she speaking all the truth. Yet the truth was somehow self-evident.

Vampire. Ruth had made herself up like a vampire from a horror film she had perhaps contrived to see, or some illustration in a library book. She looked the part.

And then she had lain down in the dark, naked but for her flimsy shawl, the window open to let in the night, and waited.

Rachaela had, again, the image of a man in a black cloak walking up the house wall. This time no sexual clenching moved in her loins, she went cold.

Was this Ruth's fantasy? Dracula walking up the brickwork to claim her?

She switched on the electric fire, the room was freezing as if hung with icicles. She went into the kitchen, washed her hands, and began to put bacon on to the grill.

Ruth went silently back behind her screen.

When she emerged she was wearing her nightdress and dressing-gown. She walked into the bathroom and Rachaela heard the clink of the pot of cold cream.

When Ruth came out, she was wiped clean of all colours but her own black and white.

'You could have kept it on,' Rachaela said.

'I was finished with it.'

Rachaela fried an egg for Ruth.

'I'm home from the bookshop now,' said Rachaela.

'Can I have a day off tomorrow?'

'Yes, if you want. You can have another bilious attack.'

'Thank you,' said Ruth.

She sat at the table, eating bread and butter.

Rachaela served the food and they ate it.

Outside snow began to fall in large fat flakes.

When they had finished, Rachaela got up and walked to one of the windows. She drew back the curtain with her hand and looked both ways along the deserted street.

'When you're out and about,' Rachaela said, 'you know you mustn't talk to anyone. I remember Emma telling you about that. It still matters.'

'I sometimes ask the way.'

'That's all right. But don't get into conversations. Always speak to women, not men.'

'Yes, Mummy.'

Rachaela closed the curtain. She looked at Ruth drinking a mug of tea at the table. She seemed like an average child, a little unusual, wonderful hair, very composed.

'Never,' said Rachaela, 'speak to men.'

Christmas came. They did not celebrate it, although with Emma they always had. Rachaela gave Ruth three books and some multi-coloured paints. Ruth gave Rachaela one of her Ruth-type presents, this time a long candle shaded through vermilion to orange, and this they burnt as their one festive token.

For Ruth's eleventh birthday, a week or so before, Rachaela had given Ruth a dress she wanted, scarlet and apple green, and Ruth wore it on Christmas Day.

They ate chicken, peas and chips, apple Danish and cream.

Outside the rain, which had taken over again from the snow, fell in grey torrents.

The day was otherwise normal. Rachaela played music, Ruth painted. There was a play on the radio about the Three Wise Men lost on the M1.

On Christmas night Ruth went for her nightly bath and came out in her nightdress.

'Mummy.'

'What is it?'

'You said I was to tell you.'

'What?'

'I've started.'

Rachaela took a moment to catch up. Then she said, 'You've got a period?'

'Yes, Mummy.'

'Did you manage all right?'

'Yes, thank you.'

'Does it hurt? Do you want a paracetamol?'

'No, it doesn't hurt.'

'That's good.'

Ruth stood looking at her. Rachaela could imagine Emma would have been all congratulations and the joys of womanhood. Ruth had begun early as she, Rachaela, had done. She thought, inadvertently, *Bleeding*.

'I'm different now,' said Ruth.

'Yes.' Rachaela could think of nothing more to say.

Ruth walked behind her screen and was gone.

Chapter Fourteen

By THE END OF JANUARY, Rachaela was working for Mrs Mantini at the antiques shop in Beaumont Street.

Mrs Mantini only wanted her in the afternoons and all day Saturday.

They did a surprisingly brisk trade, although mostly on the little things, the ewers and basins, china dogs, trays of ancient photographs. Certain of these reminded Rachaela of the Scarabae albums, the upright waxwork figures posed before palm trees – yet these people might once have been alive, the Scarabae had looked frozen dead for ever.

Mrs Mantini did not like Rachaela to sit and read in the shop. She wished her to dust the furniture, burnish the coal scuttle, and clean the windows. In spare moments she gave Rachaela boxes of jewellery or coins to sort, unvaluable items often to be highly priced.

The pay was not wonderful, but the job was fairly convenient.

Spring came early. Ruth had a phase of bringing home flowers obtained during her days of truancy:

daffodils and tulips perhaps picked from the park or swiped off graves.

'Don't steal things, you'll get caught,' Rachaela admonished her.

The flower phase died a natural death.

As the days lengthened, Ruth came home later and later. Often she was not home when Rachaela arrived from the shop.

Sometimes, too, Ruth had eaten in a snack bar, having saved up her pocket money for a beefburger.

The school sent Rachaela a letter saying that Ruth's frequent absences were causing her work to suffer. Rachaela dropped it in the bin.

'A man spoke to me in the graveyard,' Ruth announced, as they ate at the table.

'What did you do?'

'Nothing. He said I was Ruth Scaraby and I said No, I was Ruth Day.'

'You shouldn't have answered him.'

'But he was wrong.'

'All right. Then what happened?'

'He said he knew my father's family and had I ever seen them. I didn't say anything and he said he didn't think I had.'

'What then?'

'He said he'd buy me a Pepsi and I said you said I mustn't talk to strangers, and I came away.'

'Did he come after you?'

'No. He just stood there.'

Rachaela said, 'Did he have a dark coat and a woollen hat?'

'Yes. I expect he was hot.'

Rachaela tried to order herself. She had begun to

tremble with a sort of frightened and frustrated fury. How had he found them? How had he followed Ruth? How dare he speak.

Weeks since, she had tested the evening pavements for pursuit, looked from windows for watchers in the shadow. And all the while he had been creeping up on them, unseen. Of course, it was not Rachaela who interested them now. Their craving for continuance – the child—

'You must never – *never* – have anything to do with that man, Ruth.'

'Why?'

'He's bad.'

'He just looked like a man.'

'He works for the Scarabae.'

'Is that for my dad?'

'No. For the family. I told you, they're mad and dangerous.'

It was like hurling stones into water. After a moment the impact vanished, leaving no trace. Rachaela had the feeling that, rather than warning Ruth away from the Scarabae, she was intriguing her further with them. What on earth was to be done?

'I think you'd better stop roaming about. Either you must go to school or stay indoors here.' Lock her in, keep her close.

'Mummy I don't want to.'

'You'll have to. I don't want him getting at you.'

Could she go to the police? This man is molesting my eleven-year-old daughter . . . questions asked. This man is the agent of your daughter's father, his family. Your daughter's father has rights to your daughter. It could become complex, more perilous. Keep the child in. For how long? She must confront the man, drive him off. But now he never showed himself when Rachaela was there.

'You'll have to go to school. I'll take you.'

'I don't want to.'

'I know. I'm sorry. But this is serious.'

'He only said he'd buy me a Pepsi. I didn't go.'

'He might – I don't know.'

'I won't talk to him again.'

'Ruth, you must do as I tell you.'

Do as I tell you. Her mother's voice, angry, at its wits' end.

Ruth finished her food and left the table. She went behind the screen and Rachaela heard the familiar rasp of pencil on paper.

Rachaela got up and went to the edge of Ruth's sanctum.

'Ruth, if ever he catches you alone I want you to scream – scream as loudly as you can – and run away. Will you do that?'

'Scream and run away,' said Ruth. She gave Rachaela a cool and adult glance full of irony.

'I mean it,' said Rachaela.

'There was a radio programme we heard at school,' said Ruth. 'This man said daughters take after their fathers. If I'm like my dad, I must be nasty too.'

Rachaela stared at her.

Why was she trying to protect this creature? Had she forgotten the way it was, the way it had grown? Now she was acting out the ill-fitting rôle of a protective mother, and protective of what? All about Ruth, in her grotto, hung weird pictures, bits of stained glass, bells and draperies. It was a crock of shadow and dull rich colour, and Ruth crouched there like a white spider in her web, her beautiful ugly little face pierced by the blackness of the Scarabae eyes.

Rachaela swallowed.

She wanted to say to Ruth, Do what you want. Talk to the man. Find out what you like.

Ruth knew it all already in her eleven-year-old bones.

'You're not like your father. Your father doesn't want you. The family is nosy and possessive. You don't owe them anything. Do as I say.'

'Yes, Mummy,' said Ruth, and bowed her head to her drawing of a witch.

Rachaela could only take Ruth to the school in the mornings; at least she saw her to the gates. In the afternoon she had to trust Ruth on the way home.

Sometimes still Ruth was late.

'Where have you been?'

Ruth had been to the shops or round at the flat of some girl child never previously mentioned. Probably it was true, for Ruth did not lie, she only evaded.

'Has that man been near you?'

'I haven't seen him.'

'Tell me if you do.'

Rachaela tired of the stupid wardership to school. She sent Ruth off alone and followed her. No one other than herself pursued or accosted Ruth.

A sense of apathy overcame Rachaela.

The man would probably persist, he had done so before, but there were always people about. He could not abduct Ruth, even assuming he had instructions to do so, which seemed unlikely.

Rachaela did not care. *I do not care*. It was up to Ruth. For Ruth was still a burden. She must still be fed and clothed, and soon a decision must be made about a secondary school, with its uniform and other details. Ruth would become more of a problem as she grew older. For how long would Rachaela have to go on sharing her life with this being? She had got used to Ruth, that was all. It was not satisfactory.

On the street. Walk quietly and listen.

Who was this coming from a doorway? Only an old man with a bag.

Turning the corner, oversee each gap in the walls. Was anyone there?

Upstairs, Ruth not home. Go to the window in the dark, and see.

What was that?

Only a man in an anorak.

Where was Ruth? Round at this Lucile's?

There she was on the stairs now. Key in the door.

Mrs Mantini said, 'You do more looking out of that window than cleaning it.'

Who was that standing across from the shop, black overcoat, perhaps a woollen hat.

'This customer wants serving, Rachaela.'

He had gone now.

But he would not be following or watching her.

'This necklace is fifteen pounds.'

There was a frost of green on the trees. Still some light in the sky.

Ruth sat at the table eating bread and jam.

'Why didn't you wait? You'll be having dinner in twenty minutes.'

'I was hungry. Tea's always late now.'

'You're usually late.'

'I go to Lucile's.'

Rachaela faced Ruth. 'Have you seen that man again?'

'Yes.'

'I told you to tell me.'

'He didn't do anything. He didn't speak to me.'

'Where was he?'

'Outside the gates.'

'The school gates?'

'Yes. He just stood there, and I came out and he didn't move. Lucile thought he was funny.'

'Don't tell Lucile who he is.'

'I didn't tell Lucile anything. She said look at that funny old man.'

If she was with Lucile, he would not approach her – was that it? Perhaps the liaison with Lucile was a good thing.

Rachaela, at the window, scanned the street. He was there. Across the road, beneath a lamp just now turning candy red. There to be seen, showing himself.

'Stay here,' she said to Ruth.

She ran down through the house and dashed out into the street. The Scarabae agent was gone.

Above, Ruth's white face looked down on her from the window. Impartially.

Mrs Mantini picked nail varnish off her nails. 'I've been meaning to speak to you, Rachaela,' she said, 'about the way you keep being late. You were late by half an hour this afternoon. It puts me all at sixes and sevens.'

'Yes,' said Rachaela.

'I must ask you not to let it happen again.'

Rachaela reduced the fifteen-pound necklace to the prescribed fourteen pounds and carefully replaced it with the price tag face down.

Mrs Mantini ran her finger over the dustless surface of a Victorian overmantel. 'This mirror could do with a clean.'

Presently Mrs Mantini went out, to be gone for her usual two hours before closing-time.

A Japanese man came in and asked about the china ducks. When he had left, Rachaela cleaned the mirror with the glass spray which left smears, then returned to re-pricing the case of jewellery.

At a quarter to four Mrs Mantini unexpectedly reappeared.

'You'll have to close up, Rachaela. I have to drive to Brighton.'

After Mrs Mantini had gone again, the late afternoon trade began to come in, and at four-thirty, an hour early, Rachaela shut the shop in the faces of two eager customers.

Rachaela felt a sense of freedom as she walked home. She imagined Mrs Mantini in heavy traffic on the motorway. It was as if a cloud had lifted. She had given up concerning herself with the agent of the Scarabae. He could do nothing, and neither could she.

She reached the house and went up the three flights. It was an overcast day, the dark was coming.

She opened the door.

There was a strange noise. It sounded like a child crying. She knew at once it could not be Ruth.

She went around the lobby formed by the bathroom and stared at the dusk flat. Then she turned and looked into Ruth's area.

302

Ruth, who was kneeling on the floor, turned also to look at her. Her eyes were black as voids, heightened by the black eyeshadow and mascara with which she had augmented them. She was draped in a kind of Greek fashion by two of her coloured shawls and she wore round her neck Rachaela's green glass beads. Her mouth was dark red with lipstick, and smudged. It looked at first as if she had been drinking blood.

On Ruth's bed lay a brown-haired whimpering female child, also draped in a shawl and with dabs of make-up less hectically or successfully applied to its face.

On the neck of this child was a terrific black bruise.

The child sat up.

'Ooh, Mrs Day,' said the child, crying and snotty now, 'she was biting my neck.'

'For Christ's sake what have you been doing?' Rachaela seized Ruth and pulled her upright.

'Nothing. We were dressing up.'

'What were you doing to her?'

'She was biting me,' said the other child, hysterical, and began to scream.

Rachaela dropped Ruth. She grabbed the other child to shake her. The child flung herself at Rachaela, burying her snot and make-up smeared face in Rachaela's jumper.

'It was a game,' said Ruth, reasonably.

'Did you make this mark on her neck?'

'I suppose so.'

'I told her to stop,' squealed the other child, who was probably the mysterious Lucile. 'She wouldn't. She kept on and on. Am I bleeding?'

'No, you're all right. You're all *right*. Come over to the lamp and let me see.'

She dragged the howling Lucile towards the lamp, and lit it.

The mark was a bruise, purple and ripe, like a lover's kiss but worse. It looked awful.

'Nothing to worry about,' said Rachaela. 'I'll get some TCP and a plaster.'

'My mummy won't let me play with her again,' said Lucile, a note of righteousness creeping into her terror.

'I think that would be very wise.'

Surprised, perhaps, Lucile's torrent weakened to a snivel. She allowed Rachaela to dab her with antiseptic and to apply the plaster.

With luck 'Mummy' might disbelieve the dire tale, especially if the bruise went down a little before she saw it. One could not tell the child to lie to its mother. Lucile was obviously bursting to reveal all.

'You're all right now, and I think you'd better go home,' said Rachaela. 'Do you know your way?'

'Yes, Mrs Day.'

'Go and wash your face first.'

Lucile went docile to the bathroom.

Ruth said over the splash of water: 'I didn't really bite her. I could have. I didn't.'

'You're mad.' Rachaela's mother had said this to Rachaela over more trivial offences. 'What possessed you?' A foolish question. Obvious what had possessed her.

'It was a game,' said Ruth again.

'No it wasn't,' said Rachaela, 'I know what it was.'

Ruth looked at her, every inch a small vampire with her white face, reddened lips, black eyes and streaming hair. She did not look alarmed or bewildered or even scared. She looked – complacent.

Lucile emerged from the bathroom. She tore off Ruth's shawl and flung it on the bed.

'My mummy will be angry.'

'I expect she will. Well, go home now.'

The Lucile child left, blotchy and aggrieved. Rachaela had not behaved the way Mummys behaved. Another failure.

The windows were blue against the lamp's gold. Was he out there, on the street?

Ruth sat on her bed and drew towards her the unfinished drawing of lions apparently devouring people – Christians probably, from the school's Religious Knowledge.

Rachaela felt the violent urge to laugh. It was her own hysteria.

'Put that down.' Ruth released the picture. 'You've done something incredibly stupid, Ruth. You've behaved in a way that will cause a lot of trouble. You expect me to protect you. Why should I?'

Ruth looked at the windows, the coming night. She did not seem at a loss, only waiting for some boring and pointless noise to end.

Rachaela felt fury then.

It was a fearful rage, in which everything became abruptly mixed, the aversions and angers of twelve years.

'What are you, you horrible little beast?' Rachaela shouted.

Ruth looked at her after all.

The white, black, red face was surprised, just for a moment, then it settled into a closed mask. Rachaela remembered this from long ago. She had seen this expression, this lack of expression, this closing in and down, on the face of the demon baby Ruth had once been.

'It wasn't a game,' said Rachaela. 'It was something disgusting that came out of your foul head.'

'Lucile will be all right,' said Ruth, flatly.

'I don't care about Lucile, that revolting little fool. I don't care about you, either. If you want to act out this sickness you've got then I suppose you must. But why bring it here? Why involve me in it, you bloody filthy little beast!'

Ruth wriggled, like a child embarrassed in class. Then she was entirely still, passive again, almost inanimate.

'Look at me,' said Rachaela.

And Ruth fixed her eyes on her mother.

For a second there was a peculiar juxtaposition. It seemed Ruth's eyes were scarlet and her mouth black.

'Have your bath and go to bed,' Rachaela said. 'If you're hungry you can make yourself a sandwich. I don't want anything to do with you. I don't want to see you.'

'Yes, Mummy,' said Ruth.

And picking up her nightshirt from under the pillow, she went into the bathroom.

In the morning Rachaela left Ruth to get her own breakfast. Ruth poured cornflakes and milk, and ate them sitting at the table where Rachaela drank her coffee.

Ruth did not attempt to speak to Rachaela.

She took up her satchel and went without a word.

Getting to her feet, Rachaela saw her from the window, dawdling off along the road towards school.

At twenty past nine the telephone rang. Usually there were no calls save the occasional wrong number.

This was not a wrong number.

'I'm Mrs Keating, Lucile's mother.'

'Yes?'

'I suppose you know why I'm phoning.' Rachaela did not reply. She heard Mrs Keating bridle at the other end of the line. 'Your child attacked Lucile yesterday. I wondered what you had to say about it.'

'Nothing, really. Lucile wasn't hurt.'

'If you call that awful black bruise on her neck not being hurt – what is your child, some sort of monster?'

Yes, how clever of you, Rachaela thought.

She said nothing.

Frustrated Mrs Keating resumed: 'I've never seen anything like it. It's hard to believe another child could do such a thing. I think you should take her to see a doctor. A psychiatrist probably.' Still Rachaela did not respond to Mrs Keating's red rag. Mrs Keating shouted, 'I think you'd better know, I intend to write to the school about this.'

'If you like.'

'*Like*? You've got a funny way of going on, I must say. Just you get your horrible child seen to, Mrs Day, that's the only advice I can give you.'

'Thank you,' said Rachaela.

Mrs Keating swore at her and hung up.

Rachaela switched on the radio. She did not want to think any more about Ruth. She would not need to see her until tonight.

A Rachmaninov piano concerto swept through the flat, making the problem of Ruth trivial and vague.

At one o'clock Rachaela ate lunch, and at five past two, half an hour too late, she got up and left for the antiques shop.

Mrs Mantini did not upbraid her, but she pursed her tangerine lips and made a great thing of getting ready to go out in a hurry.

The afternoon was not eventful. A girl came in and tried to haggle over a nineteenth-century vase, but Rachaela told her Mrs Mantini fixed the prices fairly and never reduced items. A handsome young man and a rather glamorous middle-aged woman, perhaps his mother, looked round the shop and finally bought a small brass rocking horse.

At a quarter to five Mrs Mantini came back.

'Oh Rachaela. I hoped you'd have unloaded that crate.'

The crate was full of heavy objects that really needed the attention of a strong man. Rachaela had ignored it.

'We'll do it now,' said Mrs Mantini with much irritation.

They began to unload the crate, Mrs Mantini puffing and blowing. At five-thirty they were still engaged on the crate. Mrs Mantini shut the shop. She said to Rachaela, 'You can stay and help with this. It will make up for the thirty-five minutes you were late.'

Rachaela did not argue, and they went on unpacking the crate until a quarter past six.

Mrs Mantini straightened up and puffed out a last breath of her garlic-and-onion lunch. 'Actually, Rachaela, I want a word with you about this lateness.'

Rachaela was putting on her coat. Mrs Mantini stood hard-yellow amid brazen fire irons and fire screens. 'I spoke to you yesterday about it, but you don't seem to have heard me. I don't pay you to be late, I pay you to be on time.'

'But you don't pay very much, do you?' said Rachaela.

'If you don't like the wages, miss, you can go elsewhere.'

'Very well,' said Rachaela. She buttoned her coat. 'Give me what you owe me up until today.'

Mrs Mantini glowered, her eyes roasting.

'I certainly won't. You can come in on Saturday and I'll give it you then.'

'No,' said Rachaela. 'I'd like it now.'

She stood and looked at Mrs Mantini, and gradually Mrs Mantini broke down like an overheated fire. Cursing Rachaela as Mrs Keating had done, but in more vivid words, Mrs Mantini opened the till and counted out the abbreviated wage. She flung it on the counter before Rachaela. 'Now get out, you little bitch.'

Rachaela walked out on to the street. Her legs were trembling. She felt a wave of uncertainty and relief.

This did not matter. It was Ruth's fault anyway.

And at the flat, there would be Ruth to see. To go on with the utter silence or to break the silence, pretending nothing had happened. What did silence count for, in any case? When did they speak? Only when there was trouble.

The sky was soft and muddy, losing the light. Stars faded against the waking red eyes of the streetlamps.

Rachaela felt footloose, nearly rattling. No job. She would have to look around. That would take up her time, make her forget Ruth.

When she reached her front door, inside the house, she felt Ruth's absence, and going in, the flat was empty.

Rachaela took off her coat. She made herself coffee and switched on the lamps. She washed up the lunch things and looked into the fridge. Ruth was due to have chicken tonight. She might as well have it. Rachaela put the portions into a dish and upended a can of Heinz tomato soup over them to make a casserole. She set the chicken in the oven.

The radio offered opera or politics. She turned it off and put on a tape of Stravinsky.

The sky changed to the orange-black of city night. People came and went along the street.

At eight-thirty Ruth had not come back.

Rachaela turned the chicken on to a very low light.

At nine-thirty the soup had all evaporated. Rachaela turned the chicken out.

She sat in the flat in the silence that was not Ruth's silence.

Ruth had never been as late as this. Where could she be? Some burger bar, the Pizza Eater?

At ten thirty-five, Rachaela switched on the main light and walked behind the screen into Ruth's area.

Everything looked at first glance the same.

Rachaela examined the area carefully.

The bed was made, Ruth's way, lumpy under the dark-blue coverlet. The old bear Emma had given her sat in his corner, accorded dignity, but no longer attention. The books piled up in cranky stairways. On the wall, the painted mirror and the pictures.

The green paperweight and the blue glass cat were missing from the chest-top.

Rachaela walked into the area and squeezed up to the chest. She opened drawers. Comb and brush were not there. The vampire make-up was gone. The blue jumper and the scarlet blouse were gone. Some pants and socks, tights, the second bra, the new packet of sanitary pads.

In the bathroom Ruth's toothbrush and her little stick of deodorant were missing.

Rachaela came out and sat down.

What did she feel? As once before, nothing.

She was not astounded. Of course she had known what Ruth would do. Just as the man, the Scarabae agent, had known what she would do eventually. He had only to offer himself and wait.

Rachaela had turned on Ruth, not just the habitual cold shoulder, but with a firework of dislike and alienation. And Ruth had packed her satchel quietly in the night, gone out and gone to him. And he would have taken her, or directed her. To the Scarabae.

What should *she* do?

Nothing. There was nothing to do.

Ruth was no more. The twelve years of idiocy were over.

After four days, Rachaela cleaned the flat.

She dusted behind the books, dusted the books, scoured the cooker and did out the kitchen cupboards. She emptied the Lucozade, Pepsi and Sprite down the drain. When she reached Ruth's area, she moved the screen out into the room and took off the shawls, flowers and bells. She stripped the bed and put Ruth's treasures, carefully wrapping the glass, her books and the bear into two cardboard boxes from the supermarket, and stowed them in the bottom of the wardrobe. Ruth might send for her things. Ruth's clothes, which she would soon have grown out of, she put into bags for Oxfam. The Scarabae would have to clothe Ruth from now on.

Rachaela did not like the screen, but as with Ruth's bed it was too large to dispose of easily. She folded it and stood it in the corner behind the music centre. The bed itself she redraped in its midnight cover, and added a couple of red-and-blue cushions.

The denuded chest she pushed against a wall.

The room looked much bigger, airier. It was possible to see into all its parts freely.

She did not look for the man. He would be gone by now.

On the sixth day, she walked up to Lyle and Robbins and inquired after work, but they had no vacancies. The Pizza Eater looked over-staffed, and the girls and boys seemed extremely young and noisy. There were no advertisements for staff. She would have to look at the local papers.

On the seventeenth day a letter came from the school. Rachaela put it aside.

Rachaela sat in her chair, listening to music.

It was going to be a lot cheaper, without Ruth. Maybe she could coast for a little while.

Outside were the familiar roofs and flats, the chimneys and aerials. In the distance the park was transparently, avidly green.

It began to be hot, and the smells of petrol, geraniums and baked pavements filled the flat from the open windows.

After the twenty-seventh day, Rachaela dreamed of Ruth at the house of the Scarabae.

She seemed to be wearing Anna's evening dress, long and black and trailing on the floor, winking with spangles. Her long hair fluttered behind her as she moved about. The Scarabae clasped their hands, pleased.

Ruth was in the garden. There were red and white roses. Uncle Camillo popped up from behind a bush. He rode the rocking-horse, which moved over the lawn without effort.

He handed Ruth a letter.

Rachaela could only read the words *Come to me*.

She walked into the house. It was night, and only the ruby lamp burned in the hall. The door to the tower was ajar.

As she stood there, Adamus came out of the tower.

She had forgotten or erased his face, and so she saw it through a blur, but his body was naked, exactly as she had remembered it, golden-white, muscular and slender, the black mass at the groin and out of it the penis rising dark amber-red. His black hair fell around him. 'It's you,' he said.

'Yes. You mustn't,' she said quickly, wringing her hands in a strange melodramatic gesture.

'But I must.'

'Adamus – she's only a child.'

'No,' he said.

'Eleven years old,' Rachaela pleaded.

'A woman.'

And out of the dark Ruth stole in, enveloped in her long, black glittering gown.

She wore her make-up, but impeccably, the black eyelids blended and subtle, the red-lipstick lips softened. Her hair was like his.

She was not a child. She had begun to menstruate, she had high full breasts.

She moved towards him as though Rachaela were not there. She put her thin white hand into his.

Adamus stooped and kissed Ruth's scarlet mouth.

He leaned and picked her up, and carried her across his body, up into the breathing unlit tower.

Rachaela followed them.

They came into the upper room.

A fire glowed on the hearth. By its light Rachaela saw Adamus lie Ruth on her back on top of the piano. Somehow he climbed up after her. He kneeled above Ruth and undid the black dress slowly.

'I'm afraid,' said Ruth. She giggled, as she had done when she was a child with Emma.

Adamus bowed to Ruth's perfect breasts and mouthed and tongued them. Ruth held his head to her body. He parted her thighs and travelled down her, skin and material, and thrust the dress away, and began his second kiss.

Flames leaped in Rachaela. She longed to scream. She was invisible and unhearable, a ghost.

Ruth groaned. She pulled on Adamus. He left her ebony mound, stroking it with his fingers. He put the burning phallus there, and drove it in.

Ruth shrieked.

'You hurt me,' said Ruth, 'hurt me again.'

Unable to move, Rachaela watched them rise and fall together, their bodies mounted on a black wild horse of pleasure, galloping.

Ruth screamed. She screamed and kicked and caged him in her long white legs.

Rachaela spasmed in long aching waves and woke in the bed in the flat, staring into darkness.

It was not possible.

Father and grandfather. He could not.

But why should anything stop him?

Rachaela's day was over, she had served her purpose. Now Ruth might be the year queen.

Continuance. The mad people treasured it, and Adamus was their instrument.

Don't be a fool. If it must, let it happen.

She tried to remember his face, but as in the dream it had grown blurred and distant.

Rachaela sat up and switched on the light. Outside some drunks were shouting in the street. She was glad of them.

She got out of bed and went to make tea. That had been Emma's remedy for everything. Tea or a drop of sherry.

What would Emma have made of this?

'You can't let them get hold of her, Rachaela. From what you say, they're terrible people. Crazy, awful. Your own child. You have to get her back out of their clutches.'

'Yes, Emma,' Rachaela said.

The boiling water splashed into the mug, and the drunks sang on the street in rejoicing.

Chapter Fifteen

DRIVER NUMBER THREE WAS QUITE confident. 'Pitchley. I know Pitchley. Where the new estate is. It'll cost a bit.'

'Yes.'

'That's OK then. Jump in.'

Seeing the line of taxis at the station in Porlea she had not been optimistic, but time had narrowed the spaces of the countryside. The territory of the Scarabae had been breached.

She recollected the way, even backwards and in the early summer greenness. She recognized the broad motorway, churches and pubs.

Only the normality was unnerving.

She did not recognize the village.

A small supermarket had been built, there was a post office and a greengrocer, a new bold pub with a rainbow sign The Carpenters. Up on the hill the new estate, chocolate brown, with gabled roofs, satellite dishes, wheels of washing and model cherry trees in gardens. Somewhere in the middle lay the depression of grey stone houses. The derelict fields had gone to lawns.

'Here you are,' said the driver. 'Where do you want me to drop you?'

'At the top of the hill.'

'The estate.'

He drove her almost on to the drive of the last brown doll's house.

She paid him and got out. She watched him drive away.

The crows had gone. Where did crows go to?

It was all so different. But it was still the place. The starting point for the long walk over the heath to the house.

Her bag was light now, only packed with the bare essentials.

She had better be careful of the road. There might be more traffic.

Rachaela was correct in this assumption. Three cars went by her in her first half-hour on the road.

The sun westered as she passed the gutted farm that had now been pulled down. She saw where the crows had gone. There was a delegation here. She remembered the rook or crow sitting in the hedge the night she had come away for ever. For ever, after all, had not been so long.

The heath, when she came up on it, was alive with colours. Brown and gold among the green, purple flowers, the gorse in sunny clumps. Birds flew and circled, calling.

It was right it should look different, coming back. In her memory it was too bleak, too desolate, and that had given it an added power.

She was moving now towards the sea. She felt it, like a void before her.

After she had walked for another half hour she was

tired to the bone. She sat down on a rock. The sky was thickening. Would the daylight last? She must not rest too long.

Such parts as these Ruth had drawn, and peopled them with dragons.

A gull cried spitefully in the sky.

Presently she got up and went on. She did not have the stamina of years ago, but she would have to make it. She did not want to be marooned on the heath when darkness came. Not now.

The sound was like her tiredness at first, a long thrumming in the ear. Then she knew it for what it was. The rock jutted through the thin pelt of flowers and grass, and all at once the horizon concertinaed. She was looking out into the vault of air above the sea.

She came to it and stood and looked down into the dragon's mouth. The waves clashed along the bastions of the cliffs. She might have been here yesterday.

Darkness seeped up from the earth.

The sun was setting as she walked by the brink of the ocean.

Like a mirage she saw the blackness of the pines, and all at once, the house, small in the distance like a toy. Flawless. Its banks and slopes. One blazing emerald window.

She stopped in wonder. In wonder at herself. For she had come back.

After sunset the doors would be opened. It was the right time as she came around to the front of the house. She paused again to see its silhouette against the dimming sky. The stars were there, slightly altered, for it was a different season and a later year. She saw the tower. She felt a strange sinking in her stomach. No, she must remember, the peculiarity of the house had also to do with her perception. She must, this time, be rational.

The doors gave, just as before. As before she entered into the huge open hall or lobby, with its chessboard floor of russet-and-black marble. It was as wide as she recalled, rationality did not make it smaller. And there the shadows massed, the crouching bears that might be anything, and through the high windows dropped the occluded violet-yellow dregs of light.

The red lamp was burning on the mahogany table, catching above the chandelier with its drops of blood.

The smell of the house was the same. A church of damp and incense, old woods and musty closets, polish, oil, and sweet decay.

This time she did not turn to shut the door.

She glanced at the tower in the shadow, and dismissed it.

No one to greet her, now.

That was proper. She was superfluous and perhaps not welcome.

Could she find her way in the dark?

She walked to the stairs. The nymph guarded the newel post, holding up her blind light. A new spider had woven from her shoulder to her upraised arm, a film-set touch that was too apposite. Rachaela put her foot on the red Persian carpet and started up, out of the scarlet ambience of the lamp.

Twenty-two steps.

On the landing a soft light shone into the dark from the corridor, as in memory. The second lamp was lit, as it had been then. She recollected it falling on the face and sightless seeing eyes of Michael, the first of the Scarabae household she had ever beheld.

She entered the lit passage and there was the window in the elbow of it, dark now as then, a crowd of pictures on the walls, paintings beneath paintings.

And there the door.

How familiar it was. As known to her as the door of the flat.

Would this room be locked?

The doorknob turned easily, and the door opened on the blue-and-green room.

It shocked her, for it was just the same, as if memory had now been lifted from her head and unfolded in front of her. The green fireplace, with the black clock with angels, the dressing-table and figured mirror, the four-poster bed. The covers of the bed had been drawn back a little, the action of an hotel, to show the clean pillowcases and the white sheet.

There was no fire on the summer hearth. A fire screen of embroidered blue roses stood there. Mrs Mantini would have had an eye for that.

Rachaela tossed her bag on to the bed.

Her radio stood where she had left it, on the table.

She lifted it up and saw that long ago the batteries had leaked and burnt the wood.

She crossed to the wardrobe and opened it and saw her abandoned clothes hanging in a neat row. A faintly powdery smell hung with them, but they were not moth-eaten, would still fit her despite twelve years and the bearing of a child.

The night window loomed at the room's back. Its picture was quite evident to her, even in blackness, the leaded tree and standing figures, the apples and the unicorn.

Rachaela left the room and walked into the bath-room. Mrs Mantini would have been busy here, too. Indeed the whole house would have been a paradise to Mrs Mantini.

There were fresh soaps and clean towels.

Rachaela had been expected.

Why? They would think her maternal instinct outraged at the extraction of her child? Burning hot with zeal, the anguished mother rushing after. For what did they know of her half-hearted attempts at abortion, the years' endurance. Had Ruth described anything of Rachaela's brand of motherhood?

Rachaela took the oatmeal-coloured dress out of the wardrobe and hung it up. There was no doubt it would fit her.

She went back into the bathroom and ran a bath.

As she lay in the water, she heard the soft brisk heels of a female Scarabae pass along the corridor outside. Unice? Miriam?

The sound was so usual to her. Perhaps she had missed it in the flat, these passagings. Only the loud bad music below and the arguments on the landing.

She thought: *I am a few walls', stairways', rooms' distance from him.*

Until now she had hardly thought of Adamus. He had formed her life, as for the last twelve years she had lived it, formed her every day by the acts of one extraordinary night. Through the years she had sometimes half dreamed of it. She had never permitted herself to conjure it up. And over it had meshed a concrete slab, which now the lever of the house was painfully and irresistibly easing up.

She had known she must face Adamus, or the idea of Adamus, if she came back.

He was her reason, after all; Adamus with Ruth.

She got out of the bath and towelled herself dry. Going into the bedroom again she put on the oatmeal dress which might have been bought yesterday for fit. Its faded quality did not displease her, or the soft odour of destruction. She must camouflage and arm herself.

She powdered her face in her mirror and reaffirmed the dark pencil around her eyes.

Would Camillo leave her another gift-wrapped mouse?

But when she opened the door, nothing and no one was outside. Only the burning lamp conveyed the half-life of the house.

Did the Scarabae still dine, or had customs changed?

She would have to see.

Rachaela walked into the corridor and along to the landing, and descending the stairs she saw the lamps were lit in the drawing room as on that first night years before.

In the drawing room Michael and Maria stood like cut-out figures in their dark servile clothes.

'Michael, Maria,' she said.

They gave her stiff little bows, what she would have expected.

Michael said, 'Miss Rachaela, please go straight through into the dining room.'

'I'd like a drink first, Michael.'

'Miss Anna told me to ask you to go straight in.'

Rachaela shrugged. Something twisted in her belly, a phantom Ruth-baby.

She went towards the second door, and Michael

hurried ahead to open it for her.

She walked into the dining room, and stopped, not surprised, perturbed only by what she had suddenly anticipated.

For they were all there, as on the memorable occasions in the past.

Their known, nearly identical faces, slid by in a wave of tawdry dinner jackets, sequined old lace. Could she still name them? Yes. Alice, Peter, Jack, Livia . . . Not Camillo, never Camillo. She saw and registered all this in parenthesis. For at the table's head sat the most bizarre Scarabae of all. In an exactly similar perhaps resewn dress of dark green voile and net, a necklace that was a heart of green cut-glass, and jade ear pendants, her black hair flowing from tortoiseshell combs, her face smoothly powdered, lids black, lips crimson: Ruth.

Ruth sat among the Scarabae like a living plant among ancient statues. She had bloomed from their support.

Across the room she smiled at Rachaela her straight white teeth that had never needed a dentist.

'Hallo, Mummy.'

Almost the first time ever she had volunteered a greeting.

But then, she was at home here, not Rachaela's unwanted guest.

Rachaela did not answer.

To Ruth's right, Anna stood up.

'Come and sit down with us, Rachaela. We're so very glad that you came. We hoped that you would.'

'I had to,' Rachaela said. She said blankly, 'You stole my child.'

'Oh, no, Rachaela. Not stealing. Not that.'

Ruth said, piping up like a bright and confident pupil, 'I asked the man. He knew the way. I came by train on my own. I liked it. They sent a car to the station.'

'And you walked up the hill through the trees,' said Rachaela.

'Michael was there. He showed me the way.'

She was not afraid to speak to Rachaela. Not reluctant. It was as if it had all been planned.

Rachaela looked at the weird miniature woman her daughter had become. She did not look like a child dressing up, more like the daughter of a medieval family, dressed always as a smaller version of the adults, a woman at eleven or twelve.

'Come and sit down,' Anna said again. Her dress blinked its myriad eyes and all the dresses, Ruth's included, did the same.

Rachaela went to the table. A place had been laid at the foot, opposite across the long surface, to Ruth's place. As if they had known to the minute the time of Rachaela's arrival. Probably everything had been kept ready for weeks, prepared as soon as Ruth got here.

Rachaela sat down, and Cheta came to serve her.

It was a rabbit casserole.

Rachaela ate cautiously, not sure now she could stomach such food.

Ruth ate neatly and voraciously, like a starling.

There was wine, a deep coal-red. Cheta poured a glass for Rachaela.

Ruth too had wine which she drank in greedy little sips.

None of them had changed. This family did not.

Ruth sparkled in the midst of them like a jewel in cobwebs.

The family was pleased. It had an aura of well-being. They had got what they wanted. All of them basked, the Scarabae, Ruth.

Only Camillo was absent. And Adamus.

Rachaela left her food unfinished.

'A few days ago,' said Ruth, 'we had seagull. Jack found it.'

Rachaela said, 'The cat used to hunt them.'

'The cat is very old now,' said Anna. 'It sleeps all day and most of the night.'

Something had altered. The cat had altered.

Maria brought a strawberry tart.

Rachaela watched Ruth spoon the tart into her red mouth. She had a second helping, as she had done of the casserole. Real home-cooked fare, such as Emma had provided.

Rachaela got up. 'Excuse me.' She took her glass of wine across the room, and watched the table from there. It was obscene to pretend to be part of it.

If she, Rachaela, had been abducted as a child or teenager, would she have responded to the Scarabae as Ruth did? Who could tell, now.

The meal was finally finished with the cheeseboard and a dish of fruit. Ruth ate from these too.

The Scarabae rose and went like some collective creature, some sort of amoeba with Ruth its glowing heart, into the drawing room.

Here the old men and women deposited themselves about the room. They took up knitting and sewing, books and chess games. A mild muttering came from them like settling insects.

Maria and Cheta served tea.

Ruth stood before the screened fireplace in her duchess gown, drinking her tea, the focus for all the eyes which constantly rose and came to her, and the old smiles which lifted up the lips over the discoloured, sharp old teeth.

Ruth set down her cup and saucer by the stopped golden clock.

'Shall I go up now?'

'Yes,' said Anna from a couch. 'Go up.'

Rachaela observed her child swirl delicately from the fireplace and hurry with the well-known, swift fox-like movement from the room. Her acknowledgements to Rachaela were over. Ruth did not even glance at her.

'Where is she going, Anna?' Rachaela asked steadily.

'Into the tower.'

'Adamus's tower.'

'Adamus is teaching her the piano, Rachaela.'

A heartbeat interrupted Rachaela's breathing. She cleared her throat and said, 'How logical.'

'Yes. It seems she has a natural aptitude.'

'No doubt. Anna,' Rachaela hesitated. 'I want to talk to you.'

Anna got up like a faultless, tactful hostess. 'Perhaps you'd like to see Ruth's room?'

'All right.'

Nobody watched them go out in turn. The Scarabae were not concerned with Rachaela now. Her day was over.

They travelled by a short stairway from the morning room, up into a narrow corridor carved with horses' heads. Rachaela could not recall coming this way in the past, but she must have done, for she had surely explored all the house. At a turn in the corridor she saw a picture she remembered, a ship at sea, and under the waves a chariot racing from a previous painting.

There was an annexe beyond the corridor with two windows – blackened, impossible to decipher – and then a single door.

Anna opened the door and motioned Rachaela forward. 'It's only ethical. You're her mother.'

Rachaela entered a room of blood.

It was blood-red. The walls of embossed paper, with here and there a darkened bruise of damp, the fiery carpet, the four poster draped and covered in the colour of Ruth's velvet mouth.

Rachaela stood speechless.

Red. The blood of menstruation and the torn maidenhead. The red of the womb which bore the child. The red of the blood drunk at a feast. Which was it, or was it all of them combined?

The room had its window, too.

Rachaela gazed hard at it.

She made out a Nativity, but it was wrong. A ray from the lamp beside the bed showed that the Virgin's dress was also crimson, while the Three Kings had the heads of beasts: a horse, a lizard and a cat. Nearby, almost missed, was an ass with the bearded head of a man.

'Your symbolism,' Rachaela said, 'is always curious.'

'We have our own ways, Rachaela. This has always been the child's room, the girl-child. She is our saviour, you see.'

'Because a girl can make babies.'

'Exactly,' said Anna undisturbed.

Rachaela said, 'She's too young.'

'Not technically, of course,' said Anna, 'but I agree.

327

A few more years should be allowed to elapse.'

'When she's fourteen, fifteen?'

'Something like that.'

'It's not legal in this country, Anna.'

'Oh, this country.' Anna smiled. 'We're our own country. All our countries and none.'

'And who is the prospective male?' said Rachaela. She was sweating in the hot colour of the room.

'You know, of course,' said Anna.

'I know, of course. Grandfather and father and lover. That should be incestuous enough even for you.'

Anna lowered her eyes decorously.

'This is the best way, for us.'

'And does Ruth know what you have in mind?'

'Ruth knows and accepts she is important to us. Luckily, this time, we have been able to welcome her in her youth. She'll grow towards us, and towards her father. He already fascinates her, which is not surprising. In the end, it will seem natural to her. There is a little ceremony that will take place. This will help Ruth, as she grows older, to understand.'

'No, Anna,' said Rachaela.

'It's out of your hands,' said Anna simply.

'It isn't out of my hands. I'll take her away.'

'Even if you could make her go,' said Anna, 'Ruth would return to us as quickly as she could. Ruth has no trouble in identifying with the Scarabae.'

'It's disgusting, Anna. What happened before was bad enough, was foul enough. But this—'

'How jealous you are, Rachaela. I'm sorry for you. If you had stayed, the rôle of wife would have been yours. But you chose not to. We have had to wait in patience all these years.'

Jealous. Yes, that must be it. It was not the unliked

child she struggled to shield, but the man's flesh she would not see mingled with another's.

Anna had not changed either. Of them all, she was most like the Anna of the first meetings. But now too she was a true adversary. They did not want or need Rachaela any more. She would be allowed in as an adjunct, and kept from doing further harm. They owed her only the debt of Ruth.

'No, Anna, it's filthy and I won't allow it.'

Anna lifted her hands and let them fall.

'You fight against the tide, always.'

'She's a child. Am I to let you do this to her?'

'She will be agreeable. What alternative do you offer her? You've had your freedom, Rachaela, and what have you done with it? Yours is only a sleeping life.'

'It's mine.'

'Then live it, and allow Ruth to live hers.'

'We won't agree on this, Anna.'

'No. I expect not.'

Rachaela felt utter helplessness, as she was meant to feel, and as she guessed that Anna saw.

'Then I'm to be a spectator,' she said.

'If you wish.'

Around them the blood-red bedroom pulsed and smouldered. Rachaela imagined Ruth asleep here. Waited on by servants, her bed made, possessions carefully dusted. There on that table a box of paints and drawing pad; by the bed another box, of jewels, pearls and faceted glass. Everything had been catered for. Here Ruth could live: a pampered being, a fairy-tale princess, safe in the castle at last. And with a fairytale prince provided.

'It's all too exact,' said Rachaela. 'Something will happen. You don't know Ruth.'

'Oh yes. Ruth is like us. You were the rogue flowering, Rachaela.'

Rachaela lay in her green-and-blue bed and listened to the house shifting, and the breath of the sea.

She must make some scheme for herself, the best thing to do.

Once or twice, soft stark footfalls went along the corridor.

The tower clock by the bed told her it was five-fifteen, almost three then, if she remembered the time interval correctly. Or unless the clock had changed its pattern. But surely the clock was like the rest, changeless.

Had Adamus changed?

Did he look old now. He would be over seventy, if it could be true – foolish to reiterate any doubt. It was true, must be so.

But Ruth would not be drawn to an old man. The thirty he had looked would seem old enough to a child of eleven. But Ruth was not a child.

Rachaela saw Ruth again as she had appeared. An eldritch maiden. A mask in a dress.

She would have to speak to Ruth.

For the first time, properly speak to her.

The sea sounded louder as it claimed the beaches. The power of water.

Was Sylvian still out there, floating with the galleons and flotsam?

In the morning Rachaela bathed and dressed, and tugged on the bell-pull so that Cheta miraculously appeared. Everything was superficially as before. Toast and tea.

330

Rachaela recalled her former hypnotized aimlessness, and went out quickly.

She took the correct corridor, found the Salome annexe and climbed up to the attic.

The attic was not as it had been. The rocking-horse was gone. Webs of dust made a cat's cradle about the space. On the chests the brown bottles of Uncle Camillo's wine, many minus their corks, were wreathed and veiled.

Camillo had not been in the attic for months and perhaps for years.

The dust from the old house gathered everywhere, the powders of its grinding bones.

A cherry-and-green stuffed bird turned slowly to an icicle of dust.

She had laid the hammer there, after she had tried to break the tower window. A useless moment of violence. Let her recall and beware. The hammer was no longer where she had dropped it. Rachaela left the attic.

She began to move through the house as she had done before, opening doors, now trying to force doors which would not open. She found Alice knitting in a pale sitting room whose window was a gigantic cloudburst of primrose and grey. At the window's foot, cities burned and Alice performed complicated clicks and twiddles on her steel needles.

Had she located Alice in this room before? She had come on no other Scarabae beyond Cheta, who had brought her breakfast. Two of the doors she had forced had turned out to open the other way, and to be cupboards containing piles of bedclothes, folded.

'Alice, where is Camillo?'

Alice knitted.

'I don't know, Rachaela. Perhaps you should try the library.'

'That was Sylvian.'

'Uncle Camillo goes there now. Oh, such a lot of books we used to have. Rooms and rooms of them. I can remember Uncle Camillo playing with us, popping out from behind the chairs.'

Rachaela left Alice and wove her way through the house to the library. No one was there, but on the table stood the mutilated globe, the ink and ruler.

Rachaela looked at the ruler. It was plain ebony. She had seen Camillo scratch a skeleton on the ruler, but it was gone.

She tried the books. She looked at the lines ruled through the sentences. She found one book with single words left unruled. After much effort, she put the sentence together which the book now consisted of: *We have fled before them*.

On one wall, the north, the books were readable. No one had taken up Sylvian's work, despite the ominous ruler and ink.

Rachaela left the house and went to the steps which led down to the beach.

The sea was in, turquoise green, foaming.

She turned back to the house and resumed searching. He was the oldest of them. He had the roots of things secreted in his mind. She could not go to Adamus.

What was Ruth doing? Perhaps asleep in bed. She had liked to lie in on Saturdays and Sundays. Sometimes sitting up to draw.

Rachaela lost herself in the house as if it were essential that she must. She found another door that would not open and knocked loudly on it. When she tried again the door gave suddenly as if it had decided of itself to let her in.

There was, inside the tall yellow bed, an old man, tucked up to the chin. Between the bed and the door, a splash of red and white on the room's ochre. The rocking-horse.

'Camillo?'

The pane of the old face turned, the long white hair fanning out on the pillow.

One must be careful, too, of intentions among the Scarabae. She had meant to find him, and she had.

'I've been looking for you,' said Rachaela.

She advanced slowly. Had he come to this after all in the twelve years, the couch of age and decrepitude? There was no smell of the invalid in the room.

'Camillo,' she said again.

He looked at her. His eyes were sharp as knives.

'One night,' he said, 'the mob came. They shouted round the house and the servants ran to my mother, they were so frightened. My father picked me up. "Get dressed," he said, "put on your warmest things." Outside the sleigh was ready and the horse to pull it. They had taken off the bells. My father used the whip. We started at such a speed. I remember the white snow splashing up like a wave.'

'I don't want to hear this,' Rachaela said quietly.

'The crowd had been misled,' said Camillo. 'They ran after us and stones thudded round the sleigh. My mother was weeping. She had on all her jewellery and a great fur cloak over her nightdress. We drove from the outskirts of the town. There were men running with torches but the horse bolted past them. I was excited, too young to understand everything had been left behind. Out into the white woods we ran. Great spumes of snow roared up and the trees were like huge white candles, glowing under the moon. I sobered, thinking of sagas I had heard of wolves, but my father hushed me. My father said, "Men are to be feared, not wolves." Then the forests closed about us and there was no more light.'

'Camillo.'

'The sleigh ran all night. Once on a hilltop the trees broke, and we looked back and saw a vast red light on the horizon. My mother cried out. She said that they were burning our people. My father said the town itself was burning. Then the trees swallowed us again.'

'And in the morning,' said Rachaela, 'the light came, and you hid your head and wept.'

Camillo grinned. 'Good, good. I don't have to finish it.'

'Why did you tell me?'

'You're here.'

'Who were they, the ones that died?'

'Scarabae,' said Camillo. 'Always Scarabae.'

'Superstition, which they themselves fostered, killed them.'

'Twinkle, twinkle little star,' said Camillo, 'how I wonder what you are.'

'You were afraid of the light because you'd been taught to be afraid of it,' said Rachaela. 'You believed you were vampires because someone told you that too.'

'What is this creature,' said Camillo, 'a mouse? An elephant?'

'How can I take Ruth away from them?'

'Ruth,' said Camillo, 'that nasty child.'

Rachaela stared at Camillo.

'You don't like her.'

'A viper in the bosom.'

'Then help me get her away, Camillo. Tell me how?'

'There's no hope of it,' said Camillo from the yellow box of bed. 'She is their bud now. And you are grass cuttings, the bush that won't flower. Go away.'

'Camillo—'

'One night,' said Camillo, 'the mob came. They shouted round the house . . .'

Rachaela saw the old face close again like a crab upon its story. She went to the door and he recited the words until she had gone out and shut the door behind her. Then there was silence in the room again.

Chapter Sixteen

WHEN DINNER WAS ENDED, AND TEA had been drunk, and Ruth put down her cup, and the words had been said: *Shall I go up now? Yes* . . . Rachaela too got up. 'I'll go with you, Ruth.'

Ruth stood still, docile from the years of casual obedience.

Anna said, 'She knows the way, Rachaela.'

'I'm sure she does. But I'd like to watch the piano lesson.'

All about the room the Scarabae faintly stirred, like leaves in a light breeze. Dorian poised with a chess knight in his fingers. Alice had seemingly dropped a stitch.

'It may put Ruth off her playing,' said Stephan from the empty hearth. 'A young girl. She hasn't been learning very long.'

'Of course not,' said Rachaela. 'I'm her mother.'

A sigh appeared to go over them.

'Naturally then,' said Anna.

Ruth turned and went towards the doorway, but not quickly as on the previous night, allowing Rachaela time to follow.

Out in the hall, where Ruth's lips blended into the ruby lamplight, Rachaela said, 'Do you like the lessons?'

'Oh yes,' said Ruth.

'How do you get on with him?' Rachaela asked mundanely.

Ruth countered airily. 'You said he wouldn't like me, but he does.'

'Does he?'

'He says I learn very fast. He plays to me.'

'Yes,' said Rachaela. They had reached the door. She said swiftly, 'Do you remember the first thing he said to you?'

'Yes,' said Ruth.

'What?'

'He said, "My name is Adam. I'm your father."'

'Did you believe him?'

'Yes.'

'How old does he look to you?'

Ruth put her hand on the door. 'I don't know.'

'What do you think of him?'

Ruth looked at Rachaela, her face like paper with nothing on it, or more accurately with all the writing lined through and unreadable – one of Sylvian's books.

'He's my dad,' said Ruth.

The ghastly banal statement came between them like a cleaver blow. And Ruth turned the door handle and the door to the tower opened.

Ruth went up the stair first, to the upper room.

Rachaela climbed slowly, her body aching as if with fever.

The room.

The window was already dark, it was not credible

to see if any damage showed in the face of the lion. Candles and lamps lit the furniture, the broad black pool of the piano with its shore of keys.

By the dark and open hearth, the giant cat lay sleeping, a heap of bones beneath fur pelt. As they entered, it lifted up its lids and the blurred moons of its eyes looked on them as if from miles away.

Ruth sped at once to the cat.

She kneeled down and embraced it, rubbing her head against its face, caressing the thick fur.

Then she looked up at the man in the chair.

'Hallo, Adam.'

She was not shy, not even arch. Was she possessive? This mysterious stranger, author of her existence, who would, she had been told, care nothing for her. Now before her in all the cogency of his masculinity. Hers for an hour, or however long it was they spent together, this evening tryst of theirs.

He wore a white shirt. That was different, Rachaela remembered him only in black. Or naked, clad in skin.

The long hair was tied back, in the way she recalled. It was like Ruth's hair, so straight, a torrent.

He did not turn to look at Rachaela, looked only at the child-woman kneeling before him.

So Rachaela saw only his profile. That had not aged a moment. It was just the same. The sombre eye fixed. He did not smile at the child, he had no expression. Presently he said, 'Come to the piano.' And got up and walked across the room. And Rachaela saw his face, the unremembered face. No wonder her mind had not been able to retain it. It was too absolute, too like itself and nothing else. But there was the medium of another resemblance. For Rachaela saw now that Ruth was like Adamus more than like anything else. Perhaps this was why Rachaela had never found pleasure in her face.

As Adamus walked towards the piano his eyes inevitably met Rachaela's. She found his gaze unendurable and unavoidable, horrified that so much had stayed in her, of him.

And in that instant Ruth darted up from the hearth and came after him, and plucked at his arm.

'What shall I play?'

'I've put the Mozart out for you. Try that.'

And Ruth was the centre of the room again.

She sat down before the piano, glanced at the music, and spread her white hands. She began to play. She was deft, startlingly so. She did not fumble, but once or twice she slowed, frowning at the music. She gave the piece an eerie measured quality perhaps not suitable, but it was an interpretation. So quickly she had learned so much.

'That's very good,' he said. 'But when you misread the music, you mustn't bluff. You must stop and play it as it's written.'

'Yes, Adam,' said Ruth. And now she smiled at him.

She had smiled at Emma like that. There was no artifice, yet the smile was subtly flirtatious, sure of finding a reception.

And Adamus smiled at Ruth, a cold and quite indifferent smile, a teacher dutifully showing friendliness for a clever pupil.

Rachaela felt herself breathe, as if she had not done so for the past ten minutes. A rush of blood passed through her head.

She made herself speak.

'Ruth's very proficient after such a short time.'

'Yes,' he said, as if they had been speaking all the while, had spoken together every day for twelve years, 'it's remarkable. But I was the same. She takes it from me.'

'I take after you,' said Ruth.

'I hope not,' he said.

Ruth giggled like a happy child with a new joke.

'Play the scales now,' he said.

And Ruth played scales.

Rachaela walked away from them and sat down in one of the chairs before the hearth. She leant and stroked the cat's sleeping head. The gauntness of age had invested all of it. Easy to feel the skull beneath the skin.

So they had not infected the cat.

After the scales, Ruth played some simple pieces by Clementi. Adamus spoke to her quietly. He never corrected her while she was playing, but after, sometimes making her return and assay the piece again.

Rachaela listened to the sounds they made, and the piano, until a sort of trance had her, in which what they did seemed quite natural, as if their relationship were ordinary, or nonexistent.

Finally the lesson ended.

'Play to me,' said Ruth. 'Play the Chopin, I like that best.' She pronounced the name *Chopping*, a child's joke of her own.

Adamus began to play.

Rachaela steeled herself.

As the notes sprang round the room like flung silver daggers, she glanced at the two of them, her lover and his child.

Ruth stood at Adamus's shoulder. She did not touch

340

him. She stared at his hands, curved slightly forward like a slender branch in the breeze. Less than ever did she look like a child, in her moss-green party frock and tortoiseshell combs. She looked like a spirit, a malign fairy, the Devil's handmaiden at Adamus's shoulder.

Rachaela felt a wave of rage.

Yes, I am jealous. I have every cause to be. There is my successor.

When he stopped playing, Ruth said, 'Play the Prokofioffyev now.'

'Not now, Ruth. That's enough for tonight.'

Ruth did not remonstrate.

She twirled round and came back to the hearth, throwing herself lightly down beside the cat to stroke and caress it.

'Ruth,' Rachaela said, 'say goodnight to the cat, and then go back downstairs.'

'I'll stay here,' Ruth said.

'No,' Rachaela said, 'not tonight.'

Ruth looked up at her. She said, 'I always stay an hour after the music.'

'I told you, not tonight.'

Would Ruth obey her now? There was no reason. All the old laws were vanquished.

But Ruth got up. 'All right.'

She went back to Adamus, who sat still at the silent piano.

'Mummy says I'm to go down now.' A pause, perhaps for his contradiction. Which did not come. 'Good night.'

'Good night, Ruth.'

And Ruth bowed forward and kissed the man on the cheek.

Then she went out and down the stair, her dress slipping after her along the treads.

Rachaela heard the lower door open and close.

The cat raised its head, listened, and lay back to sleep again.

'I'm sorry to curtail your evening,' Rachaela said too harshly. 'I realize you must have a lot to say to her.'

'I have nothing to say to her,' he said. 'I teach her to play. The rest of the conversation comes from Ruth.'

'Are you defending yourself?' Rachaela said. 'You're indefensible.'

'Am I.'

'You know that you are.' She stopped, and tried to slow her breathing. 'Or have I misunderstood all of it?'

'Probably not.'

'Can it be true then, can it *really* be true, that you are to be mated to that child?'

'Mated,' he said.

'What else can it be called? Some ritualistic thing ending in the sexual act.'

'Eventually,' he said, 'presumably.'

'You're her father.'

'And her grandfather,' he said. He stood up and came back across the room to the fireplace. He stood facing her, the lamp unbearably lighting his face. 'Let's not mince words.'

'Yes, let's not. How can you contemplate such a filthy, disgusting, ludicrous act?'

'I don't contemplate it. It will simply happen sometime.'

'As it did with us. At least I was a grown woman.'

'Ruth will be a grown woman. They'll wait until she's fourteen or fifteen.'

'*They.* What *are* you, Adamus, their robot? Don't you have any say in it? Or are you just a machine?'

'Part of the mechanism of the Scarabae,' he said.

'I don't believe you accept that.'

'Of course I accept it,' he said. 'I'm here.'

Rachaela stood up also. At her feet the cat growled softly in its sleep.

'I shall take Ruth away,' Rachaela said.

'You're not strong enough,' he said, 'physically or spiritually. Ruth is part of their collective soul for good or ill.'

'You think I'll sit by and allow it?'

'You'll have no choice,' he said. 'You had power over your own life, that was all.'

'Did I? Did I, when you saddled me with that thing – that baby – I meant to abort it, flush it away.'

'But you didn't,' he said. 'Did you?'

Rachaela closed her eyes. Her weakness, her bad luck, had they truly been Scarabae reaching out to hold her to their course?

She said, 'If I'd stayed, what would have happened?'

'They would have fêted you. You'd have been the Madonna. You'd have had every care.'

'And no doctors,' said Rachaela.

'Unice and Miriam have delivered at least twenty children successfully.'

Rachaela laughed. 'Locked up in the tomb-womb of this house with two old women hauling Ruth out of me.' She thought of her hallucination in the hospital, Camillo on the beach. 'And what else? Some sort of ceremonial marriage to you, and you coming to my bedroom once every two years?'

'Something like that. They would have used us to renew the family. Very simple.'

'Very. And this is what they plan now for you and Ruth.'

'While I'm serviceable.'

'And while Ruth is able. Until it kills her.'

'It won't kill her. The family is very strong. Even you are, Rachaela.'

'Even me. The outsider. The one unincestuous birth.'

He said nothing and a wall of soundlessness rose between them.

She wanted to strike it away with her hands.

She said, 'I shall talk to Ruth. I'm going to make her understand what all this really means. Then we'll see.'

'Good luck,' he said.

'You think she won't listen. But I've lived with your child. She's interested only in herself, and what can entertain her. This is a new and fascinating game, but she'll tire of it. She won't wear it, being the brood queen of your hive.'

'Perhaps.'

'You think your Scarabae sorcery is the strongest thing of all? You're just a puppet. You have no mind. You're nothing. Their seed machine.'

'So many angry words,' he said.

The beauty of him struck inside her like a colossal chord. She longed to go to him, to lean, to lie against him. To be told this did not matter. She wanted his arms, his mouth and his body, as much as she had ever wanted them in that day and night of preposterous ecstasy. Damn Ruth, what was she – a grain of sand, a mote of dust.

But she would never let him touch her again. She would not let him have Ruth for his passionless and raging lust.

'Well, I've finished now,' she said, and she went away from him and down the stair to the door of the tower, which like Ruth she opened and closed behind her.

Two hot days passed before she found Ruth alone.

Rachaela had seen her daughter in the evenings at dinner, after which she went away to the piano lesson with Adamus, vanishing again. Rachaela had gone over the house, looked into the garden where the briars climbed the cedar tree and roses perched upon its boughs. Even into the red bedroom she had looked, and seen the window with the crimson Madonna, the tiaraed child, and the golden kings with diadems and animal faces. But Ruth was not there.

On the third day Rachaela walked out on to the heath, and Ruth was sitting by the standing stone. She wore a day dress from the turn of the century with little puffed sleeves. There was no make-up on her face and her hair was done up in a pony-tail.

Rachaela went to her and stood, letting her shadow fall into the sun-scorched grass.

Butterflies were in the tobaccoy bracken. Birds made an aerial display across the pale blue roof of the sky.

'I want to talk to you, Ruth.'

'Yes,' said Ruth.

Rachaela sat down on the grass facing her child. *Hers*. This person in the dress.

'I suppose you're enjoying yourself here.'

'Yes, thank you,' said Ruth.

'They made you very welcome. They've given you lots of presents. They let you do as you like. And no school.'

'And the piano,' said Ruth, helping her.

'And the piano of course. And Adamus.'

'He lets me call him Adam.'

'I know. Have you noticed, Ruth, that people are often kind to you, nice, when they want you to do something for them?'

Ruth looked at Rachaela. Her look was frankly speculative. And what do *you* want? She replied, 'Sometimes.'

'And that people let you down.' Rachaela waited, and thrust home the dart. 'Like Emma.'

Ruth did not flinch. Her eyes were black and impenetrable. 'Yes.'

'I want you to think about this, Ruth. The Scarabae are being nice to you because they want something.'

'They want me to stay,' said Ruth. 'I'm Adam's daughter.'

'And have they told you what they expect of you and Adamus?'

Ruth did not answer at once.

Then she said, 'They told me I'm going to be betrothed to him.'

Rachaela recoiled. She held herself level.

'Do you know what that word means? Betrothed.'

'It means bind with a promise to marry.' Ruth added, 'Anna showed me in the library, in the dictionary.'

'Do you understand what was meant?' Ruth watched her. 'That they mean you to marry him?'

'Oh yes.'

Rachaela said, too loudly, 'Daughters don't marry their fathers.'

'Yes they do. The Egyptians did.'

Rachaela cursed Miss Barrett, Mr Walker and the primary school with its unsuitable gobbets of knowledge. Or perhaps Ruth had got it from some book.

'You're not Egyptians.'

'The kings did it. The important families. To keep the bloodline pure.'

'And that's what the Scarabae told you you would be doing?'

Ruth smiled, secretively, and looked at the grass.

'Have you thought,' said Rachaela, 'about what you would have to do as his wife?' Be taken by him, broken into, forced to experience a hell of sweetness – *Don't think of it*. 'Ruth.'

'No, Mummy,' said Ruth.

'You'd have to bear his children,' said Rachaela. 'And do you know what *that* means?'

'You told me about babies.'

'All right.'

'I don't mind,' said Ruth. 'Anna explained. The line has to go on.'

'You don't mind because there's no way you can understand. My God, I can't make you realize in five minutes. It's painful and degrading, Ruth. It means your body isn't your own,' *Christ*, she thought, *I sound like Jonquil*. 'And you'll be expected to do it again and again. Do you follow what I'm saying?'

'It will be easy, Anna said.'

'Oh Anna's explained about babies too has she?'

347

'We're special,' said Ruth. 'You're different. You don't understand about *that*.'

Rachaela gathered her wits. She saw again Ruth kneeling on the floor in her shawls and lipstick, while the child Lucile snivelled on the blue bed.

'You mean this family legend about vampirism.'

'They are,' said Ruth. She corrected herself. '*We* are. There's no daylight in the house. They only go out of doors at night. Apart from Cheta and Carlo, the servants, who aren't pure Scarabae, and they have to muffle up.'

'Then why are you sitting here in the sun, Ruth?'

'I haven't changed yet.'

'And when will you change?'

'When I marry Adam.'

Ruth writhing, kicking and screaming on the black piano, Adamus on top of her, his mouth at her throat, a tiny trickle of scarlet.

'I *married* Adam. Nothing happened to me.'

'You're not like us. Your mother was a stranger.'

'Ruth, I need time with you. I want you to come back to London with me.'

'No thank you,' Ruth said, 'Mummy.'

Rachaela saw Ruth alter inside her flesh. She became concentrated, dangerous, as Rachaela had seen her once before. There was a light to the eyes, the teeth looked sharp and the fingernails long. Try to touch now, and this creature would bite and scratch. It would punch into a breast as it had when a baby, and wriggle away and get free. There was a demon in Ruth. The Scarabae demon, but given a fresh and hybrid life.

A blot of darkness on the sunlight made Rachaela turn her head.

Carlo had come out of the house and was standing, clear of the trees, without any pretence, watching them.

He wore his outdoor things, his hat and scarf and sunglasses, in the broiling heat.

Ruth turned too and jumped up.

'There's Carlo. I'm going to make an apple-pie with Maria.'

She ran towards the house, lifting up her long skirt.

She passed Carlo, who continued a moment to stare down at Rachaela on the grass, before himself turning away and back into the pines.

There was nothing else to do. She must stay. She must be their witness. That way there might be a chance.

She must stay.

He was no threat to her now.

And she would see him again.

In parting them, she would have dealings with him. The only dealings she might have.

Anna turned the key in the door of the locked room. Unice held up the lamp.

'It will be very dark.'

'We must be careful.'

The old women rustled like crisp paper.

They were all there, the women but not the men.

Rachaela stood behind them all, in her place as witness.

Ruth was beside Anna.

The lamp slid into the room and lit it crazily. It was a cave, without windows, full of stripes and bulbs of redness.

Miriam and Teresa slipped ahead into the dark and there came the noise of struck matches, little spurts of flame.

A row of candles had been ignited along the walls.

It was a neglected room. A faded magenta wallpaper appeared to be in the design of pairs of bats hanging upside down – like the graphics of Escher, other shapes seemed formed by the pale-yellow interstices. Nothing was certain. Beams poked forth in the ceiling.

The room was full of red dresses. They stood on dummies down the length and across the breadth of it.

The reds were of every depth and shade, soft and dark, coarse and transparent, like fruits, some bruised and others unripe, some left too long in the sun.

These dresses had never seen the sun.

They were old, or antique, of the styles of other centuries and other lands. They looked frail as insect wings, most of them. A few were sturdy, stuck in time. There was dust on them all.

A perfume rose from the dresses, memories of scent and flesh, through the dust.

'Come, Ruth,' said Anna. 'Look about. Several will be too large. But there are many which fitted young girls like yourself.'

Ruth went forward. In the candlelight her eyes glistened hard as jets.

If Rachaela had stayed, if she had stayed, with the child in her womb, would the Scarabae have brought her here, to choose her betrothal or her wedding dress?

Ruth paused beside a crinolined gown with huge sleeves and trailing bows, looked at it, passed on.

There were dresses like sheaths, beaded with rosy crystal. There were dresses with corseted waists and trains, and dresses with long sleeves sewn with fake red gems. Or perhaps they were real.

Ruth was half-way across the room, among the crimson pillars.

She was choosing carefully for her big day, looking at everything.

Anna had stood aside. Teresa, Unice and Miranda edged down the room after Ruth. Distracted by recollection or mere nostalgia, Alice, Anita, Sasha and Miriam wandered around the room, in their turn seeming to try to choose a gown, as maybe once they had.

Livia remained near the door. Her face contorted. She said to Rachaela, 'My Constantin,' and pressed her dry old hands to her face. It was as if she wanted to cry and could not. The rictus of pain left her slowly, and she lowered her hands, and went to a red dress, beginning to smooth its stiff sheer folds with one ringed finger.

Rachaela moved along an aisle of dresses.

Ruth had come to a standstill.

There was a rent in the ceiling above, a hole, and under it a dress posed almost alone.

It was, like the bedroom, a dress of blood. It came from a period of make-believe. The shoulders of the dummy were bare. The waist of the dress pointed like an arrow, with a line of ruby buttons to the navel. The skirt flowed, embroidered in shiny bloody thread like grapes and flowers and foliage. The ruched sleeves fell from the shoulders to the floor, and under them were other sleeves of tight red lace.

'This one,' said Ruth.

'Oh, she's chosen that one!' exclaimed Miranda. 'How lovely.'

'How beautiful she'll look,' said Teresa. 'I remember —' and fell silent.

All the women susurrated, a chorus of grasshoppers.

The skirt of the dress moved. It flaunted and bellied, as if an unseen leg had flexed beneath it.

Ruth stepped away.

She stared.

All the women stared at the dress.

And the skirt tossed again, rippled.

What was happening? Was the dress coming to life?

'No, no,' said Anna, 'no.'

She went briskly up the room. Rachaela saw her reach the dress and take up the skirt and shake it.

Suddenly a long seam burst in a puff of red smoke.

A bird flew out.

The dress had been pregnant with the bird.

It flew straight past Anna and dipped over the heads of the old women so they cried out and called.

Rachaela had never seen the Scarabae so discomposed before.

The bird rushed from wall to wall and the women screamed shrilly, warding it off with their hands which flashed with rings.

Then the bird shot suddenly upwards. It vanished into the hole in the ceiling and the beating of its wings was gone.

'The attic,' said Anna, pointing up after the bird. 'Uncle Camillo leaves the window open.'

'Will it fly out?' cried Unice.

'Will it fly away?' they asked.

'I expect it will,' said Anna. She looked at Rachaela. 'Perhaps Rachaela will go up sometime today, and see.'

'It's bad luck, a bird in the house,' said Unice.

Miranda said, 'Not for sixty years.'

'Hush,' said Anna. 'The bird's gone. Ruth. Have you chosen this one? It's just the right size.'

'There was a bird in it,' said Ruth.

The panic of the old ones had not afflicted her, but she was influenced.

'The bird has gone,' said Anna.

'I don't want it now,' said Ruth.

The old women blew towards her, statically like rags on a bush. They whispered, conceivably without words.

'Choose another,' said Anna.

'But I wanted that one.'

'Then forget the bird,' Anna was smiling and patient.

'No,' said Ruth.

Anna spread her hands and waited.

They all waited on the child-woman who was their future.

Ruth stood with her head to one side.

At last she said, 'All right, I will. This one. But the seam's torn.'

Alice said, 'I'll attend to all the seams. And Cheta will clean the dress very carefully. Especially the lace. Lace is so becoming.'

Ruth said, 'What about the veil? Will I have a veil?'

'Yes,' said Miriam, 'like a bride. A beautiful red veil.'

'And Carlo will cut red roses,' said Miranda.

'Such a special day,' said Teresa.

Ruth stood at their core, like the hub of a gradually turning wheel. She had put her back to the dress. She did not look at Rachaela.

When the candles had been blown out, they retreated from the room, to which Michael and Maria would presently come to remove the selected dummy.

Outside in the corridor the cloud of old women bore Ruth away.

Later Rachaela went up to the attic.

Within, among the chests and stands, one red dress had been stranded – the dress of Alice's mother.

She could not see the hole that led to the room below, but the window stood wide on the fierce sunlight.

Of course, they were vampires, they could not come here.

But Camillo had risen from his bed and come here and flung the window wide to attract a bird to fly into Ruth's red betrothal dress.

The bird had gone.

Rachaela stood at the window, looking across the roofs to the tower.

The sun blazed on its cone, the window glinted.

Adamus.

He had drurk her blood but he walked in the daylight. Would Ruth be disappointed when she found, after her night of metamorphosis, that the sun did not shrivel her up?

Chapter Seventeen

JUST BEFORE MIDNIGHT SCARABAE'S BETROTHED came downstairs.

She looked like a bride in Hell, in her dress of blood and the veil like melon-heart, wing-spread from its little coronet, and with two scarlet roses in her hand.

Rachaela's watch had ascertained the time, but really it was only night, the last summer light-ness compressed from the sky, the house doors open.

Lighted candles everywhere, beaded ranks of fire giving off a dense and wavering heat.

The old people had gathered in their dinner clothes, their dust and spangles. Only Rachaela in her skirt and T-shirt did not fit. She stood apart, she was only the witness.

Ruth's made-up face looked totally contained, but she shone with electricity. She was the glowing centre of the fires.

Another room had been opened up, cleaned by the servants and filled with candles and red roses on tall wooden stands.

At the far end was a table draped in red velvet, and on it a huge old book lying open. Behind the table stood Dorian in his dinner clothes and starched shirt.

In front of the table was Adamus.

To her horror, Rachaela saw that he too wore a tuxedo, a white shirt and black bow tie. He too had dressed himself as a figment of the farce. His face showed nothing and the eyes were as she recalled, dull lacquer pools without light or depth. But it was true, he was their puppet.

The Scarabae had made an aisle and Ruth walked down it and into the room.

The Scarabae moved in after her, taking up their places behind the betrothal pair, the man and the small woman-child.

Rachaela stood at the back of the room, looking across the heads of strong wire hair, and one helmed head, for Uncle Camillo had come in his armour. She and Adamus were the tallest in the room, which added to the sense of ridiculous beastliness.

Dorian unseamed his withered mouth.

'The house has come together on this night, to oversee the promising of its two children, Adamus and Ruth, to one another. This is done in the spirit of an old tradition. It is done in pledge for the house of Scarabae, in the hope that it may continue and flourish with generations.'

Rachaela's eyes dazzled from the candles. She could not follow what Dorian said, it was too distorted and nonsensical. And now he spoke in a foreign language, and after that in what was perhaps Latin.

Then Dorian put Ruth's hand into the hand of Adamus and tied them together with a white silk ribbon, an old ribbon stained along its clarity with age.

'Remember now, whatever comes, you are promised to each other before witnesses. You may take no other to you, but must keep faith until the hour of marriage and union. So are you bound.'

Ruth looked up into Adamus's face.

She smiled, cunningly.

'You must say now whether you are agreeable and will remain true to this binding. Ruth, answer first.'

'I am agreeable and will remain true,' said Ruth.

'And Adamus.'

'I am agreeable,' Adamus said, 'and will remain true.'

Dorian untied the white stained ribbon.

'Though the tie is undone, the vow is not undone. Let all here witness this.'

I witness it, Rachaela thought, *they will stay bound to one another. She will be taller when she marries him. It won't look so perverse then. Or worse perhaps.*

She thought: *What is he thinking? Is his mind a blank?*

Adamus bent and kissed Ruth on the lips, lightly. She did not close her eyes, she kept them open and drank him in.

Cheta came forward in her brooch. She carried a small cake on a plate. Adamus broke it in half and Ruth ate one half and he the other.

Michael came up with a glass of red wine. They each took a mouthful from the glass.

'Write your names in the book.'

Adamus dipped the pen and wrote, Ruth took the pen and wrote after him.

Has she put Ruth Day from force of habit?

But Dorian did not query the entry.

Adamus and Ruth, hand in hand, turned away from the table. Ruth gave Adamus the second rose; he put it in his buttonhole.

How terrifying they looked, like erroneous models on a wedding cake, the cold sheer bridegroom and his tiny sprite of a scarlet bride.

Anna stepped up to Ruth and gave her a small package.

Adamus released Ruth's hand.

She undid the gift in her usual neat, greedy way.

A rhinestone locket – it surely could not be diamonds. Ruth held out the locket to Adamus, and he fastened it around her throat.

The others approached Ruth. They gave her gifts: earrings, and books, and lengths of material, ornaments and objects of coloured glass.

Only I have nothing to give. Rachaela imagined herself as the thirteenth fairy godmother, stepping forward to present the gift of death.

Did she want Ruth dead in this moment? Was it really so bad, this idiotic ceremony and the little girl dressed like a bride?

The little girl piled the table with her trophies. Now and then she showed them to Adamus, the best trophy of all. He gravely assented.

Now Camillo was going forward. His present too was wrapped. Ruth tore off the wrapping eagerly. She was acquisitive. She ignored his figure in its armour.

Out of the wrapping came a strange metal-and-wood contraption.

Adamus said, 'Be careful,' and leaning forward took the thing away from her. It was a mousetrap.

Camillo giggled.

358

Anna said clearly, 'Uncle Camillo is very naughty, Ruth. Don't mind him.'

'Uncle Camillo,' said Ruth.

She looked at him with her jet stone eyes. Her face was pinched a little. He had tried to spoil the betrothal.

Anita came to Ruth and gave her an embroidered cushion of red flowers.

When the presentation was over, the Scarabae and their betrothed went into the dining room.

There had been no dinner earlier, now the table was laden like a medieval feast, with pies and roasts, chickens and joints gained no doubt from the supermarket in the village.

The candles filled this room too, and the roses fumed.

Ruth sat at one end of the table, Adamus at the other. Rachaela found herself seated between Stephan and Dorian. A place had been laid for Camillo, but he had absented himself. There were more women than men, and they filled Adamus's end of the table.

Selections were taken from the ready-carved joints and from the pies and dishes of vegetables.

The Scarabae ate with good appetite. Rachaela glanced to see what Adamus did, but he was eating too. She had never seen the phenomenon before. He ate slowly and indifferently, yet the food vanished from his plate. And Ruth ate carnally.

Repelled, Rachaela picked at her dish. She would not celebrate by eating.

Would there be speeches and an old champagne? Wine was served, and no one got up to speak. Yet it was the betrothal banquet. What did Ruth expect

as its end? Now and then her eyes would go to
Adamus. Her eyes were gluttonous. She anticipated
something, and there would be nothing. Perhaps it
had not been made clear to her. This was the climax
of the night.

When Adamus rose, Ruth looked up expectantly.

'Good night,' Adamus said. 'Good night, Anna.
Good night, Ruth.'

'Must you go so early?' Anna said.

'I've stayed two hours,' he said.

Anna bowed her head, and Adamus left the
table of the fairytale feast and walked out of the
room.

Ruth half got to her feet.

'Shall I—'

'No, Ruth. Stay and finish your supper.'

Ruth sank back with a peculiar glimmer in her eyes.
She forked up her chicken, but some of the vibrancy
had gone from her.

The meal went on for a long time.

Rachaela was heartily sick of it, longing to escape as
he had, but knowing she must stay, to watch.

Finally the fruits and sweetmeats had been picked
bare to stones and crusts. The company rose.

Ruth poised like a scarlet mayfly.

'Am I to go up now?'

'No,' said Anna. 'It's very late. I'm sure that soon
you'll want to sleep.'

Ruth's face was heavy, shadows under the eyes.

'No.'

'You don't feel it yet, but you will. After all this
excitement.'

'And the dress,' said Alice, 'the dress must be taken
off and put back on its dummy.'

'I want to keep the dress,' said Ruth. 'I want to wear it.'

'Oh no, no. Whoever heard of such a thing? Such dresses are kept only for the special day. You wouldn't want to spoil the lovely dress?' Alice fluttered in astonishment.

Ruth looked at Alice and abruptly radiated a beam of pure hatred.

Of course, she had been baulked. No Adamus, and now no dress. They were stripping her rôle from her. Another child would have thrown a tantrum, but this child had learned early that to make a fuss gained nothing.

Whatever else, Alice cringed before Ruth's eyes. She turned to Peter and besought him, 'It's always been done. She doesn't know. Do you remember when Jessica tore her dress and it had to be stitched as she wore it, sewn on around her, and then cut again to get it off.'

Peter nodded.

Ruth said, 'It's only an old dress.'

She shocked them. They were used to seeing her as a child but receiving the replies of a responsive adult. They did not know what to do.

Rachaela said, 'All good things come to an end.'

Ruth glanced at Rachaela. She had never looked for anything good from Rachaela, and so did not hate her for providing nothing good.

Everyone left the table, and some of the old women took Ruth away to denude her of her finery.

It was three in the morning.

In the drawing room Rachaela approached Anna.

'You should have reassured Ruth. She'll see him tomorrow, for the usual piano lesson.'

Anna embroidered a peacock.

'But she won't, Rachaela. He won't be teaching her any more. Jack has repaired and re-tuned the piano in the music room. Ruth can practise there.'

'So he's tired of the novelty already,' said Rachaela. A warm pain lit up the centre of her body.

'He doesn't communicate easily,' said Anna, as she had once said before. 'The last weeks have been something of a strain for him.'

'You used him to seduce her,' Rachaela said, 'not literally perhaps, but fundamentally all the same.'

'Ruth will have to be patient.'

'For three years? Ruth is eleven. Three years will seem a very long time.'

'Ruth is Scarabae.'

'So you keep saying.'

'It is a fact.'

Rachaela turned and went out of the room. The first thread had been pulled from the scarlet tracery. Now all the rotten fabric might come undone.

Rachaela the witness watched Ruth the betrothed.

The days grew very hot and the shut house was like an oven, burning colours coming in from its windows, an airless bath of dyes.

The Scarabae went to ground in their dyed rooms, lying in their chairs, hunted by their enemy the sun.

Ruth was on the heath a lot, and sometimes down by the sea, for she had at some moment discovered the steps to the beach. Rachaela watched her gathering treasures from the water's edge, paddling in the waves, or seated under the standing stone drawing intently. Once or twice the great black cat was with her, sleeping by her side. Ruth showed a passion for the cat, predictable and unique. On one occasion she had garlanded its neck with daisies. She was like a lost maenad. The troop of bacchantes had moved on and left her behind.

At night, occasionally, Ruth played the piano in the music room.

She played angrily and with a quantity of wrong notes.

On most evenings after dinner she deserted those Scarabae in the drawing room, and went away to her bedroom presumably to paint or read. Did Anna give her books? She had left all her own behind.

The tempo of Ruth's life was wrong. She had been accustomed to a routine which she herself might break, in truancy. But now there was no routine but idleness, and nowhere to play truant from or to.

The house had perhaps been enough at first, but then she had had Adamus. Now Adamus was denied her, and the house, not seen through his gleam, palled.

Rachaela watched this happen, she watched Ruth change. A stillness was coming over her. She was growing bored.

One night Ruth said to Anna, 'Can I go to the town?'

'The town? Oh, it's a very long way.'

Familiar conversation.

This time Stephan interposed. 'There's nothing in the town.'

'Shops,' said Ruth.

'There are shops now in the village.'

'She can go with Cheta and Carlo.'

'The walk's too long,' said Ruth. She was a child of buses and streets. She did not appear to want the wilds of the heath, empty of gravestones, burger bars and Woolworth's.

'Can I go to the cinema?' said Ruth.

Rachaela had sometimes taken her, and sometimes perhaps she had got in by herself.

'It's too far, Ruth,' said Anna, 'too far for you to go.'

Ruth looked at Rachaela, but Rachaela did not help her.

'There's nothing to do here,' said Ruth.

'You have your drawing and your music,' said Anna, 'and Alice was teaching you how to knit.'

Ruth was silent. She stared at Anna a long time, but Anna went on placidly with her embroidering, and Stephan stared into the space where the fire had been in winter.

Rachaela could suggest to Anna that she and Ruth take a hire car into the town, but Anna would refuse that, predicting that Rachaela would kidnap the child.

At some time some plan would have to be made, for Ruth was turning now, away from them. After all Ruth might have to make the night-walk across the heath.

How long before all the new toys paled? Surely already.

And the Scarabae had altered too. They no longer came to dinner in droves, but only in ones or twos, or only Anna and Stephan came. They no longer gazed on Ruth so intently. To the Scarabae-mind, Ruth had been fixed. She was safe and sound. The betrothal had set her in the precious mould, and now, although she was the apple of their eye, they were free to forget her. They looked at her, when they troubled to, in a fond pleased manner. But she was no longer the star about which they grouped.

Ruth had lost her princess status, now she was only a child in a house.

And the prince, he was gone too.

Had Ruth tried the tower door? Had she located the second door below the annexe and tried that too, to no avail? Had she written him some childish note and torn it up?

Rachaela followed Ruth.

She followed her along the winding corridors, past the furnaces of windows which did not open and which boiled the heat with ruby panes and scalding blue, so that to have their reflected lights touch one was to be scorched.

She waited at doorways, while Ruth moved around black burning rooms, thick with the honey-like smell of heated damp.

She observed Ruth try to force, as she had done, the locked doors. And watched her enter the room-worlds of the Scarabae: Alice in her sitting chamber; Eric carving a mask in a chamber whose garnet-petal window was screened by a milky blind. And Ruth held wool for Alice, and she attended while Eric carved. And later she came upon Peter and Dorian in the morning room under the vineyard Jezebel; even the green looked volcanic, and they were playing chess.

Ruth said, 'Will you teach me to play?'

Dorian, who had betrothed her to the dark prince, said presently, 'Perhaps sometime. Not now. We're busy now.' And Peter added, vaguely, 'There's a good girl.'

Rachaela heard Ruth listen to the tiresome sounds of the house, which worried at the ears like crickets.

The clicks and rasps and shifts, the rising and falling of the sea that seemed to infiltrate the skull, turning it to one huge shell.

She pursued Ruth down into the kitchen, and in the cabbage-leaf gloom where it was so hot it was hard to breathe, three rabbits lay in their fur and stank.

Ruth looked at the rabbits. Perhaps for the first time she equated meat with a living animal. There was blood.

'Does the cat catch them?'

'The cat doesn't catch anything now,' said Cheta. 'Carlo pots them with a catapult. One flick and the neck's broken. Do you want to make the pie with me?'

'No, thank you,' said Ruth.

She minded the blood, evidently. It was not human.

Outside, Ruth tried to draw Adamus. This was clear from her struggles, the pages she tore up or crumpled. She could not capture him.

Rachaela watched Ruth lying in her blood-red bed, her agile hands playing her own body, the notes of its young and partly incoherent desire. In imagination what did Ruth see? Her father-lover sweeping her up, a night-ride, formless – for she did not know enough – consolidated by dreams and images from books, brought to a mad completion in the dark, for her body knew.

Her body was ready. And her body would have to wait. Ruth would have to wait. Three years, four. Anna had explained.

All this Rachaela saw, following Ruth in her mind by day and by night.

Did mother and daughter work upon themselves jointly, each reaching the pitch of orgasm, the silent scream, to fall backwards into morbid loneliness, as one?

Maybe Ruth lay chastely in her bed.

Maybe Dorian was teaching her to play chess, or Stephan, or George.

Maybe she still made pies in the kitchen.

Rachaela had found only one drawing of Adamus blowing on the heath. The face bore a likeness but the body had not been able to form. The body had defeated Ruth.

Below on the beach, Camillo was cavorting, his white hair flopping like a flag. He was like a dog, running at the sea, and away.

Further off, above, Rachaela could see Ruth and the black cat. The cat rushed from place to place, perhaps chasing butterflies. From here it looked young and sleek, and Ruth ran after it to and fro in her 1910 dress, now and then clapping her hands.

Looking back, Rachaela saw Camillo was climbing up from the shore.

She watched him manage the perilous steps without a slip.

He glanced up and winked at her.

He came on to the heath. He saw Ruth.

'Ugh,' said Camillo. He spat on the grass. 'That child thing.'

'Why did you give her a mousetrap?'

'To catch a rat,' said Camillo. 'Did I?'

'Ruth is the hope of the family,' said Rachaela. 'But she's no longer their darling. She won't wait for years.'

'Sugar for the horse,' said Camillo. 'Poor horse. All those miles and not even an apple.'

Rachaela stared away at Ruth. The cat had lain down among the gorse tangles. Ruth kneeled there, stroking it.

'She looks like a normal little girl with her pet,' said Rachaela. 'From here.'

'Vixen,' said Camillo, 'the Devil's beast. Do you know what she's done?'

'No, Camillo. What?'

'She has a hammer. She went to the room with the dresses and broke the lock. She took out her red dress. She keeps it in her red room. I saw.'

Rachaela thought of the hammer missing from the attic, the hammer with which she had tried to break the window of Adamus's tower.

'She likes dressing up,' said Rachaela.

'The betrothal dress,' said Camillo.

Ruth sat by the cat. She seemed to be talking to it, animatedly, as she had talked to Emma when she was . . . a child.

'The cauldron's boiling,' said Camillo.

Rachaela gazed at him.

'What will happen?'

'Poor horsey and no sugar.'

'What country were you in?' she asked. 'The horse, the woods and the snow, the burning town.'

'Russia,' he said.

'I thought it might be. What was the year?'

'1703.'

'Now you tell me the truth,' she said, 'and I believe you.'

'That's not the truth,' said Camillo, 'only an answer. Better learn the difference.'

'1703,' she said, 'so now you would be almost three hundred years old.'

'Unbearable,' he said. 'I remember my childhood and my youth. But all the rest of it is nothing.'

'Will Ruth,' she said, 'live as long as you?'

'If you believe it. Longer.'

'No I was wrong,' she said, 'I don't believe it at all.'

Anna had come to dine, no one else, besides Rachaela and Ruth.

Cheta cut and served the pie.

Ruth began to eat. Suddenly she spat the mouthful back on to her plate – Rachaela was reminded of Camillo spitting on the grass – and threw down her knife and fork.

'It's bad,' said Ruth. 'It's horrible.'

Rachaela, not eating, watched.

Anna hesitated.

'Cheta,' she said, 'when was the rabbit caught?'

'Yesterday morning, Miss Anna.'

'There's no reason the meat should go off in that time. It's better for a little waiting.'

'It's *bad*,' repeated Ruth savagely.

'Don't be a silly girl,' said Anna. 'Do you think I would allow you to eat anything that was tainted? See, I'm eating it.'

'You'd eat anything,' said Ruth.

Anna said, reasonably, 'Of course I would *not*, Ruth.'

'Yes you would. You drink blood. You go out in the twilight and catch things and drink their blood.'

Anna looked startled, offended.

'Whatever put such a foolish idea—'

'You're vampires. All the Scarabae.'

369

'Nonsense, Ruth. You don't know what you're saying.'

'You drink blood,' Ruth said again, obstinately, almost proudly.

Anna was like something in a net. Her usual composure had deserted her as it had momentarily when Rachaela had spoken of sexual things. Obviously the drinking of blood *was* sexual, it had nothing to do with food. Probably Anna had never done such a thing. Adamus was the one in whom the sorcerous gene had surfaced.

'You don't know what you're saying,' said Anna. 'I would never have expected such behaviour of you.'

'You drain the rabbits in the kitchen! Old Dorian chews the bones! Alice knits with bones!' sang Ruth, standing up in a sort of frenzy, 'Livia makes bone necklaces. Jack has brown stains on his hands, they're old blood-stains, and George rinses his teeth in blood.'

'Ruth. That's enough—'

'Miriam and Unice drink blood in teacups and pretend it's tea. Stephan drinks blood before dinner. When you die you'll all go to hell.'

'Ruth!' Anna's voice rose with a cold and hard authority, and Ruth's skittishness faltered. 'You are a naughty and ignorant little girl. You may leave your dinner, since you don't like it, and go up to your room.'

'I want to see Adamus!' shouted Ruth. In her voice there was a raw shrill edge. Never had Rachaela heard a refusal bring Ruth so near hysteria, but then never had Rachaela refused Ruth anything she so much wanted.

'When Adamus is ready, he will see you,' said Anna, 'but I doubt he would want to see such a nasty, foul-tongued little brat.'

'Yes he would,' Ruth said. 'He likes me. He wants to marry me.'

'Forget about that,' said Anna, 'I have told you, you're too young for marriage and must wait. Tonight's outburst has proved it.'

'You're bad,' said Ruth, as she had said of the rabbit. Her face, like Anna's, was steely now. 'You stop him from seeing me.'

'He doesn't want to see you. He has his own affairs to attend to. You are a child, Ruth, and must act as one. Go to your room as I told you to.'

Ruth moved away from the table. She glanced once, without any emotion, at Rachaela. Rachaela might have been another furnishing. Ruth said, 'I'll go to my room, but you're still bad. You're wicked and you'll go to hell.'

Anna rose like ice and darkness.

Ruth went out of the room.

Anna sat down and sipped from her water glass. She said to Rachaela, 'You have never curbed her.'

'Yes,' said Rachaela, 'but not her spirit. It's that you'll have to fight now.'

'I shall have to fight no one. She'll see sense.'

'There is no sense,' Rachaela said. 'She wants her father, her lover-husband. You'll have to produce him for her or you'll have trouble.'

'I'm not his keeper.'

'Oh, but you are. You and Scarabae. You can make Adamus do what you want. But not Ruth.'

'We shall see.'

Rachaela shrugged. She did not touch the rabbit-pie.

Anna ate in silence.

Should Rachaela take the opportunity, go to the blood bedroom and confront Ruth now? No, for Ruth was not yet ripe. Things were grim but not yet grim enough. Ruth must come to hate Adamus before Rachaela could get a grip on her, subtract her, whisk her away.

*

In the morning Rachaela woke with a strange tension in her body, as if she had lain all night like a coiled spring, awaiting some event.

She bathed and dressed, and went down without breakfast, through the empty drawing room and dining room and out through the conservatory, bursting with huge yellow and maroon flowers, into the garden. In the morning light the dark yew tree was sprinkled with lemon tufts, the green poplar glittered. The cedar looked blue, and on fire with the climbing roses. The oaks were closed with greenness. Rachaela heard the insistence of the sea, too loud now to be a voice in the head.

By the moon dial, the black cat was lying curled on the grass and Ruth knelt beside it. She did not touch the cat. Hearing Rachaela's step, the girl raised her head.

'He won't wake up,' she said.

Rachaela looked at the cat. There was no looseness of relaxation in its posture, it appeared hard and stiff. A low hot wind went by, and lifted the long fur like a fringe.

She walked over to the cat and touched its head and back. The body was vacant.

'I'm sorry, Ruth. I think it's dead.'

Ruth said, 'No.'

'I'm sorry. I think it was very old. I remember it when I was here before. It's died in its sleep, very gently.'

'I don't want it to be dead.'

'No, I know. It was a lovely cat.'

'I don't want it,' said Ruth. She began to stroke the cat roughly, fiercely. 'Wake up.'

Rachaela left her, and went in search of Carlo. She found him out of doors in his mufflers and sunglasses, not far off, weeding around the perimeter of the grass. Perhaps he had been keeping an eye on them, Ruth and she together.

'Carlo, Ruth's found the cat and I'm afraid it's dead.'

Carlo straightened up.

He left his hoe and trowel and went across the lawn and around the trees to Ruth. Rachaela followed. She remembered him coming like that, unspeaking, for Sylvian.

Carlo bent over the cat and prodded it carefully.

'He's asleep,' said Ruth. Carlo did not speak, but he picked the cat up by the scruff of its neck, then let the head fall again. 'Don't,' said Ruth.

Rachaela said, 'He can't feel it now.' She added, 'They may burn the body. The Scarabae burn their dead.'

Ruth flung herself over the cat.

'No! No! Don't you dare burn him.'

Rachaela said to the unspeaking Carlo, 'Will you bury the cat, Carlo, please.'

'Not yet,' cried Ruth.

'It's very hot,' said Rachaela. 'He's been lying here all night.' She said, despising herself, the euphemisms, 'He's not here now, Ruth. He must have got so tired and sore, just sleeping all the time, but now he's free.'

'Where is he?' said Ruth harshly.

'I don't know.'

'At school they said everything that dies goes to heaven.'

'Maybe he's there, then.' Rachaela loathed herself.

'Except wicked things. They go to hell. Goats go to hell. He was their cat. He'll go to hell.'

'Maybe hell isn't so bad after all,' said Rachaela, rather facetiously.

Carlo had gone off, possibly to get a spade.

Ruth stood up. 'He mustn't do it till I come back. Make him wait, Mummy.'

'All right.'

Ruth sprang away.

She returned in the red dress of her betrothal, and Carlo, kept waiting by Rachaela, buried the cat beneath the funeral yew. Ruth stood at the graveside in her scarlet, crying. Rachaela had not seen her cry since babyhood. They were intensely physical, agonized tears, ending in thick hiccups of pain. Rachaela could not console her, there was no mechanism left for it. At last the spade had covered up the cat, and Carlo went away, and Ruth stood weeping at the graveside, twisting the antique red skirt in her hands, uncomforted and desolate, a figure from Greek tragedy.

Chapter Eighteen

DURING THE AFTERNOON, RACHAELA LAY on her bed under the mosaic of the window. She was so hot she could not bear to move. She wondered if Ruth had gone to the lunch served in the dining room, as she usually did. Rachaela herself could not fancy food in the heat, though once she had rung for Cheta, and Michael had come, and presently brought her a glass of water. They did not keep orange juice, not even for Ruth, let alone the soft fizzy drinks that had cluttered Rachaela's fridge.

The sight of Ruth sobbing by the grave of the dead cat stayed in her mind.

Something would happen now.

Perhaps Ruth would even come to the room. 'Mummy, I don't like it here any more.'

Rachaela made plans for the journey, the flight, as she had before. Her thoughts did not go past the moment when she should get Ruth on to the London train.

In London something would have to be done.

She did not want Ruth or the burden of Ruth, but she did not want Ruth to usurp her place with

Adamus. If she took Ruth away, she would owe her something, and how would she pay it? A sort of different panic lay in London.

She would consider it when they got there, when they were out of this madness and had merely their own to contend with.

The afternoon sweltered and dragged.

Something would happen at dinner, if not before.

They ate very late now, waiting out the going of the summer sun.

If only she could shield herself from the blazing window. The serpent in his armour on her body like burning bricks, his hand holding the apple flaming at her groin. And here she had lain with the Devil . . . Don't think of it. She thrust it from her mind.

The clocks ticked. She drowsed.

Would the door open on Ruth?

It did not.

What was Ruth doing?

Rachaela slept.

The broiling afternoon was almost over when she roused. The window had sunk to leaden shades, its whites yellowed like ivory. Her head throbbed. She took a couple of paracetamol and went out to run herself a cool bath.

In the passage an odd new shadow fell upon her. She looked up. The window of Cain and Abel, softening in the westered light, had an addition of blackness. Across the lower panes, over the grapes and wheat below the altar, a black cross had been painted.

Which of the Scarabae had done it? What new process of obscuration was afoot?

She went into the bathroom and ran cold water in the bath, the cross hanging over her mind like a cloud.

After she had soaked herself in coolness for half an hour she dressed reluctantly and returned to the bedroom, and the cross threw down its black diagonals on to the carpet as she passed.

Before all daylight had died something made her go out again, along the corridor, and back, turning into other highways. There were crosses elsewhere drawn on the window panes regardless, over the faces of figures, always low down.

She went to the landing, and above the stairs the prince at the wedding was undisturbed, but this window was placed high up. The urns above the door were similarly untouched.

When the light had gone and she heard Michael come to see to the lamp in the passage, she went out.

'Michael, have you seen the windows?'

'Yes, Miss Rachaela.'

But Michael evinced nothing. What the Scarabae did, they did, as with Sylvian and the library. On impulse, Rachaela went to the library then. A lamp burned on the table by the globe, nothing seemed changed. Rachaela moved to the north wall and took out a book. It was pristine and legible.

Rachaela turned. A book lay on the table, face up and open.

Two lines had been ruled exactly across each page, in the shapes of two crosses.

All the previous pages had been crossed. The ebony ruler lay ready, and the pen had been wet, had left a drop of ink on the table.

Rachaela felt a curious excited fear.

She came out of the library, retraced her steps and went down to the hall.

No Scarabae were about. How quiet the house was, and how loud the sea.

The lights shone in the drawing room.

Rachaela went towards the room slowly. Probably only Anna had come down. Anna the matriarch, Adamus's mother almost certainly, the mouthpiece of the Scarabae.

Rachaela was reluctant to enter the drawing room.

She hung back, looking for Cheta, Maria . . . but they had been there perhaps half an hour before, to see to the lights. Michael would come soon to serve the drinks. Was Stephan in the room . . . and Ruth . . . Ruth would not be there.

Rachaela walked into the drawing room.

She looked at the room carefully. The fine furniture in its extra years of dust, the glowing oases of polished tables, the chess game, still going on, the sofas and chairs drawn to the white marble fireplace of pillars and shields.

Anna lay on the carpet before the fireplace.

She seemed to have fallen from a chair, for her embroidery was scattered on it, the coloured silks bleeding over.

Anna lay very decorously, her dark skirts arranged and her hands by her sides. Her head was turned a little to her right and on her forehead was a vivid mark like a splash of red and purple paint.

Something protruded from her left breast.

Rachaela moved forward and stared at this thing nonsensically, until all at once it dawned upon her that it was the rounded head of a steel knitting needle.

It had been struck home with such force that only the floor at Anna's back had stopped it.

Anna's face was stupefied, almost tranquil, but her mouth had come open in the way that Sylvian's had done.

Rachaela heard a little soft noise behind her, and then a violent crash of breaking glass. A wild animal wail broke forth, like that of something caught in a trap.

She turned and saw Maria, who had dropped the silver tray of decanters and bottles, breaking most of them. The wreckage lay bloody on the floor. Maria howled, but only once, then she ran from the room.

Rachaela felt sick. The walls tilted and righted themselves. Anna was dead. Anna had been killed.

And all Rachaela could do was stand here, perhaps guiltily, looking over and over at the stigma of a blow on Anna's forehead and the needle sticking up from her breast.

The others came in quietly. They shuffled in from their nooks and crevices. The Scarabae. No one else screamed. Once or twice there was a muffled little cry. Rachaela did not turn round to see. She felt herself transfixed. Was it just that she was like them?

Finally someone came past her, and it was Stephan, who went and stood over Anna, looking down at her and making strange aimless motions with his hands, as if smoothing out waves of air.

Then Carlo came and lifted Anna and put her on a sofa.

There was no blood on the carpet. The needle had plugged the wound it made, the mark on the forehead had scarcely bled.

The Scarabae pressed round Anna on the sofa,

moving past Rachaela as if she were a chair. They did not suspect her, then.

She found herself counting them, toting up their names, Livia, Anita, Unice, Miriam, Jack, Eric, George and Teresa, Sasha, Miranda, and Stephan. And there Cheta and Maria like blind ghosts, and Carlo and Michael. And Anna.

Stephan said, 'Must have struck her first, and then when she fell, done it then.'

'Alice's needle,' said Miranda. 'Size five.'

'How?' said George.

'Struck her with the hammer. Drove it home with the hammer,' said Jack.

'Thought out,' said Miriam.

Sasha said, 'Walked towards her with the needle in one hand and the hammer hidden in the other.'

'In that red dress,' said Unice, 'the betrothal dress. And Anna would have said, You mustn't wear that dress.'

'And then she struck her,' said Miranda.

'Look how direct the blow is,' said Teresa. 'She knew what she did.'

'Do you remember Uncle Camillo,' said Miranda in a high and quavering voice, 'how he struck her down with his fist that night and drank all her blood?'

'Hush,' said the old voices.

'This is bad enough,' said George.

'Let the past lie,' said Stephan. And then, 'Anna, Anna.'

'Is she quite dead?' asked Miranda.

'Dead,' said Stephan.

His eyes came up and met Rachaela's. Stephan, but not his eyes, was dazed. The eyes peeled layers from Rachaela's face.

'Your daughter,' said Stephan, 'did this to Anna.'

'You don't know that,' Rachaela said. She knew, herself. 'Any one of us could have done it.'

'But none of us would have done it. Even you would not. Murder is there in us but comes out only in a few.'

'Like Camillo,' said Rachaela. 'You talked about Camillo. He's killed before? Why not now?'

'This isn't Camillo. Camillo doesn't care enough to kill any more. But she is young and wilful.'

'We must find her,' Sasha said.

And they grouped together like Anna's hidden blood gathering.

'She'll hide,' said Unice.

'But the house is ours,' said Jack. 'Where can she hide that we won't find her?'

'*We must tell Adamus.*'

It was Miriam who said this. The others raised their heads like night creatures snuffing prey or a foe.

'Yes . . . Adamus,' said Stephan. He turned and looked at Michael. 'Go into the tower. Tell him.'

Michael took a lamp, and moved at once away through the room, out under the archway.

Rachaela found that she followed Michael.

Something in her tried to hold her back, but did not succeed. None of the others had eyes for her.

As she would have expected, Michael climbed the stairs, and turned into the corridor with the Salome annexe. Rachaela walked a few paces behind him. He did not say anything to her, or even act as if she were there.

They passed below the gory window, the Baptist's danced-with head now black, descended the steps and went down the passage to the door.

Michael produced a key and unlocked the door.

He went up the stair inside the tower, and Rachaela went after him.

Her heart drummed.

In the upper room Adamus was standing beside the piano, as if waiting for them, for Michael.

Perhaps, through the intervening walls, he had heard Maria's scream, and this had primed him. Had Anna made no outcry?

He wore black in readiness for Anna's death.

'Mr Adamus,' said Michael, 'something—'

'Anna's been murdered,' Rachaela said. She struck home with the words like Ruth with her hammer and needle.

Adamus did not react. Then his whole face seemed to melt and come together again.

'Michael,' he said.

'Yes, Mr Adamus, Miss Anna's been killed.'

'They say it's your child,' said Rachaela. 'Ruth.'

'How?' he said, just as George had done.

Michael bowed his head.

Rachaela said, 'She hit her with a hammer and then staked her through the breast. It's the way she's been taught that you kill a vampire.'

Adamus turned and walked to the fireplace. He had turned his back to them.

'Thank you, Michael,' he said.

Michael moved about and left the room. His blindman's eyes showed nothing.

Adamus said softly, 'And is it Ruth?'

'Probably. They seem to think so.'

He shouted: 'She's yours!'

'And you're her father,' she said coldly.

He swung round from the mantelpiece and his

whole person had changed. He burned with a white fury that was quite terrifying, banked, controlled, lethal.

'Anna was your mother,' Rachaela said.

'It doesn't matter to you.'

He came forward and she threw herself out of his way. He went by her and down the stair.

When the noiseless radioactive thunder of his passing had stilled, Rachaela ran after him, through the door and down the stair.

So the Scarabae hunted Ruth through the house.

Upstairs, downstairs, and in my lady's chamber . . .

Cheta had brought keys, and where a door was locked they unlocked it.

They did not find Ruth.

They found paintings smeared with red crosses.

They found Alice.

She was in a pale bedroom behind the pale sitting room. She lay on the pale bed in a pastel afternoon dress with another of the needles, size five, implanted in the left side of her bosom. No other blow had been necessary, perhaps Alice had been asleep. Her eyes had opened however, they were full of wonder.

Adamus shut Alice's eyes.

Later, in the room with the angel window of blue and yellow, they found Dorian and Peter.

The blow to Peter's head was from behind, there was a great deal of blood. Dorian had been struck between the eyes. Both were rolled on the floor, side by side, beneath their chess game, decorously, and the steel needles pinned them to the carpet.

Dorian had not, it seemed, died immediately. His left arm was outslung and his face constricted. She must have been very quick and unexpected, her blows *one*, *two*, like that. Who knew how strong they were, these ancient men? But then Ruth was strong, too. She was Scarabae.

They searched the house like a pack of silent dogs. Almost silent.

Miranda said, 'Where did Uncle Camillo hide?'

Jack said, 'He didn't hide. He came out and told us. What he'd done.'

'No,' said George.

Adamus said clearly, 'Ruth isn't Camillo.'

There were no other dead ones to find, for now they had all been accounted for. Save Camillo.

Rachaela moved behind them.

She was numb, afraid. She had known that Alice, Dorian and Peter, missing from below, were also dead.

Through the long hot afternoon, this was what Ruth had been doing, in her blood-red dress. And in the evening, after the lighting of the lamps, Anna.

She could have killed me, too. But Rachaela was nothing to Ruth; Rachaela was not a vampire.

Their glamour had turned rotten for Ruth. Ruth was no longer the vampire princess, but the vampire hunter. Each time she struck them down, she proved that they were real—

The blue rooms and the brown rooms, the yellow room like an autumn leaf – they did not find Camillo. To Ruth's bedroom they went, Adamus leading the way. With lamps and candles. But Ruth was not found.

Why did they think she was hiding in the house? Because they themselves would have gone to earth here. They knew Ruth. Even what she had done. Themselves in a distorting mirror.

Had they ostracized Camillo all these years, these hundreds of years, for his obscure and disgusting crime. Rachaela had said to him: *You believed you were vampires because someone told you that too.*

She knew Ruth had not gone near Camillo.

She *knew*. Did she then know where Ruth was hiding?

Yes.

Rachaela knew and perhaps all of them knew, this search being only some ritual they performed among the black windows Ruth had smeared with crosses, and under the carvings, the paintings and painted mirrors which had lipstick crosses like blood.

And now they were here, and Cheta took out the key, and put it away again, for the lock of the door had been broken.

Adamus flung the door wide.

And there again, in the prancing lamplight and candle flash was the mildewy paper of bats, and the countless red gowns upon their stands.

The Scarabae stood in the doorway, muted, and put their old dry hands up to their lips and throats and on each other's shoulders.

It was as if they could not enter.

But Adamus went in.

As if he knew it all, had been told of the scene, as perhaps he had, the bird hiding in the skirt of the gown.

He strode forward, and as he passed the dresses he thrust at them and sent them spinning. He was the centre of a red whirlwind, and as they thudded down their gauzes shattered and crimson smoulders and sprays of beads burst up from them. He the wind and they the red sea, parting.

The Scarabae women gave tiny cries, as some of them had done on finding Anna and Alice, Peter and Dorian. It was another sort of death.

But Adamus came to the dress in the corner, a dress with a full skirt, a train.

He did not push the dress over.

He reached out and delicately pleated up the material, ounces of rose satin that crushed together in his hand.

And there at the heart of the dress, like a child in a flower in a fairy tale, was Ruth.

She was crouched very small in her garment of blood, darker and richer than her hiding place. Her black hair spilled round her. There was no blood on her that was visible and her hands were empty.

She turned her head like a snake, looked up and saw Adamus standing above her. And then she smiled, the sweetest smile Rachaela had ever seen upon her face. And the face, always that of a hobgoblin, broke into beauty like a star.

'I hoped it would be you,' Ruth said. 'I thought it would be. Adam,' she said, 'they tried to keep us apart.' Like a heroine in some third-rate book.

Very gently, almost daintily, he reached further into the dress, and with both hands he lifted her out.

And Ruth, seeing only him, put up the star of her face to be kissed.

Adamus transferred her to his left hand. He held her by a grip upon the waist of her dress, up in the air.

And then he struck her with his right hand, across the face and neck, a blow that should have smashed her in pieces.

His own blow tore her out of his grip and the bodice of the red dress ripped and came away and Ruth flew backwards to fall upon the floor.

She lay there, partly stunned, and the torn away bodice had left bare her breasts, which were white and perfect with buds for nipples, and now a tiny thread of scarlet spilled there, not from the dress but from the corner of her mouth. And for a moment Ruth looked, as she lay there, the flawless image of the media vampire, before her pale face turned puce on one side and began to swell.

'Get up,' Adamus said.

'No,' Ruth said through her thickening lips. 'You'll only do it again.'

'Get up,' he said, 'and face them.'

So then Ruth got up, and holding one arm across her breasts, she stared at the Scarabae.

She stared and they stared back at her.

They did not ask her if she had done it, or why. She did not deny anything or boast of anything. All their faces were the faces of icons. Something was conveyed between them perhaps, without look or word.

The silence was very long.

When Rachaela looked at Adamus, his face too had become like theirs. He left Ruth where she stood and came towards the doorway. And all of them parted to let him by.

Only Rachaela caught at his arm.

'*No*, Adamus. You can't go – what will they do?'

'Take your hand off me,' he said. 'Don't force me to make you do it.'

Her hand fell and he went by her and away into the dark of the corridor.

She said to the Scarabae loudly, 'What will you do?'
And she was frightened, but it seemed for herself not
Ruth. '*Stephan* – what will you do?'

Stephan said, 'We must confine her. That was what
was always done.'

Miranda said, 'In the attic.'

'Locked in the attic out of harm's way,' said Miriam.

Sasha said, 'For many years.'

'You're crazy,' Rachaela said, only a repetition.
'She's just a child. A sick child. She needs help.'

'Locked away,' said Stephan. 'Carlo,' he said.

And Carlo went forward to Ruth, and as he did so he
took off his jacket, and when he came to her he offered
it.

But Ruth spurned the jacket, only keeping her arm
firmly across her naked breasts.

Carlo put one hand on Ruth's shoulder, arresting
her.

She put up her head arrogantly, and let herself be
propelled towards the doorway. And as she passed
through the Scarabae, or perhaps as she saw Rachaela,
Ruth smiled again. But now it was the smile of a
clown, lopsided from the damage of the blow. With
difficulty she enunciated: 'You deserved it.' And was
taken away to the attic above in the dark.

*

'Stephan,' she said, 'you don't understand.'

Stephan sat staring at the hearth, where the fire had
been in winter.

Rachaela sat down facing him. 'Stephan, what Ruth
did was terrible. Can't you see that she's psychotic?
To lock her up in your attic will solve nothing.'
Stephan watched the phantom of the fire. 'She needs
attention. She needs a hospital.'

Dark Dance

'Anna,' Stephan said.

'Anna can't be helped. Let me help Ruth.'

'We have our own ways.'

'Ruth isn't yours. She's mine.'

'Ruth is ours.'

The bodies lay in their bedrooms, Peter and Dorian together on one bed. Soon, when the tide turned, they would be taken to the beach. Burned. So much Stephan had told her.

'You must listen to me, Stephan.'

'Oh, Anna,' he said.

Rachaela got up and went to her room.

She sat listening to the sea, trying to hear the moment when it changed.

It had happened.

Ruth would hate Adamus now. And he was finished with Ruth. So much passion between them. More than there had been between Adamus and herself.

But she must get Ruth away. Now it was possible. Only the locked attic door to prevent it.

Why? Why must she rescue Ruth?

Ruth was the demon Rachaela had always envisaged.

Better to wash her hands of Ruth and all that blood.

But something would not let her.

After all there was some bond between them. Like the unbilical cord, unsevered. No love, never that. But . . . something.

She could not leave Ruth to the Scarabae.

The tide, surely the tide had turned now.

She listened, no longer for the tide, but for the minute noises of the Scarabae as they went down to the cremation of their dead. Like beetles in the woodwork, creeping. She heard them go, or did she imagine it.

Finally she went out, and from the landing she saw them, filing into the lower rooms, in their summer clothes, as if to a midnight garden-party.

What a bonfire there would be on the beach.

Had Adamus gone with them?

Rachaela turned and went into the left-hand corridor.

When she reached the foot of the stairs she expected one of them after all left on guard, but no one was there.

She climbed to the attic door. It was firmly closed. The lock must be more hardy than that to the room of gowns or they would not have trusted it.

She tried the door. It shook and did not give.

Rachaela stood there at a loss.

What should she say, to an eleven-year-old murderess who had killed four times over?

'Ruth – Ruth? It's me. Ruth, answer me.'

A bell of silence formed, in which Rachaela seemed to hear dim bat-like squeaks, the rush of sparks in a great fire miles away.

'*Ruth.*'

A voice answered from beyond the door.

'Hallo, Mummy.'

It was calm and still, the voice, muffled by the swollen lips, and very young. It was a child's voice.

'Ruth. Are you afraid?'

'No,' said the voice. And then, solemnly, 'Yes.'

'Did they leave you a light?'

'Oh yes. They left me candles.'

'Be very careful with them,' said Rachaela.

'Yes, Mummy.'

'I'll make them let you out. Then we'll go back to London. I don't know how long it will take.'

'They won't let me out,' said Ruth. 'They didn't let out Uncle Camillo for twenty years. That was in another house. Sasha told me.'

'Sasha meant to scare you. Did they hurt you?'

'No, just my face. I cut my mouth on a tooth.'

'Are your teeth all right?'

'Yes,' said Ruth. 'But my eye's swollen up.'

'He might have killed you,' said Rachaela.

'He was angry.' There was a second silence. Ruth said, 'I didn't mean to do it. It was like the book. They were bad and I wanted to punish them.'

'Don't talk about it now,' said Rachaela. 'We'll find you a doctor. You can talk to him.'

'Yes, Mummy,' said Ruth. After a moment she said, 'They brought my clothes, and my drawing book and paints. There's a stuffed bird. All this wine Uncle Camillo made. I drank some. It made me feel funny.'

'Don't drink it,' said Rachaela.

'I can see Adam's tower from the window. The lamp's burning. I can see the yellow lion.'

'Does the window open?' Rachaela asked quickly.

'No. They locked the window too. They brought me dinner on a tray. It was a piece of old fish. But the jelly was nice.'

Rachaela thought, incongruously, *I haven't eaten all day*.

'Ruth, try to trust me. I promise I'll get you out.'

'All right,' said Ruth.

The third silence formed.

Rachaela thought of Ruth at the grave of the cat, weeping.

Blinding, searing tears filled Rachaela's eyes, sliding through like razor blades.

'Don't be afraid, Ruth,' she said. 'There's nothing to be afraid of.'

And now I am the liar after all.

'Will he forgive me?' said Ruth.

'No, Ruth, he won't.'

'No,' said Ruth. She said, 'I did it to make them sorry. But I didn't really mean it.'

'Yes, I understand.'

'I'm sorry, Mummy.'

When she went out, the sky was bright with fire.

When she looked over at the steps, it seemed to be touching heaven.

There was nothing left to see of them, Anna and Alice, Peter and Dorian. They had gone up in smoke.

Without a prayer or a song, like old clothes or refuse, so they cremated their dead at the rim of the water.

Far out, the sea made white flounces.

The Scarabae, those who were left, stood in their erratic circle, like old kiddies at a Guy Fawkes party.

She looked from her height and saw them all, Teresa and Anita, Unice and Miriam, Sasha, Miranda and Livia, George, Stephan, Jack and Eric. And to the side the humble retainers, the not-quite Scarabae, Maria, Cheta, Michael and Carlo.

Adamus was not with them. And Camillo was not.

The fire burned on and on like all the fires of the world.

Chapter Nineteen

BOTH DOORS TO THE TOWER were locked.
The woman stood before each of them in her
skirt and blouse and deluge of black primeval
hair. Then she went back to her green-and-blue room.

Rachaela stood looking at herself in the winged
mirror, breast-high amid the hedge of lilies, the rayed
sun and swallows.

Who am I?

She did not know. She saw herself as a stranger,
beautiful and far away. In looking at the faces of others,
she had forgotten her own.

It would be easy to go. To leave them all to each
other.

But they would travel with her.

She could not leave Ruth, poor insane little animal,
snared in their rites and ceremonies where even
murder was accorded a kind of ritual place.

Rachaela went down to the kitchen.

Cheta and Maria were scouring pots; Michael sat at
the table, cleaning silver methodically.

'Michael, I need to see Adamus. You must let me into
the tower.'

'When Mr Adamus locks the doors he wishes to see no one.'

'I realize that. But this is important. And you have a key.'

'I take his meals, Miss Rachaela.'

'If you won't let me in, I'll come with you.'

He could not refuse her. She was Miss Rachaela. And Anna was not there to countermand the order.

She waited until lunch-time, in the kitchen.

When the tray was ready with cold, supermarket chicken and salad, biscuits and cheese, the glass of wine, she followed Michael, as she had followed him before.

They went via the Salome annexe, down the stair and along the passage, to the door.

'If you will wait, Miss Rachaela, I shall tell him—'

'No. I'm coming in with you.'

Michael did not argue.

She went after him, into the tower and up the steps.

The room, burning from its window, tawny, gold, amber, was empty.

Michael put down the tray on a table.

'I'll stay,' Rachaela said, firmly.

Michael left her in possession.

Half an hour passed in the golden syrup of the room.

She examined books in a bookcase, there was nothing she recognized. No music stood on the piano. There were no ornaments in the room. On the mantelpiece the clock whirled backwards. Overhead the beams were like old toffee, sticky with webs, and with hooks in them for vanished lamps.

Rachaela left the upper room and walked down the stairs to the two closed doors beneath. She knocked and tried one, and found a white bathroom with a seahorse window. Hesitating, she knocked and tried the other door. It opened on a small bedroom, very dark, for the window showed a tower in a storm, like something from the tarot pack. The bed was ordinary, without posts. Adamus lay on it, looking at her.

'You know why I'm here,' she said.

'No.'

'Of course you do. Because of Ruth.'

'Why because of Ruth.' It was too flat to be a question.

'Adamus, I have to take her to London, to some hospital.'

'Why?'

'She's deranged. I must get her help.'

'Again, why? They'll care for her and keep her locked away. What more do you think your doctors will do for her?'

'There's a chance she can be – cured—'

'No chance at all.'

Rachaela said, 'I treated her like a sort of monster, so maybe it's my fault if she is one.'

'Don't you think,' he said, 'that we're all monsters.'

'Perhaps you're right,' she said. 'If I say that the Scarabae drove Ruth to do what she did, I suppose you'll disagree.'

'I don't care why she did it,' he said.

'I'm surprised you take it so hard. You spend no time with them.'

'Rachaela,' he said, 'she took a steel knitting needle and hammered it through Anna's breast. After she had practised on Alice, Dorian and Peter.'

'Yes, I know. Which is why I say she needs help. They've locked her in the attic as if this were some old "B" horror movie.'

'Instead of a nice hygienic padded cell. Do you think,' he said, 'that Ruth would let you put her into some institution?'

'Ruth's frightened by what she's done. She knows she needs—'

'Ruth knows nothing. Ruth is a collection of instincts and primal talents. You let her grow like a weed. Plenty of callousness to make her strong, and no guidance, to make her a law to herself.'

'Then it *is* my fault.'

'Probably.'

'Let me shoulder it. Give Ruth to me.'

He sat up. In the storm light of the window he was white and hard as marble.

'If it had been left to me, I'd have broken her neck.'

'She's your child, too.'

'I know.'

'How long will they keep her in a cage? What will happen when they release her? The Scarabae aren't able to deal with this.'

'They've dealt with plenty of things like this, and worse.'

'That story about Camillo—'

'The story is true. He was married in the family tradition to a girl, and he savaged her on the wedding night. She bled to death.'

'It isn't relevant.'

'No. Probably what Camillo did was an accident.'

'Ruth didn't know what she was doing.'

He stood up. He came towards Rachaela and stood over her. She did not let herself draw aside.

'Please help me, Adamus. Help me get her out. I'll take her away. You can forget her.'

'It's unforgettable,' he said.

'Then you can't want her to remain.'

'I don't care,' he said, 'any more.'

'All the more reason—'

'About Ruth, or the house, about them. What does any of it mean? Nothing.'

She took after all an involuntary step backward, and he reached out in an instant and gripped her arms.

'And you,' he said, 'the brave mother battling for her child. You would have had her cut out of you like a cancer.'

'And *you*,' she said, 'you served me like a bull does a cow. And then you were done with it. You would have done the same for Ruth.'

He held her so she could not move away, and he grinned at her with dead black eyes.

'Nothing means anything,' he said again, 'but I know why you're here. All right, then.'

He swung her round before she could struggle and thrust her on to the bed.

She tried to writhe away but he dropped on top of her. His weight crushed her. Every forward surface of her body was covered by his. What she had feared was happening.

Rachaela freed her right hand and struck the side of his head as hard as she was able. He caught her hand and pinned it down. She attempted to bring up her knees but he was too heavy on her.

His face was a blank but he frowned slightly with concentration. His eyes were flat as jets – Ruth's eyes.

As he bowed his head towards her she sank her teeth into his neck. She bit hard and thought she tasted his blood.

A terrible thrill uncoiled in her like a serpent.

He jerked back from her and she hit him across the

face with her left hand.

She seized his body and as he let go of her right wrist she grasped the fall of black hair. She struck him and pulled on him, filling her fingers with his spare hard body, as if she climbed a mountain. She wrapped him with her legs, splitting her skirt along the seam.

She screamed his name again and again.

At the last moment she buried her face in his neck, her open mouth against his skin. Erupting shudders ran the length of her, she was molten, clinging, tossed and flung backward. The delirium deserted her and she fell down into the bed.

When she opened her eyes he had left her. He stood against the occult window.

'So much for that,' he said.

A sort of shame ran over her. She got up, shaking and dizzy, her skirt absurdly flapping open.

On his neck was the mark of her teeth. She had not drawn blood.

What had happened had robbed her of speech, but she said, 'I'll never bother you again.'

'I believe that.'

'There was never anything between us,' she said, 'Ruth was a mistake.'

He watched her, waiting for her to go.

A hundred sentences filled her head, none able to be spoken.

She went out of the room and going to the outer door, moved on into the passageway.

A fearful light was in it, red and dying like the sunset of some diseased planet.

I got what I went for.

It was as if she had made love with a corpse.

*

Rachaela stood watching the sea. It drove in long green breakers to the cliffs, and broke and was sucked away.

The repetition of the sea was like life. The endless, fruitless attempts, the failures and fallings back. Even when the sea claimed the beach, the tide turned and the water was thrust away again.

Their bones were in the waves.

She could not think what else to do. A deep apathy was settling on her. But if she wanted to take Ruth away from them, she must fight.

She walked along the shore. The heat of the day was merciless, and she thought of the attic up under the roof with its locked window. Chastisement as well as confinement. And in winter, how could one keep warm? Perhaps they would let her freeze, for what she had done.

She pictured Adamus, and sent the picture from her mind.

Rachaela turned and went back towards the house. And as she approached it, she thought how curious it looked, so grey and untended, its lines leaning, and the ranks of windows with their glims of red and emerald.

Camillo was sitting on the floor outside Rachaela's door.

'Here I am,' he said.

'There you are.'

'No horse,' he said, 'I am without the horse.'

'Yes.'

'But I've brought you something.'

Rachaela stayed still. Camillo blocked off the door from her, sitting cross-legged like a tailor. Under the black cross on the window.

'That's very kind of you.'

'Yes. The boy wouldn't help you, would he? Adamus. You and he, the same. Dark horses.' Camillo got up. 'It should have been you, not that child.'

'Should it?'

'I tried to pretend once I was like Adamus is. I slit her neck with a table knife. But the gene didn't come out in me.'

'I'm not a vampire,' Rachaela said. 'None of you is. Not even Adamus. It's something he does. A sickness. And Ruth caught the sickness.'

'Nasty,' Camillo said. 'Take her away. She'll cause trouble, up in the attic. The attic was mine. But she hasn't got the rocking-horse.'

'I want to take her away,' said Rachaela.

'Good. Then here's the key.'

He held out something to her that shone dully in the window glare bisected by the black-paint cross.

'The key,' she said, 'the key to the attic?'

'One of them. It works.'

Rachaela reached out slowly and took the key.

'Thank you, Camillo.'

'Take her away,' he said.

'I will.'

Camillo went down the passage. He said, 'Don't suppose it will do any good.'

Rachaela's hand clasped convulsively on the key.

Steady now. It would take all her care.

*

Rachaela entered the dining room and no one was there, no one had come to dine but herself.

All afternoon she had seen no Scarabae. They had slipped into compartments of the house, perhaps hiding themselves.

Cheta served Rachaela. It was lamb cutlets, from the supermarket, carrots, peas and new potatoes.

Rachaela ate hungrily. She would need the food. Michael had not appeared and she had asked Cheta for a glass of wine.

After the lamb there was an apricot jelly, perhaps the remains of yesterday's meal.

Cheta served her tea in the drawing room.

It was strange, not to see Anna sitting there, or her embroidery. Her death had not sunk in. Once before she had been absent.

Rachaela stayed Cheta as she was leaving the room. 'Has Ruth been fed?'

'Oh, yes, Miss Rachaela. Carlo took up Miss Ruth's tray an hour ago.'

They would not clear the tray until the morning, when breakfast was taken to the voracious incarcerated child.

Rachaela hoped Ruth had been able, with her battered face, to eat her dinner. She too would need it.

Rachaela was leisurely over her tea. She left the room when her watch told her it was almost ten-thirty.

She went up to her bedroom. She waited another half hour, hearing no Scarabae, having seen none beyond Cheta.

At five past eleven she went out, and made her way up to the attic.

The key turned easily in the lock.

She went in slowly, prepared almost for anything. But the room was as she recalled it from her last visit, and brightly lit by candles standing in holders on the chests.

Ruth sat in the rocking-chair, and behind her was the black-night window, reflecting candles.

Ruth had a distorted clown's face, and one of the brown bottles in her lap.

'I told you not to drink that,' said Rachaela, alarmed.

Ruth stared at her.

'Did they let you come?'

'No, Ruth. I got a key. How much have you drunk?'

'Only a little. It tastes foul.'

'Good.' Rachaela shut the door. 'I'm taking you away tonight.'

Ruth nodded. She stood up.

She wore the 1910 dress, but she could walk in it, and everyone wore anything nowadays, particularly the young. The wounded face might draw some comment.

'I'm sorry, you'll have to leave your things behind.'

'That's all right,' said Ruth carelessly. 'I don't want anything.'

'I don't want you to go to your bedroom. If there's anything light up here, I can carry it.'

'Nothing,' said Ruth.

'We'll have to walk across the heath. It's a long walk I know, but it's the only way.'

Ruth looked sulky for a moment. Then she said, 'I don't mind.'

'It should be easy to get a car from the village now, once the shops open.' Ruth took another drink out of the brown bottle. '*No*, Ruth.'

'It's only wine.'

'Don't drink it. I want to take you down now to my room. Be very quiet. If we meet any of them, hide, if there's time. If not, well, we'll see. I don't think it will happen.'

Rachaela remembered her own night of going,

and how they had all of them gathered in the hall, but given before her, followed her, without protest, knowing. Would they give up Ruth the criminal so strengthlessly? Yes. Why else the key, the vast silence of the house? They wanted to be rid of Ruth, whatever they might have done or said.

Rachaela moved out of the attic and Ruth came after her. Rachaela locked the door again, when they were on the outside.

They descended the stair, went through the annexe and came out into the corridor. Nothing else moved. The Scarabae had cleared the ways.

They negotiated the corridor, came along the landing, went into the other passage, to Rachaela's door.

The house might have been vacant.

Ruth looked round at the blue-and-green bedchamber.

'It's nice. What's the window of?'

'The temptation of Eve.'

On the bed, packed, sat Rachaela's bag. Her boots stood by the hearth, for walking.

Ruth still wore her shoes from school. That was a blessing.

Ruth said, 'It will be nice to go home.'

Rachaela saw the flat, Ruth's area dismantled, and all her things in boxes. At least nothing had been given away, not even the clothes for Oxfam.

She's trying to keep on my fine side, Rachaela thought. *She doesn't think of the flat as home. Perhaps not anywhere.* She thought, *Christ, what will become of her?* And she visualized Ruth borne screaming into a tiled tunnel by men in white coats.

'Ruth, you must stay here now. Don't go out of the room. Do you need the bathroom?'

'No, Mummy.'

How in God's name had they managed that, in the attic?

'I'm going to go down and see if anyone's about on the ground floor. I won't be more than ten or fifteen minutes. And then, we're leaving.'

'Yes,' said Ruth. She sat down in the chair, where once Adamus had sat.

'Be ready, Ruth.'

Ruth nodded, and swung her legs. They did not quite reach the floor.

Rachaela went out again. She walked along the corridor softly. She felt a peculiar buoyancy.

On the landing she paused. All was quiet. The house murmured, muttered to itself. The sea sounded.

In their nests the Scarabae kept close.

Down in the hall all the lamps burned, the ruby lamp, the lights of the drawing room.

Rachaela went into the drawing room, the dining room.

She opened wide the door to the conservatory, and so the door to the garden.

The air was full of scent, roses and jasmine and the salt of the ocean. She experienced a sudden tearing in her, nostalgia for something soon to be past. She had never truly understood what she felt for this house.

The yew was very black. The cat lay beneath, morphing itself into putrescence and bone. And out there, Anna and Dorian and Peter, Alice and Sylvian, rocked in the tide.

And behind her in the tower, Adamus.

Adamus.

Her feet on the lawn, she turned and stared towards the cone of the tower's roof, and in that second a great chord of sound was struck, as if upon her own body, shivering up from her soles into her spleen, her heart and cranium.

It was like a metaphysical note, like the breaking string in *The Cherry Orchard*. Did it likewise portend some loss, some irreversible cruelty of fate—

Rachaela threw off the cloak of sensation which had settled bat-like upon her.

She ran back into the house, across the rooms, the hall, and quickly climbed the stair.

On the landing she paused again. Again she heard only the silence of faint noises.

She walked to her door and opened it and Ruth was gone.

There was only one place that Ruth would go. Into the tower. To Adamus.

To Ruth it had not counted, his revulsion and his violence. They were irrelevant. Only seeing him mattered.

Rachaela tried to control her galloping pulse, her terror. After all, Ruth would be with him now. What, what would happen, between them?

She had run to the room, now she flew, along the landing, through the annexe, down the stair. Had the door been locked, and Ruth left waiting at the door? But Ruth was not there. And the door – stood ajar.

Rachaela entered. There was light in the room above.

She climbed sluggishly now, as if a boulder were on her back.

She came to the door, and into the doorway, and looked through.

Ruth was crouching in the middle of the room, by a table with a stand of candles that lit her as if purposely.

She was quite still, her hands drawn up under her chin, and her black hair falling to the floor. She did not turn to look at Rachaela. All her attention was caught.

From a beam above the piano something dark was hanging, moving slightly to and fro. It seemed to have no form, but as it moved, there was a pale shape, a sort of face, unrecognizable, dangling off the neck from a short black cord.

His feet had struck the piano as the stool went over. That had been the sound Rachaela heard.

He hung there formlessly, like a cocoon, swinging slightly, but all the time more heavily and more slowly.

Ruth moved. She stood up.

'Is he dead?' she said in a high thin voice.

Rachaela tried to speak. And no words came.

'I think he's dead,' said Ruth.

And she hiccuped loudly, and covered her mouth in fear.

Rachaela tried to go forward, but she could not take a step.

'Adam,' said Ruth. She picked up the candle-branch and went closer to the hanging, swinging thing. She lifted the candles up to see. Then she screamed. She screamed continuously, and the horrible spiked soprano bleats went through Rachaela's brain. She must make Ruth stop screaming. She took a step forward, and Ruth lifted the candles and touched them to the hanged man, and rivulets of light ran over him. He was alive with fire.

'*No*—' Rachaela floundered in the slough of poisoned air, and Ruth turned to her the face of a demon.

'We burn our dead,' said Ruth.

And she flung the candles round the room like flaming flowers.

The curtains went up in a fountain of fire, the chairs beside the hearth began to burn.

Ruth still had one candle. She darted at Rachaela and Rachaela cowered aside.

Ruth burst past her, the burning candle in her hand, pressing it to the doorway and the wall as she went. The door blazed up.

Rachaela stood in a room of fire.

The house was burning.

It was like a forest. Things scuttled underfoot, the fleeing mice. Ceilings broke with a great crack. Wooden objects fell, alight, and broke like blossoms.

There was so much light, like sunlight, scalding.

Rachaela ran down a burning stairway, between walls of flame.

She did not know where she was, she had lost track of direction. The fire ran and sprinted before her. Ruth – Ruth was the fire.

Ruth must be stopped, but Ruth was unstoppable.

The rooms burned. It spread so fast. The house, summer-dry in its mummy dusts, the old curtains catching like pergolas of flame, the floorboards snapping.

Was this the annexe? A huge window, its leading melting. A fissure spread across the glass like a green lightning.

Rachaela ran.

The fire bit at her arms, there were splinters of flame in her hair – she beat them out.

Out of the furnace and on to the landing. She could still recognize the landing although fire hopped along the balustrade, and below the nymph was burning, her dead lamp lit up with fire.

Rachaela turned, she looked about her, but she was no longer herself. She was only terrified. She ran down the stairs over the carpet bobbing with little crackling lights, out on to the chequerboard of the floor, all as reflective now as a lake, a lake of fire.

The drawing room was burning too, the arch was filled by flames and something burst there with a great hiss and sigh.

She saw Scarabae at the dinner table, and the flames on their plates, the flames unstitching them, and their clothes burned off their bodies, which were like medieval paintings of the dead before the flame consumed them.

Rachaela shrieked. She ran across the fiery floor and out of the first and second doors of the lobby, into the night.

She stumbled through the trees of the garden. Her body was blistered, her hair was burning again, she swept it out. Her hands were burned, and her legs had been needled by fire. She coughed and wept, the black water running from her eyes and nose.

She saw Uncle Camillo riding his horse across the flames, waving his sword, as he burned.

She saw them in their boxes of beds, burned up like papers.

Rachaela sank on her knees among the oaks, crying and blind, while the house blazed like a festival, in a coronet of golden light.

Mice ran like a flow of ink from the well of fire into the sheltering darkness.

The house fell in at about three in the morning.

It gave like a well-laid hearth, centre crumbling, the roofs descending with a whoosh of smoke and sparks.

Windows exploded like fireworks.

By then the ones who had survived were out on the heath.

Rachaela, from her distance, counted them and named them.

Miriam and Sasha, Miranda and Eric, Michael and Cheta. No others came from the pyre.

No others except, of course, Ruth. But Ruth had come and gone long since, scuttling over the darkness like an imp. No longer with a lighted candle, her work accomplished. She fled towards the heathland, towards the dragon parts, and vanished.

What would she do in those wild places, that demon child, without streets and shops, without Woolworth's and the graveyard?

Rachaela, seated on the ground, her back against a tree, could only watch, the witness, as now she watched the Scarabae.

Her body was a medley of pains and she wept from pain, but the Scarabae, with half their garments scorched off them, only stood in a little loose group above the house, and watched it flame and watched it fall, as perhaps they had watched other fires and fallings.

Rachaela, in her agonized exhaustion, did not go near them, did not consider them. Did not care.

Yet at her wrist her watch ticked on.

The darkness was on the land like mourning, but in an hour it would be dawn. The sun would rise.

What then?

An excerpt from
Heartbeast
by
Tanith Lee
Coming from Dell in September 1993

PART ONE

I

The blinds, which were down, filled the room with the yellow color of the inside of a peach. Within this globe of yellow the man and woman wove about each other like two naked icons of amber.

It was the height of the day. Outside, above a familiar hubbub, the bodiless voice uncoiled from a minaret, calling the faithful to prayer.

Marjannah's black hair hung over the side of the bed in three sliding ropes. Her arms, flung backward, clenched the tawny pillows, and her mouth, mulberry in the light, parted on a low scream. Her slender legs locked the back of her partner, and her anklets of thin gold clicked together.

Daniel Vehmund rode her body, making upon it the immemorial stabbing motions of the sexual act. His hips were narrow and hard; smooth, like his back, as ivory; and from his frantic head the hair rained golden as the aura of the room.

Marjannah cried again and arched her pelvis upward.

Disturbed by mysterious carnal currents, or some breath of air through the lattice, little bells rang on a slender chain. And in a cage a topaz bird let out a chirp.

"Kill me," said Marjannah.

Her arms poured from the pillows to clutch the assassin's back. She uttered two wild and sobbing shrieks that each pierced all other sound, soared, and sank to nothing. Gasping, Daniel hung above her, then sank on her motionless body.

"Death," said Marjannah. "My beloved."

They lay still for perhaps fifteen seconds, and then Daniel eased away from her and turned onto his spine.

Marjannah sighed.

"For those moments you are mine," she said.

Daniel smiled. For those moments it seemed to him he was no one's, not even his own, but possessed solely by the demon of pleasure, a blind, spasming thing of fires.

Marjannah stroked Daniel's hair, cheekbones; and the bird in the cage began to trill, fluttering on its perch.

"I shall have the girl fetch us coffee and sweetmeats."

"Not today, Marjannah."

"Can you be this heartless as to leave me so early?"

"There's someone I have to meet."

"You lie to me. You do not wish to stay with me."

That was true. "It would be paradise on earth to stay with you. But God makes us perform our duty."

"You have no duty."

"Yes. I expect a man with a letter from my mother."

"I do not believe in your mother."

"I have one."

Marjannah rose from the bed and stretched her beautiful body, her hair rippling and her anklets clacking.

Daniel watched her in a silent, holy appreciation of her splendor, which in no sort would detain him further that day.

In acknowledgment, the girl put on her embroidered robe, and touching the tassels of the blinds, let them up.

Parched light burst in. Certain shabbinesses of the room were revealed, torn threads, a mousehole. The topaz bird had turned to a virtuous white, and strutted up and down.

Daniel rose. As he dressed himself in his underlinen, shirt, and breeches, he glimpsed outside the close-hung roofs that scaled like counters to the sukh. Across the sukh, far away, tall slender towers arose with teardrop domes of colored mosaic.

He was not happy exactly, but the thought of the probable letter excited him. He knew that when he had read it, a descent would come, as if from strong wine. He would be filled with yearnings, rage, and hatred. But these he held at bay. He had given way to great anger once before, and that had brought him here, to this strange, exotic environment of brilliant dyes and alien sounds, its smells of spice and vice, its ornamental women, and surges of a religion that, to the cold churches of his earlier youth, was like a blast of burning air.

"Shall I see my lord after the sun sets?" asked Marjannah, with what he took for the humility of her false repertoire. Doubtless she would put him from her mind as soon as he was gone.

"No, sweetheart. Not tonight."

"Alas." But she smiled.

Perhaps she would entertain instead the rich Turk who courted her. Daniel did not much care. Marjannah was a spirit of the exotic environment.

He took a fruit from a pottery dish and went out of the room. "Farewell," she said. In the corridor he saw "the girl" —the old servant woman—in her cubicle, preparing thick, sweet coffee. She grunted but did not speak to him.

On the outer stairs, where sometimes the prostitutes brought their customers by night, were broken flowers and sun, and the tang of urine. He passed the vacant room of the porter known as the Black Giant.

The great heat had waited.

He passed along an alley of brown shadows, over which fig trees hung their waxen bulbs. A concertina of narrow steps ran down between the walls that almost touched, overhung by a vase of red roses on a balcony. High up floated rags to dry, and then the dried sky, which looked less cerulean than indigo.

Daniel Vehmund moved out into the sukh, under its crimson and ocher hangings. Today the market seemed full of camels. They trod between the stalls in the midst of an open square, stinking and proud, accoutred like brides. The man with the letter would not have come with a caravan from the mountains, but up from the port. He was to be found where the agent always sent them, at the French Inn on the edge of the sukh's southmost quarter.

The crowd was, as ever, mostly heavy and idle. Daniel pushed his way through. There were no women but those of the lowest sort, beneath modesty, servants, or slaves. Once or twice one saw a carrying chair borne through, its veiled entrance strung with beads, smelling of jasmine and musk.

A man flung five daggers in the air, flashing, catching them by their hilts. The usual snake charmer was at the turning of the booths, by the doll makers. The serpent swayed from the pitcher, sinisterly following the motion of the pipe. Beyond, the dolls were giving a puppet show, and Daniel paused to watch a turbaned warrior embattled with a jinn. The warrior whacked with his crescent sword and the jinn collapsed in a clashing of copper disks: The battle between good and evil was always easily resolved in stories. But the crowd cheered and clapped.

Across the layers of the sukh a wall of the inn was growing visible, its sign of a ship, European and incongruous, above the stars and blades and magical tokens of the market.

Daniel eased through a knot of hagglers and stepped around a gambling party on the ground. He was by now accustomed to the occasional exclamation or pointing of fingers. Fair northern skin was not unknown here, but his blond hair elicited comment, and his eyes had sometimes caused a little trouble. The evil eye was feared by ignorant and wise alike, it seemed, and any uncommon thing concerning the eye might suggest it. Daniel's eyes were an odd color, tawny, like washed brass. Hazel, his mother had called them.

A tall man in a dark robe stood in a little space, looking fixedly at Daniel.

Before the man was a board, and on it three earthen cups. A few of the idlers stood about, to see the ancient trick performed, but none willing to bet on where the object, to be hidden beneath one cup, would next appear.

The man had a long and bony face, pockmarked and sallow. His head was wound in a faded white cloth. He beckoned to Daniel peremptorily.

Daniel would have walked on, but a fellow in the crowd, perhaps the man's accomplice, took his arm and urged him suddenly forward, "Come, come."

Daniel shook him off. "No."

The pockmarked man had produced something that shone and flashed as the knives had done. A jewel of glass, most probably. He slipped it under the central cup, and moved the vessels rhythmically about over the board, circling one another, finding new places.

When the cups stopped moving, the idlers laughed. No one would guess where the object now lay, certain that it would not lie where it seemed to—for at this trick, old as antique Greece, the bystander was always wrong.

Daniel shrugged and walked off across the sukh. The fellow did not snatch at him again.

Hungry dogs clustered at the foot of the French Inn, and even as Daniel approached, someone kicked them away, a drunkard come out into the air, who hailed Daniel like a long-lost brother. Daniel maneuvered past him and entered the pungent darkness of the tavern.

At once a kind of fear dropped over Daniel. He knew it, and paid it no heed. He reached the counter and addressed the one-eyed man. "A sailor from the *Algerac*. Is he here?"

"Over there, monsieur. The bearded one in the corner."

Daniel proceeded through the gloom, jostled by rough shoulders now and the languages of three or four nations. He got to the table and sat down facing the bearded sailor.

"You have a letter for me?"

"You are to give your name," said the sailor.

"Vehmund."

"I have a letter for Vehmund."

The dirty fingers went into the dirty coat and came out bearing a sealed paper. So it had traveled, this thing from his mother, in God knew what makeshift and filthy resting places, gripped and passed by what foul and feckless paws. A wonder it had reached him.

Daniel held out his hand.

"You are to pay me."

"The letter first."

The sailor grunted, gave up the letter, then took the fistful of sous.

"You aren't generous, Monsieur Vehmund."

"I gave you what you were promised."

How many times this, or like, dialogue.

The sailor slurped his vinegary wine and turned away to look at the women displayed on the gallery. One, an Arab girl with a fringed shawl and kohl-black eyes, drew his attention. He got up sullenly and sidled off.

Daniel broke the seal of the letter. His hands shook and, after all, he did not want to read it, to begin again. To go back. But the closely written, educated lines were already before him. *My dearest* . . . Sometimes the handwriting was altered, girlish, and not her own, as if she were too tired and called another to form the letters for her—but who was there to call on?

A wave of sorrow poured through his body, numbing his limbs. She wrote in so ordinary a way, as if nothing were amiss. News of the farm, which his brother was managing, the seasons, the winter lambs, a spring storm. As if he must pine for all this, which in any case was not properly known to him. He had come back to her that first time a stranger, as it seemed she had meant him to. He remembered how he had seen her at the doorway of the house, milk-white in her pale gown, and her hair turned gray. A madonna of smoke.

And after the words of the farm, her truths and lies of herself: "I am quite well these days and Janet and I have been baking, up to our chins in flour. All the cats have had their kittens and we are overrun with cats worse than the mice. I let them sleep their sleeps on my bed now, if they want." By that message alone assuring him of the vast change that he had wrought, striking off her shackles—and at the thought, his heart beat fast, almost choking him. He pushed memory away, and read of the small things of the farm, and so came to the glimpsed soul of the letter: "I miss you so, more with every day. But I am content to miss you as long as you prosper. Write to me soon and tell me everything. Is there money enough still, and does your employer grant you a better wage? Is your health good?" And then, "I fear you must stay away some months longer, to assure your success."

What had it cost her to pen these words? To couch the fact in such general and evasive terms?

Some months . . . It was a year since he had left her; they had known he must be absent at least so long, and much more. For his brother, though a brute, was not quite a fool. But she was safe from the brute, it seemed; she had promised to tell him otherwise. Would she keep her promise? How many eons had gone by, his childhood, his years at the city school, when she had hidden everything, and he, conniving, had not seen it.

In the hot and shadowy inn he read her farewells to him, and the letter was over, ended.

A boy glided to his table, knowing infallibly the moment. "Urak."

The boy slid away and returned instants later with the misleadingly small jug of spirit and the deceptive little glass.

Daniel Vehmund drank the liquor, and a terrible darkness, deeper, steeper than the shadow of the inn, enclosed him. No longer a creature of the sunlight with his pastel tan and golden hair and eyes, but black as night in that corner the sailor had vacated for the quim of the Arab girl.

And the inn drew off and left him in his darker darkness.

When he had finished the jug he turned it, as was traditional here, mouth down on the table, got up and left the tavern. He was steady enough, the drunkenness from the urak had sent him only inward to the core of an unbearable pain that, at this time, he must always touch in order to resist it.

Remote now, the clustering sukh, its notes and smells.

The man in the faded turban had remained at his board. His crowd had drifted off, yet still he moved the vessels over and about one another. Daniel stopped to watch him, and a fascination held him there. Hypnotically the cups moved, like the snake to the charmer's music. Where was the glass jewel?

The cups ceased their motion. The pockmarked man looked up and met Daniel's gaze with his own black eyes. Daniel shook his head.

The man turned up the cups one by one. Nothing lay under any of them.

The sukh, pressing on every side, seemed distant, a mile off. But this man was close, and the board empty.

Then the pockmarked man opened his lips and out ran his tongue. It was gray and horrible, like the tongue of some lizard. And on the tongue, a waterdrop on a diseased petal, rested the jewel of glass. It gave off one huge spark, like lightning. It was pure and cold, more real than anything— the sukh, the sky, the earth, or the air.

"By Christ, a diamond," Daniel Vehmund said.

The tongue, lizard-like, snapped back and the jewel vanished.

The man waited, mysteriously.

"What do you want?" Daniel said.

The man, the jewel pent in his mouth, jerked his head and raising his hand beckoned Daniel forward, as if he knew him and were his guide.

Daniel reached into his coat, drew out a coin worth more than he had paid for the letter, and tossed it against the empty cups. "A clever trick."

He walked away quickly, through the unreal sukh. The image of the diamond did not leave him. It was printed like a blot of darkness on the day, a blot of white fire within his lids.